Bayou City Burning

D. B. BORTON

Boomerang Books

Published by Boomerang Books, Delaware, OH

This is a work of fiction. Many of the characters are based on actual historical figures, but most of their actions and all of their dialogue are the inventions of the author.

Print ISBN: 978-0-9993527-2-4
Ebook ISBN: 978-0-9993527-3-1

To Diane Moore Lynch
and in memory of Robert Carpenter

Acknowledgments

The author wishes to thank Louise and Joe Musser for their comments on a draft of this novel, and my editor, Rebecca Langley. I'd also like to thank Ohio Wesleyan University librarian Jillian Maruskin for all her help in my research.

Author's Note

Many of the events and characters in this work of fiction are based on actual events and people. All of the dialogue outside of the prologue is fictitious.

Prologue—July 20, 1969

It was there, and then it wasn't: a grainy, pockmarked triangle slashed by a dark shadow. First the edges blurred into an impressionist dream of earth tones and light, then the cut of a thin shadow skimmed across the surface, and then—darkness. Nothing to see, no matter how I strained my eyes.

Static, like a windstorm against a microphone, accented by high-pitched beeps.

A calm male voice: "Contact light. Okay, engine stop."

Then another voice, a familiar twang, Texan: "We copy you down, Eagle."

The first voice again: "Houston, Tranquility Base here. The Eagle has landed."

Later, I heard that about five million people all over the world were doing exactly what I was doing at that moment. I had a summer job as a day camp counselor at the local Y, but they sent everybody home early that day—kids, counselors, and staff—to watch two men land on the moon, just like President Kennedy had promised they would eight years before.

In the thrill of the moment, it was hard to predict what people would remember afterward. Probably they'd remember the words, "The Eagle has landed." But I'd remember the part that came before. I'd remember the first word in that announcement: Houston.

If it hadn't been for my old man, that word might have been different.

Some people regard my father Harry as a two-bit shamus. They see him as a licensed peeper with a gun under his coat and the ethics of an alligator lizard. I've seen him that way myself. But he's got his principles. And I knew as I sat in our chilly living room, curtains drawn against the blazing star that lit up the lunar surface and melted the Texas sidewalks, that this was his gift to me: that word.

He didn't have to do it. The other side was safer, and they paid better, too.

But I was his little girl, and he wanted to make me happy.

Book One

Harry – May 12, 1961

Chapter 1

I was sitting at my desk reading the *Post* when the light changed and I looked up to see a man standing in the doorway. The rain hammered against my windows and the air conditioner was grinding away at my back and I thought, not for the first time, that someday somebody was going to get the drop on me and I wouldn't even hear it coming.

This bird could have been the one, too, because he had a slight shoulder bulge in his otherwise well-tailored gray pinstripe suit—the kind of bulge that was supposed to draw your eye and strike fear in your heart. His display handkerchief was silk and light blue and showed some style. The suit meant that he was no cheap torpedo, and if he'd financed it with the heat he was carrying, I'd need to be cautious. A well-dressed button man is still a button man. He had brown hair cut close, a hairline that was older than he was, and eyes with lids like blackout shades. The fear he was supposed to inspire was undercut by the oversized white handkerchief he was dragging across his sweaty, bright red forehead.

"Jesus! How do you stand it?" he said.

An out-of-towner. I made no comment. I didn't even offer to take the dripping raincoat he had draped over one arm. This was another mark of the outsider: somebody who didn't know that when it rains in Houston in the summer, you strip down, you don't wear another layer.

His eyes made a tour of my office. It was a short tour.

"You Harry Lark?" He pocketed the handkerchief.

"That's me," I said.

"Where's your secretary?" He angled a thumb over his shoulder toward the outer office. Two rings winked at me, a diamond and a signet.

"She must've stepped out," I said noncommittally.

Jeanie had "stepped out" about six months ago when I'd traded her salary for a set of braces for my son. I liked to keep up appearances, though, so I hung an old sweater from the back of Jeanie's chair and sprayed it with perfume from time to time—mostly rejects from my daughter's Christmas gift exchanges. I filed some things on Jeanie's desk instead of in the wastebasket and kept a page in the typewriter.

But what did he care, unless he was worried about witnesses?

I nodded at the wooden chair in front of my desk and angled a packet of Winstons in his direction. "What can I do for you?"

He slung his raincoat over the arm of the chair. It dripped small dark stains onto the rug. He took a cigarette and we lit up. Then he settled back in the chair and grimaced. I studied his tie, waiting for him to speak. It was the same slate gray as the suit and thin as a razor blade.

"I need some information about an event that's taking place here next week," he said. "In town, I mean." He waved his cigarette in the direction of the window and grimaced. The grimace told me that he'd never consider promoting Houston from a backwater berg to a city. His voice was flat and forgettable—the kind of voice that could have read the daily stock report.

"And what would that be?"

"Two men are coming down from Washington, DC. I want to know what they're doing here, where they go, who they see. Pictures, too."

"What's the beef?" I said.

"Let's say that I suspect these men of conspiring to defraud taxpayers by engaging in certain underhanded practices that stand to damage my business interests and those of my associates." He was looking at Dwight D. Eisenhower, who was hanging on my wall, when he said it. If Ike didn't like this story, he didn't say so. I didn't like it, but I was in hock to a certain orthodontist, so I refrained from comment.

"Let's say that," I said. "And you would be Mr.—?"

"Smith." His gaze returned to me and his eyelids dropped to half-mast over the cigarette smoke. "My name is Smith."

"Well, Mr. Smith," I said, "I get fifty dollars a day plus expenses."

"Isn't that a little steep?" he said.

I shrugged. "I have to pay for the air conditioning." Besides, his suit told me he could afford it.

He gestured with his cigarette. "And I suppose all the other private dicks in Houston have to pay for air conditioning, too."

I grinned. "You're welcome to go ask them."

I left it up to him to imagine spending the hours between now and his departure time sitting in a Houston office without air conditioning instead of cooling his heels in a lounge near the airport. I felt sure he was doing it, too.

"Yeah, all right," he said.

My marks were Philip Miller and John Parsons. Their work had something to do with space research.

"What kind of space research?" I said, frowning. "You mean for business expansion?"

"Hey, that's right." He pointed the cigarette at me. "Business expansion. But the business is space—outer space."

My phone rang. The voice on the other end was accusatory. "You were supposed to pick me up ten minutes ago for the orthodontist."

Since he'd become a teenager, my son Hal addressed me in one of three tones of voice—bored, superior, and disgruntled. He'd found it harder to manage since he'd acquired a mouthful of metal and rubber bands, but not impossible.

I pretended to check my desk calendar and make a notation. "Yes, that's fine," I said. "I'll be there."

"I'm going to be late for the orthodontist," Hal said.

"That's all right. Happy to help out. Thanks for calling." I hung up and raised my eyes to my visitor. "Where were we?"

"Space."

"I don't know anything about that," I said.

"I don't, either," he said. "But there's business involved, and a lot of money. That's all you have to know."

The two men were due to arrive the following Tuesday at Houston International. He didn't know the time or the flight, but he gave me photographs of the men. The photographs looked like my kind of photograph—stuff taken with a telephoto lens when the subject didn't know he was being photographed.

He glanced out the window next to the one with the air conditioner. City buildings gleamed in the rain but there wasn't much else to look at except the Weather Ball on top of the Texas National Bank, which blinked to show that precipitation was expected. It didn't matter to him; he was blowing town anyway, the sooner the better.

He counted out four twenties and laid them on my desk. "That enough to get you started?" he asked. I nodded. He told me he'd come back in a week at the same time.

He was already swabbing the back of his neck with the wet handkerchief as he stood up.

"What if I have to get in touch with you before then?" I said.

"Save it." He turned his back and headed for the door.

I stood at the window and watched him emerge from the building downstairs, his raincoat over his head like a pup tent. The Chinese laundry on the first floor was kicking up a lot of steam and he gave it a wide berth, stepping gingerly to keep his Italian leather shoes out of the puddles. Then he disappeared around the corner, so I didn't get to see his car, if he had one. It was probably a rental, anyway. I had already decided that tailing him at this point was a losing proposition. He'd paid me enough to start the work he wanted me to do, but not enough to give me the trouble of tailing him. Besides, I had a date with my surly teenaged son.

I pocketed the twenties and hoped that my daughter's teeth all stayed as straight as a drill sergeant.

Dizzy – May 13, 1961

Chapter 2

I was resting my dogs on a military footlocker, perusing a Flash comic book, and listening to B.D. squawk about the heat. I had a side conversation going with Mel about whether I'd rather be the Green Lantern or Flash, though I didn't much care about being either one of them. What I really coveted was Wonder Woman's bracelets and Lasso of Truth. But when you're pinching your reading material from your brother's strictly forbidden comic book stash, you can't afford to be choosy.

"I wish you'd just shut up about it," Mel said to B.D. "It's May. In Houston. It's supposed to be hot. It's been hot every summer since I was born, and that's thirteen summers."

"Thirteen for you," I said. "Twelve for me and B.D." Not taking a side, just clarifying.

"But look, y'all," B.D. complained. "The crayons liked to melt all over our business cards. And I can't color inside the lines with my eyes full of sweat." For the millionth time, she slipped the bandeau off her head and pushed back her hair with it. Her blond ponytail was wilted. "And it's only Maaaaaaaay!"

I sympathized. If I didn't watch out, I'd come away with Flash imprinted upside-down on my sweaty knees like a tattoo and when my brother Hal saw it, he'd know I'd been sneaking his comic books and the jig would be up.

Mel sighed. "Well, I know what you mean," she said. "I'm fixin' to march down to the barber shop, Dizzy, and ask for a haircut like yours." She tried to shape her dark curls, but they sprang from her head like Medea's snakes in my mythology book. She wore her hair in a Raggedy Ann, cut short across her neck, but she still had about five times as much hair as I did. I ran a hand over the short brown hair on my head and felt it stand up like possum fur, which was why my brother Hal sometimes called me Pogo.

"Lucille," B.D. said, speaking to my tabby cat, who was stretched out full length on the garage floor, snoozing. "I don't know how you can stand to wear that fur coat."

"At least it's not raining," Mel offered. Lately we'd been plagued by storms that flooded the ditches at one end of the street and sent tidal waves all the way down to the circle at the other end, where crawdads fetched up when the water receded, beached and confused.

"Not yet," B.D. said.

"Let's see the cards," I said, to take their minds off the heat.

B.D. handed me some and I peeled them off her fingers. Mel studied them over my shoulder. At the top, they said, "Looking for Something?" Some of the cards were lettered in Mel's neat round printing and some in my loopy handwriting. Under that was B.D.'s drawing of an eye behind a magnifying glass, the kind Sherlock Holmes used. Under that was the name of our business, Spring Branch Lost and Found, and our business address—my garage.

"This eye looks kinda bloodshot." Mel pointed.

"My pink Crayola slipped," B.D. said, "so I had to fill it in."

"Looks kinda like Harry's," I said.

"It does," Mel agreed.

In defense of my parents, I want to point out that my mother was the only parent in our group who had allowed us to open a business in the family garage. It's true she'd been pretty distracted lately, getting ready for her trip to England, and probably also true that she was thinking along the lines of a Kool-Aid stand. My father Harry, who better understood our line of work, wasn't required to voice an opinion since he didn't live at home anymore, and had no official say in the commercial use of our garage, but he'd voiced one anyway, which he usually did. He said we were setting up as the neighborhood pawnshop, and he was all for it. "Just don't take any hot ice, girls," he'd told us.

"I'm serious, y'all," B.D. moaned. "I know where I can find a lost fan on the Danners' breezeway."

"It's not lost," Mel said.

"It will be once I fetch it here," B.D. said.

Billy Wayne Abbott showed up then and I was glad for the diversion, even though he was dumber than a box of rocks. We saw him coming up the driveway, adjusting the ball cap on his head like he was signaling a base runner. Billy Wayne was a pudgy kid. If you dropped him off a water tower, I suspect he would have bounced, filled up the way he was with hot air and ego.

He stopped outside the garage door, hands on his hips, and squinted in at us. "Y'all find my kickball?"

"What's it look like?" B.D. said.

His mouth hung open as he looked at her. "What you think it looks like, Cootie? Looks like a kickball."

B.D. gets teased a lot on account of her last name, which is Cooter. She gets it way worse than I do, even though my given name is Desdemona, because the average Texan doesn't know Shakespeare's Desdemona from Miss Hogg County or the Azalea Queen. Which is fine with me, because I've read the play my mother wrote her dissertation on, and the only worse name she could have given me was Iago.

But if you pitched to B.D., you'd better be prepared for a line drive up the middle that could drill a hole in your gut. "We might have a kickball," she said, "but how do we know it's yours, Ab-butt? If you can't describe it, we sure can't hand it over."

"How'm I s'posed to describe it?" He said raised his voice in frustration. "It's a kickball. If Dizzy found it in the Maynards' yard, it's mine, and y'all know it."

Everybody knew it. Most everybody was there when he kicked it into the Maynards' yard, and everybody also knew he was too yellow to climb the fence and face Bevo, the Maynards' Great Dane.

So I did it later. Bevo was a pal of mine, seeing as I regularly took him something from the ice cream truck. Harry always said, "You pay to play."

"What you got for us?" I asked.

"I got a nickel," he said.

"Don't waste our time." I went back to my comic book.

He sighed, reached into his back pocket and brought out his collection, but then he just held it, fingering the rubber band.

"Show us what you got," Mel said. Baseball cards were her department. If Mel died young, she'd arrive at the Pearly Gates—or wherever it was Jewish people went—in a good position to negotiate.

"Uh-uh," he said. "I ain't showing you what I got." He raised the cards to his chest as if we were playing Go Fish. "Tell me what you want and I'll tell you if I got it."

Mel rolled her eyes. "Okay. Clemente, Ford, and Cepeda. Juan Marichal."

"Juan who?"

"Marichal. Rookie pitcher for the Giants."

He slipped off the rubber band and studied his pack. A furrow of concentration split his forehead and channeled the sweat down his nose. "I can give you Clemente."

"And?" Mel said, holding out her hand.

He took a step back, clutching his cards. "And what?"

"Don Zimmer? Johnny James? Dick Farrell? Zolio Versalles?"

He gave her a sly look. "I got James and Farrell."

"Okay," she said, "you can have your kickball in exchange for Clemente, James and Farrell."

He handed over the cards and I retrieved the ball from the air conditioner box where we kept the sports equipment—or where we would keep it, when we found some more to keep.

He tucked the ball under his arm and retreated a few steps, grinning at Mel. "That just shows what you know. That Johnny James card has a mistake. He's wearing the wrong hat."

"Billy Wayne, they all have mistakes," Mel said. "Zimmer, James,

Farrell, and Versalles. That's going to make 'em more valuable someday, you wait and see. We'll wave to you from our limousine while you're pedaling your bike down Long Point Road."

His face fell. But then you could see him turning it over in what passed for his mind, and refusing to believe he'd been had. "I'll wait and see," he said at last. "But I bet I got a long wait."

"He is so aggravatin'," B.D. said as we watched him retreat down the driveway. "If he wasn't so full of himself, he might could squeeze some brains in there."

A few other kids saw the sign at the end of my driveway and stopped by out of curiosity, but the only one who had lost anything was Billie Jo Skelton, who told us she'd lost one of her favorite barrettes at the beach.

"Y'all got any barrettes?" she asked. She held up a thumb and forefinger. "It was this big and it looked like a candy cane, 'cept it was a bow."

I opened my mouth to give her a geography lesson but B.D. cut me off. "Sugar, we don't go as far as Galveston." She gave me a look that was supposed to remind me about our customer relations talk.

Mel said gravely, "Somebody else has that territory."

Billie Jo frowned. "Then how will I find it?"

"Maybe you should check the Yellow Pages under 'lost and found,'" I suggested with a straight face. "Or even under 'barrettes.' Look for a company with a Galveston address, and give them a call. They'll recognize it from your description."

"Oh," she said. "Okay."

Our last customer of the day was Pammy Crowder. She looked around with her hands on her hips and said, "Y'all don't have much stuff."

She was right, of course. We were just getting started. And since we spent our weekdays in school, that left only the weekends for scavenging. The blue law meant we couldn't open the store on Sunday, and Saturday temple for Mel and Sunday church for B.D., along with the family meals afterward, made serious dents in the time we had to search for new merchandise.

"We need more inventory," B.D. said when Pammy had departed.

"In three more weeks," I pointed out, "it will be summer, and then we'll have all the time in the world. Harry always says to bide your time."

Harry – May 16, 1961

Chapter 3

On Tuesday I went to the airport to pick up Parsons and Miller, the two birds Smith wanted me to tail. I'd hired the Gonzalez brothers, Danny and Turk, because I couldn't afford to miss my marks. They drove one car, in case somebody needed to get out and hoof it, and I drove another. I gave them a Motrac unit so that we could communicate, and copies of the photographs Smith had given me. I'd acquired the Motrac walkie-talkies after a successful River Oaks divorce case fattened up my bank account, and they were worth every penny on a case like this one. The morning flight from DC was due in at nine, so we got there early and parked in front of the art-deco terminal, all rounded white shoulders below and bronzed green angles above—like a high-fashion hat. The rain had stopped during the night and there was already a small crowd milling around the observation deck, but I didn't like the percentage. If Miller and Parsons happened to be wearing hats, I'd never recognize them from above. Danny took the doors at one end, Turk took the doors at the other, and I took the main doors in the middle. There was an evening flight as well, but I was banking on the morning flight, since most business travelers liked to arrive early and get out of town at the end of the day.

Sure enough, about nine-twenty, here came our pigeons. I happened to be watching the door when they opened it and hit the wall of hot, humid, Houston air. They flinched when they stepped out the door as though they'd been slapped by a hot, wet towel, and then the handkerchiefs came out. The bird in the lead had a long face split by a long nose. His hair was dark and combed back from his forehead revealing a hairline that must've been drawn by a ruler. He had wide comical eyebrows and a well-shaped upper lip that made you think of stage actors with plummy voices. The other guy was balding with a forgettable face, but he was wearing a bow tie and I made him for Miller, since the only picture I had of Miller showed him in a bow tie, and bow tie aficionados don't usually switch hit.

I smiled to myself at the handkerchief routine, but when they cleared the door and I saw the two men who were flanking them, I stopped smiling and turned my head away. I'm not on intimate terms with the city's power brokers, but our paths cross from time to time, and I couldn't take a chance that I'd be recognized.

I whistled for the Rodriguez brothers and headed for my car. Over my shoulder I saw Turk rounding the corner of the terminal building. I had my door open and was watching our marks when Danny jogged up to me.

"Four of 'em." I nodded in the right direction. "Two rows back. Looks like a white Caddy."

He looked, nodded. Turk pulled up behind us.

"You boys take the lead," I said.

After a while, the walkie-talkie crackled. Danny said, "You paying us extra to tail the head honcho at Brown & Root?"

I should have warned him to be more discreet; I didn't trust the unit not to break into every radio program from here to Texas City. "Let's avoid specifics," I said. "Not for broadcasting. But look at it this way, boys. Maybe you'll get some information to sell him, and you'll make your fortunes."

Brown & Root was the largest construction company in Houston. You couldn't drive a block in the city without running into something that the Brown brothers, Herman and George, had built, and that included the freeway we were driving on. They divided their time and their living quarters between Houston and Austin so they could keep an eye on the politicians they owned in both places. They owned a couple of congressmen and senators, too, and a vice president, Lyndon Baines Johnson. It wasn't their fault they didn't own a president; their boy had been upstaged by a good-looking Boston blueblood with a political legacy that no bootstrap Texan could compete with.

"Turk wants to know who the other guy is," Danny said. "Looks familiar, but I can't place him."

"Don't know him. Couldn't tell you if I did, not on the radio."

"Do we need talk in a secret code?" Danny said. "Ten-four. Over and out."

We drove north on the Gulf Freeway toward downtown. I let them take the lead in case I might be recognized.

Then Danny's voice broke in, "We got company. Gray Plymouth Belvedere, Virginia license plates. You know him?"

I shook my head. "Didn't I warn you to be discreet?"

"He ain't looking for us, boss," Danny said. "He ain't listening to the radio. He's practically sitting in their back seat. If they're watching for a tail, they can't miss him."

"Write the number down," I said.

We got off on South Main, and I hung back. I imagined George was showing off his handiwork, since there were at least three skyscrapers going up downtown that he probably had a hand in, unless he was too busy building the new freeway southwest of town.

Danny's voice crackled. "Take a guess where we are. Go on—take a guess."

"You're at the tiki bar at Trader Vic's sipping a fruity drink with an umbrella," I said.

"No prize for you, hombre," he said. "We're in a parking lot at Rice Institute."

"University," I corrected automatically.

"That's right, they changed it," he said. "Come on up Main Street and take the first entrance past Sunset. We're in the first visitors' lot you come to. Our boys went into that big wrap-around building that looks like the Palace of Versailles."

That was a good description of the administration building,

Lovett Hall. It was an imposing three-story structure with more arches than Notre Dame Cathedral and more flagpoles than the UN. It had two massive wings that flanked a courtyard of walkways, emerald lawn, and clipped hedges. Turk had already returned from a reconnaissance trip when I pulled in.

He was the older and more solidly built of the two brothers. He had an impassive face and x-ray eyes that came across as sleepy. Danny stood with his hands on his hips. He was wiry and full of suppressed energy, like a cobra in a snake charmer's basket.

"They're in the president's office," Turk said.

"Where's Virginia?" I asked.

"Studying the portraits of past presidents," Turk said. "Fits right in. They never going to guess he ain't a student or a professor."

We had to watch the office somehow without attracting attention. The building was immense and it had too many exits; if they went wandering around inside, we'd lose them until they returned to the parking lot.

I said to Turk, "You'll have to go in. Do you have a jacket and tie?"

He grimaced. "Yeah, and I got a hat and shades, too, but this is going to cost you extra."

"Too bad you don't have your machete, hermano." Danny took a swing with an imaginary tool. "They'd figure you was going to trim the hedges."

"I went in there with a machete, I'd be arrested for sure," Turk said.

When he was gone, Danny and I settled in to wait. Between us we had enough cigarettes to last a while. Virginia hadn't put in an appearance.

"Like I told you, man," Danny said, "it's almost like he wants to get noticed. They can't miss him."

"I don't guess you recognized him," I said.

He shook his head.

It was almost an hour before our party of four left by the back entrance with the Rice president in tow—an elderly geologist named

Carey Croneis who'd taken on the job when the former president got sick. He hadn't wanted the job and so had the perpetual air of a man scanning the horizon for reinforcements through his rimless glasses. Virginia came hot on their heels, turning to snap photos of the building like a regular tourist. Turk caught up with us.

"They took a tour of the building," he said. "That's why it took so long. They were looking at the laboratories. Sounds like George wants to build 'em some more. The government men, they're talking about government money from NASA. But seem like they've got a race problem. That right?"

"Who doesn't?" Danny said.

I nodded. "Yeah, it's in their charter. Old Man Rice funded a school for whites only. But you'll be glad to know that they do admit Mexican-Americans like yourselves."

"Okay, but if the negroes start protesting, I ain't crossing their picket line," Danny said.

Our party went into the faculty club, and it was no mystery what they were going to do there since it was now lunchtime.

"I can't go in there," I said. "I'm the ex-husband. There are folks around here who would enjoy throwing me out."

My ex-wife Fran was a Rice English professor and Shakespearean scholar, publishing as "D.F. Lark," who had gotten where she was by sheer grit. Marrying me was the craziest thing she'd ever done, and she'd lived to regret it. On the plus side, we'd gotten two great kids and a precarious friendship out of it. Not to mention the bonds of alimony.

Danny pretended to be shocked. "You mean you ain't got no disguises in your trunk? No wigs or false noses? What kind of shamus are you? Hombre, you're a disgrace to your profession."

I ignored him and turned to Turk. "You're wearing a jacket and tie. You go. Tell them you're a Mexican engineering professor looking for your amigo, Professor so-and-so. Pretend you don't speak much English, so make them let you take a look around to see if he's there. We just need to know if anybody else has joined the party."

"Better not say Mexico," Turk said. "They wouldn't believe there's engineering professors south of the border."

"How 'bout Venezuela?" Danny said. "Everybody knows they got oil in Venezuela, they must need engineers."

As Turk entered the building, Virginia came out. He narrowed his eyes at Turk, but Turk just nodded at him. Virginia had just learned a lesson about segregation—nobody could eat in the Faculty Club except faculty members, administrators, and their guests.

Turk wasn't gone too long. He returned shaking his head. "Just our boys," he said. "Nobody else at the table. Ol' Droopy Lip is doing most of the talking." He meant George Brown, whose fat lower lip makes him identifiable even in profile.

I'd sent Danny to Youngblood's for fried chicken and we sat on the lawn and ate it, which cheered me up. I felt so cheerful, in fact, I strolled over to where Virginia was lounging against a tree and offered him a drumstick. Up close he looked even younger. His nose appeared to exert some kind of magnetic pull on the rest of his features so that they clustered in the middle of his face, even drawing down his eyebrows and widow's peak. Only his blond hair defied the trend and stood up in resistance. He wore a charcoal gray suit a size too big for him, which made him look like a kid playing dress-up.

"Go ahead," I said, extending the drumstick wrapped in a napkin. "There's plenty."

He eyed the drumstick suspiciously and curled his lip at me. "I don't eat on the job," he said, then immediately looked regretful about having admitted he was on a job.

"Suit yourself." I took a bite of the drumstick. "But it's a shame to come all this way and miss Youngblood's fried chicken."

He tried ignoring me. He stared at the entrance to the Faculty Club.

I turned around and stared with him, chewed and swallowed. "They're not coming out for a while," I said. "Those good ol' boys, they'll order at least three double bourbons for a confab like this one."

He took the bait. "A confab like what? What are you talking about?"

"Your two countrymen, and my three," I said. "They've got a lot to discuss."

"Such as?" He sneered.

"Well, this building they want to put up, for one thing," I said.

"How do you know they're building something?" he asked.

I tossed the chicken bone to the squirrels, wiped my fingers on the napkin, and stepped closer. "Because one of them is a builder," I said, lowering my voice to a conspiratorial stage whisper.

"What kind of builder?" he said.

I shrugged. "What kinds are there, sonny?"

He was tempted beyond his limit. "Lots of kinds," he said, nettled by that "sonny." "We ain't talking about no housing development here. You don't hire no ordinary contractor to build a space center. I bet there ain't ten companies in the country could do it."

"You could be right," I said placidly.

"Sure, I'm right," he said. "You've got to have the right place and the right builder and the right everything. You've got to have a port they can ship things in and out of, too." He was getting up a head of steam when a mosquito stopped him in his tracks. He slapped the back of his neck and evidently knocked some sense into his own head. "Anyway, I'm not talking to you. But if you think they're going to build this thing here and make everybody pack up and move out here to cow country, well, you're crazy, is all."

I laughed. "You're not the first person to tell me that."

"Aw, buzz off!" he said. "Go soak your head!"

Those suggestions weren't original, either, but I didn't tell him so. Instead I handed him a business card. "If you think we can help each other out, let me know," I said. "I like to keep things friendly."

He shoved the card in his pocket without looking at it.

Chapter 4

Eventually, our party emerged. The president walked them to the parking lot and shook hands with everybody. We all got back in our cars and followed the Caddy down the Gulf Freeway to Ellington Air Force Base. Our two cars hung back and let Virginia take the lead. He kept tight as a coondog's tick on the Caddy's bumper all the way.

These days, apart from its radar facilities, Ellington was mostly a reserves training base, so it wasn't heavily populated. We knew we couldn't get in without being spotted. We parked on the perimeter and watched through binoculars as our four met up with somebody who showed them around in a Jeep. The somebody appeared to be a brigadier general, but I couldn't trust my eyes at this distance, least of all through a chain-link fence. The two out-of-towners kept their handkerchiefs at the ready as the sun beat down. The general didn't appear to notice the heat.

Virginia was conspicuously crouching behind an antiaircraft gun until a guard came and shooed him away. He didn't look like an eager reservist, I guess. I wondered, though, how he'd talked his way past the guards on the gate. Probably he'd just waved his hand in the direction of the Caddy and said, "I'm with them." At least, that's what I would have done.

After the tour of Ellington we followed our boys down the Gulf Freeway to a small crossroad and turned toward Seabrook and Galveston Bay. I could see the Caddy in the distance and the gray Plymouth between me and the Gonzalez brothers on this stretch of road, which was flat here at sea level. It was quite a parade for a road that wasn't used to the traffic. The rabbits and copperheads must have been getting an eyeful.

I saw the Gonzalez mint-green Pontiac Chieftain off to the left, parked under a sign warning us that we were entering private property owned by Humble Oil and Refining. The Plymouth slowed to a crawl but didn't stop. I did.

Turk was leaning against the Pontiac rolling a cigarette. Danny was studying the retreating Caddy through a pair of binoculars.

"Not much place to hide in there." Danny scanned the landscape. "What you want to do, boss?"

I went over to survey the scene. All we could see was scrub brush and the distant shapes of oil wells. Now that the rain had stopped, somebody had cranked up the sun so that it could dry things out.

Danny said to Turk, "I bet he wants us to use our Indian skills to sneak up on 'em."

"Aw, man, you're full of shit," Turk said. He licked his cigarette paper. "Our people weren't hunters, they were farmers. If he wants us to find cow flop, we're all set."

I peered through the binoculars, but I couldn't see anything but the Plymouth, which was making a U-turn and heading back our way. Turk whipped out a map and we were all three studying it, pointing in different directions, when the Plymouth roared past us.

"You get that plate number?"

Danny nodded and handed me a scrap of paper.

"He's a long way from home," I said.

"Yeah," Danny said. "You wouldn't think they'd be all that interested in the oil bidness in Virginia."

I pocketed the slip of paper, shed my jacket, and reached for my camera. "All right, I'll go," I said. "Makes more sense than splitting you up."

Danny grinned at me. "Got your suntan oil, gringo?"

"Hold on, Harry." Turk reached into the car and pulled out a straw cowboy hat, which he set on my head. It was large for me, but I appreciated the cover it would give me in the brush.

“Yippee-ki-yay, podner,” Danny said. “Watch out for the rattlers, copperheads, and cottonmouths.”

I handed him my car keys and a five-dollar bill and told him to park the car by one of the small frame houses up the road and pay the owners for the parking space.

I wasn’t happy about how little cover was available, and if our men had come out here to look for a potential building site, they weren’t going to be studying their shoelaces, either. There were cattle grazing, but I wasn’t getting paid enough to try that old Indian trick of hanging from an animal’s belly so that you could sneak up on your enemy. I could have used a pair of cowboy boots, if I’d owned a pair; this was the kind of country they were made for, overstocked with cactus, burrs, brush, and copperheads. I ran in a crouch, the cowboy hat bouncing around on my head and sweat running down the back of my neck like some Chinese water torture. From a distance I probably looked like a jackrabbit wearing a Stetson. Every now and then my feet sank in muddy hoofprints.

I couldn’t hear anything except the loud buzz of insects. But sometimes a small breeze stirred the nearby salt grass and brought in the salty, heady scent of Galveston Bay.

Suddenly, the scrub gave way to green lawn. In the middle of the lawn was a mansion—a two-story sandstone Italian Renaissance house with an adobe roof. It was big enough to park a couple of cargo ships in, if you wanted to run them up the bay and portage them across the grass.

I knew where I was. This was the West Ranch property, former home of lumberman, cattleman, and oilman James West, publisher of the *Dallas Journal* and *Austin Tribune*, and former Chairman of the Houston City Planning Commission. He’d made a fortune he didn’t need when he’d sold this property to Humble Oil years ago. It was a huge tract of land located at the epicenter of the annexation war between Houston and its neighbors.

Along one side I could see a tree line that marked the undulations of Clear Creek as it wound its way to Clear Lake, a tongue of water protruding from Galveston Bay. I could see the water glinting in the sun.

I moved from tree to bush to pillar to hedge until I was squatting at the base of a stone wall. All the windows were closed, but some of the panes were broken and I could just make out voices. I took my hat off and risked a look through the window, but my efforts were rewarded with a great view of an empty room. I worked my way around the house until the voices got closer, and I knew they were standing on the veranda.

Somebody was saying, "At least you wouldn't have to start from scratch. All you'd have to do would be to tell George here what you'd need, and he'd fix it up for you. Isn't that right, George?"

"Sure," George said. "Be a mighty straightforward proposition."

There was a scuffling of shoes and one of the visitors said, "It's a beautiful house."

The first voice was saying, "Designed by an architect named Joseph Finger. It took three years to build and cost two hundred and fifty thousand dollars, which was a lot of money in those days. It has twelve bathrooms, do you believe that?"

The other visitor said, "We'd need good plumbing if we decided to put some labs in here."

They talked about the plumbing for a while and whether it had been damaged by vandals.

Then the first voice said, "You can see how close the water is—that's Clear Lake right there."

The first visitor said, "We're talking about some pretty heavy cargo, though. We can't just float it across a lake on rubber tires."

George said, "I reckon we can accommodate you. Let's take a look upstairs."

The second visitor cleared his throat. "It'd be kind of hot up there, won't it? I don't know that we need to—."

"We'll make it quick," said the first voice. "Don't worry, Mr. Parsons. The next time you see the place, it will be air-conditioned. You have my word on that."

They shuffled inside and I went back around the front of the building. I didn't see any percentage in risking the game to get inside. The government men—if that's what they were—wanted to build something—something that might include laboratories—and George Brown wanted to build it here, that much was plain. But how was Rice University involved? I felt certain that Mr. Smith already knew what the "something" was. I gathered it involved heavy cargo transported by ship. Smith had mentioned space, and Virginia had called it a space center, so maybe the government was going to start sending meteorites or radioactive rock samples up Galveston Bay. It didn't sound like big business to me, but I didn't know much about it. I supposed the right rocks could be worth a lot of money.

The house tour lasted another fifteen minutes, and then they got back in the Caddy and drove off down the road. If they were going to tour the property, I couldn't see myself dogging them on foot the whole way. I found a broken window, broke it some more, and slipped inside the house to look around, but there wasn't much to see—just the abandoned remains of a once-elegant mansion like Scarlet wearing the curtains and waiting for Rhett to return. I snapped a few more pictures, then more or less followed the road back to the entrance. I didn't want to be caught taking a stroll when the Caddy circled back, if it hadn't done that already, so I counted on Turk and Danny not to lose our foursome.

The boys were parked up the road across from a small weather-beaten frame house the color of dust. Its gutters sagged and one of its windows was broken and patched with cardboard, but a riot of zinnias lined the cement wall along the front porch. In the shade of a live oak, the Rodriguez brothers were surrounded by kids, all barefoot and suntanned, still wearing their school clothes. They were kicking around a flabby soccer ball and giggling. My blue Impala was parked in the dirt driveway, nose out, and three of the kids were sitting on the hood.

"They're taking the long tour," I reported and wiped the back of my neck with a handkerchief.

"Hombre," Danny said. "You are one hot, tired, cranky gringo." He turned to one of the kids. "Chiquita, can you bring my friend a glass of water?"

The kids saw the camera and suddenly everybody wanted their pictures taken, so Danny snapped pictures. I was sorry I hadn't brought the Polaroid so that the kids could see the pictures, but they seemed content to mug in front of the lens. My daughter Dizzy would have given me a lecture about getting organized and being prepared. I drank the water given to me by an obsidian-eyed girl in a ruffled pink dress. I reflected that I'd maybe never seen my own daughter wearing anything so feminine as a ruffled pink dress.

"No sign of Virginia?" I asked.

"No," Danny said. "But his car's parked up the road."

"Yeah?" I said.

"Go take a look," Turk said. "You can't miss it."

I looked around. I didn't want to get caught in the road when the Caddy returned, but I wanted to see the Plymouth up close. I decided to risk it.

I jogged up the road until I came to an abandoned auto shop. Its sun-bleached sign—Al's Auto—was clinging to a single rusty nail. The Plymouth was parked by a skeletal gas pump, like a hippo hiding behind a flamingo. The car was locked but I couldn't see why he'd bothered since his whole life was spread out on the front seat for any curious passerby to see. There were a map, a crumpled Marlboro pack, a Thermos, a Shipley Do-nuts bag, a bottle of insect repellant, a newspaper clipping folded to show a large black-and-white photograph of Parsons, and a key to room 8 at the Ramble Inn Motor Court on Telephone Road. There was even a file folder labeled "STG" and under that, "CONFIDENTIAL." "Confidential" was underlined three times either to discourage nosy birds like me or to draw our attention. I deduced that I might be interested in the contents. I deduced that Virginia was staying at a dive on Telephone Road while he was visiting the city. I couldn't see what was inside the Thermos or the donut bag, but I deduced that he'd already consumed some of the contents of each. Harry Lark, Ace Detective.

I jogged back to the house, where I was met by my barefooted friend, who gave me a reproachful look over a soccer ball. That was all right. I'd disappointed most of the women in my life at one time or another, so if she wanted to make me feel guilty about abandoning her, she'd have to get in line.

After a while, Turk spotted the Caddy coming, and we hid behind the house while the kids lined up along the road and waved. Then we followed the Caddy back to the airport and reconvened in the parking lot.

"What happened to Virginia?" I asked.

"We didn't see him," Danny said. "We thought maybe you let the air out of his tires."

"I'm not that kind of guy," I said. "Besides, I didn't think of it."

We watched our four men disappear into the terminal building.

I said, "If I were to say the words 'space center' to you, what would it make you think of?"

Turk's deadpan didn't change. Danny frowned. "What do you mean, 'space center'?" he said. "You talking about outer space? Where the Russian astronaut went?"

I nodded.

He and Turk looked at each other. He shrugged. "So what's a space center? Like a museum?"

"More like a laboratory, for studying things."

"You mean out there near Galveston Bay, they're going to build a big laboratory?"

"That seems to be the idea," I said. "But they need access to the water—maybe even a deep water channel. Something for heavy cargo."

"You think they've got some giant meteorites to look at?" Turk said.

"No, wait," Danny said. "Maybe they've got a UFO, like that one in the movie that crashed into the North Pole."

We looked at him.

"Listen," he said, "if that's what they've got, and they bring it to Houston, we're in big trouble. Those flying saucers carry seeds, and the seeds grow up to be space invaders, like Marshall Dillon in that carrot costume. You see that movie? *The Thing*?"

Turk looked at me. "He's full of shit, but he's right about one thing. They wouldn't need that much land or that much water just to look at some space rocks. That Mercury capsule they sent Alan Shepard up in—that wasn't so big. But the rocket that got it up there—that thing was big."

It hadn't been two weeks since NASA had succeeded in sending Shepard into space, and the excitement hadn't died down yet. We hadn't matched the Russians, of course, but we were breathing down their necks. Our president was encouraging us to think that way.

"It might explain George Brown's involvement," I said. "The Browns made their first million on shipbuilding. Maybe they're going in for rocket-building now."

"Sure," Danny said. "And that could explain the Humble connection, too. Rockets need fuel. Maybe they're going to build a rocket factory and a launch pad right there in the middle of the oilfield."

But we didn't have anything else to do except speculate on the basis of limited evidence, so we went home.

Chapter 5

I was sitting in front of the fan in my undershirt, drinking a beer and writing up my notes, when the phone rang. It was Carillo, an HPD detective I knew.

"What do you know about a guy name of Claude Arthur Dunwoody the Third?" he said.

"Nothing," I said. "What am I supposed to know about him?"

"You tell me," Carillo said. "He's got your card in his pocket."

"What's he look like?"

"He's a baby-faced blond kid, as far as I can tell," he said.

"What's that supposed to mean?"

"Snakebit," Carillo said. "Rattler got him."

I whistled. "Dead?"

"He'll probably recover," Carillo said. "They got him over at Hermann."

"Where'd you find him?"

"I didn't. Some kids found him out near the West Ranch property. Say, do you know this bird or don't you? How come you're asking all the questions?"

"I might have run into him at that. But I never saw him before today and I only talked to him for five minutes. He didn't tell me his name."

"Did he tell you what he was doing in town?" Carillo said.

"No, he didn't seem to want to talk to me."

"I can sympathize," Carillo said. "I haven't been talking to you for five minutes and already I don't want to talk to you."

"You're just saying that to hurt my feelings," I said. "You asked what he was doing in town. Does that mean he's from out of town?"

"See, that's why you're such a successful dick," he said. "Yes, genius, he's from out of town. You want to guess where?"

"His car tags said Virginia."

"What a coincidence. His driver's license says the same thing."

"So you have his home address, and his injury is the clear result of a chance encounter with a snake. Why are you calling me?"

"That's a good question. I've been asking myself the same thing. Mind telling me where he was when you were trying to hold a conversation with him?"

"Not at all," I said. "He was hanging out by Lovett Hall at Rice."

"At Rice?"

"Yeah, you know. Big school on South Main Street. They've got a stadium and everything."

He let a few beats of silence pass before he said, "Mind telling me what you were doing there?"

"My ex-wife works there," I said.

He waited. I waited. I took a swig of beer. He sighed.

"You're telling me that a gumshoe from Virginia came all this way to snoop around campus at Rice and then took a drive out to the country to look at the West Ranch?"

"That's what it sounds like," I said. "If he was a gumshoe. Do you know that he was?"

"He had a license in his wallet. Ink was still wet."

"Standards must be lower in Virginia."

"I wouldn't know. They seem to be pretty low in Texas. Anyway, I don't guess the standards say anything about snakebite training either place."

"You could be right. Was he packing?"

"Just a pocketknife."

"Use it on the snakebite?"

"Tried to. Cut it open, anyway, but it's hard to suck on the outside of your ankle."

I hadn't told him everything I knew, but he hadn't told me everything he knew, either. I didn't think the rattler had made off with the confidential file sitting on the front seat of Virginia's car, so unless he'd eaten it, the cops had it, which put them one up on me.

I felt guilty—not a lot, just enough to sour the beer on my tongue. Poor sap. I pulled on a clean shirt and a jacket and went out.

The Ramble Inn Motor Court was just the kind of dump I'd anticipated—peeling paint in a brown that had probably never looked good but must've looked better before the sun spent some time on it, weed-choked walkways and untrimmed bushes, blacktop with cracks an armadillo could fall into. What few lights remained intact blinked in a desultory, end-of-the-universe sort of way, as if they couldn't be bothered to illuminate anything. It was fine for me—plenty of cover from the bushes and the grinding of the window air conditioning units. The walls themselves were so thin I could've put my elbow through one and got in that way, but I have standards. So I pushed the "Do Not Disturb" sign out of the way, picked the lock on number 8, and went in.

The room smelled of mildew and cigarettes—that cheap motel smell like the funk of an old man who's given up bathing because his own familiar smell reassures him that he's still alive. The cops had already been here, I was sure. I doubted that Virginia was a high priority for them, just a minor inconvenience. He wouldn't even have been that if he hadn't been found half dead with a PI license up the road from Humble Refining property.

The room could have been ordered from some cut-rate motel supply catalog about thirty years ago. The gray carpet had been beaten down to its threads. The only thing holding it together was a bunch of stains running the gamut from wine to coffee. Metal frame bed with a gray corduroy bedspread racing the carpet to the finish line. Battered nightstand, coffee table listing like a drunken sailor in a sea squall, and desk with cracks in the cheap pine surface. Two utilitarian lamps missing their shades. Walls that had been painted when Hannibal was still training elephants, and chips showing where a couple of pictures used to hang. I tried to imagine some art lover stealing them or some honeymoon couple taking them as souvenirs of a dump that didn't run to monogrammed towels, but I couldn't do it. The built-in radio worked, but the knob came off in my hand. I wondered what would happen if I picked up the telephone receiver but squelched the impulse.

A cheap cloth-and-cardboard suitcase lay open on the bed. Either Virginia was a messy packer or the cops had wanted him to know they'd seen it. It held the usual assortment of underwear, socks, shirts and ties. In the breast pocket of one of the shirts I found a couple of business cards for C.D. Dunwoody, Claims Adjuster, Capital Life and Casualty, and in another I found cards for Claude Dunwoody of the *Groveton Herald*. Virginia was spreading himself thin. There were no more file folders—or anything else, for that matter—hidden under the clothes.

I checked the desk and blessed the cop who'd passed on the notepad with a scrawled note that said "Ronny" and a phone number. I didn't recognize the area code, but I was willing to bet it was a Virginia code, and while I was in a benevolent mood I blessed Ma Bell for giving us direct distance dialing. A chipped glass on the nightstand smelled of whiskey, but Virginia hadn't been hospitable enough to leave the bottle. There weren't any other glasses, and all of the butts in the ashtrays were Marlboros, so if he'd had any visitors it wasn't obvious. Next to the ashtray was a book of matches from the Starlight Lounge up the street.

A couple of mosquito hawks followed me into the bathroom and commenced to do the bump-and-grind with the low-watt light bulbs on either side of the cracked mirror. The light startled a pair of cockroaches and they scuttled off through a hole in the wall behind the sink where the pipes came in. The roaches were smaller than my shoes, but not by much. If one of them had stood on the other's shoulders, he could have spit in my eye. Somebody's fifth-grade insect collection already lay scattered about the sink, along with Virginia's razor, shaving cream, toothbrush, toothpaste, deodorant, and hair oil. The smell of mildew was stronger in here, and the sink was iron-stained. A faded green shower curtain clung in desperation to two rusted rings.

I returned to the main room and examined its surfaces from eye level. They were all furred with dust, undisturbed except around the note pad and by the telephone on the nightstand. I squinted at the nightstand, then thrust my hand under the pillow on that side and came up with a gun. It was a Smith and Wesson .38 with a short barrel and wood grip. It would have taken care of the rattlesnake and then some. I'd had a few of those "if only" moments myself, and I felt another surge of sympathy for the poor schmuck. I replaced the gun where I'd found it. The cops hadn't taken it, neither would I.

I found the dead soldier in the battered metal wastebasket, along with an empty Marlboro package and the wrappers from a Moon Pie, a Clark's, a Chuckles, and a Hostess Donettes. I felt a deduction coming on: Virginia had a sweet tooth. Also he drank. At the bottom of the bin, there was a crumpled bar napkin on which he'd been doing some calculations. I hoped he hadn't been calculating his wages, if one of those numbers represented his day rate, but considering the dump he'd landed in, I was probably hoping in vain. The next time I got an opportunity to give him advice, if there was a next time, that would be at the top of my list.

I took a last look around and let myself out. To preserve what was left of his pride, I locked the door behind me and straightened the "Do Not Disturb" sign.

Dizzy – Saturday, May 20

Chapter 6

On Saturdays, if he wasn't working, Harry sometimes took us to Whataburger for lunch. By "us," I mean B.D. and me, since Mel went to temple on Saturday mornings and Hal usually spent Saturday mornings in Greg Buchanan's garage, where they were building a soapbox racer. But the trips to Whataburger didn't happen very often, since Harry was nearly always working. Or so he said.

If left to our own devices, we'd case the neighborhood and scavenge items we could put in the Lost and Found. It was better on weekday afternoons when Mel was along because she had a real knack for finding things. Before we'd ever even opened the shop, she'd found an intact snow globe with a cowboy inside it, a hubcap that was only slightly dented, a retainer inside its plastic case, and a five-dollar bill that we cashed in for change to put in our cigar box. Mel was the goods, all right, and we always felt a little disadvantaged without her. But this one Saturday in May, after we'd collected our usual haul of loops for toy looms, Tinker Toys, jacks, grubby tennis balls with teeth marks in them, barrettes, and a plastic bandeau or two, our luck turned, and we found a Tiny Tears bottle, a metal pan for an Easy Bake oven, a sneaker, and a small silver heart with "Margie" engraved on it.

This last item was too important to put in the Lost and Found, and we knew it, but we were excited to find it anyway, hidden in the tall grass along the road where it would never have been found by anybody who wasn't on their biscuit and poking around with a stick. We took it to the Monaghans' house on the next street and turned it in to Margie's mother. We didn't want to be accused of boosting it. That was a good way to wind up in the hoosegow. We turned down the one-dollar reward Mrs. Monaghan offered us, and left her with some of our business cards instead, which she promised to pass out at her bridge club. Harry always says it pays to invest in good will. He is chronically disorganized and can't remember a softball game or doctor's appointment to save his life, but he remembers every favor he ever did for someone.

We stopped by Mel's and collected her. She still smelled like the cologne she wore when she got dressed up for temple.

When we got back to the shop, we found Howie Sunderland waiting for us, sitting cross-legged in front of the garage door as if he expected it to open from the inside. Howie wore baggy shorts, a striped tee shirt, and a frown. Whole galaxies of freckles blurred together on his cheeks, and his red hair looked like it had been Brylcreemed into submission by the barber that morning.

He got to his feet. "Open up, y'all," he said. "I lost Buddy."

"Who's Buddy?" B.D. said, while I yanked on the door handle.

"My cat," he said. "He ain't been home."

When I got the door open, he walked in and began peering anxiously into the boxes.

"He's a yaller cat," Howie said. "A tiger. About this big." He held up his hands and looked at us as if this description would help us distinguish Buddy from all the other cats we had rounded up. Maybe he thought we'd arrange a lineup.

Lucille chose this moment to make her entrance from wherever she'd been sleeping under the bushes. She stood on her hind legs to check out the footlocker before jumping on it, wrapping her tail around her paws, and looking at Howie.

"He's bigger than her." Howie pointed at Lucille. "He could beat her up, easy."

"It's rude to point," B.D. said.

"We don't have any lost cats," I added.

He looked around. "Ain't this the Lost and Found? Buddy's lost."

"And if we find him, we'll let you know," I said.

"Whyn't you go find him?" he said.

"That's not how it works," I said.

"It's a lost and found," he complained. "Buddy's lost, and he needs to be found."

He was getting on my nerves, but there was a note of real desperation in his voice, and his lower lip quivered.

B.D. heard it, too. "Well, maybe we could help you look for him," she said. "Why don't you sit down and tell us how he came to be lost?"

As he was planting his bottom in a lawn chair, I said, "Was he a boy cat? I mean, was he *still* a boy?"

He took offense. "Of course, he's a boy!"

B.D. shook her head at me, but I raised my eyebrows and spread my hands. If Buddy still had all his original equipment, he was probably off romancing lady cats from here to Long Point Road, and there was no way we'd get him back until he was good and ready to come home. Harry always said that in most missing persons cases, the hard part wasn't finding them, it was talking them into going home.

I angled my head at B.D. and we retreated to the back of the garage.

"We could try," she said. "We've read enough detective novels between us, plus you've got Harry."

"Harry says that the most important thing a detective needs to know is human nature."

"So?"

"So in this case, we're talking about feline nature. And what we know about tomcats is that they run off. You remember my cat Spike. That's what he did—he skipped."

"Diz, just because Spikey ran off, it doesn't mean that every boy cat will do that," B.D. said patiently. "You can't judge every boy cat by one boy cat, any more than you can judge every man by what Harry would do."

I knew that she'd mentioned Harry because he was the one with the reputation for taking a powder.

"You *can*, though," I insisted. "That's what the vet told me when Spike disappeared. It's what they do—it's how they're made. They go looking for janes and forget to come home."

She sighed. "Well, even so, we ought to try and help him. I mean, look at him."

We both turned back to Howie, who was slumped in the lawn chair. His sneakered feet dangled short of the floor. A tear slipped from the corner of his eye. He rubbed it away with his fist and snuffled.

"If we're going to make this business work, we need to become the neighborhood experts on lost things," B.D. said. "It will be a good experience for us."

"It won't help our reputation if we fail," I muttered.

"Come on, Diz." B.D. patted me on the arm. "You can't think that way. You've got to have a positive attitude."

I shrugged, and she took it for assent. We returned to Howie.

We got the dope on Buddy's disappearance: he'd missed three meals, which meant he hadn't been seen since Thursday evening.

"Do you have any pictures of Buddy?" I asked.

He frowned in thought, then lit up. "I could draw you one now!" he said. "You got a yaller crayon?"

"She meant a photograph," B.D. said. "Do y'all have any photographs of Buddy?"

He didn't know, so we sent him home to look. I retrieved a notebook and pencil, the magnifying glass Hal had given me for Christmas and a can of tuna fish and can opener from the house.

"We might could take Lucille," B.D. said, "for bait."

Lucille was sprawled full length on the footlocker and gave us a baleful look.

"Up to her," I said. "She might come, or she might not."

"If you opened the tuna fish, she'd come," B.D. pointed out.

So I punctured the can with the can opener and put them both in a paper bag. Lucille sat up and looked interested.

Howie came puffing up then and handed me a snapshot. I wasn't expecting much, and not-much is what I got: a great picture of a grinning Howie, arms spread, partially obscured by a blurred form that could have been a cat, extended in the act of jumping down. All I could tell from the photograph was that Buddy was a big boy, probably not a longhair.

To B.D. I said, under my breath, "Do we bring the kid or send him home?"

"Bring him," she said. "He might have more information than he's given us. Besides, he's so pathetic that folks will take one look at him and go out of their way to help us."

In the end, Lucille came too, trailing a good distance behind us as if she just happened to be going in the same direction. Howie lived on the next street, so we began with the neighbor that lived behind him on my street. Since it was a sunny Saturday afternoon, lots of people were home, washing their cars or working on them in the garage, or painting things laid out on sawhorses on the driveway, or gardening, or playing catch with their kids. We circled Howie's house. Most of the neighbors knew Buddy.

"Whenever he comes over in the evening," said a man with a face like crumpled paper, "why, I give him a little milk."

"Buddy don't drink milk," said his neighbor. "Don't appear to like the taste. Now, a little bit of hamburger, that's more to his liking." He punctuated this declaration with the wrench he was holding.

The first man looked at the second. "Maybe you got the wrong kind of milk," he said. "Buddy's crazy for what we give him. Never seen him eat hamburger, though."

"Hamburger's what he eats at my house," the second man said.

A third man had meandered over. He was holding a soapy sponge. "I'll tell you what he really likes—tuna fish. I give him a little bit of tuna fish, and he don't hardly let it hit the plate."

Clearly, Buddy was an accomplished moocher with an elaborate con going. I added five pounds to the weight I'd assigned him in my head. We moved on.

"Oh, I know that yaller one," said a woman two streets away. She was wearing a scarf over her curlers and washing her windows. "That one's feisty. Him and my Sugarpuss, they're always getting into it. I got to turn the hose on 'em to get 'em to stop."

Two doors down, we found a man sitting in a lawn chair on his front porch, smoking a cigar and listening to a ballgame on the radio. "I don't pay much attention, tell you the truth," he said. "But sometimes seems like I can't hear the radio or the television for all the caterwauling. Just the other night, them cats was going at it again. I don't know whether your boy was in it or not, but it was a doozey. You never heard such a racket."

"Would this have been Thursday night?" I asked.

"I couldn't tell you, hon," he said. "I was watching *The Tonight Show*, and Jack had that fellow on—what's that fellow's name, now? Something foreign. He was in that big Roman movie, with the chariots and all. I never thought that fellow was so funny, but he is, and anyway that's when the fight busted out. Like I said, I don't know who-all was involved, but if your boy lost, you best be looking for the b—."

He stopped himself just in time. He glanced at Howie. "Well, that's all I know."

"Were they in the front yard or the back yard?" I asked.

"Front yard." He gestured. "Right out here."

I turned around to look at the street from his vantage point. My gaze swept the houses, yards, and street. There were plenty of bushes to look under. Unless—.

I looked up. Plenty of tall pines as well. If I were losing, that's where I'd go. And in a crisis, I wouldn't worry too much about how I was going to get down.

"I've got to go get something," I told B.D. "Wait here." I gave her the paper bag to hold.

"Should we start looking under the bushes?" B.D. said in a low voice.

We both looked at Howie. "Why don't you wait?" I said.

I returned with Hal's binoculars, and began scanning the treetops.

"You think he could climb way up there?" B.D. said.

"If he was desperate, he could."

"I see him! I see him!" Howie shouted. "There he is! Up there!" He pointed.

I aimed the binoculars where he was pointing, and there, sure enough, sat a yellow tiger cat.

Howie began to dance under the tree, jumping and reaching and calling Buddy's name.

Buddy looked down and moved his mouth but we couldn't hear over Howie's din if he made a sound. He closed his eyes and meowed again. But he didn't budge.

Lucille sat on the grass, looking up with apparent curiosity. Then she meowed, at nobody in particular.

"We'd better call the fire department," B.D. said. "I don't reckon he's going to come all that way for one little can of tuna. I'll go call."

"Hang on," I said. "He's on the move."

Buddy stood and stretched, as if he was used to living in trees and found it pretty comfortable after all. He meowed again, and Lucille meowed again, and then he looked down, head cocked, and appeared to assess the situation.

"I'd better go call," B.D. said. "I'd better tell them to bring one of those trampoline things." But she didn't go. She didn't want to miss anything, I could tell.

The man with the cigar came and stood with us. "I'll be derned," he said.

Buddy had stretched down and dropped to the next branch, slipping a little and hugging the branch until he was steady. We heard the scrape of his claws as he scrabbled for purchase on the bobbing branch. It had been a traumatic experience he didn't seem to want to repeat. He crouched on his new branch, looked down, and meowed at us. He'd done his part, he seemed to be saying. Three more kids showed up, took in the situation, and asked for the cat's name. They added their voices to the cheering section.

"Come on, Buddy," they said. "It ain't that far to the next branch. You can do it!"

"Nyow," said Lucille.

"I can get a ladder," the cigar man said. "Maybe if I stand at the top, it won't seem so far."

By the time he'd returned with the ladder, Buddy had gained the next branch, and a small crowd had gathered. The cigar man set up the ladder and climbed it. This seemed to cause Buddy some trepidation and he eyed the branches above him. But the cigar man, the man who claimed not to take any notice of the neighborhood animals, started to sweet-talk him.

"We ought to call the fire department," somebody said.

After a few minutes, Buddy appeared to be persuaded by the cigar-man. He descended one branch, then two, but slipped again on the second and dangled for a minute before he got his legs under him and scrambled back onto the branch. He hunkered down and closed his eyes.

"Here." B.D. handed me the bag she'd been holding. "Offer him the tuna fish."

I opened the can, put it back in the bag, and gave it to the man on the ladder. But Buddy appeared to be more interested in survival than tuna fish.

That was when the fire truck arrived. So somebody had called them after all. Two firemen joined the crowd and assessed the situation, arms folded. The owner of the house with Buddy's tree couldn't be found, and they didn't want to drive the fire truck onto the grass without permission. They could back it into the driveway, but the ladder wouldn't stretch to the tree.

"Let me and Lucille try," I offered.

I picked her up and climbed the ladder, which wasn't easy, given Lucille's state of panic when she looked down and saw the ground falling away past her thumpers. She dug her claws into my shoulder, so that we were both yowling by the time we reached the top of the ladder.

This performance drew Buddy's attention, and he decided to take a closer look. While I wrestled with a wriggling Lucille, he began making his way cautiously, branch by branch, down the tree. Every time he slipped, the crowd gasped, but he appeared to have made up his mind now that Lucille was involved in the rescue effort. I heard B.D. ask the firemen for a trampoline to catch him, but one of them said that he'd probably land on his feet in the grass and wouldn't need it.

In the end, that's just what happened. He was about two feet above Lucille and me when he fell, and as he passed us Lucille leaped out of my arms. The crowd gasped. Buddy landed with a soft thud and Lucille landed on top of him. There was a beat of silence as they picked themselves up, looking a little dazed, and then the crowd cheered. B.D. scooped up both cats and handed Buddy over to Howie.

"Oh!" Howie said, hugging Buddy hard enough to give the cat second thoughts about abandoning the tree. "Thank you, thank you, thank you!" His eyes shone with tears. "Y'all found him and then y'all rescued him! You're just like Superman!"

I wiped at the blood on my shoulders with a licked finger and grinned at B.D., who was handing out our business cards. She'd been right, after all. If Harry had been here, he would have said, "You can't buy that kind of publicity."

Harry – May 20, 1961

Chapter 7

The morning after I tossed Virginia's motel room, I called the number on the note pad. I didn't get anyone then, or in the afternoon, but around six o'clock, a woman with a tired voice answered the phone. There was a baby screaming in the background. She handed me over to a male voice.

"Ronny?" I said in a conspiratorial whisper.

"Yeah, who's this?" he said. "Jeannette, can't you take her for a walk or something? I'm trying to talk on the phone."

The woman said something in a go-to-hell voice, and then the screaming faded.

"Who'd you say you were?" Ronny said.

"A friend of Claude's," I said, "from Houston. Look, he's had some trouble down here."

"Claude Dunwoody? Is that who we're talking about?"

"Right. He's in Houston, and he's had some trouble."

"Houston?" He didn't add, "What's he doing down there?"

"That's right, Houston. And he wanted me to call and let you know about the trouble because he doesn't know when he'll be able to get to a phone and call you."

"What happened to him?" He'd lowered his own voice to match mine. I could hear the wheels turning. "He didn't get arrested, did he?"

"I don't think so," I said. "I'm not sure."

"Jesus! I told him not to go and do anything stupid! Jesus!" Then his mind caught on something. "How come you're not sure if he's been arrested or not? Where is he?"

"He's at Hermann Hospital," I said. "A rattler got him."

"A rattler?"

"A rattlesnake."

"Rattlesnake?" His voice rose with his skepticism. "Say, what is this? If this is—."

"I'm not kidding," I said. "He followed some fellows onto some old ranch property down here and a rattler bit him and he just made it back to his car." I wasn't about to give him a full report; he wasn't paying me. Wasn't paying Claude much, either.

"Well, why would he get arrested for a snakebite?" he said.

"It's not that," I said. "The ranch is private property, and I guess somebody called the cops. Well, by the time they found him, he couldn't give them his name or anything, so they went through his wallet and found his ticket—his PI license, I mean. Now the cops are curious about what he was doing out there."

"Jesus! I knew something like this would happen! I knew it! It always does with Claude. Snakebite!" I heard a sound like a palm slapped against a hard surface. "Jesus, if I wasn't related to him I'd come down there and bite him myself. PI, my ass! Probably ordered his license from the back of a comic book." He engaged in some heavy breathing and low-level profanity for a while, and I didn't interrupt. Then he wound down, and the suspicion returned. "Wait, you talked to him afterward?" he said. "How do you know Claude?"

"I met him in a bar down here," I said. "We're drinking buddies. But I guess I'm the only friend he has in town, so he called me up this morning."

This was the thin part of the story. If he could call me, he could have called Ronny—collect, of course—but Ronny didn't sound like the kind of guy I'd call collect for sympathy after I'd botched a job for him.

"What'd he tell you?" he said.

"Just what I told you. He's doing better because they've shot him up with painkillers and all." This was probably true, since I'd checked on his condition earlier and learned that he was in serious but stable condition. He was bound to be feeling better than he'd been feeling when they found him. "But he asked me to call you because the cops are hanging around and asking him questions about the ranch."

"What ranch?"

"Like I told you." I let some impatience into my tone. "The ranch where the rattler bit him."

"What's it called?"

"What difference does that make?" I said in pretend exasperation. "It's not a ranch anymore. It belongs to the biggest oil company in Houston."

"Jesus!" he said. "That's all I need."

"Well, he wanted me to tell you." Then I added, "Oh, yeah, he wanted me to tell you that he lost Parsons and that other guy because of that rattler. So he doesn't know whether they went anywhere else, but he thinks they might have left town already."

"Jesus, I know that much. I saw Miller at Langley this afternoon."

"Yeah, well, that's all I know," I said with the air of somebody who'd already lost interest. "I guess I'll call again if he asks me to, but you shouldn't count on that. He's just a guy I met in a bar."

"I understand," he said. "Listen, I didn't mean to be rude before, I was just surprised, you know? I appreciate you calling. I do."

Half an hour in the library on Monday morning suggested that "Langley" probably didn't refer to the CIA headquarters but to the Langley Research Center in Hampton, Virginia, headquarters for NASA's Space Task Group—the "STG" on Virginia's file folder. Another couple hours revealed that the Space Task Group managed NASA's manned spacecraft missions, including Alan Shepard's recent space flight. A call to Langley in the guise of a shipper trying to read the signature on a delivery confirmation netted me two candidates for "Ronny." Two more phone calls, one to each of my candidates in which I pretended to be calling the other, identified my pigeon: Ronald F. Gardiner, an engineer in the Systems Integration Section, whatever that was.

Amateurs. The world is full of them.

On the other hand, everybody's an amateur at something. I couldn't launch a rocket to save my life.

Around eleven I showed up at Claude's hospital room with a potted plant wrapped in tinfoil and a Texas-sized smile. I was having a hard time thinking of him as "Claude" instead of "Virginia," but I was making the effort because I didn't want to be accused of insulting a man when he was down.

"Howdy," I said. His head was propped on a pillow but the sheet was pulled up to his chin, which made him look younger than ever despite the shadow of a beard against his pale skin. His short blond hair pointed in all directions and his eyes drooped, but they opened a little wider when they saw me.

"Jesus!" he said. "You're all I need."

I continued to smile at him in what I hoped was a disarming fashion as I sat down in the wooden visitor's chair and hitched it closer to the bed. His roommate—a geezer I might mistake for a corpse in poor light—stopped snoring, stirred, fluttered his eyes, said something unintelligible, and fell asleep again.

"I figured I was probably the only guy in town who knows you," I said. "Sorry to hear about your injury. There but for the grace of God and all that."

"You don't know me," he objected. "And I don't know how you managed to wander around out there and not get bitten, but I don't think God had much to do with it."

This counted as witty repartee for Claude, and I upped my estimate of his IQ.

"I brought you something to brighten up your sickroom."

He eyed the plant with a sour expression. "What is it?"

"A plant."

"Swell."

"There's a bonus." I said peeled back the tinfoil to show the pint of Scotch I'd nestled in under the red flowers.

He brightened, then looked suspicious. "What's the catch?"

"No catch," I said, and set the plant down on his nightstand next to a glass of water and a small dish of something bright green that might have once been Jello. "Professional courtesy. Shamus to shamus."

"Well, thanks," he said grudgingly. He wasn't going to give me the satisfaction of reaching for the bottle, but his fingers twitched and I knew he wanted to.

"Also, I called Ronny for you."

That raised his eyelids. "How do you know about Ronny?"

"A cop I know found my card in your pocket and called me."

"Carillo?"

"That's the one."

His mouth turned down and for a minute I thought he might cry. "Christ, they've probably tossed my motel room."

"I wouldn't be surprised," I said. "Also your car."

"Yeah." He sighed and looked out the window. The rain was back, drumming against the pane. The old man in the next crib snored on. "About Ronny—did he say he was coming to get me out of here at least?"

"He didn't say." I lit a smoke and offered it to him. He struggled to sit up, grimacing. "I get the impression he doesn't especially want to be a known associate of yours."

"Christ, he's my cousin. It wouldn't kill him."

"Maybe when he calms down. Anybody else you want me to call?"

"Hell, I didn't want you to call him. Now I'll never hear the end of it."

"Maybe the cops have called him by now anyway."

"Why would they?" He flashed me a sharp look, or as sharp a look as a man can muster who's been shot full of dope. He had already forgotten that I'd told him, or rather implied, that the cops had given me Ronny's name.

I shrugged. "They've got the file."

"What file?" He was working up to belligerence again.

"The file you left on the front seat of your car," I said. "The one marked 'STG' and 'confidential.'"

He crumpled at that. His shoulders drooped, his chin dropped, his mouth sagged, even his hair stood down. He looked at his cigarette as if he was wondering where he'd get the energy to stub it out in disgust. "Aw, hell," he said, "maybe I should go back to delivering produce for my Uncle Elmer."

"Don't take it so hard, kid," I said. "Everybody's got to start somewhere. Was this your first job?"

"Second," he said morosely. "My first was for Aunt Constance. I found out who Uncle Elmer was screwing on the side."

"Sounds like a burned bridge, you ask me. Like I said, put it down to experience." I knew I should be discouraging him. I didn't think he was cut out for this work. But you don't kick a man when he's down. "How did you get your license, anyway?"

"Lied."

"Oh." I wanted to cheer him up but he wasn't making it any easier. "I tell you what you do, you find yourself a local shamus who needs an operative and go work for him for a while—get a little more experience under your belt. You can't learn how to be a detective just by reading Ross Macdonald, you know."

"Who?"

"Skip it."

"No, you're right," he said. "I need more experience. I oughta come work for you, except I couldn't stand the weather." He glanced at the window again. Water streamed down the glass.

It was a near miss. If he'd asked to work for me, I might have come up with a few dozen phony excuses, but I would have taken him on in the end. He would have looked at me the way Dizzy's cat Lucille had looked at me when she was just a muddy furball with big eyes, and I would have caved and then cursed myself every day until I found a way to get rid of him. I repressed a shudder.

"Your cousin Ronny belong to Elmer and Constance?" I asked casually. I offered him another cigarette, and he took it. Now that his hands were outside the sheet I let him light it himself.

He shook his head. "Judy and Orson, my mother's side of the family."

"So he's, what, afraid they'll pick Houston for the new space center? Why does he care?"

"Why do you think?" He was irritable again. He gestured at the window. "Jesus, who in their right mind would want to live here?" Then he relented, and added, "No offense."

Since I'd had the same reaction when my wife announced that she was accepting a teaching job at Rice, I couldn't afford to take offense, so I just said, "He'd have to move?"

"They all would." He frowned at his cigarette. "It's not a popular idea."

"You get used to it," I said. "And when your kids are going barefoot in January, you might even decide that you like it. I mean, not you personally," I corrected. "But you might want to tell Ronny that air conditioning has done a lot for the city. Houstonians view roaches as just another breed of livestock. And when the bayous overflow and the crayfish wander onto the patio, we just look on it as a fresh seafood delivery. Hurricanes keep us on our toes and make us appreciate the garden-variety thunderstorm. Like I say, you get used to it."

He shifted in the bed and grimaced.

"Hurting?" Not a serious question for a man with a rattlesnake bite. It was an invitation to unload if he wanted to.

For just a second, his features relaxed into exhaustion and the suffering showed. Then the impulse passed and he gained control again. "Yeah," he said. "I'd offer to show it to you, but if I had to look at it again, I'd probably pass out. Jesus!" The corners of his mouth turned down in disgust. "Who gets bitten by a rattlesnake when they're working as a private eye?"

"Welcome to Texas," I said. "Just because we've got more guns, registered and unregistered, than any other state doesn't mean that's all we've got."

A nurse bustled in then and made shooing motions so I said goodbye and went to the door.

"My sister," he said.

I turned back. “Sorry?”

“Maybe you could call my sister.”

I wrote down the sister’s number and left. I called the sister when I got back to the office and she said she’d come right away. I figured I’d heard the last of Claude Dunwoody the Third. I wished him well, as long as he went back to Virginia and stayed there.

Chapter 8

Mr. Smith showed up when he'd said he would—same suit, same bulge under his armpit, same powder blue handkerchief.

"Your secretary's still out," he said.

"Summer cold," I said.

He grunted, took the report I offered him, and started to read.

It was a good report, detailed and accurate if badly typed. The only thing it left out was Claude. Call it professional courtesy to a guy who's been laid out by a rattlesnake, or call it caution. I didn't know what the game was yet; I didn't even know the players. I didn't know if Smith was connected to Langley or if he was running his own game. But I'd given him his money's worth. I'd even identified the fourth man in all the photographs, the other tour guide. It was Ed Redding of the Houston Chamber of Commerce.

He took his time with the report—so much time that I began to wonder if I'd used any words too big for him to handle. Finally, he looked up.

"Pictures?"

I nodded and handed him an envelope. He shook them out and studied them one by one.

Then he put them back in the envelope, crossed his arms, and leaned back.

"So how did they seem—Parsons and Miller? Your impression."

I stroked my chin. "Hot."

He studied my face. "Unhappy?"

"Miserable."

"Really?" He smiled. It was the smile of a vampire contemplating a nice neck.

He paid me in cash without a squawk, adding, "There might be more later." And then he was gone.

I watched him disappear around the same street corner as last time, and thought that I probably wouldn't see him again.

I was wrong. The next day, May 25th , President Kennedy addressed a joint session of Congress. Among other things, he said that we were in an all-out race with the Russians to control outer space, and that he was committed to putting a man on the moon by 1970.

I saw some of the speech on the news that night. I was watching it with my kids at their house. They both sat up a little straighter when they heard it. Hal said, "Gee whiz!" in a voice heavy with awe and maybe something like longing. Dizzy sat with her fork suspended between the TV tray and her mouth, forgotten. "Jeez!" she said. "The moon! Do you think they can?"

I passed my hand over the top of her head. "Maybe next time around they'll send a woman, Sis."

She set the fork down. "Yeah, I guess they'll have to. They'll need somebody to clean up the mess."

Hal and I exchanged a look. Neither of us pointed out that, in this house, the messiest room belonged to Dizzy—that Hal's room was almost compulsively neat, the pennants on the wall, the books on the desk, and the shoes in the closet lined up like members of a military band.

"Don't worry, Pogo," he said to her. "You'll get your chance, if you want it. You can do anything you set your mind to."

She ducked her head and smiled a little then because she understood him. He didn't mean that anybody could do anything they set their mind to, he meant that Dizzy could, and he was probably right. I winked at him.

Personally, I felt a little light-headed, as if the earth had shifted under my feet. A man on the moon would change everything for my kids. Their universe would expand.

About a week later, Mr. Smith caught me in my office again. I was looking over some photographs I'd taken in an insurance fraud case. I hadn't given Smith a thought except when I'd called the hospital to check on Claude, who had been discharged. We were having mild weather for a change, but the Weather Ball still blinked green. Mr. Smith had learned his lesson and was carrying a black umbrella, no raincoat. Without the shoulder bulge, you might have taken him for a banker.

"Some cold," he said, by way of announcing his presence.

"It's turned into pneumonia," I agreed.

"Got another job for you," he said. He sat heavily in his chair and fished out a small notebook. "Ever hear of the 8-F Club?"

I nodded.

"You a member?"

"Not hardly." I laughed. "Anyway, it's not a real club. Local reporters usually call it 'the 8-F crowd' or the '8-F group.' They don't carry membership cards like Communists or Elks. It's just an informal group made up of Houston bigwigs. They get together over at the Lamar Hotel, in the Brown brothers' suite, 8-F, and engineer the city's future. I don't think they have regularly scheduled meetings."

"Your congressman's coming to town," he said. "Albert Thomas. Know him?"

"I've met him. So has half the city."

"I think there's going to be a meeting of this 8-F group while he's here this weekend."

"Seems likely."

He leaned forward. "I want to know everything—who's there, what they talk about, what they're planning, how much it all costs."

"You don't want much," I said.

"Can you plant a bug?"

"That's illegal."

He held my gaze. Finally, he said, in a conciliatory tone, "You're a taxpayer. How do you feel about your money being spent on crooked back-room deals that cost you more in the end because of all the palms being greased? How do you feel about secret arrangements that never make the newspaper, about phony bidding processes that never give honest businessmen a real shake because the fix is already in?" He conjured up some righteous indignation and injected it into his voice, where it sounded like a gospel singer in a cathouse quartet.

But I wasn't about to listen to a gun-toting thug from New York or Chicago or Miami lecture me on ethics. "Is this related to the space center?"

"That's right," he said.

"Listen," I said, as if I were allowing him to convince me, "maybe I could get a man in there, undercover. A room service waiter."

He nodded his approval. "They sure don't pour their own drinks."

Given the crowd, the drink pourer was probably a curvaceous blonde but I didn't tell him so.

"I suppose I can get what you want," I said, "one way or another."

The trick was to keep him hooked while promising as little as possible. I didn't want him to go out and hire another PI. He left me another retainer and went away satisfied.

I called up a desk clerk I knew whose brother I helped beat a vehicular manslaughter rap by tracking down a witness who said that the victim was dead drunk at the time and jaywalking. Of course, the brother had been drunk, too, but the judge didn't know that. I did, and that gave the clerk an extra incentive to help me out.

His greeting was tentative.

"I need to know about 8-F," I said.

"I see, sir." His professional voice wobbled. "Well, I'm sure we can accommodate you if you'll tell me what it is you require."

"Okay," I said, laughing. "I'll do the talking. There's going to be a party this weekend. I assume that means booze and food. Would that be tomorrow or Saturday?"

"Saturday might be a possibility," he said, as if considering. "Yes, sir."

"Lunch?"

“Certainly, sir.”

“Will there be a Brown in residence Friday night?”

“I believe so, yes.”

“And your people will set up in the morning?”

“Around eleven—yes, that should be no problem.”

“Give my regards to your brother,” I said, and hung up.

This suited me just fine, since I’d promised to take Hal to a Houston Buffs game on Friday night—the last game of a home stand against Omaha.

On Friday afternoon, I went to see a man I know who rents highly specialized electronic equipment out of the back room of his pawnshop. The shop itself is as dusty as the inside of a crematorium, but the back room is immaculate. The window unit there purrs like a contented cat. The lock is unpickable. Very few people know that the room exists. I went to collect a Protona Minifon Special that was probably worth more than I was.

“You’re giving me the PI discount, right?” I said to him.

Simon Grossman was a large man, but stooped and shambling with age. He had a squinty left eye and a schnozz from which hair sprouted like grass. He was draped in a threadbare suit and a slim apology of a tie that looked like it could be better put to use tying up tomatoes, and in fact maybe had been.

“You got a client?” he said.

“In a manner of speaking.”

“What manner would that be?”

“I’ve got a client, but I’m not sure he’s one of the good guys.”

“And you are?”

“I’m not telling him about the wire until I hear what’s on it.” Grossman was as close as a miser’s pocket so I never worried that anything I said to him would end up on the street. “Afterward, I might tell him, I might not.”

“But you’ll charge him anyway.”

I grinned.

“Give me thirty,” he said. “You get a discount for entertaining me.”

I left with my bug. Good to know I could always fall back on a career in stand-up.

I happened to have a passkey to the Lamar that I'd bought off a disgruntled employee who was still serving time at Huntsville for other items he'd boosted on his way out the door. I wondered if I should have sprung for the full bellman's uniform while I was at it, but it wouldn't have worked. There were too many hotel employees around who wouldn't recognize me.

So around ten on Saturday I put on a pair of beige uniform pants and a matching shirt with "Larry" stitched over the pocket in red thread and "Acme Air" stitched on the pocket itself. I put on a small moustache and a pair of black-framed glasses and a hat with the same Acme Air logo stitched on it. I changed the battery in the recorder and tested it. I got out a leather tool satchel and removed the tools from it—wire cutters, gauges, crimpers, clamps, screwdrivers, and wrenches of varying kinds. I placed the recorder and its microphone in the empty case, then a folded towel on top. I replaced the tools.

It was eleven when I went through the service entrance at the Lamar and boarded the service elevator, which was empty. On the eighth floor I passed a couple of swells dressed for a day on the town. They were already bickering over the kinds of things married couples bicker over—she wanted him to wear the other jacket, he hadn't wanted to eat lunch with her friends in the first place. I gave the marriage another six months, tops. In the meantime, they were too preoccupied with their own grievances to notice me.

Room 8-F was up the hall. The door stood open and there was a trolley parked outside piled with tablecloths and napkins and silverware and dishes. I wished I could have the place to myself, but you don't always get what you wish for. Inside two young men in starched white jackets were setting up a table in the living room. It was a nice corner suite, tastefully furnished in Modern Hotel down to the ham-handed landscapes on the walls. Even the Browns didn't rate a Salinas, apparently, though I was willing to bet there was one on the wall in their corporate offices. This was where they came to smoke and drink and play cards, and even if they did business on the side, they didn't want it to look like an office. Two bedrooms, living room, dining area, and a kitchenette. There were already several bottles of hooch lined up on the pass-through bar. The morning sun filtered through the blinds and lit up a richly hued faux-Persian rug. The colors in the room ran to dark blues, greens, and reds, except for polished brass lamps you probably couldn't lift a fingerprint off of. The air smelled of cigar smoke, bourbon, and power.

I rapped on the open door. "AC check," I said.

They looked at me, shrugged at each other, and went back to maneuvering the table into place.

In Houston, nobody messes with an AC repairman.

I skirted the table. I found the wall thermostat, fingered it, squinted at it through my glasses. I could hear a voice coming from one of the bedrooms behind me, and guessed that somebody—probably Herman Brown, since he didn't own a house in Houston—was on the phone. I turned my back to the two waiters, knelt by the mahogany end table closest to the thermostat and opened my kit. I plugged the microphone into the Minifon, then affixed some gum adhesive to the backs of both pieces. Behind me, I heard the waiters step out into the hall. I pressed the record button and reached up and attached the equipment to the underside of the table.

I gave the waiters a thumbs-up sign on my way out, but only one of them noticed. I'd made it in and out inside of three minutes, everything neat as a sailor's bunk. The Minifon would record for five hours and then stop without a sound, like a sleeper's heart attack. I went home, ditched the satchel, glasses, and moustache, and changed into a suit. I splashed on some cologne to encourage the impression that I had an important lunch date. Then I drove back to the hotel garage, parked, and went into the lobby to sit.

I bought a paper off the news seller. Then I found a nice inconspicuous chair to sit in and read my paper. The house dick paid me a visit before I finished page one. I stood to shake his hand.

"Harry," he said. He was a geometric solid with shoulders and torso like a concrete retaining wall. He wore a nice navy suit that fit him perfectly but he moved uncomfortably in it, like a boxer dolled up for an awards ceremony. He was more than muscle, though. I knew a few wiseasses who had underestimated him until they woke up in traction at Ben Taub.

"Marty," I said. "How goes it?"

He shrugged. "Can't complain, I guess. Kids okay?"

I nodded. "Yours?"

He nodded. "Bunny just turned fourteen, you believe that?" His eyes made a quick circuit of the lobby and returned to mine. "You got a teenager, right?" He pointed a meaty finger at me.

"Mine's fourteen, too," I said. "Difficult age."

"Christ, they're all difficult," he said. "But I might not survive the teen years."

"Long's everybody else does. Lot of drama to get through."

"I can't make any promises. If I catch some pimply faced boy putting the moves on her, he's history. You better tell your boy."

"I don't think my boy has noticed girls much yet."

"Jesus, how can he miss 'em?" he said. "They take up so much space."

I spotted George Brown crossing the lobby to the elevators with another man, Big Jim Abercrombie. George, ever the salesman, was talking as usual, but he looked around, spotted us, and waved. I nodded and waved back. Abercrombie was a big, square-chinned man in a straw Stetson and big dark-framed glasses. He had made his first fortune running an iron works before he took up drilling.

I looked at my watch and let Marty see me looking.

"Gettin' old." Marty's eyes followed them. "Hell, everybody's gettin' old."

"Way it works," I said.

"What brings you down here?"

"Oh, I'm supposed to be meeting a client. I'm a little early."

"Dame?"

I winked at him. "Confidential information."

"That's good," he said. "I spot her, I'll pretend I don't see her."

"You don't miss much."

He gestured at my chair. "Just don't wear out your welcome. I'll have to charge you rent."

We shook hands but I hadn't sat down again when Congressman Albert Thomas made his entrance. He toured the lobby, shaking hands all around, until he came to me.

He had an isthmus of a widow's peak in a receding hairline, a prominent nose that was brother to LBJ's, and a broad expanse of chin to match. When he smiled, his upper lip disappeared over a tidy row of even teeth with a single disarming gap. He was wearing a dark suit and one of his signature bow ties, a dark red polka-dotted one.

"Hi, podner," he said, extending his hand. "How you been keeping?"

"Fine, sir, fine," I said. He had the knack many politicians have of conveying intimacy in the clasp of a hand. He added his other hand to the pile. "Yourself?"

"Oh, I'm fine. Daughter's getting married in a few weeks. You've still got that to look forward to, I believe."

"Yes, sir," I said, though I found it difficult to visualize Dizzy marching down the aisle in a wedding dress.

"It's Daisy, isn't it?"

I gave him points for getting so close. "Dizzy."

"That's right, Dizzy. Shakespearean, if I remember. And how about your boy? We're going to recruit him to go to Rice one of these days, me and George. Interested in science, isn't he?"

"That's right."

He winked at me. "I know you have a family connection. And the tuition's still free, though it might not be for long if George gets his way. But if your boy gets in and you're still short, why, you go see George. He's chairman of the board of trustees, you know. There's going to be a lot of opportunities opening up for bright young men.

If we're going to send a man to the moon, we'll need a whole heap of scientists."

"I appreciate that, Congressman, but right now he's only interested in earning some money working at the Y."

"Well, it's never too early to start that, is it, daddy?" He chuckled and clapped me on the back. "Business going okay? I know Mrs. Ramperson was real pleased with the work you did for her."

"Business is fine."

He spotted someone over my shoulder and leaned in, lowering his voice. "I'd better go. That fella over there is probably going to be the next governor of Texas, and I believe he's aiming to finance his campaign from what he takes off me in a poker game tonight."

I watched him catch up with a dapper bird in a dark blue suit, who turned to shake hands. This was John Connally, former naval secretary and another of LBJ's cronies. He probably would be the next governor of Texas now that the current governor had submarined his own political future by pushing for a state sales tax. They were joined by Gus Wortham, a well-fed-looking insurance executive and cattle rancher who'd taken a turn or two as president of the Chamber and had a hand in everything from Rice Stadium to the rodeo. A step or two behind Wortham was a well-dressed negro man carrying a shopping bag. His eyes met mine, categorized me, measured me, and dismissed me; his expression didn't change.

I sat down again and looked over the paper. Bobby Kennedy was predicting a negro president within fifty years, which seemed pretty unlikely given that the Freedom Riders were still locked up in Mississippi and Alabama. A likelier event was the seamen's strike that the maritime union was threatening—an event that would bring the Port of Houston to a standstill and undermine the local economy. I frowned at the paper. No businessman likes to contemplate the prospect of less money in local circulation. A small item buried on page ten reported that a handful of young negroes from Texas Southern University had picketed a movie theatre downtown. The local papers conspired to promote the illusion that we didn't have a race problem in Houston, so reports on the local civil rights movement were hard to find and short.

Over the paper I saw two men cross the lobby. Both wore sport jackets and sport shirts, but I didn't have any doubts that they were headed to 8-F. One was a pleasant-faced man with a broad smile and wavy hair. This was Homer Thornberry, LBJ's Congressional successor in District 10. The taller man I didn't recognize, but he was a serious-looking bird with a close-cropped moustache tucked under the overhang of a large nose.

I stayed another half hour. I had spotted several more candidates for the 8-F party, but nobody I recognized. When Marty's eyes drifted my way, I stood up, stretched, looked at my watch again for good measure and shook my head. I caught Marty's eye and shrugged. Then I tucked the folded paper under my arm and sauntered off.

Chapter 9

I left the Minifon in place until Monday, when Herman Brown would probably have returned to Austin and the presence of an air conditioner repairman would be less noticeable. The room had been cleaned when I went in, but the odor of booze and tobacco smoke was stronger than before. I retrieved the equipment, buried it in my bag, and left. Nobody said boo to me.

I went back to the office and played the wire, taking notes on the cast of characters. I'd been wrong about the curvy blonde; somebody named "Lester" was pouring the drinks, and they all seemed to know him. I wondered if this bird was Gus Wortham's negro shadow. I didn't play back the whole five hours, and after the first half hour or so, when they'd discussed the space center enough so that I didn't think they were likely to spend much more time on it, I did some paperwork and typing and filing and ate my lunch while I half-listened to the rest.

Then I called a reporter I know, Sam Jeeter at the *Post*.

"I hear you're the resident expert on the 8-F crowd."

"Probably true," he said. "What you need?"

"I need to figure out who was there on Saturday for lunch," I said.

"Not me. My invitation must've gotten lost in the mail."

"I was in the lobby," I told him. "Nobody asked me in."

"Probably better for your bank account that way."

"High stakes?"

I could hear the shrug in his voice. "Not for them. But for you and me, brother? Way out of our league."

"Both Browns were there," I said. "Albert Thomas, Homer Thornberry, John Connally, and Gus Wortham. Big Jim Abercrombie, too."

"The politicians," he said. "That's interesting. Most of the time, I don't know how these guys can remember which meeting they're at, swear to God. If they have cards in their hands, they know they're playing cards. If they have guns in their hands, they're hunting. Otherwise, how can they tell if they're discussing banking, insurance, construction, the oil business, or the goddamn ballet?"

"Can I try you on a couple of names I overheard?"

"Jesus! Where were you? Under the sink?"

"Professional secret. How about Morgan?"

"Morgan Davis. Humble Oil. But he's not a usual participant. He's a friend, and he plays footsie with them, but not cards. Wonder what they wanted with him."

"All right. Somebody named Ed?"

"Ed Clark, probably. Lawyer from San Augustine. He does some of Lyndon's legal work."

"Lester?"

"Lester Randle, Wortham's driver and factotum. You want the real expert on the 8-F crowd, he's it, but you'll never get anything out of him. Word is he's incorruptible."

I thanked him.

"Hold your horses, mister," he said. "What else did you hear while you were under that sink? Anything I can use?"

I laughed. "I was in the lobby, remember? But if I had been under the sink, I'll bet I wouldn't have heard anything that you don't already know. I'll bet they're all backing Connally for governor, I'll bet they wish Lyndon was president, and I'll bet they're worried about the Freedom Riders. Oh, and I bet they think we need a better stadium and a better baseball team to play in it. And a better airport. Just a hunch."

"Thanks for nothing," he said, and hung up.

I worked the rest of the afternoon on a transcript of the wire recording. It went something like this, minus the calls for drinks.

Somebody said, “That was some speech the president gave the other night—shootin’ for the moon.”

Somebody else said, “Yeah, that old tomcat’s really out of the bag now. The buzzards going to be gathering.”

“What do you hear about that, Al?” somebody said. “What’s our competition look like?”

“Early days, boys, early days,” Thomas said. “I reckon the folks in Florida are excited. I reckon they figure anything new that gets built will get built there. But George’s the one to ask. Ever since Lyndon put him on the Space Council, he’s had the inside track. I’m as curious as y’all are to find out what he knows.”

“What about that, George? We can’t be the only people who know NASA’s thinking about a new facility.”

“Yeah, George. How many people knew that those two fellas from NASA came out to see the Clear Lake property?”

“We didn’t take out any ads in the newspapers,” George said.

“No.” Thomas again. “But there were folks at Langley who knew about it, and other folks at Goddard and Ames, where those fellas came from. And I have to tell you, boys, those folks at Langley are concerned. They don’t want to move to Houston.”

There was a general reaction to this—a mix of indignation and laughter.

“Well, I know.” I could hear the smile in Thomas’s voice. “We’ll win ‘em over in the end. I’m just saying, there’s resistance. So we got to get all our ducks in a row.”

George said, “Morgan’s got his people on board, right, Morgan?” Morgan must have nodded, because George went on. “One thousand acres of prime real estate between the Ship Channel and the airport, right next door to an Air Force base. And we’re donating it, free of charge, to the American people.”

“Well, Rice is,” somebody said, probably Herman. “I still don’t know what we’re going to get for it. Bobby Kennedy’ll probably come to town and help 'em organize an astronauts' union." Herman was a rabid opponent of unions, and I could picture his florid face turning redder.

"Albert, I know you're the appropriations man,"—this might've been Connally talking— "but why do we have to donate it? Didn't you give NASA enough money to pay for it?"

This was met with laughter, and Thomas said, "I told Mr. Glennan that NASA wouldn't see a goddamn dime unless they built us a space center in Houston. I was so riled up when they gave Goddard to Maryland. I like to never gave them another penny."

"And look what happened," somebody added. "He resigned."

"I believe Mr. Webb knows my sentiments," Thomas said.

"To answer John's question," George interjected, "we're trying to set up a win-win situation here. Albert says there's going to be competition, and he's right. Florida wants this thing—hell, even Kennedy's own state wants it. So we're sweetening the deal. We're making an investment. Humble gives the land to Rice—that puts Rice at the center of everything."

"And gets Humble a nice tax write-off," somebody said.

George continued. "Rice makes NASA an offer it can't refuse—free land."

"In return for which Rice becomes intimately connected with the space program," somebody else said.

"Rice students get moon rocks to play with," said the first somebody.

"More than that," George said. "Rice laboratories serve the space program, our undergrads and grads intern in NASA facilities, our faculty works with NASA scientists and engineers."

"And Brown & Root makes a bundle building the damn thing," Gus offered.

"There'll be plenty to spread around," George said.

"Ever'body's boat gets floated," Thomas said, and you could almost hear the wink in his voice.

"How about that little race problem they got over at Rice?" A new contributor. "What's Lyndon say about that?"

"Well, now, that ain't none of Lyndon's affair," Thomas said, and the irritation in his voice reminded me that even if he and LBJ were cronies, they drew their financial and political support from the same well, and that was bound to encourage competition.

"I'm working on that," George said. "In order to convince this fellow Pitzer from Berkeley to be our next president, I had to get the board to agree to move on desegregation. I won't say they're happy about it, and they'll likely drag their feet, but we'll get it done. I've discussed it with Ed here, and Ed thinks we can get a court to agree to a reinterpretation of the original charter, on this and on the tuition thing as well. We're talking about the future here, and we know that, like it or not, the colleges of the future won't be segregated."

"Well, I don't know about that," someone objected, "and I hope it's not true."

"I know your feelings," George said, "but as things stand, we can't get a nickel for Rice out of the federal government—hell, we can't get a nickel out of the foundations. The Ford Foundation gave us money for a summer workshop, but it's got to be integrated. And they all say the same thing: come back when you've stopped discriminating against nigras."

"Well, I don't like it," Gus said. "I don't like to see us cave in to 'em. And if those Freedom Riders come down here, I'm sure we've got some nice accommodations at the Harris County jail for 'em."

At this point, the talk turned to desegregation and all the uppity, ungrateful nigras who didn't know their place and were being stirred up by Yankee commies to challenge the benevolence of their rich white benefactors, among whom the 8-F gassers counted themselves. It was pretty predictable stuff, but I wondered what Lester Randle made of it all. The wire ran for another two hours, but nothing more substantial was said about the space center. I heard Thomas leave, though, and as he did, he said, presumably to Davis, "Next time I see you, podner, I'll have a dotted line for you to sign on."

I stood up and stretched. Then I took a half-empty bottle of Wild Turkey and a pack of cigarettes out of my desk drawer and sat down to think. Mostly I was thinking about what to put in my report to Mr. Smith. I was thinking about what it would mean to my own kids if Alan Shepard moved to Houston, and if he was joined by other astronauts. I was picturing Hal, who was building a soapbox racer in a friend's garage, working to build a spaceship. I wasn't sure where Dizzy fit into the picture, but she was a talker and a writer, and I figured they'd need a few of those at NASA as well. If I had to choose sides, the choice was clear. As for Smith, I didn't know whose interests he was representing, but I was pretty sure it wasn't the West Ranch cows'.

When Mr. Smith showed up the next day, I was ready for him. He read my report. It didn't take long, so he read it again.

He looked up. "Not much here," he said.

I shrugged.

"I thought you were going to try to get a man in there," he said.

"I went up and looked around," I said. "Wasn't possible."

He looked down at the report. "I don't even know what they talked about."

"I'll bet you do," I said.

He scowled.

When I had his attention, I gave it to him straight.

"Look, you come in here with your phony indignation, trying to work me up about back-door political dealing," I said. "But this is Texas. Political rodeo is the national sport of the Republic of Texas, right behind football, and the rougher and goofier and more entertaining it is, the more we like it. You try to take the corruption out of Texas politics, you've got nothing left. We might as well move to Nebraska. I know they're scheming to get a space center in Houston and you know it. So what? If you can beat them at their own game, go to it. Only leave me out."

He narrowed icy eyes at me. This was supposed to make me tremble in my boots only I didn't own any boots.

"How much do I owe you for this?" He lifted the single page between his thumb and forefinger and curled his lip at it.

"It's on the house."

He left without looking back.

Chapter 10

I locked the wire in the safe—not the conspicuous one behind Eisenhower's picture but the one under the floorboard—along with a carbon copy of the transcript. The original I folded up and slipped into my glove compartment.

On a hunch, I sat in my car that night and watched the office. If Smith was coming back, I was betting it would be tonight so that he could blow town tomorrow. I didn't figure him for a stiff who would stick around for a slide lecture on the Battle of San Jacinto and a tour of the *Battleship Texas*. I'd grabbed a few hours of sleep and a cup of coffee and parked under a busted streetlight about half a block down.

The noise of the city quieted down to a hum after midnight. Every now and then a siren split the silence, the sound magnified by the walls of the concrete canyon. But there was no movement on my street. The streets were slick with rain and oil from an afternoon thunderstorm, and they reflected the sultry streetlights and the neon from the bar up the street. A wisp of steam rose up like a ghost from a grate in front of the laundry. Behind my building was an old house where Mrs. Gunderson spent her retirement tending her roses, and I could smell their heady scent on the still, moist air. My daughter Dizzy has no patience for stakeouts, and no wonder—they are duller than sorting socks and demand less energy. I'd already read the *Chronicle* twice through by the inconsistent light of the moon. The papers were still full of the Texas Chief wreck at Cleburne the week before, and by now I could practically recite the casualties list. The Freedom Riders were relegated to a back page and the local demonstrators had disappeared from the paper altogether.

I was draining my Thermos at two o'clock when I spotted the dark figure striding up the sidewalk on the opposite side of the street. He didn't see me; he wasn't looking for me. He had me figured for a hick Houston gumshoe putting the cross on him for the extra dough. He disappeared into the shadow of the entryway, and I couldn't see if he made it in or how. My eyes drifted up to the third floor corner windows as I sipped from my plastic cup. I waited. The longer it took him to get in, the more damage he was likely doing to my lock. I would have left it open for him, but that would have been suspicious. I checked my watch. Then I spotted a thin thread of light coming through the windows on the third floor. I watched it wink out as he closed the blinds. I wondered if he'd turn on the air conditioner.

I settled in to wait but in less than five minutes, two more dark shapes appeared on the sidewalk opposite and disappeared through the entryway into the building. I sat up and wondered whether anybody else was going to show up for this convention. It was maybe twenty minutes before two men emerged. I couldn't be sure, but I thought that they were the two latecomers, which would mean Smith was still inside.

My original plan had been to follow Smith, even though I thought he'd probably just lead me to a motel, and I'd have to decide where to go from there. But the new players complicated things, and if I waited any longer for Smith, I'd lose the chance to tail them, so I started the car and took off after them. Around the corner, they got into a Ford sedan, so I circled the block and followed them.

They took me home. I idled at the corner and watched them park in front of my apartment building, get out, and go in. As I drove past, I saw one of them leaning into the squawk box. Probably he was talking to the super, pretending to be me or any of the other names he could read by the buzzers. Security is only as good as the brains it depends on.

I parked in my space, took my .38 out of the glove compartment, and went in through the back door and up the stairs. My apartment door was closed and the whole building was quiet as a Trojan horse. I unlocked the door and stepped in with my gun drawn.

The blackjack came down on my wrist with a crack and I dropped the gun before he caught my jaw on the rebound and slammed me against the door. He moved in to backhand me but I kneed him in the groin, so the blow didn't pack much force. He fell back with a grunt and I followed up with a body blow, but it was like punching a sea wall. He took another step back and brought up the automatic in his other hand and pointed it at me. His eyes were watering from the blow to his nuts but he looked like he could see well enough to plug me. I raised my hands in surrender.

"Your round, brother," I said.

He was beefy with wide-set small eyes and fleshy lips and a birthmark high up on his temple. His face shone with sweat, and I could smell his sour odor from this distance. He wore a brown suit and a red tie so loud I thought he must have picked it out blindfolded.

His partner was taller and older and better dressed. He had gray eyes the color of fish scales. He had shadows like oil slicks under his eyes and they matched the shadow on his upper lip, camouflaged by his dark complexion. His expression said that he could barely be bothered to take an interest in the little squabble between his partner and me.

"Lark," he said in a flat voice, as if maybe I didn't remember my own name. "Let's talk."

Beefy waved me toward a chair, but I didn't sit down.

"Do I know you?" I said. I brought out a handkerchief and touched it to my cheek, where it came away with a small red blot the color of Beefy's tie. Then I put it away and got out a cigarette. Beefy narrowed his eyes, as if that would help him focus, but his eyes were so small to begin with, he couldn't narrow them much without blinding himself.

"We came for the dough," the partner said.

"I get it." I gestured with the cigarette. "He's the muscle, you're the mouth." I couldn't see a gun on him, but that didn't mean he wasn't wearing one. "Okay, I'll play. What dough?"

"You know what dough," the partner said. "We got no time for games."

I shrugged. "I didn't call this meeting. You don't have time, why don't you boys hit the road and come back when you do?"

Beefy took a step and backhanded me with the pistol, casually, as if he were flagging a cab. In the morning I'd have a matched set of bruises, one on either side, and I'd catch hell from Dizzy, who says I have masochistic tendencies. I don't know where she picked up that word—probably from her mother—but she can pronounce it and even spell it.

I staggered a little, just for show, and stumbled toward him. Then I landed a blow to his midriff and an uppercut to his chin that rocked him back on his heels but otherwise didn't do him any more damage than a pillow in a pillow fight.

"Sit down, Lark," the partner said.

Beefy had the gun pointed at me again, so I sat.

"We want the money," the partner said. "We're not leaving here without it."

"Go ahead, search the place." I made an expansive gesture. "I don't know what the hell you're talking about, but help yourself."

The partner came alive then and gave me a look so menacing that it could only mean he didn't know what he was talking about, either. Bluff was his game, and he got paid for doing it well.

"No." His voice was flat. "That's not how this is going to work. We want the five hundred grand, and we'll tear you apart to get it."

"The five hundred grand?" I looked surprised. "You mean the—."

He didn't take the bait, probably because he couldn't. "Yeah. *That* five hundred. Or any five hundred, it don't matter to us."

"I give you five hundred and you take your pea shooter and go away, is that it?"

"That's it," he said. "Or you don't, and we leave you in little pieces on the floor."

"Well," I said, "when you put it like that."

I stood up and headed for the bedroom. The partner angled his head for Beefy to follow me. Beefy trailed me to the bedroom closet, where I opened the door and reached up for a cash box on the shelf. My right hand slipped under a sweater sitting next to it and palmed my Detective Special. Glancing back, I saw that Beefy's gun hand had cleared the door. I turned and yanked the door shut, then brought the Colt down on his wrist. He dropped the gun and I scooped it up. Then I threw myself against the door. He grunted, lost his balance, and fell backward. I shoved the door open, stepped over him, and went for the partner in the front room. The partner, a surprised look on his face, was reaching into his coat when I shot him. I rushed him and found the gun half out of a shoulder holster but he wasn't moving and I knew he was dead.

I heard footsteps in the hall then and somebody pounded on the door. "Open up!" he shouted. "Police!"

Then he tried the door, found it open, and walked in. It was Carillo. He looked at me, looked at the stiff on the floor, then heard moaning from the bedroom and looked in. "Did you really need three guns?"

He had his own gun drawn. "Now you're here we could hold a gun show," I replied, laying the guns on the coffee table.

He holstered his own Detective Special and went into the bedroom to cuff Beefy. I heard him using the phone. I went and retrieved my other gun from the corner where Beefy had kicked it and laid it next to the others.

He returned to the front room, came closer and studied my face. "How'd you let them get the drop on you?"

"You mean why," I said. "How was the easy part. I wanted to find out what they were up to. That kind doesn't scare easy. They don't talk unless they have the upper hand."

"And what were they up to?"

I shook my head. "I don't think they knew. They were looking for money—a lot of it. Five hundred grand. They thought I had it. That's all I know."

"What five hundred grand would this be?" he said.

"Beats me."

He crossed his arms and found a wall to lean against. His bloodshot eyes and the stubble on his face said he'd been up for hours. "What do you know about the stiff in your office?" he said. "He looking for the same five hundred grand?"

He'd surprised me, and I'm sure it showed on my face. "Stiff as in dead? Brown hair, medium height, tailored suit, two rings?"

"That's the one."

I fished out a cigarette, offered him one, and lit them both. I was buying time and he knew it. I'd figured, of course, that the two goons hadn't just stopped by at that hour to read me a bedtime story. And I hadn't seen Smith leave the office.

"He was a client of mine," I said. "Said his name was Smith. I can spell that if you want me to."

Silence.

"My guess? Your murder weapon's there." I pointed at the three guns. "Not the Colts. Those are mine."

"Why'd you think it was Smith got offed? You only got one client or were you watching the building?"

"Lucky guess," I said.

"Who tossed your office?"

I shrugged.

"What did Smith hire you for?"

I shook my head. "Can't tell you that. You know it's confidential."

"Your client's dead, Lark," Carillo said, "which can't be good for business."

"Look, all I can tell you is that the job didn't have anything to do with five hundred grand," I said.

"You haven't raised your rates?"

I ignored him. "I would have said that Smith searched my office because he thought I was holding out on him. In the end, I couldn't find out what he wanted to know and I didn't charge him. But where the dough comes into it, I'm damned if I know. Say, how'd you find out there was a stiff in my office, anyway?"

"Your landlord, Mr. Lum, called with some cockamamie story about going down there in the middle of the night to look for something. My guess is he's got an illegal relative or two dossing down in the back room."

I nodded. "He's got a lot of cousins."

"They all do," he said. "Who gives a shit? I'm not going to bust him. Too much of that going on in my own family. Anyway, somebody heard something and got nervous. Probably saw something, too, though they'll never admit it. Uniform called it in, and the desk sergeant caught me on the way out."

"You got here fast. I'm touched."

"Don't be. You're suspect number one."

I grinned at him.

He took me back down to my office then and I confirmed that the stiff on the floor was the man I knew as Mr. Smith. He'd been plugged in the chest and if I had to characterize his expression, I would have said resigned, but that's probably imagination. The techs had already left and the meat wagon boys were hanging around, smoking and looking bored. Once I'd pegged Smith, they zipped him into a body bag and carted him off.

"Anything missing?" Carillo said. "Want to check and see if the boodle's still where you stashed it?"

They'd made a pretty thorough job of it. There were papers strewn all over the floor—everything from client files to the menu for the Chinese joint up the street. Even got the safe open, though the only intact thing that I could see at first glance was the Eisenhower portrait. Even button men don't mess with the general, I guess.

Carillo gestured at the mess. "Give you a chance to catch up on your filing."

They hadn't found the wire, of course. They wouldn't have known that the wire existed, unless they'd had me followed, and I would have spotted the tail. They didn't know what I had, they just thought I had more than I'd given them. I would have thought the same in their shoes. They'd thrown the typewriter on the floor but it was built like a tank and my typing didn't look any worse. Didn't look any better, either. What made me sore was the broken glass on the kids' pictures.

Later, around the time I was finally dropping off to sleep, it occurred to me that I'd been thinking of the three of them as "they." But that didn't square with Smith's murder. And I wasn't even sure that they'd been looking for the same things. They might have all been the same type, but that didn't mean they were playing on the same team, or that they even knew each other.

How had it played out, then? Up till now, I'd been assuming the two latecomers had joined the search. But it probably wasn't like that at all. Either they'd walked in, plugged Smith, and tossed the place themselves, or they'd let Smith do all the work and then plugged him. But I was damned if I could see where the five hundred large came into the picture.

I suspected the money was mob money, and my suspicion was confirmed when Carillo told me that Smith had been a mid-level wise guy from Chicago named Graziano. The guy I'd iced was the same, only from Tampa, and his name was Neroni. His sidekick, who got sprung by a shyster within twenty-four hours in spite of the murder rap, was a Fabiano Landi, of Miami, who was related to Neroni. Cousins. They're everywhere.

The slug they took out of Graziano let me off the hook for that beef, but I got the third degree anyway when I went down to the station to make my statement. We don't have organized crime in Houston, and the cops like to keep it that way. When the mob stages a shootout on their turf, they get nervous. But Carillo didn't get much more out of me than he had the night before.

I knew more than Carillo, but I didn't know much. I couldn't figure the mob angle. I couldn't connect the Chicago Mafia to NASA, no matter how I looked at it, unless they wanted the franchise for casinos on the moon. And if the dough was some kind of bribe, I couldn't see who it was intended for or why it had ended up in Houston—or why anybody thought I had it.

The next day I got an earful from Dizzy, as I expected, and her mother insisted on doctoring my wounds. I said that I wasn't aware that a PhD gave somebody a license to practice medicine, which is the wrong thing to say to a woman who's coming at you with a bottle of iodine.

I cleaned up my office and Mr. Lum put a new lock on my door. I gave him a fin for any insomniac nephew he might have on the premises who was willing to report an intruder in the middle of the night. For a week or so, I kept on the lookout for any gun-toting Italians who might have joined the hunt for the five hundred grand, but I didn't see any.

I wished the Texas boys luck on their space center and put the whole thing out of my mind. After all, they wouldn't be thanking me for drawing them into a mob trial. And I wasn't going to give up Smith/Graziano and Claude Dunwoody to the Brown brothers. For one thing, that would raise uncomfortable questions about how I'd come by the information I had. I didn't want Herman Brown sore at me. There are a couple of dozen labor organizers in the state of Texas who could testify to the consequences of that, and I didn't want to end up feeling like one of Herman's paving jobs. Besides, you don't build a company the size of Brown & Root and not feel the crosshairs on the back of your neck.

But the real reason was principle: you don't rat out your clients. Not even the rats. Word gets around, and pretty soon nobody wants to hire you. Even the ones who believe the rats deserved what they got will worry about whether you might not do the same to them.

Anyway, they were all rats, just rats running in different packs.

On June 13th, the *Post* ran a front-page article reporting that Houston was being considered as a possible site for a new space center. Congressman Albert Thomas, who was about to review NASA's latest appropriations request, said he'd been trying for years to get NASA to locate some of their facilities in Houston. He was quoted as saying, "If lightning strikes our road, this could involve the expenditure of millions in the Houston area and the direct employment of several thousands of people." It was an interesting way to characterize the political machinations he'd been engaged in, but I didn't put it past him or any of the 8-F crowd to conduct side negotiations with God Almighty.

Meanwhile, I had my own problems. In two weeks, I would become a full-time father again.

Dizzy – June 28, 1961

Chapter 11

Sure enough, we got plenty of neighborhood publicity out of Buddy's happy recovery and by the time school had been out for a week, we were doing a good business. With more time to canvas the neighborhood, we'd managed to accumulate a respectable inventory. We had plenty of slow times, but on the whole we thought that the Lost and Found had been our best idea yet for how to spend our summer vacation.

We were discussing our business practices one Wednesday, with B.D. and me maintaining that we could change into our bathing suits after lunch, play in the sprinkler, and still keep an eye on the Lost and Found. Mel argued that it wasn't professional.

"Look here," she said. "Dizzy, when Harry goes to work, he wears a suit and tie, right? Every day, right?"

"Unless he's under cover," I said.

"And a gun in a shoulder holster, right, Diz?" B.D. said.

Mel ignored her. "Unless he's in disguise he wears a suit and tie because it tells his customers that he's a professional."

"He wears a suit to hide the gun, right, Dizzy?" B.D. said. "You can't stash a gun in your swim trunks."

"He wears it because it's *professional*," Mel repeated. "You don't want to be waiting on customers in your bathing suit."

"In this heat, I do," B.D. insisted. "Besides, we aren't wearing suits and ties, we're wearing shorts and tops. We're already unprofessional."

"Y'all have got to be willing to make sacrifices," Mel said. "You know what the president said, 'Ask not what your country can do for you.'"

"We're not doing anything for our country," B.D. objected. "We're just running a l'il ole bidness."

"Like my daddy always says, what's good for General Motors is good for the country," Mel said.

"What's that supposed to mean? No bathing suits?" B.D. turned to me and added, "Even Nancy Drew packs a bathing suit in her emergency travel kit, and nobody ever accused *her* of being unprofessional."

But I'd already noticed a new customer coming in, and they turned to see what I was looking at.

I didn't recognize her with the sun behind her. "We help you?" I said.

She took a few tentative steps forward. Lucille raised her head to stare. I shifted my chair around to get a better angle, and that seemed to spook our customer.

I could see now that she was as pale as a ghost, skinny and little, maybe six or seven, with short, fat pigtails like blond commas tied up in big pink bows. Her hair was so pale it was almost white, like spun silver. She wore a pink sunsuit with ties on her bony shoulders like butterflies perched there, and pink thong sandals and a little pink beaded necklace. She kept her hands behind her back, making her look even smaller and more vulnerable.

"Is this the Lost and Found?" she asked finally.

"That's right," I said. "You lost something or found something?"

"I lost something," she said, staring at me. She had big blue eyes that were made for staring. "You're Dizzy."

"Right again." I waited for her to work up the nerve to say whatever it was she wanted to say. Harry always says it pays to wait.

"I need you to find something," she said, still staring.

"Okay," I said. "What'd you lose?"

"My daddy," she said finally. "I want you to find my daddy."

In the silence that followed, you could hear the insects buzzing in the summer heat, and a dog barking, and a train whistle, sounding lonesome in the distance.

This was what came of branching out from happening upon random things that were lost to going out and looking for specific things that were lost.

"I recognize you," B.D. said at last. "You're Sissy Heffelman, aren't you? Live over on Cedarspur?"

The little girl nodded.

B.D. said gently, "Sugar, your daddy passed. He died in that awful train wreck a few weeks back. To us she said, "Mrs. Moseley went to the service and she was telling my mother about it." She gave us a look that said, "More later."

Sissy shook her head and the pigtails smacked against her cheeks. "He's not dead," she insisted.

"He is, though," B.D. said. "Didn't your mama take you to the cemetery to say goodbye to him?"

Sissy blinked. "He's not dead," she repeated.

I decided to try a different tack. "What makes you think he's not dead?"

"He sent me a birthday present."

"Uh-huh," I said.

"Do you mean that he sent something with his name on it?" Mel asked.

"It didn't have his name on it but I know it was from him. My birthday was last week, and it came on Monday."

"Whose name did it have on it?" Mel asked.

She turned her eyes on Mel. "It didn't have nobody's name on it. But I know it was from him."

"What did your mama say?" B.D. asked.

"She said it must've come from somebody who knew us, and knew about my birthday, and wanted to make me feel better 'cause I lost my daddy," she said. "But it didn't," she added, scowling.

"Did it come in the mail?" I asked.

She nodded.

"Then it must've had a return address."

She shook her head. "It didn't have no return address."

"It was just a package, with no return address, addressed to you?"

She nodded again.

"Did you recognize the handwriting on the package?"

"It was typed."

"It had a typed mailing label with your name and address on it and no return address?"

She nodded.

I felt a prickle on the back of my neck.

"You know what a postmark is?"

She shook her head.

"You still got the paper it was wrapped in?"

She became more animated. "I got the paper and the string and the box and everything. You want to see?"

"Yes, that was real smart, to keep those things," I said. "We can figure out where it was mailed from."

"What was in the box, sugar?" B.D. asked. "What was your present?"

Now she brought her hands out from behind her back to reveal a Barbie doll, elegantly dressed in a pink formal gown and a white fur stole.

B.D. gasped. She was the only Barbie fan of the three of us. "It's Enchanted Evening! That stole is real rabbit fur!"

Even Lucille was impressed. She sat up and stared at the doll with interest, probably at the piece of dead rabbit that Barbie was wearing. She opened her mouth and sniffed the air.

Sissy extended the doll to me and took another step closer. "You want to see it?"

"Sure," I said. I looked around the garage, spotted a pair of gardening cloves that weren't too dirty, brushed them off and put them on. I took the doll gingerly. "Did it come in a box like you see at the store?"

She nodded.

Mel pointed. "Who changed her clothes?"

"What?"

"Who changed her clothes?" Mel repeated. "Barbie doesn't come in those clothes, she comes in a black and white striped bathing suit. That's what she's wearing in the box." Mel took no interest in Barbie, but you couldn't be a thirteen-year-old girl in America and not know the fundamentals. For one thing, Mattel made a point of interrupting all of your favorite afternoon TV shows with Barbie commercials.

"Daddy must've changed her clothes," Sissy said.

B.D. took up this line of questioning. "So she was dressed like this in the box you got? Was her neck stuck in one of those cardboard thingies? 'Cause I don't see how you could get a thingie around her knees in that dress, and that's how they come." The last was said for our benefit. She demonstrated with her hands to her neck. "Either they've got a cardboard collar thingie around their neck or there's one around their knees, to hold them in place."

"It was around her neck," Sissy said.

"So you think your daddy changed her clothes and put her back in the box," B.D. summarized. Under her breath, she said to us, "That's creepy, y'all."

"Who else has touched it, besides you?" I asked. "Since it came in the mail, I mean."

"Nobody."

"Not your mother or your sister or your best friend?"

She looked confused. "I don't have no sisters."

I sighed. "Has anybody besides you touched the doll?"

"No." Her forehead wrinkled as if she was afraid of saying the wrong thing.

"So here's what we need, Sissy," I said, leaning forward. "I can dust everything for prints—for fingerprints. You know what fingerprints are?" She looked doubtful, but I went on. "I might find something, I might not. I won't get anything off the packaging unless there's some on the plastic. If somebody changed Barbie's clothes and put her back in the box, I'll maybe get a print off her. But none of that will do any good unless I have your father's fingerprints to compare. So I need you to go home and find some things that belonged to your dad—things he touched with his fingers. They have to have hard surfaces, though, understand? Like plastic. Like a hairbrush or a cigarette case or an ashtray or—." I tried to picture Harry's bedroom.

"Or a box where he kept his cufflinks," Mel put in.

"Yeah, or maybe a framed photograph with glass," I said.

"Or any photograph," Mel said. "Or a pocketknife or a lucky coin or something."

"The best things would be things that nobody has touched since your father died." She opened her mouth to object and I amended, "Since the train wreck, I mean. Not your mama, and not you. But we'll take your fingerprints for comparison." I wasn't likely to confuse her prints with an adult's, but I like to be thorough. "And you should bring me something of your mama's, too—something you don't touch usually. You got a pair of gloves?"

This last was a rhetorical question. Every Southern girl owns a pair of gloves, even me, although mine are stuffed in the back of the drawer so my mother won't see the grease from my bicycle chain and the fingerprint dusting powder.

"I got gloves," she said.

"Okay," I said. "You put on your gloves before you collect the things I asked you for, and then bring it all back this afternoon. Remember to wear the gloves, and remember—hard things, not soft." Then I added, "You'd better bring us a photograph of your daddy while you're at it."

B.D. spoke up. "Sugar, are you sure you're allowed off your street?"

She drew herself up to her full height like the mayor of Munchkin City and said, "I'm seven years old now."

B.D. didn't pursue it. But she did say, "Best leave the Barbie with us. You'll get her back."

As we watched her go, B.D. said, "Dizzy, are you sure we should be encouraging her? Her father's dead."

I shrugged. "She won't be back, if her mother gets wind of it. But if she is, maybe we can prove to her that her father didn't send the package."

B.D. shook her head. "Diz, we ain't never going to prove nothing to that one."

Mel said, "Somebody sent her that package, and they don't want her to know who it was. If it turns out to be her mother and we prove that, her mother might have a conniption."

B.D. sighed. "It was probably like her mother said—just some good Samaritan, a neighbor or a family friend, who wanted to cheer her up on her birthday."

I turned to B.D. "You said Mrs. Moseley went to the funeral service. When was this?"

"I don't know," she said, "but it was right around the time school let out, so—end of May? Beginning of June? That just seemed real sad to me, to have something like that happen right before summer started."

"Was it a regular funeral with a coffin and everything?" I asked.

"Seems like it wasn't." B.D. shut one eye to help her remember better and aimed the other at the dart board on the back wall. "I believe there was an explosion and a fire when the train wrecked, and I think Mrs. Moseley said there wasn't much left to bury. But I wasn't supposed to hear that part, so I didn't catch it too good."

Mel stayed for lunch, but B.D.'s mother called her home. B.D.'s mother stands on their front porch and hollers B.D.'s name, which is Brenda Diane, in a voice that B.D. says gets on her last nerve. B.D. has to run home just to shut her up.

As we passed through the kitchen, Rose was fixing tuna fish sandwiches and paused to tell us to wash our hands. "He up yet?" I asked, nodding in the direction of the master bedroom.

"I think he's in the shower," she said. "Don't be messing in his things." To herself she added, "And don't be telling me if you do."

Rose is our housekeeper. Rose used to be our maid and come once a week like the other maids on the block, but what with teaching her classes at the university and writing her book, my mother didn't have a lot of time left over for housekeeping, so she asked Rose if she'd be willing to come to work for us full time, and Rose agreed. Now Rose runs the house. My mother calls it a "managerial position," and pays her a salary that annoys the other women on our block. They're afraid their maids will get ideas from the civil rights protesters and make a picket line across Bingle Road or worse, get ideas from the seamen and go on strike. My mother says, "If they don't like it, they can lump it," but she doesn't say it to them.

Rose is a very pretty negro lady about my mother's age with a lovely singing voice when she chooses to use it. But she can also be what my mother calls tempestuous and when she is you don't want to cross her or your dinner's liable to be burned to a crisp or your ears, one. Everybody's a little afraid of Rose—everybody but Harry. Harry's not afraid of anybody.

The door to the bedroom was closed, but when I cracked it open, we could hear the water running in the shower. I saw his old army duffel on the bed and slid my hand inside till I found what I wanted: Harry's fingerprint kit. Mel was looking at his shoulder holster, which hung on the back of a chair.

Because Harry's a shamus, he's got lots of useful equipment I covet and sometimes borrow. I was borrowing some now. B.D., who goes to Sunday school every Sunday, says covetousness is a sin, so the way I see it, I'm saving my soul. Once I pinch something, I don't covet it anymore.

I stashed it behind a sofa cushion in the den on the way back to the dinette.

He came in while we were eating lunch. He was wearing his pants and an undershirt. He had a cup of coffee in one hand and a cigarette between his lips. He smelled of English Leather aftershave.

He ruffled my hair, the way he likes to do, though there's not much hair to ruffle.

"Hi, girls," he said. "Fenced any valuable merchandise today?"

Women seem to think my father is good-looking. He's got brown hair combed back, deep-set glittery dark eyes and heavy eyebrows. He's got high cheekbones and a wrinkled forehead whenever he's thinking or frowning or if he has a cigarette in his mouth, like now. He's on the short side for a man, but you can tell he never gives it a thought. Personally, I like the way he looks, but I don't understand why women throw themselves at him, which is what my mother says they do.

"I wish you'd go smoke that thing somewhere we're not eating," I said, though Rose was already handing him an ashtray. He and Rose always act like they're in cahoots. Because he doesn't live here, he gets special privileges when he does show up, even now when he was living with us temporarily while my mother was in England doing research for her book.

He left the room and went, of all places, to the den, where he sat down on the sofa and started reading the newspaper.

When we finished lunch, I said to Mel, sotto voce, "We've got to retrieve the dingus."

"The what?" Mel said. I shot her a look. "Oh. The dingus."

"I'll distract him and you get it," I said, but she put a hand on my elbow as I was turning toward the den.

"How 'bout I distract him and *you* get it?"

She went and perched on the arm of the sofa on the other side of him and started asking him when he was going to take her to the shooting range and what kind of gun he'd recommend for her. He said he'd take her to the range when her mother wrote him a permission slip, which we all knew would happen at the dawn of never, and the gun he'd recommend for her was a water pistol. This was a sore point with me because Hal had a Daisy Air Rifle, and it was a beauty, with a wood stock and a black metal barrel and a 30-BB magazine and pump action. Hal was three years older than me, but I was willing to bet I'd be a better shot if I ever got the chance. The few times Harry had taken me to the shooting range, I'd been pretty good—even Harry admitted that I had a good eye. Besides, Hal was more interested in how things worked, and I was worried he was going to take the air rifle apart to see how it was made before I ever got my mitts on it.

I stuck the dingus under my top and gave Mel the high sign. Over my shoulder I said to Harry, "I got a game tonight."

"I'll be there," he said.

"Do you think he'll show up?" Mel asked when we were out of earshot.

I shrugged. The thing about Harry was this: if you never counted on him, you never had to be disappointed. That way, you could just be pleasantly surprised when he came through. He was usually there when it mattered most, and I'd decided that was good enough for me.

We went back to the garage. I'd also brought out my Brownie camera and my gloves, but I knew from experience that I had to be careful or the bicycle grease on the gloves might mess up the fingerprints.

"I thought you had your own fingerprint kit, Diz," Mel said. "Why'd we have to steal Harry's?"

"His is better," I said. "Mine's just for play. We should have taken one of his cameras, too."

B.D. showed up wearing a tee shirt over her bathing suit.

"Just in time," I said. "You get to undress Barbie. Here, put on these gloves."

She wrinkled her nose. "Diz, is this your only pair? They're a mess."

"You're not going to a tea dance."

"But I'll get grease all over her gown," she grumbled.

"Then turn 'em inside out."

I spread some newspaper on the footlocker and we knelt around it. B.D. laid a naked Barbie on the paper after carefully setting aside her dress, stole, shoes, and necklace. Lucille came over and nosed her way in to see what we were doing, but I didn't want her to get black fingerprint powder all over her white paws, so I had Mel hold her.

"Maybe you better wrap Barbie's head," B.D. said, "so you don't mess up her hair. She's got a perfect bubblecut."

So I went and got some Saran Wrap and a rubber band. B.D. winced when I slipped the rubber band around Barbie's neck, but she didn't say anything.

I started with her front. I wished I'd thought to ask how many times Sissy had dressed and undressed the doll, but it turned out to be a non-issue. I only found one complete kid-sized fingerprint on her chest over her boob, where the low-cut dress exposed her skin.

"She hasn't even played with it, y'all," B.D. whispered. "That is so sad!"

I turned up plenty of adult partials, though. B.D. was the best artist, so I handed off my magnifying glass and Big Chief tablet. Hal had given me the magnifying glass as a joke, but it was one of the most useful presents he'd ever given me. B.D. drew the fingerprints, along with a sketch of the doll to show where we'd found each fingerprint. I took some pictures with my Brownie, too, but Mel noted that we should take some outside in the sun since I didn't have a flash. I picked up the newspaper, laid it out on the driveway, and took a few more. I was a little anxious that she might melt down to a little plastic blob with a bubble cut because once when I was little I'd left my Mickey Mouse guitar in the back of the car and it had melted into a misshapen lump of plastic. But now the sky was already working itself up to an afternoon thunderstorm, and the clouds cut back on the light considerably. We turned Barbie over and I dusted her again. She had a complete adult print right across her butt on the side without the Barbie brand name and another one on her back.

"If that print on her fanny belongs to Mr. Heffelman," Mel said, "then he is one sick man and we ought to think twice about finding him."

"Cheese it," I said. "Here she comes."

Sissy was trekking up the driveway with a Barbie make-up case that was bigger than her head. Just for good measure, she was wearing white gloves and carrying a pink Barbie umbrella. She looked like a pint-sized Avon Lady.

B.D. wrapped Barbie in the newspaper so that Sissy wouldn't see what we'd done to her and we all went back into the garage. Sissy carefully placed her make-up case on the footlocker and unzipped it. She'd done better than I thought she would. From her mother she'd lifted a small hand mirror and a perfume bottle, and from her father's things a hairbrush, a cigarette case, a bottle of hair tonic, and a small framed snapshot of the Heffelmans posing with a pony at a kiddieland, from the look of it the one on South Main Street—Mama, Daddy, an older boy—maybe Sissy's age now—and a younger Sissy. She'd brought another picture of her father as well, a snapshot of her sitting on his lap so you could see his face better than in the kiddieland picture. But the face was so ordinary—just a middle-aged man with medium-length hair combed back from a forehead that wasn't too wide and wasn't too narrow over a nose that wasn't too fat and wasn't too skinny and eyes that could have been light brown or gray. The only thing you could tell for sure from the picture was that he loved Sissy with all his heart.

We had her take off her gloves so that I could take her fingerprints. I warned her not to try and help me as I rolled her inked finger pads on the paper form, one by one, but she frowned in concentration anyway, as if I'd given her an egg to hold on a teaspoon. Afterward, B.D. handed her a wet rag to wipe her fingers clean.

"Okay, kid," I said to her. "Nice work. We'll be in touch. Give B.D. your phone number."

"What are you going to do?" She rubbed the back of one calf with her sandal as if she was reluctant to leave.

"Investigate," I said. "It's what we do."

"Can't I watch?" she said.

I shook my head. "This part is just for the professionals."

She eyed B.D. in her bathing suit, but in the end she went away without a fuss.

The first big drops of rain splattered on the cement as she

retreated. B.D. wanted to call her back in out of the rain, but she already had her umbrella up. "Leave her," I said. "She's a tough cookie, that one."

Mel photographed everything she brought us with the Brownie. We had a time trying to keep the sweat from rolling down our faces and splattering everything.

By now the rain was coming down like Niagara Falls and the wind was blowing it in so we closed the garage door, which trapped all the heat and humidity inside and brought out the earthy smell of things that grow in the moist darkness, along with the chemical smells of paint and turpentine. Thunder boomed and cracked overhead and rattled the jars of nails and screws on the workbench. Lucille was pretending to snooze but she had her ears pinned back.

I examined the packaging Sissy had brought us. The postmark was from Topeka, Kansas, June 22. The address label was typed, but I knew it could still come in handy in case I ever found a typewriter to compare it to—like maybe the one Mrs. Heffelman used.

Harry stuck his head in to tell me he was leaving. I stood between him and the fingerprint kit and nodded as if I wasn't paying him much attention, but when I heard the sound of his car engine die away, I said, "We need a better camera. I hope he left us one."

The duffel was still on his bed, where he'd left it. I found what I wanted inside: a Polaroid Land camera. I wondered if Harry had brought it home with the idea of recording this fatherly adventure for posterity. He doesn't like to think of himself as a sentimental guy, but he's not immune.

B.D.'s eyes widened when she saw it. "A Polaroid! Do you know how to use it?"

I got out the brush and the carbon powder and dusted everything Sissy had brought us. We laid it all out on the workbench under the hanging fluorescents and opened the garage door again to let in all the light we could. We studied the results under the magnifying glass. Most of what we got was disappointing—smudges and partials—but there, in one corner of the Vaseline Hair Tonic label, was a complete adult fingerprint. I set it down next to Barbie's heinie, and we all leaned in.

They looked the same to me.

Chapter 12

"What now?" Mel asked.

"We need an expert," I said.

"Harry?" B.D. looked at me over the magnifying glass.

"He'll do for a start, I guess. But even if the prints are a match, there could be another explanation." I knew better than to jump to conclusions, especially when our jump had to clear an obstacle the size of a man's coffin.

"Such as?" Mel said.

I shrugged. "He could've mailed it from Topeka before he died, and it got delayed. That's the simplest explanation. My mother once received a birthday card from her sister that came two months after her birthday, even though my aunt said she'd mailed it a week before."

B.D. nodded. "That happens sometimes."

"Or maybe he arranged in advance for somebody to send the present to her on her birthday," I said. "If it was a clerk in a store, they might not even know he was dead."

"Why didn't he just buy it and give it to her himself?" Mel persisted.

"Maybe he was afraid he'd forget." That was the voice of experience talking. The only reason Harry never forgot my birthday anymore was because my mother didn't let him.

"So he set something up a month in advance?" Mel said.

"Or, listen, y'all," B.D. said. "Maybe he had a premonition, or he went to a fortune teller, or something like that. Like he somehow knew something bad was going to happen to him."

"Where'd you get that idea?" I said.

"It was in one of Gin's books she bought at the drugstore." Gin was B.D.'s older sister. She worked at the drugstore soda fountain, but spent all her earnings on books featuring steamy babes and smoldering men on their covers, so the drugstore probably came out even. "There was a gypsy fortuneteller, and she told Elvira Lovelorn that she would never promenade down the aisle in her white dress, which turned out to be true, although not for the reason you might think, but I won't tell you why because I don't want to spoil it for y'all in case you read it some time."

Mel nodded seriously. We knew all about gypsies from reading Nancy Drew, because gypsies were always crossing Nancy's path. I was dying to meet a real-life gypsy, but I was beginning to think they never traveled this far south. You would think that people who lived in tents and wagons would appreciate some warmer weather from time to time, especially in the winter, but I'd never laid eyes on a gypsy in the Bayou City.

"What was he doing on the train anyway?" I said. "B.D., you know?"

She nodded. "He was a traveling salesman. Mama says he traveled all the time."

"So there could be another explanation," I said.

"Which we don't really believe," Mel said.

"What do we do next?" B.D. said.

"We'd better find out everything we can about Mr. Heffelman's death," I said. "We'd better go talk to B.D.'s canary, Mrs. Moseley."

"Are we going to tell her we don't believe he's dead?" B.D. asked.

"No, we're going to pretend we're—." I tried to think of something believable.

"Selling Girl Scout cookies," Mel offered.

"It's the wrong time of year for that," B.D. countered, "and everybody knows it."

"Maybe we should just tell her about our business," Mel suggested. "Maybe we should just tell her we're visiting people in the neighborhood to advertise."

So we picked out the best of our business cards and went to see Mrs. Moseley. I dug out some umbrellas, and Mel said that we could use them for emergency flotation devices if we needed to. I had to loan B.D. a pair of shorts to put on over her bathing suit, but you could still tell she was wearing it because the ties around the back of her neck stuck out from under her tee shirt. We posted a sign on the closed garage door to let our customers know we'd be back in an hour. The rain had let up some, so we put out a lawn chair in case they wanted to cool their heels and wait.

"Well, aren't you just the cutest things!" Mrs. Moseley exclaimed when we'd rung her bell and explained our business. "Come on in out of the rain and tell me all about it."

You could tell she was thrilled to get our story straight from the horses' mouths, so to speak, in spite of the puddles we were leaving in her entryway. Mel and I left our sandals there, but B.D.'s bare feet made little dark prints on Mrs. Moseley's beige carpet. Mrs. M. didn't turn down the volume on *Guiding Light*, so we practically had to shout to make ourselves heard.

We sat on the couch and drank lemonade and chinned with her about some of our customers. We didn't start with Sissy, because we didn't want to give anything away, but when we finally mentioned her, we hardly had to say a thing.

"Oh, that poor little child!" Mrs. Moseley pressed one hand to her chest and shook her head. She was a large lady with a big bosom, which she'd upholstered in red flowers. She wore her dirty blond hair in a limp pageboy, with the bangs pulled back to give us a good view of her eyebrows tweezed as straight and thin as a knife's edge. "You know she lost her father just a few weeks ago. Isn't that sad? It was a train wreck. A whole lot of people were killed, and—."

She was drawing breath to give us all the gory details, and then she caught herself. You could see it dawn on her that we were just kids, and she clammed up. We could hear the thunder grumbling as the volume dropped on the television.

B.D. leaned forward and said in her most grown-up voice, "We heard that it was real messy. We heard that they couldn't hardly put all the bodies back together."

"They couldn't." Mrs. Moseley took the bait. "You see, it was a tanker car they hit, and there was a big explosion. Well, you can just imagine!"

"We heard they had a hard time identifying all the bodies," B.D. said, "what with pieces of everybody flying every which way." She was making this up as she went along, but that was the advantage of being a reader—she had a head full of stories to draw on. Not that her usual reading material featured flying body parts, so I gave her extra points for imagination.

Mrs. Moseley's hands flew up for emphasis. "Sugar, it was a mess! Everything got all mixed up with everything else, if you know what I mean, and they had to go through pockets and purses—when they could find pockets and purses." She gave us a meaningful look and scanned our faces to see if we were keeping up with the scene as she was painting it.

"I reckon they found enough of that poor man to put in a coffin, because Mrs. Heffelman's niece Alberta told me they buried him out at Woodlawn," she said. "I believe they found his wallet." A happy brunette with a perky flip started singing about laundry detergent on TV, and her eyes shifted to the screen.

"When did all this happen, Mrs. Moseley?" I asked. "Do you remember?"

"Well, now let me think," she said. Thinking apparently required the effort and concentration of a yogi master. She slumped forward, tilted her head till her ear brushed one flowered shoulder, planted her cheek in one hand, and raised her eyes to study some old water stains in the ceiling. Her forehead creased like a plowed field. "It was the end of May..." She thought some more, then nodded. "I believe it would have been the thirtieth, a Tuesday, because I always get my hair done on Wednesdays, and everybody was talking about it down yonder at the beauty parlor. I hadn't heard anything about the wreck till I went to get my hair done."

She beamed at us as if she'd just guessed the secret in the first round, but I was hung up on the idea that she went to the beauty shop every week. I thought about advising her to sue them for malpractice, but then I skipped it. We had to keep her talking.

"Did you see the coffin, Mrs. Moseley?" I cranked up the volume on my voice to compete with the commercial.

I snagged her attention. She shook her head, as if regretful. "I never did. They didn't have it at the service for some reason, only at the burial, and I didn't go to that. But Alberta told me it was a real nice one."

"That's good that they could afford a nice one," I said. "Did Mr. Heffelman have life insurance?" Out of the corner of my eye I could see B.D.'s reaction, and I knew I was stepping over the line of propriety by asking a question about the deceased's financial affairs.

But Mrs. Moseley never noticed. "Why, yes, he did," she said eagerly. "And don't you know he had just bought a fifty thousand-dollar policy in March? Now wasn't that lucky?"

I agreed that it was. "How come Mr. Heffelman was on that particular train?" I asked. "I mean, do you know where he was going?"

"He wasn't going, darlin', he was coming home. From Chicago. Mr. Heffelman was a salesman, and he traveled a good deal. It was a Chicago company he worked for, if I recall."

"What line?"

"Oh, now let me think." She cradled her chin in her hand again. "Cleaning products, I believe it was."

"Where was the train wreck, Mrs. Moseley?" I asked.

"Up yonder at Cleburne," she said, pointing as if we might need directions to the crash site. "You know, they get a lot of trains through there. I'll tell you what, girls. I always liked to travel by train. Why, you couldn't pay me enough to get me up in an airplane! And I don't mind the car for short trips, but for long trips, why, the train is more relaxing. I like to think it's safer, too, but after this, I just don't know. I told my husband I believed I'd just stay home from now on."

We thanked her, and tried to blow, but she had something else on her mind.

"You're Desdemona Lark, aren't you, sugar?" She tried to stroke my hair and frowned at it disapprovingly.

"Yes, ma'am."

"You poor thing," she said. "I hear your mama's gone on a trip and left you and your brother on your own."

"No, ma'am," I said, annoyed. "My father's staying with us."

"Oh, yes, your father." Her skin tightened across her cheeks and I thought that if she bit her tongue any harder she'd have to swallow it or spit it out, one. "Well, I don't know what the world's coming to, what with all this divorce and mothers going to work and leaving their children at home to fend for themselves."

"Well, ma'am," I said, "the way I see it, we'll be running the world one of these days—us kids who learned to fend for ourselves. I expect we'll be good at it, too."

I'd just drawn breath to say more when Mel dragged me out the door.

Mrs. Moseley stood on her porch clucking as we started down the front walk and somebody turned a hose on our umbrellas, but B.D. just waved and said, "Oh, we like the rain. It doesn't bother us a bit."

Turning away, B.D. gave my arm a squeeze. "Don't mind her, Diz," she said. "Everybody knows she's just an old gossip who minds ever'body else's business 'cause she doesn't have any of her own."

We sloshed down the street.

Mel said, "About that life insurance—do you believe in that kind of luck, Dizzy?"

"Stranger things have happened, I guess."

"Well, *I* don't believe it," B.D. said. "I'm telling y'all, he got some kind of premonition and went right out and bought life insurance."

"What are you thinking about now?" Mel asked me. She'd caught me frowning.

"Why *did* he take the train?" I said. "When's the last time you went down to the train station to see somebody off? I don't even remember what the place looks like. These days, most people fly or drive their car."

"Maybe he couldn't find a flight to suit him," Mel said. "They don't have but a couple of flights a week to most places."

"Maybe he brought back merchandise to sell," B.D. said. "Couldn't take it on the plane."

"Or maybe he had stops to make along the way," Mel said, "seeing as he was a salesman."

"Then why didn't he drive?"

"Maybe it's like she said," B.D. offered. "The train was more relaxing. And if you have work to do, you can work on the train."

"How far is it to Chicago?" Mel said. "Maybe the train is faster than driving."

"We'll have to find out," I said. "The doll was mailed from Topeka, Kansas. We should find out whether the train makes a stop there."

"So if he didn't die in Cleburne," Mel said, "and if he's alive in Topeka, what does that mean?"

"It would mean that he did a bunk."

"And abandoned his family?" Mel said. "Why would he do that?"

I shrugged. Hal and I were the only kids I knew with divorced parents, so I realized that divorce was unimaginable to most kids my age, even my closest friends. Dads were supposed to sit at the head of the table every night and carve the turkey on Thanksgiving and play catch with their children after supper. They were supposed to wear sweater vests and hand out advice like Ward Cleaver or wear a sheriff's badge and take their kids fishing like Andy Griffith. To my friends, my dad was the exception that proved the rule.

Mel quickly realized what she'd said and tried to make amends. "That's not what Harry did. He didn't just disappear. He'd never do that. He loves his kids."

"But here's the thing, y'all," B.D. said. "If Mr. Heffelman did a bunk, like you said, Dizzy, who's in the coffin they buried?"

I nodded. "Yeah, or what?"

"And what now?" B.D. said. "Are we going to talk to Mrs. Heffelman?"

"Not just yet," I said. "She might not be all that eager to talk to us."

"What do you mean?" B.D. said.

"I mean she's just collected fifty thousand clams, or she's about to."

"You don't think she'd be happy to hear that her husband was alive?" B.D. said.

"Maybe not. Look, Harry makes his living off cases like that," I said. "It's called insurance fraud. Mostly people pretend to be injured so they can collect, but every once in a while the companies get a hinky life insurance claim. He told me about a case where the husband and wife were in it together."

"What do you mean?" Mel said.

"They take out an insurance policy, then pick up some poor bum, and arrange for him to have a fatal accident. The husband disappears and the wife goes boohooing to the cops that her hubbie's been killed. They have a funeral and everything. Then she tries to collect the insurance—a hundred and fifty grand, I think it was. The company hires a pal of Harry's to look into everything, and he finds the husband living it up in Acapulco, waiting for his wife to show up."

"Jeez!" Mel said. "What happened to them?"

"They're both in the slammer."

"It's hard to picture Sissy's mom doing a thing like that," B.D. objected.

"Maybe so, but we better find out more about that train wreck first. And I wonder what funeral parlor handled the funeral. If it was Mumford's, maybe Digger can tell us something." Dudley Mumford, whom everybody called Digger, was in Hal's class in school.

"How are we going to find out more about the train wreck?" Mel asked.

"We'll start at the library downtown," I said. "The newspapers."

B.D. kicked at the water streaming along the gutter. "Mama won't let me go downtown on the bus till I'm thirteen."

"Maybe I can get Harry to take us," I said. "He could go to his office and babysit at the same time."

B.D. perked up. "And after we go to the library, can we go to the picture show? You know they're showing that new Hayley Mills at the Lone Star."

"I'll ask Harry," I said. "I bet he'll do it."

On the way home we collected another barrette, a five of spades playing card that probably fell off someone's bike wheel, a paddle with broken elastic and no ball, a bent and soggy View-Master disk, and a pristine Barbie-sized red high heel. B.D. didn't want me to take the paddle, but I pointed out that if we found a ball someplace, we could maybe attach a new piece of elastic and unload it for five cents. Everything was muddy.

Hal rode me to my softball game on his bike that night. The rain had stopped and the field was wet but if they called the games for mud there wouldn't be a softball season in Houston. Harry showed up late while my back was turned, which it almost always was since I played catcher. He did his best to look like he'd been there a while, but I'm wise to his tricks. I know he missed my base hit in the second inning and the runner I tagged in the third, so if it wasn't for the ride I needed on Saturday, I'd have given him the silent treatment all the way home.

Chapter 13

It wouldn't have worked anyway, the silent treatment, because we didn't go directly home after the game, and when he told me we had a stop to make, I had to give him a piece of my mind. "A stop" was Harry's way of saying he had work to do. If I was lucky, it would just be a meet and not a stakeout, but I'm not usually lucky that way.

"I wish you'd just tell me beforehand," I said, "instead of springing it on me now, when I'm hot and sweaty and I got most of the infield stuck to my face. I don't even have a book to read. I told you before: for stakeouts, I need a book."

I peeled my team shirt away from my chest to let some air in. The shirt was red, with the team name, Sockets, on the front and the sponsor's name, Spring Branch Towing, on the back. "Sockets" was supposed to rhyme with "Rockettes," not "rockets." It was a stupid name for a team in the first place, and then some dope misspelled it. But nobody asked me. I pulled off my sneakers and socks.

"There's a telephone directory on the back seat," he said, "and a road atlas."

In the dark car he couldn't see the withering look I gave him. "At *home*, I have *The Mystery of the Fire Dragon*, which I waited months to get."

"Look at it this way, Sis," he said. "You could be reading some bogus story about Nancy Drew or you could be living the real thing with me."

"You're not going to Hong Kong," I retorted. "And I bet you're not involved in a kidnapping. You're probably just going to some hot-sheet motel to catch somebody in the sack with the wrong person."

He started. "Where'd you get that language? Not from Nancy Drew, I bet. Anyway, you know I don't do that kind of work." But we both knew he did, especially since Hal got his braces. "But you could show a little respect for what I *do* do, which puts food on the table and books on your nightstand."

"Mostly it's the Houston Public Library that puts books on my nightstand," I pointed out. "But I'll forgive you if you take us downtown on Saturday."

"What's going on downtown?"

"We want to go to the library and the picture show. Don't worry, you're not invited."

I couldn't see his face but I could imagine him thinking that he'd gotten off easy.

"Deal," he said. "Show's on me."

"Deal."

When we got to the address he was looking for in the Heights, a small frame house, he passed it and pulled over on the edge of a ditch. He reached into the backseat and when he turned around again he was holding a camera and looking at me.

I let my head drop back in frustration. "Why do you always do this to me? You know I'm terrible at it."

"No, you're not. Give yourself some credit." He was screwing on a telephoto lens. "Besides, it's good experience."

I once made the mistake of telling him that I might want to be a private dick when I grew up. Now he called everything from stuffing envelopes to sitting through stakeouts "good experience."

"One of these days," I grumbled, "I'm going to get arrested." But I took the camera. I pictured myself in the sneezer in my Socket tee and sneakers. Maybe the hookers would pass me a fag and I'd take up smoking just to spite him.

"I'm going to try to get him to come out on the porch," he said, "but if I can't, just get what you can." He reached past me and took a high-powered flashlight out of the glove compartment.

My bare feet felt stones in the grass alongside the ditch. "I don't know why we didn't just stay home and shoot from there," I muttered, squinting at the house across the dark expanse of two front yards. A pale, flickering light in a side window indicated that somebody was watching television. I squatted down behind a bush in the neighbor's yard and pressed my eye to the viewfinder. I couldn't see a thing.

Then I found Harry's blue suit on the porch, ringing the doorbell, and the porch light flicked on. Harry gestured toward the street, and after a minute a man wearing dark pants and an undershirt opened the screen door and stepped out onto the porch. Harry hooked him under the arm and brought him to the edge of the porch, talking the whole time. I snapped a picture and the flash popped and the man looked startled. He craned his neck and peered into the darkness, but Harry kept talking, the way he does, while I screwed in another flash bulb. Harry was showing the man a package wrapped in brown paper and string that he'd produced from his pocket. He fumbled the package and the man instinctively reached down and caught it. I snapped another one and the flash popped but this time the man had turned his face away because Harry had practically knocked heads with him. I wasn't going to risk another one, so I just sat tight until the man went back inside and the porch light went out. Harry got back in the car and drove off. When I figured the coast was clear, I walked to the corner and waited for Harry to circle back around and pick me up. I figured it was a case of insurance fraud—it usually is when Harry drops the package—but I didn't give him the satisfaction of asking him.

At home when Harry sat down to watch the news I brought out the two Polaroids of fingerprints. I handed them over, along with the magnifying glass, and asked if they were the same.

There was no way to hide the fact that I'd borrowed his camera, but I could see him decide not to comment on it. Instead, he just said, "What's this for?" as he took the photographs.

"It's confidential," I told him. "I might tell you later if anything comes of it."

His eyebrows went up in surprise. "You photographed Barbie's tush?"

I didn't comment. He studied the photographs. "They look pretty similar to me," he said at last, looking up, "but I'm no expert. Anyway, what you really need are enlargements."

I frowned. "Can you do that with a Polaroid?"

He handed the photographs back. "Sure, if you have the right equipment."

I thought I knew somebody who did, so I accepted the photos without comment.

The next day B.D. and I rode our bikes up to Long Point Road to see Digger Mumford at Mumford's Funeral Home. Mel volunteered to mind the store, but I could tell that the funeral home creeped her out. Digger was wearing a tee shirt and jeans and washing a black hearse in the driveway in front of the garage. The exertion had turned his skin pink and made his freckles stand out.

"Can we see inside?" B.D. asked.

"It just looks like a station wagon," he replied, "only fancier." And he opened up the back so we could see.

"Look, Diz, it's got curtains," B.D. said.

"You ever drive it?" I asked Digger.

"Few times. Not out on the street, though."

"You got your license yet?" I asked. Digger was fourteen, Hal's age, so he could get a driver's license. Hal was working on his.

"Yeah, I got it," Digger said. "They still won't let me drive the hearses, though, because I look too young and they don't want to insult anybody. Like somebody thinks I'd go joy riding in a hearse."

B.D. was lying down in the back of the hearse with her hands crossed over her chest. "It's not too comfortable," she reported.

"Well, of course it's not comfortable," I glanced at Digger. "You're supposed to be lying in a lined coffin, with a cushion under your head." I didn't know much about it, really, except what I remembered from my grandmother's funeral.

"And deceased," he added. "You're not supposed to be comfortable, you're supposed to be dead."

This made us all giggle. I waited until he'd wiped the whole car down, and we were helping him dry it.

"We wanted to ask you about Mr. Heffelman's funeral," I said finally.

"What about it?" he said.

"Did you see the body?" B.D. asked.

Digger seemed kind of taken aback. He frowned. "We call them 'remains,'" he said. "We don't talk about bodies."

"Okay." She was unfazed. "Did you see the remains?"

He looked at me quizzically. "Why do you want to know that?"

"His daughter Sissy doesn't believe he's dead," I explained. "She asked us to find out. We heard that you buried a coffin, but—well, we just want to make sure he was in it is all."

"Sissy Heffelman?" he said. "You mean—?" And he held out his hand, palm down, at about her height.

"That's her," I said. "Just turned seven."

"But she's real determined," B.D. said.

He had stopped drying and was folding his towel. "I saw the remains. But if you're asking me if it was Mr. Heffelman or somebody else, I couldn't tell you. I only saw Mr. Heffelman a couple of times, so I might not have known for sure it was him if—well, I might not have known. But the man in the coffin had been hurt real bad. His head was crushed and so his face—." He looked at us as if wondering how much he should say.

"Would anybody have been able to recognize him by his face?" I asked.

"Well, no," he admitted. "I don't think so."

"Then how did they identify him as Mr. Heffelman?" I said. "Like, was he wearing Mr. Heffelman's clothes? Or Mr. Heffelman's cufflinks? Or did he have Mr. Heffelman's wallet in his pocket? Or did he have a mole or a scar that Mr. Heffelman had?"

"Oh," he said. "I guess he was wearing Mr. Heffelman's clothes and carrying Mr. Heffelman's wallet. And I think he was wearing a ring."

"No mole or scar?"

"Not that I heard of."

"And Mrs. Heffelman said it was him?"

"Well, sure." He looked around and lowered his voice. "She was balling her eyes out, so she must've known it was her husband. I don't see why Sissy thinks it wasn't."

"She's got her reasons," I said. "We just wanted to make sure she was wrong."

"Well, she is."

Next we went to see Alice Song, a friend of ours from school who had been in my Brownie troupe in second and third grades. Alice's dad was a photographer, and Alice was a photographer, too. She always had a camera slung around her neck. I had called her the night before to tell her what we needed.

"Is this Barbie's fanny?" she said, studying the photos.

"It's the fingerprints we need," B.D. said, "for comparison."

"Okay," she said. "Like I told Dizzy, because this is a Polaroid, I'll need to make negatives first, and then enlarge them. Come back tomorrow, and I should have 'em ready."

We rode our bikes back to my house and reported to Mel. She was sitting cross-legged on the garage floor, playing jacks by herself. Lucille was sitting on the footlocker, watching her. Lucille's head bounced in time with the ball.

"So according to Digger, it was probably Mr. Heffelman in the coffin," she said, "but it's not one hundred percent certain. But he had Mr. Heffelman's wallet and wore Mr. H's ring, so it's ninety-nine percent certain, especially since I can't see any reason why somebody else would be pretending to be him, can you?"

"Well," B.D. said, glancing at me, "I don't want to give anything away since you haven't read it yet. But in *The Mystery of the Fire Dragon*, somebody is made to look like somebody else who's missing."

"B.D.'s right," I said, "The thing is, all the things they used to identify Mr. Heffelman—those were all things that could be faked. You can put somebody else's clothes and ring on a body, and put somebody else's wallet in their pocket."

"But why would anybody do that?" Mel asked.

"No idea," B.D. said.

"Mr. Heffelman was just a traveling salesman," Mel said. "He wasn't an international jewel thief or a mob boss or anything like that."

"You're right," I said. "It doesn't make any sense. So it probably didn't happen the way I said."

"We'll know more tomorrow, maybe, when we look at Alice's enlargements," B.D. said.

"So are we going to talk to Mrs. Heffelman now?" Mel asked.

"Not just yet," I said. "I want to read up on the train wreck first."

"Which is why we're going to the library on Saturday," Mel said.

"And then to the picture show," B.D. said happily.

Chapter 14

"Wow, would you look at that!" B.D. said. "No wonder Mr. Heffelman lost his face."

She was sitting with her head propped on her elbows, leaning on the polished wooden library table. I was standing in the middle so that I could turn the pages of the newspaper, and Mel was leaning across me to see the picture.

"It's a mess, all right," Mel agreed. "You see a list of victims, Dizzy?"

"They call them 'casualties,'" B.D. put in.

"How come?" Mel demanded. "Doesn't seem like there'd be anything casual about dying in a pile of metal and glass like that."

"This was only the first story," I said. "The list comes later. This article says they couldn't even get to some parts of the trains yet because they were still too hot from the explosion."

"How did it happen?" Mel said.

"Says here that somebody didn't switch the passenger train off the same track as the tanker car."

"Man, oh, man," B.D. shook her head. "How'd you like to be that somebody?"

We fell silent. We were probably all thinking that we'd forgotten to do a few things in our time—I know I was.

I laid the newspaper aside and picked up the next one. This one had another front-page picture of the wreckage. The headline read, "36 Confirmed Dead in Cleburne Train Wreck," and underneath was a smaller headline: "Dozens Injured in Wreck of the Texas Chief."

"I bet the names are on an inside page," I said. "They don't like to put the names on the front page out of respect for the families."

We read the story, then turned to where it continued inside and found the list of names at the end. B.D. and Mel stood up and leaned in till all our heads were touching. I scanned the list, then started over, putting my finger on each name as I went.

"It's not there," Mel said excitedly. "Diz, it's not there."

"The story says that the list is only partial because of 'difficulties with identification,'" I pointed out.

"Yeah," B.D. said, "difficulties like missing faces."

"But if he had a wallet..." Mel said.

"You're right," I said. "He should be there."

I laid that paper aside and picked up the next one. "We should have asked Digger when the body arrived at the funeral parlor," B.D. said. Then she made a face. "Excuse me, the *remains*."

We skipped ahead to the end of the article and scanned the names.

"Here it is." Mel tapped the page. "Leo A. Heffelman."

We went back to the beginning and read the article through, then flopped back into our chairs.

"I wonder if they accounted for everybody," I said.

"You mean, like, if they had any arms or legs or bodies left over?" B.D. winced.

"Or if they know what happened to everybody on the train," Mel suggested. "Not just the passengers, but the engineer, the conductors, the porters—everybody."

"It doesn't *say* they had unidentified bodies left over," B.D. said. "And it doesn't say that anybody's missing, either. Wouldn't they have to put that in the paper if it was true?"

I looked at her and realized that hanging out with Harry had given me a head start when it came to skepticism. "Not if somebody leaned on them to dummy up."

B.D. frowned at me and scratched at a mosquito bite on her arm. "Why would anybody do that? The police would have to identify all the bodies to make sure the right families got notified. The families would be pitching a fit if they had somebody missing and nobody could tell them whether the person was dead or alive."

"Yeah, but I could see if they had some spare body parts laying around and they didn't know who they belonged to, they might just box 'em up and hand 'em to a family and say, 'Here. Here's your dad.'" Mel was frowning in concentration. "You think someone's going to look at a foot or an elbow and say, 'No, that's not him'?"

"I cannot believe we're having this conversation, y'all," B.D. said. She slipped her bandeau off and put it back on again.

"Well, that's kind of what Sissy did," I said. "She said, 'That's not him.' Which is why we're having this conversation."

"Except that Sissy never saw the body," B.D. said. "At least, I hope she didn't. And her mom did."

"Probably," I admitted.

"Personally," Mel said, not without sympathy, "I think what that girl needs is a shrink."

"Well, we can't shrink her," B.D. said. "We're in the lost and found business."

"Rose has some relatives who work as Pullman porters," I said. "I wonder if any of them work on the Texas Chief."

"What is it you think they could tell us, Diz?" Mel said.

"I don't know," I said. "They might know if anybody's missing and not on the list. Or maybe they just saw something funny. You never know till you ask."

"Do you think they'd talk to us?" B.D. said. "We don't have licenses or anything."

"If Rose asks them to, I bet they will. I'll ask her."

We had quite a few blocks to walk to the movie theatre. The pavement felt hot through our sandals. The sun was blazing away but you could see some clouds rising up in the direction of the Gulf. We stopped at the Foley's lunch counter on the way and ate burgers and fries and drank Dr. Peppers. Sitting next to B.D. was a colored lady with a baby who played peek-a-boo with B.D. over his mother's shoulder.

The Lone Star was an old theatre, worlds away from the drive-in where we usually saw movies from the backseat with a speaker clipped to the window. The Lone Star was a movie palace, fancy with gilt carving around the screen and Roman ladies holding up the balcony. It smelled the way old buildings do when the plush seats have worn down and the velvet ropes get kind of moth-eaten and the tops of the curtains get furred with dust thick as a cat's coat. We bought some popcorn and candy and some more Dr. Peppers and moved up close so we could see the whites of Hayley's eyes.

It was her best picture yet, with Hayley playing twins who had been separated when they were little and their parents divorced until they meet at summer camp and plot to reunite their parents. This one twin grew up on a ranch out West, and the other grew up in an old house in Boston. Hayley sang and played the guitar, too.

When it was over, B.D. said, in her Hayley voice, "It was so sort of marvelous," and Mel and I agreed.

But when we got back to the lobby, we heard a commotion outside. An older boy wearing a short red jacket and a bow tie and cap took hold of Mel's arm and pulled her toward the door.

"Just stick close, y'all," he said over his shoulder to B.D. and me.

Outside there was quite a scene. A small group of negroes and two white girls— older kids—were walking around, carrying signs. The boys wore jackets and ties, and the girls wore dresses and stockings. They were partly surrounded by a crowd of white people. Like us in our sundresses and sandals, most of the white people weren't as dressed up as the negro group. Some of them were shouting at the colored kids to go home. One man pushed a negro boy and made him stumble, but he recovered and kept right on walking. The crowd kept moving in, forcing the colored kids back toward the building.

The kid from the theatre was still pulling Mel through the crowd like a security escort but I stopped in my tracks when I saw Rose's niece Juney. She was carrying a sign that said "Theatre Management Unfair."

"Hey, Juney," I said. "What's going on?"

B.D. bumped right into me. She looked over my shoulder. "Hey, Juney," she said. "What are y'all doing?"

"We're picketing." Juney didn't look happy to see us. "Y'all go on home, now."

I fell in step with her. "Picketing about what?"

Her eyes shifted around and she hissed at me, "Dizzy, it isn't any of your business. Go on home, now, like I told you."

"Black bitch!" somebody snarled in my other ear.

A hand reached out as if to grab Juney, but I batted it away. "Oh, go soak your head," I said as I trotted to keep up with her.

"Juney," I called.

"Hey!" B.D. said, and I saw her elbow somebody who had elbowed her.

A negro boy stepped between her and the other elbow and put a hand on her arm. He had a nice face and dark framed glasses that made him look intellectual, like a college student.

"We're picketing the theatre because it's segregated," he said to us. He glanced at Juney, but she was busy trying to ignore us. "Negroes pay the same price as whites for their tickets, but we have to enter by a different door and sit in the balcony, whereas whites can sit anywhere they want."

B.D. and I had taken in the other signs they were carrying by now: "Lone Star Unfair to Negro Patrons," "Equal Treatment for Equal Pay," and "End Segregation."

Mel, who had apparently shaken her escort, popped through the front row of onlookers and joined us.

The college boy looked around uneasily. The crowd was growing.

"You girls had best run on, now," he said. "There could be trouble."

"But we support you," I said. "We should join your protest."

"We're not afraid of trouble," Mel said, as a glass bottle sailed past us and shattered against the building.

"We appreciate your support," the college boy said, "but you're too young. It could be dangerous."

The usher reappeared and tried to get a grip on Mel's arm again, but she shook him off.

"We're joining the demonstration," B.D. told him. In her Hayley voice, she added, "These people are getting gypped, and we think it's lousy."

"Yeah," Mel said, in her own Hayley voice. "It stinks."

"Yeah," I added, "It stinks."

The usher looked worried, and I felt a little sorry for him. If he didn't get us away, he could get blamed for whatever happened. But I turned my back on him anyway and locked arms with the college student.

I felt something wet hit my shoulder, hard. I thought at first that someone was spitting on us, but then I looked up and realized it was starting to rain—big, heavy drops that meant a gully-washer was coming. We kept marching.

"Little sister," the college student said, "I wish you'd go home."

But I could barely hear him now over the blare of the police sirens bouncing off all the cement and metal and glass of the downtown buildings. As the lights flashed from the police cars and the brakes squealed, most of the crowd fell back, but I saw a white woman kick a negro girl when she thought nobody was looking, and an old white man in a business suit spat on one of the boys.

The cops rushed in with sticks raised and herded the demonstrators into a tight knot. At that moment, the sky opened up and dumped the Gulf of Mexico on our heads. Most of the white crowd scattered, but a few stayed behind to see how things played out.

A blond cop grabbed me by the shoulder and shoved me in the other direction. "Beat it, kid," he said.

Furious, I slugged him, though my aim was off and I didn't hit any targets worth hitting. Still, he stumbled—probably from surprise—and fell to his knees.

"Here's a news flash," I said. "We're with them."

Mel grabbed me and we ducked under some blue-uniformed arms to rejoin the group of demonstrators.

Juney had a small cut on one cheek and her hair was mussed, but she turned on us in a rage. "Would you get out of here?" she hissed. "I'm in enough trouble without having to answer to Aunt Rose for all of y'all."

Our clothes, soaked through, clung to us. The starch Rose insisted on using in my petticoat had given up the ghost. I latched onto the college boy again, and Mel latched on to me.

The college boy frowned at us. "Come on, now. Y'all don't want an arrest record before you're teenagers. What would your daddies say?"

"My father has a rap sheet of his own," I said. "He'd better not have something to say about mine."

A red-faced cop handcuffed the college boy and put us in the paddy wagon with the others when he couldn't get rid of us. The cop skipped the bracelets on us, which probably would have fallen off, anyway.

"I hope y'all get the spanking of your life," the cop said.

"Oh, dry up," I said.

They took us down to the slammer and locked us up in a holding cell with two white girls from the demonstration. They put Juney and the other colored girls in a separate cell right next to us, which seemed pretty idiotic. I don't know where they took the boys, including my new pal, but I hoped they weren't all down in the basement getting the third degree, which, according to Harry, involves getting hit with phone books. I had a new scratch on my hand, B.D. had lost her bandeau, and Mel had lost a button from the front of her sundress, but we were in better shape than the colored girls. We were in a room full of cops and desks and other people who might have been criminals or might have been citizens trying to report a crime or, I now realized, citizens like us exercising their constitutional rights. Mostly, nobody paid any attention to us. We looked daggers at the cop who went through our purses, but he never even looked up.

"What's Harry going to think when he turns up and we're not there?" Mel said.

"He'll figure it out," I said. "He's a detective."

"Don't worry," one of the white girls said to B.D. "They'll let you call your parents to come pick you up. They won't file charges."

"I don't believe I want to call my parents just now," B.D. said.

"How often have y'all been arrested?" Mel asked the girl. You could tell Mel was impressed by how much she knew.

The girl laughed. "A few times. I lost count. The worst thing is they keep your cigarettes."

"So you've had other demonstrations?" I said.

"Sure, lots of them," a colored girl joined in. "Last year it was lunch counters. This year we're working on movie theatres and bus stations."

"How come you switched?" B.D. said.

At the same time, I said, "How come I haven't heard anything about your demonstrations?"

"You haven't heard anything about them," said the first girl, "because the business owners got together with the newspaper owners and decided it was bad for business to print stories about us in the papers."

"And we switched," said the second girl, "because some of those same business owners decided that it was bad for business to have us sitting in at the lunch counters all the time, even if it wasn't in the papers, so they agreed to integrate."

"They were probably afraid we'd do something worse, and then the papers would have to cover it," the first girl put in.

"Anyway," the second continued, "there are still some holdouts, but most of them agreed."

I thought about the colored woman with her baby, sitting next to us at Foley's.

"But we never read about that either," I said. "We read about the Freedom Riders in Mississippi and Alabama, but we never read anything about Houston."

Another colored girl spoke up. She was rubbing a bruised wrist. "That's because in Houston, the hot shots—the business owners and politicians—have agreed that we don't have a segregation problem."

Everybody laughed at this, but I didn't see the joke.

The second girl said, "That's why we want to get arrested."

B.D. shook her head till her ponytail whacked her in the face. "Wait. Y'all *want* to get arrested?"

"Sure," said the third girl. "If we just protest, the papers ignore us. But if we get arrested, it's news. They've got to print it."

You can learn a lot in stir.

It wasn't too long before Harry showed up. A gray-haired cop walked him over. He was shaking his head, but he didn't look mad.

"The three pipsqueaks are mine," he said, pointing. Then he spotted Juney, who was trying to avoid eye contact. "I'll take that young lady, too."

"She a relative?" the cop asked skeptically.

"That's right," Harry said.

So they signed us all out and returned our purses. Juney objected to taking a ride, but in the end she let Harry drive her home. He didn't say a word in the car—not even about the large damp spots we were leaving on the seats—and she didn't, either. She just smoked a cigarette and looked out the window. Finally, as if she couldn't help herself, she said, without looking at him, "I told her to go home."

"I'm sure you did," he said.

"More than once," she said.

"Uh-huh."

"I told her there could be trouble."

"Trouble is her middle name," Harry said.

"Will you tell Aunt Rose what I said?" she asked, and now she did look at him.

"I'll tell her," he said.

He pulled up in front of Juney's house, and she thanked him when she got out of the car.

"Don't mention it," he said.

He turned around and looked as us then. We were lined up in the back seat.

"So how does it feel to be embarking on a life of crime, girls?"

"You should know," I said.

He tried to hold on to his frown but he couldn't help himself. He grinned at us in the rearview mirror, shook his head, and drove home in amused silence.

I knew there'd be more to it later, and there was, in the form of a lecture about avoiding dangerous situations and trying not to make my old man gray before his time and also—most importantly—about not telling my mother.

"My mother," I said, "has always taught me to have the courage of my convictions."

"That's because your mother spends all of her time in an ivory tower," he said. "Don't get me wrong—she's a tough cookie. She wouldn't be where she is today if she couldn't compete against the men in her profession. But she hasn't tried to test her convictions in the outside world. Maybe she will. The way things are going, maybe we all will. But if I could keep her safe in her ivory tower, I'd do it."

"And me too?"

His eyes went soft and he reached out and stroked my hair, the way he likes to do. He sighed. "No. No, Sis, I don't guess I have that option with you."

"Because I'm too much like you?"

"That's about the size of it."

I cuddled up against his shoulder. I matched my palm against his to compare them and then curled my fingers through his.

"Anyway," I said, "nothing happened really, just some pushing and shoving."

"You got off easy this time."

I thought about what the girl had said in the jail. "This isn't Alabama or Mississippi. It's Houston."

"Plenty of angry crazy people in Houston. You never know what they might do."

That night, somebody firebombed the Lone Star Theatre.

Book Two

Dizzy – July 2, 1961

Chapter 15

We didn't hear about the firebombing right away, because it didn't make the morning paper. Harry took us to Shipley Do-nuts for breakfast, and we overheard some people talking at the next table.

"Isn't that where you went yesterday, Diz?" Hal said.

Harry and I exchanged a look, but didn't comment. We'd agreed that the less Hal knew about my hitch in the slammer, the better.

But Rose knew, and I caught heck from her on Monday morning, as I knew I would. It didn't take me long to figure out that Rose had mixed feelings about the picketing.

"If Juney wants to make a fool of herself parading around holding a picket sign," she fumed, "that's her business, but it ain't none of yours. She's almost grown up. You're not. And if your mama finds out about it, there's going to be you-know-what to pay!"

I thought my mother might have joined the picket line herself, but I held my tongue. When it suited her purpose, Rose made my mother sound like General MacArthur, even though the inclinations toward military discipline were all Rose's. That was one of the things my mother liked about her. "Did Juney go to the lunch counters last year with the others?" I asked.

"She been part of that group ever since she went to college." Rose was shaking her head. "They always up to some kind of mischief."

"Mischief? I heard a bunch of lunch counters downtown got integrated, and it was all because of those sit-ins. That makes Juney a hero in my book."

Rose hesitated. You could see she was proud to hear Juney called a hero, and in her own heart, she probably knew it was true. But Rose never liked to show all her cards.

"Well, you keep that book to yourself, hear?" she said. "You too young to be mixed up in those things, and the older kids don't want you there."

"Because I'm white?"

"Because you're too young. They don't want to be worrying about you all the time if things get ugly."

This was more or less what Harry had said. Nobody had come right out and said that picketing was the wrong thing to do or the wrong way for negroes to get what they wanted, they just didn't want *me* to do it.

"I wish everybody would quit worrying about me."

"Well, you got a few years to wait before that happens. And your mama and daddy ain't never going to quit worrying about you."

After all that talk about worrying, I didn't think the time was right to ask about Pullman porters on the Texas Chief, so I waited till B.D. and Mel arrived a little later. Mel's mother had sent over some potato salad. Harry was at work and Hal was at his summer job at the Y.

"She told me to tell you she knew it wasn't as good as yours, Rose," Mel told Rose as she handed over the potato salad. "But she wanted to make a contribution because you're feeding me all the time."

This was the right tack to take with Rose, who said, "Tell her I appreciate it, but it's no trouble. I got to make Dizzy's lunch anyway, I might as well feed all of y'all."

She sat down with us at the kitchen table and made a big show of tasting the potato salad.

"Rose," I began, "don't you have some relations that work on the trains as Pullman porters?"

"Mm-hmm," she said. "My brother Lucius, my brother-in-law Louie, my nephew Paul—that's Pansy's oldest. Let me see. Is that everybody? Oh, yes, my cousin Augustus. My cousin Harley—Augustus's father—used to work for them, but he's retired now. My nephew Gideon used to work for them, but he lost his job. A lot of folk have lost their jobs now that so many people are taking airplanes instead of trains. My uncle George used to be a porter, too, but he's retired, and he say he's glad he retired before things got so bad."

"Jeez Louise," Mel said. "You sure have a big family, don't you, Rose?"

"Well, it was five of us girls and two boys," Rose said. "But my mama had a big family, too. My daddy didn't have but one sister, Aunt Tildy."

"Were any of your relatives working on the Texas Chief when that big wreck happened up by Cleburne?" I asked.

She nodded. "My brother-in-law Louie—the one that's married to my sister Pansy—he was on it. He got banged up pretty bad, and— well, he hurt his arm." Her eyes swept our faces and I could tell we were getting an edited account. "He hasn't been able to work since it happened. He can't hardly lift his arm, and his knee has been paining him. It was a terrible thing."

"Do you think he'd talk to us about it?" B.D. asked. Her voice shook just a little when she said it. You never knew what might set Rose off.

Rose frowned at her. "What you want to talk about it for? You fixin' to write a book?"

"I just thought it would be interesting," B.D. said meekly.

"*Interesting*?" Rose repeated. "You think a train wreck with folks lying on the ground and moaning and flames shooting up and burning folks alive is interesting? That ain't what *I'd* call it."

She drew a breath, but I cut in before she could get up a full head of steam. "We have a missing persons case. We have a client. There's this little girl named Sissy Heffelman."

That deflected her assault on B.D. "That little bitty thing come waltzing up the driveway last week?" Rose doesn't miss much.

"That's her. She's convinced her father didn't die in the wreck, like everybody thinks."

"Including her mother," Mel put in.

"She thinks he's just disappeared," I said. "She's got her reasons for thinking the way she does, and she's asked us to find him. We need to convince her that he's dead. We've read about the wreck in the newspapers, but it would help a lot if we could talk to somebody who was there."

"An eyewitness," B.D. said.

"Right," I said. "An eyewitness."

Rose looked puzzled. "Didn't they bury him?"

"They buried somebody," B.D. said, and when Rose's frown swung her way, she added, "It was probably him."

"Funeral?"

"Yes," I said. "Closed casket because of the damage."

"His name listed in the newspaper?"

We nodded.

"So everybody think he's dead except this one little girl?"

"That's about the size of it," I said.

"Then what you want to go around bothering folks for? The man is dead. Her mama think so, the funeral parlor think so, and the newspaper think so. I'm sorry for this little girl, but sound like what she need is a good cry, not no lost and found to be finding somebody that ain't lost."

"What we really want to know," I said, "is whether all of the missing passengers were accounted for."

"And whether they had any—." B.D. made a vague gesture with her hand. "Any body parts—you know—left over, ones they couldn't—." Feeling the weight of Rose's stare, she stopped.

"Identify," Mel finished for her.

"Y'all been reading too many of those mystery books," Rose said, shaking her head. "It's turned y'all's minds as sour as old milk. Why don't y'all go out there and run your store and mind your own business?"

Because she'd never read Nancy Drew, she didn't know any better. Nothing this bad ever happened in a Nancy Drew book. Nancy might get kidnapped or tied up by a menacing counterfeiter or thief or she might even get conked on the head, and somebody might sprain an ankle, but people almost never got plugged, much less iced. There was no mention of unattached body parts in Nancy Drew.

"This *is* our business," I said. "We run a lost and found. Sissy believes her father is lost and she asked us to find him. We need to convince her that the only place she can find him is under the headstone in the cemetery. That's all we're doing—looking for more evidence."

"Well, a headstone in a cemetery would be enough to convince most people," Rose said.

"Will you take us to talk to your brother-in-law?" I asked. "We just want to talk to someone who was there."

"I don't know what you think he can tell you. He was likely laying on the ground himself, not wandering around checking dead folks off the passengers list."

In the end, we wore her down, and she agreed to take us. I asked her brother-in-law's name.

"Boudet," she said. "Mr. Louis Boudet, from out Baton Rouge way."

So after Rose made the arrangements, we put on sundresses so we'd look more grown up, and because we were paying a call on somebody. Most days, Rose rode the bus to our house, but today she had driven her car, a big white-and-gold DeSoto that made her look small behind the wheel.

Most of Rose's family lived in Fifth Ward, northeast of the city, due east of where we lived in Spring Branch. Rose had two children, and she used to bring them with her to work sometimes in the summertime, but they were older than we were and liked to stay home with their older cousins. We liked her daughter Eula, and she was always nice to us, but you could tell she maybe thought we were juvenile, like she felt a little superior. That was okay; she was still aces with us. We envied her sophistication, her beehive hairdo, and her pierced ears. When we passed Rose's house, Eula was sitting on the porch with some other girls, and we could hear rock and roll music coming from a radio. She waved back when we waved at her. One of the girls was dancing with a toddler wearing diapers, and she made the baby wave, too.

The Boudet house was up the street and around the corner from Rose's house. It was a two-story white frame house built on cinderblocks and shaded by tall oaks on two sides. There was a little patch of grass in the front yard and flowers, most of them marigolds. There were tall ones and short ones, big ones and little ones, round ones and flat ones, in all shades of orange and yellow. There were other flowers I couldn't name, looking wilted even in the shade of a chinaberry tree.

Mr. Boudet was a big man. He sat on a porch swing, which hung low under his weight. He wore dark blue pants, a button-up white shirt, a red vest, and a red and blue tie. A blue jacket was draped across the back of his chair as if he wanted to be ready for church at a moment's notice.

It made me hot just to look at him, but he didn't seem bothered. He had a long face and kind eyes framed by laugh wrinkles like cat's whiskers and gray hair trimmed close to his head. He stood up, holding onto the swing chain, and shook hands with each of us but the hand he offered us hung low like the porch swing and he didn't look too steady on his feet. There was a cane leaning up against the wall nearby.

I knew he was married to Rose's younger sister, but he looked older than Rose. Maybe it was because of the gray hair, or maybe it was because of the trouble he'd had with his health since the wreck. Or maybe it was because you could never really tell how old Rose was by looking at her.

"Why don't you go on in the house and fix us some lemonade, Rose?" He settled himself in the porch swing again, making it creak with his weight.

I sat in a lawn chair and B.D. and Mel took the glider. There was no breeze but it was surprisingly cool there in the shade. A cardboard fan rested next to him on the swing, probably from one of the neighborhood funeral parlors, but he wasn't using it, maybe because he only had one and couldn't share it four ways.

"I know your daddy," he said to me.

"Yes, sir," I said. "He sends his regards."

A lot of people knew Harry. I figured that between Harry and Rose I could get in to see just about anybody I wanted to see in the city of Houston, white or negro, minus those they'd ticked off, which added up to a big exception.

"Well, you tell him the same from me. He is a good man." He had a different accent from most of the colored people I knew, and I couldn't place it but assumed it was a Louisiana accent.

I nodded.

"You girls enjoying your summer?" he asked. His gaze took in B.D. and Mel in the glider. They were sitting up tall as if they were having their picture taken.

"Yes, sir," B.D. said. "We surely are."

"Yes, sir," Mel said.

"Not too hot for you?"

"No, sir," Mel said.

"It is mighty hot," B.D. said.

"But not here," I added.

"No," B.D. agreed, "it's nice out here on the porch."

"It's the oaks." He said pointed with his good arm and squinted up at them. "God's air conditioners."

We all smiled.

"Rose said you were in that bad train wreck, Mr. Boudet," I said. "How are you feeling?"

"Well, I'm still here," he said. "I got to give the good Lord credit for that. There's a lot that died, you know, but I reckon it wasn't my time, no."

"Were you hurt pretty bad?" B.D. asked.

"Well, I got thrown pretty hard on my shoulder." He said touched it gingerly with the fingertips of his good hand. "My arm ain't been right since. And I got pretty banged up when the car turned over. My knee and my ankle don't seem right neither, and they hurt all the time, so I've got to use that cane. But I ain't complaining, me. No, ma'am, not when so many people died."

Rose returned with a tray of lemonade, and we all took a glass. She sat down on another lawn chair in the corner. She put the squint on each of us to make sure we were behaving ourselves.

Mr. Boudet looked around like a satisfied host. "Y'all want some soda crackers?" he asked. "Rose, you should've brought some soda crackers."

"We're fine," B.D. said.

"We're not hungry, honest," Mel said at the same time.

"They'll spoil their lunch," Rose said, also at the same time.

After a beat of silence, I asked, "What was it like afterward? After the collision, I mean?"

"Oh, Lord, sugar," he said, "I don't know. I was knocked out, you know. And then when I opened my eyes—why, I reckon it looked like Armageddon at the end of the battle. There was people lying all around, covered in blood and moaning and crying out. And it was smoke everywhere and ash till you could hardly breathe. And the smell of it—not just the burning oil and hot metal but—."

Rose broke in. "Why don't you ask him about the man you're looking for?"

He sent her an apology with his eyes and then looked at me. "Y'all looking for somebody?"

"We're looking for a passenger who was listed as killed in the wreck." I handed him the picture, leaning forward and stretching my arm so he wouldn't have to get up. "Do you remember him?"

He fished some wire-rimmed half-glasses out of his shirt pocket and took his time putting them on, hooking the ends around his ears. He studied the photograph carefully. "Mr. Heffelman," he said, to my surprise. "This his little girl?" When he looked up, his eyes were shiny.

Here was another surprise. I was hoping Mr. Boudet might

recognize Mr. Heffelman, but it hadn't occurred to me that he might actually have known him and cared about him. I guess it should have. Mrs. Moseley had told us that Mr. Heffelman traveled back and forth to Chicago a lot, so if he was taking the train he was probably a regular passenger on the Texas Chief. I supposed that even a man as ordinary in appearance as Mr. Heffelman could have made an impression over time. Till now, I hadn't even thought that a porter might feel emotional over the death of a passenger he'd come to know. Harry wouldn't have made that mistake.

"I didn't see him after the accident," Mr. Boudet said, "if that's what you're asking me. I'd like to oblige you, but I can't."

"Was there anything special you can tell us about Mr. Heffelman?" I asked. "Did he ride the train often?"

"Pretty often. He was like a lot of salesmen—sometime he rode all the way from Chicago and sometime he got off the train along the way, got back on when the next one come along. One of the younger porters, a loose-mouthed fellow name of Bert Meacham, he said one time, 'That Heffelman—he's got a girl in every port,' and he winked at us, but he was just talking foolishness. I reckon what he had was customers."

I leaned forward. "What else do you remember about him?"

"Oh, he showed me pictures of his kids sometime," he said. "I sure hate to think of them kids without a daddy. And his wife was real pretty, I remember that. He dressed kind of flashy, but a lot of the travelers do, you know. I don't know what else I can tell you. He was a gentleman, friendly enough but quiet, didn't give us any trouble. One time he gave me a five dollar tip for shining his shoes, said he'd just made a big sale."

"Did he say anything about a Barbie doll he was giving his little girl for a birthday present?" B.D. asked.

"Not to me," he said. "I knew he had a little girl, though."

"Would you happen to know where he was sitting when the wreck happened?"

"Well, now, I can't say for sure. He was sitting in the lounge car when I come back from the diner—that was, oh, half an hour before the accident. A gentleman from my car left his cigarette case in the diner and asked me to fetch it for him. I hadn't seen Mr. Heffelman before that so I don't know where his seat was. Of course, he could have been in another sleeper, you know. We generally carry four, so he wasn't always on my car, and a porter don't generally have much of a chance to walk through the train unless, like I say, a passenger leave something in one of the other cars and ask the porter to fetch it. But seem like Mr. Heffelman used to ride my car more often. Here lately I believe he took to getting on the train at Kansas City or Wichita early in the morning, and sleeping in the chair car. Can't say that for sure, though, because like I say, I didn't always see him."

"Or Topeka?" B.D. asked. "Could it have been Topeka?"

"Could have been," he agreed.

"Where was the lounge car in relation to the front of the train?" Mel asked.

"It was—," he began, then looked around and spotted the notebook I was writing in. "Here, hand me your notebook and I'll show you."

He raised his head to get the right angle through his glasses and drew slowly and awkwardly with his bad arm. He drew a line of boxes and labeled them with letters, then motioned for us to gather around. He pointed at the cars labeled "D," "L," and "S."

"Look here," he said. "I went from this second sleeper to the diner, so I walked through the lounge car coming and going."

"So if you passed him," I said, "that means that all you know is that he was closer to the front of the train at that point than you were. I guess most of the passengers who were killed were at the front of the train." I frowned. "But the sleepers are pretty far back."

He pointed again with the pencil. "You understand, there's only workers at the head of the consist. The passengers are farther back."

"The head of the what?" Mel said.

"The train," he said. "The consist—that's just another word for all the cars in the train. You see, there's the locomotive up front, and then you have your mail cars and baggage cars. Oh, they might put another chair car on from Houston to Galveston, but up north at Cleburne it wouldn't be any cars up front but RPOs and baggage."

"RPOs?" Mel echoed.

"Railway Post Office," he said. "Mail cars."

"And do people work in those while the train is moving?" she asked.

"That's right," he said. "There's clerks on those cars, and a baggage master on the baggage cars."

"So how far back is the first passenger car?" B.D. asked.

"That depends on the run," he said. "I don't pay much attention. But there might be, oh, eight or nine cars before the first passenger car." He ran his forefinger along a line of cars marked with *B*s and *M*s and stopped on the first car marked *C*, which he tapped. "So the people in the first chair car—they would have the worst time in a collision like that one, with the gas explosion. But some other folks died when their cars derailed and fell over."

"How did the crash happen?" We knew what the papers had said, but I wanted to hear his angle.

He shrugged. "Brakeman threw the wrong switch, that's all. We were mighty lucky on two counts, though. We were already slowing for a stop at the station, and they was only one tanker in the yard. That's not normal. Usually, they got a whole row of them tankers lined up. If we'd hit one of them lines, why, I don't expect there would be nothing left to investigate. I reckon the whole town would've been blown to kingdom come. I wouldn't be sitting here talking to you now, that's a fact."

"Were there other porters working on the train that day—the day of the wreck?" I asked.

"Oh, yes, we had four sleepers on that train, three regulars and an extra. That makes four porters. There was Robert Hamms, he lives up in Chicago. Then there was a fellow named Dooley Grayson, who died in the wreck—he was the extra. And Amos Anderson, who's still in the hospital, and me."

"But not Bert Meacham."

"No, not that time," he said.

"If we wanted to talk to the others, do you think they'd be willing to meet with us?" I had reclaimed my notebook and I was writing down names.

He thought a moment. "Well, you know, folks don't like to relive a tragedy. It's hard. But I believe they would if I asked them to. I wonder, though. You might do better to talk to the chair car attendants if he wasn't on a sleeper that run."

"Would the railway ticket office that sold him the ticket have a record of his seat assignment?" Mel asked.

He shook his head. "They know which seats they sold, but they don't write down the passengers' names."

It was just as well. I could see us marching into the railway office in our sundresses, trying to convince the chump behind the counter into spilling the dope about Mr. Heffelman's seat assignment on the wrecked train.

"Do you know their names—the chair attendants?" I said.

"No, I wouldn't know that," he said, shaking his head. "There must have been, oh, seven or eight of them, and they work a shorter run, so you don't get to know them like you do the porters." Then he raised his good hand. "No, now, I take that back. Johnny Foster was on that run. You know him, Rose—Althea Graham's grandson? Go to church with the family over to Fifth Ward Church of Christ? He was in the hospital but I believe he's back at work already." He shook his head and smiled. "Young bones."

He flattened his palms against his thighs, leaned forward, and asked us if we'd like to see the rabbits and chickens he had out back. B.D. and Mel were getting up when I thought of one more question.

"Mr. Boudet," I said, "was there anything else unusual that happened that day? Anything else that might have made the day stand out even if the wreck hadn't happened?"

Harry always said you had to give a horse its head, which meant you were supposed to give your witnesses a chance to answer the question you hadn't asked.

Mr. Boudet was struggling to his feet. Once he got the cane in place, he leaned on it and thought. "No, . . . no, I can't think of anything like that. There was a mother with five little ones—I reckon the oldest wasn't no older than seven or eight. I believe they were visiting her mother in Galveston. They got banged up some, but they survived." He looked off in the distance. "There was a couple on their honeymoon. They was always holding hands. They came through all right. That's all I remember."

I didn't go with them to see the animals because I didn't want to pet a bunny living on borrowed time before it showed up on a dinner plate—something I think hadn't occurred to Mel and B.D. When they returned, I asked Mr. Boudet if he could call any of the other porters who might have known Mr. Heffelman to see if they'd talk to us.

"You mean right now?" he said.

"Yes, sir, if you would, please. I'd be particularly interested in visiting Mr. Anderson in the hospital, since he was there that day, if you think it would be okay."

Rose frowned and B.D. looked at her feet and I figured I'd just committed one of those social sins that were always tripping me up.

"I mean, if you don't think it would be too much trouble," I said. "Or if you don't think he'd be offended."

"No, I guess it would be all right," he said.

"We'd love to talk to anybody who knew Mr. Heffelman, whether they were on the train that day or not. I think you said Mr. Foster and Mr. Meacham knew him?"

"I don't know if Mr. Foster knew him. Mr. Meacham did," he said, frowning. "But—." He was searching for words. "Mr. Meacham, he kind of—he like to talk, him. And when he talk—well, you get the wheat and the chaff all together."

We all managed to shake hands with him before Rose hustled us down the steps and into the car.

"Did I mess up?" I asked Rose.

"Not too bad," she said. She glanced over at me as she put the car in gear. "Anyway, you got your daddy's killer smile. Folks going to do whatever you ask them to."

I grinned at her. "'Cept you."

"'Cept me," she agreed.

Chapter 16

"I hope Mr. Boudet wasn't all dressed up on our account, Rose." B.D. leaned forward with her hands on the backs of the front seats. "I felt so bad for him. If he'd put that coat on, I believe I would have fallen right off the porch in a dead faint."

"He always dress like that," Rose said. "All the porters do. It's what they're used to."

Rose fried hamburgers for half the people in the neighborhood, including Eula and her friends and us. We sat in the yard under a chinaberry tree and ate off paper plates.

"So what do we know now that we didn't know before?" Mel asked.

"Well, we know that Mr. Heffelman was seen on the train before the crash," B.D. pointed out. "That proves he was on the train. But he wasn't as close to the front as we might've thought."

"If he did a bunk," Mel said, "it wasn't planned in advance. He couldn't know the train was going to wreck."

"The porters must've all known him," I said, "so it's not as if Mr. Boudet could've mistaken somebody else for him. It was definitely him."

"We should have asked if they spoke when he saw Mr. Boudet in the lounge car," Mel said.

"Yeah," I agreed, "although he probably didn't say anything like, 'Remind my wife about the life insurance policy.'"

"Or we could've asked if he was talking to anybody that Mr. Boudet recognized," Mel said.

"We found out about some of the other people on the train," B.D. said. "At least, some of the ones who didn't die."

"Yeah," Mel said. "It's one thing to see a list of names in the paper, but it's another thing to know that they might have been mothers and kids and honeymoon couples."

After lunch Rose came out to tell us that Mr. Boudet hadn't been able to reach Mr. Foster and Mr. Meacham was in Chicago, but we could visit Mr. Anderson, who had been sent home from the hospital.

"But I got the impression that Mr. Anderson wasn't too crazy about talking to y'all," she said. "Mr. Boudet did you girls a favor by talking him into it, so you best behave yourselves."

"Will you take us, Rose?" I said. "Please?"

"Yes, but I don't know what y'all are going to eat for supper if I spend my day gallivanting all over Houston with you."

"I can scramble eggs," I offered, "and fry some bacon."

"Humph," she said, and I knew she was remembering the last time I made bacon, when she arrived in the morning to find the house full of smoke. Cooking wasn't my racket.

Mr. Anderson lived in a little white shotgun house in a row of houses that all looked alike. His house was raised up on cinder-blocks and had a narrow set of cement steps leading up to a small front porch. His daughter Marcelle led us through the living room and kitchen to the bedroom. She wore a pale green uniform with her name stitched across the pocket, and it swished when she walked in her rubber-soled lace-up shoes. She said in a low voice, "He's embarrassed y'all have to come back to the bedroom but I told Louie, 'If they want to talk to him, they going to have to come to him. He ain't exactly entertaining visitors. He broke his leg in the wreck and he don't get around so good on crutches yet.'"

B.D. said that we didn't want to inconvenience him any, and that we'd only stay a few minutes.

"As far as that goes, he'll probably be glad of the company," she said, smiling. "Any of y'all know how to play pinochle?"

The house was like an oven, despite the fans set in the windows at either end to create a breeze. It also smelled like a hospital—alchohol and sweat and sickness. Mr. Anderson was propped up in the bed, a sheet pulled up tight across his chest and anchored by his arms, one of which was in a cast. He was wearing a brown bathrobe over a brown plaid pajama top. His skin wasn't brown so much as gray like ashes, and he had a ring of gray curls around an otherwise bald head. He was clean shaven, and as we got closer the scent of his aftershave made my head swim. He looked skinny and sunken like the last survivor of a famine. If he'd closed his eyes, Digger could have been sent to pick him up and wouldn't have given him a second look. But open, his eyes were bright and lively.

The room was small, so it was crowded with just a tall bureau, a nightstand, and the single bed. On the wall next to the bureau there were pictures of Jesus, Abraham Lincoln, and a colored man in a high collar and bow tie.

Rose introduced us, and we shook hands. There were one folding chair stamped with the name of a church and one ladderback kitchen chair and no place else to sit, so we stood around the bed.

Rose started the conversation, "How you been keepin', Amos?"

He shook his head sadly. "Poorly, Rose, poorly." He had a high, thin voice like the chirp of an insect.

"Can you walk?" she asked.

"I can walk a little. Just enough to go to the toilet is all. But my shoulder got banged up some, and the crutch hurt my shoulder too much to use it."

"Is the company going to compensate you for the work time you're losing?"

"I don't know." He said shook his head. "Marcelle say she going to sic the union on them, but I don't know can they get me anything or not. I believe my portering days is over, though."

From the doorway, her arms folded, Marcelle said, "What I *said* was, 'What the union done for you lately?' Seem to me if they was paying attention, they'd be calling a strike right now while the maritime union is on strike. You couldn't get nothing in or out of Houston without the sailors and the railroad men. Then maybe you get some compensation."

"Marcelle, you don't know the first thing about it," he said to her. "That's a whole different union from the porters' union. Porters don't load the freight trains."

"I know," she said, in a tone that said she didn't know but would not be contradicted. "But them unions could get together on a thing like this, and then y'all might see some real change. And if I see Mr. Asa Philip Randolph, I'll tell him so myself." She turned away, swatting at the air with a dishcloth. "But didn't nobody ask my opinion."

Mr. Anderson looked at us, nervously I thought. "She just talking. She's not serious." To his daughter, he said, "These girls going to think you're a communist, talking like that."

"They better think I'm an American citizen that know her rights, and yours, too," Marcelle said. She planted her hands on her hips, and said scornfully, "Communist. Somebody call me a communist, I'll communist them." She took herself into the kitchen, where we could hear her banging pots and pans around.

"I'll talk to her," Rose said. "Maybe I can help."

I thought that before Rose was through with the railroad, Mr. Anderson would have a pension or a new job that a man could do sitting down.

"The girls want to talk to you about the train wreck," Rose said. "They're looking for somebody. Would that be all right with you?"

His eyes scanned our faces. "Well, I don't know," he said. "I told Louie I didn't know nothing. I couldn't tell nobody nothing about the accident. One minute I was leaning over, adjusting the curtains for a young lady, and the next I was waking up in a hospital bed. That's what I know." He said this as if he was delivering a speech he'd memorized, and now the speech was over and he could sit down. It wasn't the kind of speech that was supposed to be followed by questions from the audience.

I asked one anyway. "How close to the front of the train were you, Mr. Anderson?" Harry says to start with the easy questions, the ones people don't mind answering, to put them at their ease.

He turned his eyes on me. "I was in the first Pullman back of the lounge car, so I was pretty far back. I just wasn't lucky. Some folks that far back—why, they walked away without a scratch, or so I heard. Mr. Dooley Grayson, who was killed—he was in one of the chair cars, farther up."

"Would you look at a photograph and tell us if you recognize the man in it?" I said. I slid the picture out of its envelope and handed it to him. I didn't want to give him a chance to refuse.

He hesitated for just a second and then reached out to take it. His hand was trembling. At first he just held it, not looking at it, as if he didn't know what to do with it.

"You need your glasses, Amos?" Rose said.

He turned his eyes to the nightstand where Rose was picking up his glasses. He took his time putting them on, then reluctantly raised the photograph and looked at it.

"Why, that's Mr. Heffelman," he said. "I read that he died in the wreck." He studied the photograph, then handed it back to me.

"Did you see him on the train that day?" Mel asked.

He turned his eyes on her. "Now, let me think." His eyes drifted off to a corner of the room. He thought for a good long while as the fan whirred behind him and sweat trickled down the back of my neck. It occurred to me that Nancy Drew was always cool as a cucumber, even when she was in Hawaii or at Shadow Ranch, and I wondered if she had been born with built-in heat tolerance, like my cousin Frieda. B.D. looked like she might melt into a puddle right there on the flowered rug.

Finally, he said, "I just can't recollect. My memory doesn't work too good now, since the accident. I can't hardly recall that day at all, just the curtain, like I told you. I'm sorry."

"But you saw him on the train plenty of other times," B.D. said.

"Oh, yes, he rode often," he said. "He was a salesman, you know."

"Did he ever mention buying a birthday present for his little girl?" B.D. asked.

"Not that I recollect," he said. "I'm sorry."

This was said with finality, as if he hoped to close the subject.

But I persisted. "Have you talked with anyone else about the accident? I mean, railroad investigators and insurance investigators—people like that."

"No," he said quickly. "No, I ain't talked to nobody. I was in the hospital, you know. And anyway, they wouldn't have talked to me—them insurance people. I couldn't tell them nothing. I don't know nothing."

I smiled at him. "In that case," I said, "how about a game of pinochle?"

He lit up. "You girls play pinochle?"

"I do," I said. "We can teach Mel and B.D. Rose, you want to play?"

"No," she said, "I'll go sit with Marcelle in the kitchen." But as she turned to leave the room she gave me a look that said she knew I was up to something, and I'd better behave.

"They's some more chairs in the kitchen," he said. "Why don't y'all bring some in here so the girls can sit down?" To me, he said, "The cards are in the drawer there."

I thought I might catch it from B.D. and Mel later, but for now, B.D. just took off her bandeau and put it back on and Mel swiped at her forehead with the back of her arm.

It was a little awkward balancing the cards on our knees until I gave up and sat cross-legged, and so did Mel and B.D. Mel had to move so that the fan didn't blow her cards all over the room and my foot kept going to sleep but I couldn't move it because I had melds on one knee and tricks on another.

After a while, Marcelle came in with glasses of lemonade, looked around, and said, "Daddy, why didn't you tell Rose to get out the card table?" She went to the front room and came back with a card table and set it up next to the bed. Things went better after that.

"Is it interesting work, being a porter and traveling around all the time?" I asked Mr. Anderson once the girls had gotten the hang of the game.

"Well, now, it can be," he said. "I reckon it's got its ups and downs like any job. At least I have seniority, so I've been holding this line on the Texas Chief for eight years now."

"I guess traveling all over isn't what it's cracked up to be," Mel said.

"Not when you have a family, it's not," he said. "Oh, when you're young, it can be a fine thing to see the country. But a Pullman porter, why, he doesn't see much of the country because he's not supposed to leave his car, you know."

B.D.'s head popped up at that. "You mean you never got to get out and look around in any of the places you went?"

He smiled at the indignation in her voice. "Well, sugar, just between us, the porters sometimes help each other out in that regard. So I might watch another man's car while he went out and looked around the town, and then he'd watch mine a while. It's against the rules, but we do it. Sometimes we might be on a special hired car—you know, like if a group of performers or musicians was touring the country. We might be parked in the yard for days and that's one time when we might help each other out. Of course, that doesn't happen to me anymore, it only happens to the extra porters—the ones gets put on for the special car."

I saw Mel opening her mouth to ask about extra porters, but I wanted to head in a different direction, so I said, "I imagine it takes a lot of tact to deal with the passengers. I suppose that could be one of the biggest drawbacks of the job."

"Well, now, most of the ladies and gentlemen who ride the train are a fine class of people," he said. "But there's always a few bad apples, same as in any job."

"So you have to be a diplomat?" Mel said.

He nodded. "That's right. We're there to serve the public, and the company. They insist on courtesy at all times. The customer is always right."

"Except they're not," B.D. said, a little indignantly.

"No, but we're expected to behave like they are," he said.

"That stinks." B.D.'s Hayley voice crept in.

He smiled at her again. "It's part of the job. If you can't hold your temper, you won't last long as a Pullman porter." You could tell he was proud of his work and his own success. I knew from listening to Rose that Pullman porters were highly respected in the negro neighborhoods, so I figured he had a right to be proud. It seemed to me like a pretty glamorous way to make a living, like being an airline stewardess. But I knew I could never hold my temper with bums and pills and phonies.

"Was Mr. Heffelman one of the good guys, or a bad apple?" I asked, studying my cards. "We didn't know him, and we're trying to find out what he was like."

"Oh, he was a very nice gentleman. Never gave me a bit of trouble."

"Was he a big tipper?" I asked. I felt B.D.'s bare foot bump my ankle, but I didn't look at her.

"He was about average," Mr. Anderson said. He didn't look offended, but I guessed that a Pullman porter couldn't afford to be offended much, or if he was, to let it show.

"Did he have a lot of friends on the train," I said, "him being a regular and all?"

"Yes, he knew quite a few of the other salesmen."

"So he was a friendly sort of man?" B.D. said.

"Oh, yes. I reckon that's maybe what drew folks to him. A man like that can become popular by being a good listener, and that's what Mr. Heffelman was. One time my wife was sick and I had to leave her to go on a run, so I was worried about her. Mr. Heffelman asked me what was wrong. I thought maybe I messed up or didn't do something I was supposed to, but it wasn't that. He just looked at my face and he knew."

"Did he talk about his family much?" Mel asked.

"I saw pictures of his little girl once, and the baby," he said. "You could tell he loved his family."

We were all staring at him. "The baby?" B.D. echoed. "What baby?"

"His baby," he said. "His little boy." He suddenly realized that we were staring, and you could see him pull back.

"Sissy has a brother named Tommy," B.D. said. "Could that have been the baby?"

"Yes, Tommy," he said, relaxing. "I believe he said that was the name."

"When did he show you the picture?" I asked.

"Oh, I don't recall now."

"Was it recently?" Mel asked.

"I'm sorry, I just don't recollect. I told you that my memory hasn't been too good since the accident. I probably have Mr. Heffelman mixed up with somebody else."

"Do you remember anything else unusual that happened on the train that day, Mr. Anderson?" I said. "Or anybody who stood out to you?"

He was already shaking his head before I finished the question. "No, I don't remember anything about that day, except what I already told you." He had been sitting up to play the game but now he eased himself back against the pillow and closed his eyes. "I'm sorry, girls, but I'm getting mighty tired. Maybe you'd better come back and finish this game another time."

We folded our hands and laid the cards on the card table.

"I hope we haven't worn you out," B.D. said. "We enjoyed talking to you about your job."

"No, sugar, it's not you. The accident wore me out. Y'all come back another time."

We said we would and headed for the door. He cleared his throat behind us.

"You know," he said, "a lot of folk don't like to talk about what happened."

I turned. "Why not?" I got it out before B.D. could pinch my arm.

He did look tired now, and the shrug he gave us was a tired shrug. "I don't know, sugar. Could be lots of reasons. People got they own reasons. I know you girls don't want to make anybody mad or offend anybody, but you might, even if you don't intend to." He gave us a weak smile. "I'll bet y'all got lots better things to do on a summer afternoon than play pinochle with a beat-up old man."

"Dizzy, was that a warning?" Mel asked later, when we were finally out of Rose's earshot.

"If it wasn't," I said, "it missed a good opportunity."

"He's afraid of something," B.D. said.

"And it's not the company," I said. "If he was afraid of the company, he wouldn't have told us about breaking the rules."

"And besides," she continued, "whoever it is he's afraid of, he thinks we should be afraid of them, too. We should have asked Marcelle if he'd had any other visitors asking about the wreck."

"If they came to the hospital, she might not know," I said.

"So who is he afraid of?" Mel said. "That's the question."

"If we answer that one," I said, "the duck's going to drop from the sky and give us a hundred smackers."

As soon as we got home, we walked over to Alice Song's house to retrieve the enlargements.

She nodded at the envelope she handed me. "Daddy helped me, so that's the best you'll get out of those Polaroids."

As agreed, I paid her two unopened packs of baseball cards that somebody had traded for a pogo stick, and a box of flash bulbs. Back at the lost and found, I laid the enlargements out on the workbench and we studied them again under the magnifying glass.

"They're fuzzier than I thought they'd be," Mel admitted.

"Hold on." I rummaged in the workbench drawer and found a tape measure. I gave B.D. a Big Chief tablet and asked her to make a drawing of each fingerprint. Then I started measuring, point to point, and writing down the measurements on the drawings.

We studied the results.

"This makes my brain hurt," B.D. admitted. "They look pretty close."

"They do," Mel agreed. "I think they're the same. But we're not experts."

"And we don't have the best equipment," I pointed out.

"But even so—," B.D. began.

We looked at each other. "We're pretty darned suspicious," Mel finished.

Chapter 17

"We need a ride in the morning," I said to Harry when he finally showed up for dinner that night. I was standing at the stove scrambling eggs and keeping an eye on the bacon, relieved to be barefoot and out of my petticoat and back in my shorts and tee shirt.

"Where to?" He had just sat down at the table and his lap was full of Lucille, who was doing her little dance, circling and smacking him in the nose with her tail.

"Train station," I replied.

"Who's leaving?"

"Somebody we need to talk to."

"Somebody you need to talk to?" When I didn't say anything, he said, "What kind of a somebody?"

"He's a Pullman porter on the Texas Chief," I said.

"And why do you need to talk to a Pullman porter on the Texas Chief?"

It ticked me off, the way he kept repeating everything I said, but I needed him. "We have a case, if you must know." I turned the bacon over and saw that the under side was a little black, so I decided I'd skip the top. I forked the two pieces onto a paper towel and then dumped the eggs on a plate.

"A case?"

I could hear Lucille's purr from where I stood in the kitchen, and when I turned to look at him I could see that the hand that wasn't holding the cigarette was stroking her under the chin, just the way she liked, so I forgave him and said, "It's a missing persons case.

We're trying to find out whether somebody who's missing really died in the Texas Chief wreck a few weeks back."

He smiled down at Lucille, but I knew it was really for me. I set the plate in front of him, pulled the toast out of the toaster and handed it to him.

"Who thinks he's dead?" He put down his cigarette to take the toast. It was the right choice. His other hand still stroked Lucille.

"I didn't say it was a he," I pointed out.

He grinned at me. "Who says this bird is dead?"

"His wife," I said. "The funeral parlor that buried him."

He nodded. "Who thinks he isn't?"

"His daughter."

"How old is this daughter?" He started eating his eggs. I'd turned the bacon black side down so he couldn't see the scorched part.

"Seven."

"And she thinks he's not dead because—?"

"Somebody sent her a Barbie doll for her birthday, and she thinks it was him. There was no card or note, and no return address on the package."

"So she just turned seven," he said, looking at me. "And *you* think he might not be dead because—?"

"His fingerprint is on Barbie's butt," I said, "under her fancy outfit." I set down the spatula, extracted the enlargements from my pocket and placed them next to his plate, along with the magnifying glass.

His eyebrow shot up and he put his fork down. "How old are you?" He picked up the magnifying glass and began studying the photos.

We both knew this was a rhetorical question, but I answered it anyway. "Twelve," I said. "And a half—almost three-quarters."

"My God," he said to Lucille, "in two years your mama will have her driver's license, and there will be no stopping her."

"Judy Bolton has a cat named Blackberry who rides around in the car with her all the time when she's investigating her cases."

He looked at me and then at Lucille. "Does Lucille know about this?"

I nodded at the photos. "What do you think?"

He looked at them again before replying. "I'm no expert," he said, shaking his head and making me wait for his verdict, "but they look pretty similar."

"You know an expert?" This was a rhetorical question. Harry knew experts on everything.

He nodded.

"So . . . will you give us a ride?" I repeated.

"Okay," he said. I knew that he was secretly proud of me. He might have been less enthusiastic if he'd known that I'd boosted his fingerprint kit in the course of my investigation, but then again, he'd probably already figured that out. "What time?"

"Six o'clock."

He frowned as he worked it out. "In the morning?"

"Uh-huh."

He made a face.

"You promised," I reminded him.

"Well, Jesus, I didn't pinky swear or whatever it is you do these days. Christ, it's the Fourth of July—it's a national holiday. Who works on the Fourth of July?"

I just looked at him.

"Okay, I'll do it," he said. "But you'll owe me."

I had bugged Rose until she'd agreed to call Johnny Foster for us. She had spoken to his wife, who had told her that Mr. Foster was asleep, and that he'd sleep until he got up for work on the Texas Chief in the morning. Apparently, Mr. Foster had been promoted to porter after the wreck, and Rose said that porters hardly get any sleep when they're working. They had to show up early to clean their cars and get them ready for the passengers. So I'd called the ticket office and found out that the train left Houston at seven-twenty in the morning. We'd just have to go find him at the station.

Johnny Foster was a long shot, and we knew it. Once we'd

studied Mr. Boudet's diagram of the consist, we'd come to appreciate just how many cars there were on a train. And even Mr. Boudet didn't know for sure how many cars the Texas Chief had on the day it wrecked. We were gambling that Mr. Heffelman had been sitting in Mr. Foster's car before he went to the lounge car or that he'd passed through Mr. Foster's car on his way to the lounge car. But what would that tell us? We already knew from Mr. Boudet that he'd probably been sitting in the lounge car at the time of the accident. Still, Harry says to keep an open mind and keep asking questions. We might meet up with somebody else who saw something that day.

It was a feat getting Harry up and out the door in the morning, but I did it. B.D. and Mel were already sitting in the back seat when I pulled him out the back door and shoved him into the front seat with a cup of coffee in his hand. At the station, Harry went into the office while we checked the board for the right platform.

"You girls know what he looks like?" Harry asked when he came out. He was putting his wallet away, and I knew what that meant.

"No," I said. "You?"

"I'd probably recognize him if I saw him," he said.

We found the Texas Chief but the doors to the first and second passenger cars were locked. I saw a negro man in a white coat and tie coming down the platform and asked about Johnny Foster. He didn't know Mr. Foster, but we talked him into letting us on the train to look around. Maybe the fin that Harry slipped him had something to do with it, maybe it didn't.

"Put it on your expense report," I told Harry when he made a big show of pocketing his wallet again.

"Sissy is loaded, is she?" he said.

The white coat had told us that if Mr. Foster was a porter, he'd be some ways back, past the chair cars, the diner, and the lounge car. We trooped through the cars like a train-within-a-train. All of the men we saw were colored, and a few of them asked if they could help us. Nobody tried to throw us off the train, they just kept directing us farther back.

As we passed through, I wished we had more time to look around. I'd only been on a train once in my life, and that was to see my grandparents off. In the movies, they made it seem like such a luxurious way to travel. Hal had a Lionel train set, all put away now, but that was another sore subject. I'd have traded every doll I'd ever been given for a Lionel train set, with its distinctive oily odor, its hum and clack, and its long line of cars, from the elaborate engine that blew real smoke, past the coal car and flat cars to the red caboose at the end.

Harry spotted Mr. Foster up ahead and recognized him. When Mr. Foster straightened up and turned toward us with a cleaning cloth in one hand and a bottle of polish in the other, he looked so astonished that we might as well have been a band of train robbers out of the Wild West. He had to switch the cleaning cloth to his other hand to shake hands with Harry.

He was younger than the other porters we'd met, with wavy reddish hair and long, thin eyebrows over chocolate eyes. If he'd had antennas, they'd be quivering. He was wearing a white coat and a dark blue tie.

Harry asked after the family, the way he does, but Mr. Foster cut him short.

"I'm sorry, Mr. Lark, but I'm not allowed to have personal visitors while I'm working," he said. "It's against the rules."

Harry put a hand on his shoulder. "That's okay, Johnny, I squared it with your boss," he said, which was true. "The girls are investigating the train wreck a few weeks back. They'd like to ask you some questions."

Mr. Foster's eyebrows lifted as he looked at us.

"We can talk while you work," I offered.

"That's right," B.D. said. "You just go on about your business and we'll ask questions."

He glanced up and down the aisle as if he was expecting his boss to materialize and contradict Harry's assessment of the situation. He transferred his cleaning cloth to his free hand and turned back to his work.

"But first—." I held out the photograph of Mr. Heffelman. "Maybe you could look at this picture and tell us if you recognize this man."

He paused. The eyebrows settled into a pair of flat arches. "Why, that's Mr. Heffelman."

I nodded encouragingly.

"Did you see Mr. Heffelman on the train the day of the wreck?" Mel asked.

"Yes, he was on my car." He seemed to have forgotten his cleaning.

"Do you remember where he got on the train?" I asked.

He shook his head. "I couldn't tell you that. I didn't get on the train until Fort Worth, and he was already in his seat. Well, not in his seat—I believe he was in the diner having lunch. But then he come back from lunch and took his seat."

"Were y'all in the first chair car in the consist?" B.D. asked. We were beginning to learn a thing or two about trains.

"Oh, no," he said. "We were in the fifth car back."

"The fifth chair car," Mel said. "Past the mail cars."

"That's right," he said.

"Mr. Boudet told us that he saw Mr. Heffelman walking up the aisle right before the accident," I said. "Was he in his seat when the accident happened or had he left the car?"

He gazed off into space. "Yes, now I believe that's so… He wasn't in his seat. I expect he went to talk to somebody or else went to sit in the lounge car."

"He had a lot of friends who rode the train regularly, like he did," B.D. said.

"Yes, the salesmen get to know each other, after a while," Mr. Foster agreed.

"Did he have any particular friends that you know of?" I asked.

"Well, now let me think." He stared off into space the way people do when they're trying to visualize a memory.

"We don't want to interrupt your work," B.D. said. "We know you just got promoted."

She pushed the right button with that "promoted" bit. He turned to the closest seat and began wiping it down in double time.

I expected his speech to speed up as well, but it didn't. He moved to the next seat up and said, "I believe that Mr. Hightower and Mr. Flanagan were friends of his, and maybe Mr. Seltzer."

I had my notebook out and I was writing down names.

"He was friendly with a lot of folks, Mr. Heffelman was," Mr. Foster went on.

"These men you mentioned, were they all salesmen?" Mel said.

"I believe so, but I couldn't tell you what it was they sold."

"Do they all live in Houston?" I asked.

"Mr. Hightower and Mr. Flanagan do, or somewhere hereabouts. I'm not for sure where Mr. Seltzer live."

"I don't guess you know their first names," I said.

"They call Mr. Hightower Bob. I believe they call Mr. Seltzer Andy. Mr. Flanagan—." He paused a moment in his cleaning frenzy, in suspended animation, frowning at the seat. "Stan, maybe? No, no, it's Donny. Mr. Flanagan is Donny."

"You've got a great memory," B.D. said.

"You got to have a good memory in this job." He spotted something between the seat and the wall and knelt down to pick it up. It looked like a ticket stub.

"Did you see Mr. Heffelman after the wreck?" I asked.

He shook his head as he stood up. "No, I didn't. I was busy helping the passengers in my car and anybody else who was close." Maybe he was expecting an accusation, so he anticipated it. "Maybe I should have gone looking for him, though. He was one of my passengers. Maybe I should have checked the lounge and the diner, too. You don't stop to think in a situation like that. You just help the next person and the next person and the next."

"I'm sure you were a help and a comfort to many people," B.D. said.

"We'd better get out of Mr. Foster's way, girls," Harry said. "It's getting late. Any more questions?"

"Did anything else unusual happen that day that you can remember?" I asked. The Harry question. "Anything at all?"

He shook his head. "Not that I can recall."

"Is there anybody else working on the train today who was working on the day of the accident?"

"I saw Herman Fairchild earlier," he said. "He was working that day. I haven't seen Arthur Petry, but he might be working."

We thanked him and headed back down the aisle.

When we got to the chair cars, I had the photograph in my hand and began asking if any of the attendants recognized him. The first attendant we met, who looked harried, said that he recognized the man, but didn't know his name. He wasn't working on the train the day of the accident. The second attendant said the same. We found Herman Fairchild in the third chair car back. He was a tall, gaunt man who stooped over, maybe from spending so much time in the confined space of the train. He listened, head bowed, and responded without looking at us. He knew Mr. Heffelman, he said, but couldn't remember whether he'd seen him on the train that day. He couldn't remember anything else. Nothing unusual had happened that day. He repeated this last part several times. He was sorry he couldn't help us. When I looked back at him, I noticed that he was limping slightly.

When we asked about Arthur Petry, we got sent back down the aisle to the Pullmans. We found him frowning over a stack of towels. He was shorter than Mr. Fairchild, and solidly built. He had an expressive face that shifted quickly from one emotion to another. We asked if he was on the train when the accident happened, since Mr. Boudet hadn't mentioned a Mr. Petry.

"Mr. Boudet told us that the only porters were himself, Mr. Anderson, Mr. Hamms, and Mr. Grayson, who died," Mel said.

He nodded. "Mr. Hamms took poorly—that's what happened. I was in Kansas City, so they put me on at the last minute. Bad luck for me, good luck for him. But this other porter—this Mr. Anderson—he might not know about that. It's a lot to keep track of, when you're a porter. You can't be keeping track of everybody else's business—just got to tend to your own."

We showed him the photograph of Mr. Heffelman, but he shook his head. "I'm usually the extra man," he said. "I go all over—wherever the company send me. So I don't get to know the passengers. Or the other porters, either. But now I'm hoping to be a regular on the Chief."

We didn't know what else to ask him, so I asked the Harry question.

"I don't remember anything unusual." He frowned deeply. "Unless maybe the gentleman with the briefcase. A jeweler, I think he was, or a salesman, maybe. The man that I relieved in Kansas City, Mr. Hamms—he's the one told me about it."

"A gentleman with a briefcase?" Mel said.

"Mr. Hamms, he said, 'There's a gentleman in Upper 13—that's the berth number, you know—a gentleman in Upper 13 with a briefcase. You better not go near that briefcase.' Well, I didn't think nothing of that. Lots of passengers are particular about their things—don't want nobody to touch them, you know. They always suspicious we going to steal something. I didn't really see the gentleman until the next morning when I seen him going along to the toilet in his undershirt and pajama pants. He had the briefcase on a chain locked to his wrist. Every time I saw him, why, he had that briefcase."

When he didn't say anything more, I asked, "Had you ever seen anything like that before?"

"Once or twice I had. Another fellow told me that the gentlemen who did that was jewelers, carrying jewels to sell or use in they work. That's why I say he was either a jeweler or a salesman." He shrugged. "I only mention it because this gentleman wasn't as ordinary as the other passengers. But I don't know that I'd call him unusual, either."

"Can you describe the gentleman?" I said, pencil poised over my notebook.

He glanced at the notebook. "Oh, I don't know," he said. "I didn't notice much about him, except for the briefcase. He was a dark-complected gentleman with dark hair and a gold ring on his finger—not a wedding ring, you know, but another kind—like a lodge ring, something like that. That's all I can say."

"Do you remember his name?" B.D. asked.

"No, I can't say as I do." He scratched his chin. "Seem like it was something Italian, but I don't really know. Could be if you went looking for him you'd find out he had a French name, or Spanish." He smiled a little. "Most porters—they real good with names, you know. It helps with the tip if you can look a gentleman in the eye and call him by his name. I expect I'll get better now if I can hold this line. When you an extra, you always rushing off somewhere, last minute, and you don't hardly have time to remember where you headed."

We could see passengers beginning to gather on the platform outside, and Harry said it was time to go, so we thanked Mr. Petry and left.

As we walked toward the station building, I looked back at the Texas Chief. Mr. Fairchild was helping an elderly lady up the steps to the train, smiling a polite smile, but even at a distance I could see that over her head, his eyes were on us.

Chapter 18

Harry took us for breakfast in the station coffee shop. Turning on the charm, he steered the hostess toward a table in the corner. I could tell he wanted to talk as much as we did.

He wanted to hear the whole story, and we gave it to him—about Sissy Heffelman and her Barbie doll, about Mr. Heffelman's burial, and about our interviews with the Pullman porters. He was playing it cool, as usual, but I could tell we surprised him. He never expected, for example, that we might know so much about the condition of the body.

"You've got your connections," I told him. "We've got ours."

"I can see that," he said. He looked at the cigarette in his hand as if he didn't know what it was there for. He'd taken it out at the beginning of our story and forgotten to light it after that. He twiddled it, turning it over, end on end, the way he does when he's thinking about something.

"This fingerprint," he said. "We need an expert opinion."

I nodded. "I'm betting it's his, though."

To his credit, he just nodded.

"Could be an insurance con," he mused. "You haven't seen the widow yet?"

We shook our heads. "We were waiting until we had a case," B.D. said.

"We don't want to be given the bum's rush as soon as we open our mouths," I said.

"Just because she cried at the funeral parlor and the service," Mel added, "doesn't mean she wants her husband back."

"Fifty grand is a lot of dough," I said.

"And she might be in on it," B.D. said.

He grinned at us. "You girls are pretty young to be so cynical."

"I caught it from you."

He pointed his cigarette at Mel and B.D. "What's their excuse?"

"They caught it from me."

The waitress brought us our food then, and asked us if we wanted anything else. Harry winked at her, and she almost dropped her tray. I rolled my eyes at him, but he ignored me, as usual.

"So what did you learn from the interviews this morning?" Harry stuck the cigarette in his shirt pocket and turned to his eggs.

We looked at each other.

"Well, something isn't right," I said. "We just don't know whether it's related to our case or not."

"Why do you say that?" Harry looked up over a forkful of egg.

"Because Mr. Fairchild makes the second witness who didn't want to tell us something," B.D. said. She was breaking off pieces of her donut and eating them with her little finger crooked as if we were having high tea with the vicar in an Agatha Christie novel.

"But we don't know whether the thing he didn't want to tell us is the same thing that Mr. Anderson didn't want to tell us," Mel said.

"Uh-huh," Harry said.

"They were both nervous," I said. "But about what? We got to thinking maybe we weren't the first ones coming around to ask about the wreck."

"Probably not," Harry said.

"Mr. Anderson warned us off, though," B.D. said. "Told us to stop asking questions. Mr. Fairchild didn't do that, he just—well, stonewalled us."

"We played pinochle with Mr. Anderson," I pointed out. "Maybe he got to liking us. Mr. Fairchild didn't have that opportunity."

"Okay," Harry said, "I think we can stipulate that Mr. Fairchild would have liked you if he'd played pinochle with you, so what?"

"If Mr. Anderson thought we were really headed for trouble," I said, "that might've made him decide to tip us off. Mr. Fairchild didn't care one way or another."

"But it's still possible that what they're hiding doesn't have anything to do with our case," Mel agreed. She was biting a corner off one of her toast triangles. "There seem to be lots of rules on a train. They could've both been doing something that was against the rules, and they're worried about getting into trouble. If I worked on a train, I'd be breaking the rules all the time, I bet—especially the one about not sleeping on the job."

"So we just don't know," I agreed.

"What about the man with the briefcase, y'all?" B.D. said. "Are we interested in him or is he just a whatchacallit—a red herring?"

"I'm interested in him," Mel said. She'd eaten a second corner and was working her way to the middle.

"Me, too," I said.

"Me, three," Harry said.

"I mean, he could've been just an ordinary jeweler," B.D. said. "But whatever he had in that case had to be valuable or he wouldn't have it chained to his wrist."

"It could've been money," I said.

"It could've been plans for a top secret weapon against the commies," B.D. said. "I read a book like that once."

Mel shook her head. "If you're carrying plans for a secret weapon, you don't go advertising it by chaining a briefcase to your wrist. Everybody knows that. You have to hide them someplace inconspicuous, like on microfilm in a cigarette case or in a false bottom in your shoe or sewn into the lining of your hat."

Harry looked at her in mock admiration. "Is that what they do with those things? I've always wondered."

I ignored him. "Yeah, it was probably jewels, like Mr. Petry said."

B.D. said, "But why you'd want to go and advertise that you had anything valuable is anybody's guess. I'm with Mel. It's a pretty dopey approach to security."

"The question is, what happened to the briefcase full of whatever it was after the accident?" I said.

"That," Harry said as he fired up a smoke, "is a very good question."

At that point we felt a kind of stir in the air around us. B.D., who was facing the door, looked up from licking her fingers and said, "Uh-oh. Y'all, this is déjà vu."

We turned toward the door and saw four negro kids walking toward the counter. Juney wasn't one of them, but I recognized one of our cellmates from the sneezer. They were dressed as if they were taking the train, in suits and ties and dresses, and carrying books that looked like schoolbooks. They found four seats at the counter, two on one side of a white man and two on the other, but the white man made a big deal out of getting up and leaving, so then one of the negro kids sat in his seat.

The quiet in the room gave way to an indignant buzz, like a beehive in an earthquake. Mel opened her mouth to say something, but Harry cut her off. "No," he said, "you do not have my permission to get arrested. If you girls want to add to your jacket, it won't be on my watch."

The counter man heaved a sigh audible across the room, put his hands on the counter, and looked down his nose at them. "I keep telling you kids, you can't get served in here—not yesterday, not today, and not ever. It's the Fourth of July, for crissakes. You want to spend it in jail?"

One of the young men said, "I suppose if an ordinary citizen can't get served in a public establishment, then jail is a fitting place for him to spend the Fourth of July." He said it calmly, as if he was just making an observation, not trying to provoke a fight.

"Aww, hell," said a man with an exaggerated drawl, "Why don't you go ahead and serve the kids, Bert?" The man was wearing a white Western shirt, string tie, and cowboy boots, and his Stetson was on the table in front of him.

This drew a reaction from the other customers—a mixture of agreement and angry contradiction.

A man stood up, red in the face. "You do that, and—and—and I'm leaving!" he sputtered.

"Ain't nobody stopping you that I can see, pardner," said the cowboy. If he hadn't been such a big man, he might have faced more than surly mutterings, but nobody seemed to want to take him on. "Now, why don't you just ask the kids what they want?" he said to Bert.

"I know what they want," said a woman with big hair. "They want to turn this place into a pigsty." She fingered her pearls and glared.

To my astonishment, Harry waded in. "Ask 'em what they want," he said over his coffee cup, "and put it on my tab."

The cowboy hat smiled at him. "Now, that's a real nice offer, Mister. I bet there's a lot of folks here would like to contribute."

"Here," said an older lady, holding up a quarter. "You can have the counter man's tip."

"Well, I don't see any call for that," Harry said, and I noticed he'd put on the folksy voice he uses when it suits his purposes. "Bert's just trying to do his job. Isn't that right, Bert?"

"We can pay for our own meals," said one of the negro kids, and you could tell he was miffed.

My cellmate gave Harry a dazzling smile. "That's right," she said, "but we sure do appreciate the offer."

By now the negro cook had come out of the kitchen, and all of the waitresses and kitchen staff and the bus boy were standing around frozen in place.

The counter man sighed again and looked at the cashier, a sour-faced lady with teased hair and cat's-eye glasses with little gold chains attached. She was frozen, too, with somebody's change in her hand. "Lorraine, go call the cops," he said.

She laid the money down and bustled out the door to find a flatfoot. Because we were all watching her, we didn't notice the negro cook until he laid down his apron on the counter. "I quit," he said, and followed Lorraine out the door.

"There goes breakfast," a man said, and got up to leave.

"Come on, Martha," said another man to his wife. "There's a coffee shop across the street." They herded their kids out in what had become a small stampede for the door.

We stayed until the cops had tried to talk the kids into leaving and then finally led them out in handcuffs. I knew that Harry wanted to make sure everything was on the up and up, and nobody got hurt. The cowboy and the woman with him stayed, too. The cowboy, now wearing his Stetson, shook Harry's hand on the way out.

"I like your style, pardner," he said to Harry.

Then he put his hand on B.D.'s head. "Little ladies," he said, "it's gone be a different world some day. I hope y'all live to see it."

"Me, too," Harry said.

That night, in the middle of the night, six hours after the Texas Chief discharged its Chicago passengers, somebody bombed Union Station.

Harry – July 5, 1961

Chapter 19

I smelled her before I saw her—a scent like a rumor wafted in through the open door. I was contemplating the state of my bank account, which like Florida was sliding into a bog and would soon be invisible to the naked eye. Then I caught the faint tapping of heels against floor. I got up and went out to the reception area.

She wore a beige suit that couldn't disguise her nicely sculpted form. A flowered neckline and a thin gold necklace called attention to the bare brown skin at her throat. Dark hair was swept up from her nape into some kind of twist at the back. She wore a dark brown hat with a narrow brim at an angle that invited speculation, so I speculated. She turned dark, assessing eyes on me. She had a brown leather bag slung over one of her squared shoulders.

"Mr. Lark?" she said.

I nodded.

She advanced, offering a well-manicured hand. "I'm Leda Wardlow, Mr. Lark," she said. "I'm an attorney."

Her handshake was firm and cool. She gestured with her free hand, no wedding ring in sight. "I believe you know the others—Mr. Halsey and Miss Armbruster."

I turned my head reluctantly to notice Sly Halsey and Juney Armbruster behind her, and Halsey's smile said he noted the reluctance and that now I knew he knew it. Halsey was a man of medium height and build, with skin the color of milk chocolate, wearing a light summer suit and a discreet tie. He had wavy dark hair and there was something oriental about his eyes, though I couldn't put my finger on it. He wore dark-framed glasses that I suspected were an affectation, and didn't hide the pale thin knife scar on his upper lip. The scar did nothing to spoil one of the best poker faces in the business. I ought to know. I'd played poker with him, among other things.

"Sly." I shook his hand.

Juney did not appear to be in a hand-shaking mood, so I skipped it and gave her my friendly dog smile. She bit her lip and looked away. She was wearing a crumpled yellow shirtwaist with a Peter Pan collar that made her look younger in spite of the low heels that were probably intended to make her look older. Maybe it was the light in my office, but she looked beat, as if her last friend had just put the snatch on her milk money.

"We don't have an appointment," Leda Wardlow said, "but perhaps you know why we've come. We were hoping you might give us fifteen minutes of your time?"

Considering Juney's involvement, the situation was unlikely to make my bank account happy, but on the up side I'd get a quarter of an hour to look at Leda Wardlow, gratis. I ushered them into my office.

I unhooked the sweater from the back of the secretary's chair and wheeled that in as well. Leda Wardlow frowned at it. "Won't your secretary need her chair?"

"Oh, she's out running errands," I said. "I don't expect her back any time soon."

As they settled themselves in the three available chairs, Halsey said, "Something's come up and Mrs. Wardlow thought we might want to engage the services of a white detective."

I knew that he was tipping me off about the "Mrs." part, and I was grateful—even though I could tell by his grin that he was enjoying himself. Anyway, she could have been divorced and still using the "Mrs.," but I knew he wasn't going to give me *that* much help.

Mrs. Wardlow crossed her legs but the air conditioner drowned out the whisper of nylon on nylon.

I turned to her. "You said that I might know why you'd come," I said, "but I don't." My eyes went to Juney, and I was on the verge of making a joke about rap sheets, but Dizzy says that I need to take women, especially young women (especially Dizzy herself), more seriously, and this seemed as good a time as any to start. So I just said, "Please explain."

"You know what happened last night, don't you?" Mrs. Wardlow said.

My eyes drifted to the morning paper, folded on my desk. A private investigator doesn't like to admit that anything has happened without his knowledge, which makes him appear to be caught flat-footed, but I was damned if I knew what she meant. I'd taken the kids to see fireworks the night before, but they had gone off without incident, and if other fireworks displays hadn't been so lucky, I hadn't heard about it.

"It hasn't made the paper yet," Mrs. Wardlow said, "so of course there's no reason you should have heard of it, except that you work downtown, and also live downtown, I believe?"

"Not downtown," I said, "but not far."

"So we thought it might have awakened you—the blast and then the sirens," she said. "But of course with air conditioning—." She gestured at my window unit as if it was Exhibit A: true to character, the AC roared like a squadron of Superfortresses with a spanner in their engines.

We all contemplated my air conditioner. "I've been meaning to get a new one," I said.

"In any case, what happened was that someone bombed Union Station," she said. "The damage was worst in the restaurant—it was destroyed. Within a few hours the police were rounding up members of the Progressive Youth Alliance, to which Miss Armbruster belongs. The group had staged a sit-in at the counter there earlier in the day—that is, yesterday."

"I know," I said. "I was there."

She raised an elegantly arched eyebrow at me, but decided not to pursue it. "Miss Armbruster was not there. Nevertheless, the police seemed to think that she knew something about the incident. She was only just now released after several hours of questioning."

"I'm sorry to hear that," I said. I gave Juney a sympathetic look, but it was wasted on her, since she was still avoiding eye contact. I hoped that it was not wasted on Mrs. Wardlow.

"Two properties have been bombed in two days," Wardlow said. "Before the bombings both sites were targeted by PYA demonstrations. You can see why the police think what they think."

This was too much for Juney. "But that just shows what idiots they are," she burst out. She stood up in agitation and circled behind her chair so that she could rest her hands on it, and maybe so that she could have something handy to throw if the mood struck her. "They don't listen to us, they don't read our literature, they don't read our press releases. We're *nonviolent*, for crying out loud!"

I suppressed a smile at the old fashioned expression. Juney had been raised in an upstanding Christian household, and no matter how frustrated and angry she got, she couldn't bring herself to cuss. What would a girl like that be doing with a bomb in her purse?

"If they haven't read your literature before this, Juney," Mrs. Wardlow told her, "they're certainly reading it now. But even if the police understand that the group's official position is nonviolent, that doesn't mean that everyone in the group accepts that position wholeheartedly."

"So the cops are going to be looking for someone who doesn't," Halsey said.

"Especially since there's been so little coverage of the group's activities in the papers," I said. "The cops are bound to suspect someone on the inside who knows where the group has been demonstrating."

She turned on me, and I thought I might get the chair. "But that's ridiculous!" she spat. "Just because you and your white friends don't know where we've been demonstrating doesn't mean that nobody else does. It's not a secret. Lots of people in the negro community know."

"That's neither fair nor productive, Juney," Wardlow said mildly.

"As a matter of fact," I said, "I was on the scene for both demonstrations, as you know. If I were a cop, I'd pull me in for questioning."

"Right," Juney said. "As if they'd ever take a white businessman in for questioning." But she sat down.

I bet the cops had a hard time thinking of me as a businessman. There were plenty of flatfeet who would love to put the collar on me. But if Juney had an exaggerated sense of my importance, I wasn't going to be the one to correct her. "So where do I come in?" I said to Wardlow and Halsey.

"We think the cops have it backwards," Halsey said. He leaned forward and talked with his hands. "Ain't some disgruntled young negro college student trying to blow up the white establishment. It's some racist yahoo think they got the right idea in Alabama, want to see the cops get tougher, maybe break a few skulls. It's somebody who wants to discredit the movement."

"Okay," I said, "but they're taking a lot of trouble and risks. What do they get out of it?"

"They want a continuation of the status quo—a segregated South," Wardlow said. "At the very least they want to intimidate the demonstrators by setting some very angry policemen after them."

I stroked my chin and shook my head. "I don't like it. It's not a bad theory as far as it goes, but the payoff isn't big enough. The theatre was right around the corner from the Lamar Hotel—that's some mighty expensive real estate. Union Station isn't exactly deserted at—what time did you say the bomb went off?"

"I didn't," she said, "but it was around two-thirty."

"Okay, even so," I said. "Even if it was on a timer, the torch had to drop the ticker in a public place. Let's say he made sure that there wouldn't be many people around when the bomb blew. Was anybody hurt?"

"Janitor," Halsey said.

"A negro janitor," Wardlow added.

"And a couple of brakemen," Halsey said. "Doesn't look like anybody died, but we don't know the condition of the casualties."

"Okay," I said, "so he risked a murder beef, but maybe he had enough confidence in his work to think that was unlikely. As far as we know, he hasn't been arrested yet. Cops went after the kids first, isn't that right?"

"So you're saying he was good," Halsey said, "and he knew he was good." He was squinting at a spot over my head and I could see he was tracking with me. "A pro."

"Uh-huh," I said.

"And pros aren't usually in it to express their political beliefs," Halsey said. "Ain't doing no pro bono work for the John Birch Society or the KKK."

"Uh-huh," I said.

"So what we need to do is follow the dough," he said.

"Who has enough dough to pay a torch to take those kinds of risks and get it right?" I said. "Be an expensive job, you ask me. Union Station isn't some privately owned office building that somebody wants to collect insurance on."

"Man's got a point," Halsey said to Wardlow as he sat back in his chair.

"If you were going to investigate, Mr. Lark, where would you start?" Wardlow asked me.

"I'd start by collecting a retainer," I said.

Wardlow didn't blink. "Of course. What are your rates? Please keep in mind that our funds are not inexhaustible."

"I'm trying to forget it," I said. "Please keep in mind that my son has a mouthful of very expensive braces."

"Touché," she said, and marked the accent with a tilted eyebrow. "We're not without resources, but if we're forced to match our opponents dollar for dollar, and they hired an expensive professional, as you say, then our cause is hopeless." She smiled at me.

That smile knocked another fin off the rate I was going to quote her. "Let's say thirty a day plus expenses."

"Thank you," she said. "That's a generous offer." I got another smile that almost had me offering to do the work for free, but the good angel on my left shoulder conjured up my latest bank statement and I squelched the impulse. "So where would you start after you collected the retainer?"

"I'll work some contacts in the PD," I said. "Somebody might know something."

Juney made a noise of exasperation that I could hear over the AC. I looked at her, and then went back to Wardlow, who was easier on the eyes. "An experienced arson investigator gets to know the local talent," I said. "Whether they've got evidence that will stand up in court or not, they usually have a favorite suspect."

"Then why don't they go after him and leave us alone?" Juney complained.

"Maybe they have. But like Sly said, these guys don't work for free, and the cops probably figure it's easier to break the guy that hired the perp than the perp himself. After all, the perp's probably been sweated lots of times—it's old hat to him. He wouldn't last long in his profession if he caved every time a bull put the muscle on him."

Wardlow looked at Halsey. "What do you think?"

Halsey nodded. "It's a good place to start." He spread his hands. "I don't have those kinds of contacts."

"On the other hand," I said, "I could start following the kids around to every demonstration and staking out the targets afterward, but I'd be damned conspicuous if I did and I figured you wanted to hire me to do something that Sly can't do."

Sly grinned at me. "Yeah, whitey," he said, "that be a waste of your talents."

"I'm still not persuaded that the bomber isn't just a racist with some crack-brained plot to destroy the local movement," Wardlow reiterated.

"I'll keep an open mind," I said.

"Can you give this case the attention it needs?" she asked. "So far, nobody's been killed, as far as we know, but that could change at any time."

"I have a few things I'm working on, but I'll make time for you."

She wrote me a check and asked me to keep in touch with Halsey as well as with her, shook my hand, and headed for the door. I crossed the room to show them out.

Juney got up to follow, but I said, "I'd like a few minutes with you, Juney—in private."

As the door closed behind the others, Juney slumped in her chair and regarded me with suspicion and irritation. She was still a teenager, so I didn't hold it against her. I knew I was getting practice for later, when Dizzy hit her teenage years and became even more of a pain in the ass than she was now.

"We're not kids, you know," she said before I could get a word out.

I leaned on the edge of my desk. "Fair enough," I said. "But you know you'll always be a kid to your parents and your parents' friends. That's just the way it is." I extended the cigarette box by way of a peace offering and she took one, but she looked guilty about it.

"Were they rough on you at the station?" I asked.

She shrugged. "Nothing I couldn't handle. But it wasn't fun." Then her bravado wavered and she yielded to the temptation of a sympathetic ear. "They have special tactics for girls, you know. Like, they might not beat you up, but they look at you like you're dirt, and they don't let you go to the bathroom." She looked down at her hands as she said this, and her voice quavered a little. "And after a few hours you feel like dirt and you're afraid you're going to—you know, embarrass yourself." She swiped at a tear that was fighting its way out.

I moved to one of the other chairs and pulled it closer. I held out my handkerchief.

"Oh, heck," she said, and took it.

"You're a brave girl," I said. "You keep going back."

"It was worse this time." She was talking through the handkerchief. "The bombs made it worse."

"Like Mrs. Wardlow said, if anybody gets killed, it will get even worse," I said.

"I know," she whispered.

"So if you know anything, or suspect anything—anything at all—this is the time to come clean."

She glanced up at me, ready for a fight, tears or no tears.

"I'm not saying you know who's behind the bombings," I said carefully. "And they may not have any direct connection to your group, like Mrs. Wardlow says. But there's a chance, and it's not a bad chance, that somebody in your group knows something. Not the leaders, probably. But since the bombings just started, maybe there's a new member you don't know very well yet. Maybe this person doesn't strike you as entirely trustworthy. Maybe he's secretive, or a little too passionate—it could go either way."

Her head was down but I saw her blink and the handkerchief she'd been kneading went still.

"I bet you've got good instincts about people, Juney. I'm just encouraging you to trust your instincts."

She moistened her lips with her tongue.

"You think it over." I caught my hand on its way to patting her knee. "If you have any suspicions like the ones I've mentioned, you don't have to tell me about them, you can tell Mr. Halsey. But you have to tell somebody. And whatever you do, don't try to confirm them on your own. The bomber's playing a dangerous game, and he wouldn't think anything of coming after you. Understand?"

She didn't say anything.

"Can I get a nod on that?" I said. "It's really important. Don't put yourself in danger. Understand?"

She nodded.

"Okay, that's it." I slapped my own knees. "End of lecture. You'd better catch your ride home."

“Thanks, Mr. Lark,” she said, her voice still thick with tears. “I know I’m not the easiest person to get along with right now.”

“Skip it,” I laughed. “I get a lot of practice.”

Chapter 20

I tracked down the man I wanted to see at Union Station in the afternoon. The trains were running, but the station interior was off limits to passengers, who were crowded on the platforms, corralled by barriers and crime scene tape. Makeshift ticket booths had been set up on the street in front of the station, where long lines of people waited in the sweltering heat. I didn't know what they'd do when our daily thunderstorm blew up, but I was glad I wasn't trying to go anywhere by train.

I asked for a cop named Draper, and got waved past the yellow tape. One look at the building's interior told me why the place was off limits. The damage appeared to be worst at the far end where the coffee shop had been, but the roof was supported by two rows of tall columns, and they'd all need to be checked for cracks. A scaffold hugged one of the columns to my right, and I assumed that the man on the platform was doing just that. The air conditioning either hadn't survived the blast or had been turned off and the acrid, smoky air created a miasma through which people moved like underwater swimmers. I removed my jacket and hung it over my arm.

I spotted Draper talking to several other men, and hung back until he was finished. He wasn't the man I'd come to see, but I knew he could introduce me to the man I'd come to see, and did.

James Robert "Jumbo" Stubbs was the size of a tractor-trailer truck. He had mousey thin hair combed over his bald pate, but it was the thinnest thing about him. He was chewing on a fat cigar, unlit, and mopping his face with a red bandanna the size of the King Ranch. His massive arms protruded from tight short sleeves ringed with sweat. His tie had been pulled loose. His suit and cowboy boots were covered with ash. He looked like a man with bad digestion and a worse disposition.

I shook one meaty paw and thanked him for seeing me. My hand came away black.

"Well, don't be too thankful," he said. He extracted his hand and continued with the mopping operation. "If I wasn't desperate, you wouldn't be here, but I am. I don't have a goddamned thing."

He knew who I was working for. I could have played it cool and clammed up, but I didn't think it would get me anywhere. Insurance investigators were thick on the ground after an incident like this one, and I was coming late to the party. A late insurance investigator would be marked down as incompetent, and that wasn't the impression I wanted to make.

I didn't want to waste his time or mine. As he turned toward the hole where the coffee shop had been, I said, "Who do you like for it?" As the smoke began to scratch my tonsils, I wished I'd replaced the handkerchief I'd sent out the door with Juney that morning.

Stubbs shook his head. "Hell, I don't know."

"Not the kids?"

"Oh, hell, no," he said, and glanced at me. "Just look around." He waved a hand at the rubble. "If they'da tried they would have blown themselves to hell and gone."

"Professional torch?"

"Had to be." He nudged something with his foot, then bent to pick it up and examine it. I couldn't tell what it was, but then he held it up for me to see. It was a fragment of black plastic, part of a record from one of the tabletop jukeboxes.

"The Big Bopper," he read. "I love that sumbitch." He dropped the record and a puff of dust rose to engulf it.

"Understand, I'm not ruling the kids out," he said. "They could've hired the bastard. They're not all kids, either. Their leader—Stearns—he's in law school. You met him?" When I shook my head, he went on. "Like I said, he's older—late twenties. We picked him up on suspicion a few years back, and he squawked to city council about police brutality."

"Suspicion?" I said. "Suspicion of what?"

He gave me a sour look.

"Oh, sure," I said. "Suspicion."

I followed him as he picked his way through the rubble. He squatted awkwardly over a hole in the floor, like a trained elephant balancing on a stool. He pointed with his cigar. "Here's where he stashed the bomb—under the counter."

"Timer?"

"Who the hell knows? Be weeks before we sort through all this crap. And we've still got the movie theatre to deal with."

I squatted next to him and got a heady whiff of sweat. "Must've been an expensive job," I mused.

"You damn right it was expensive."

"You think this group of college students have that kind of money?"

Palms on his knees, he heaved himself upright. "Depends on what kind of friends they got."

I stood, too. "What kind of friends might that be?"

He stared at me. "The usual kind, son. Don't you read the papers?"

"Communists?" I ventured.

He didn't dignify this with a direct response. Instead, he said, "It beats everything how some folks with a lot of money want to give it to pinko anarchists squawking about private property and capitalism and I don't know what-all, but they do." He hitched his pants up over his vast middle, leaving a new set of black handprints on them. "Hell, I ever get rich, I'll be giving my money to the John goddamned Birch Society and anybody else defending my right to keep it. You got to dance with them what brung you, ain't that right?"

I tried to look sympathetic but let this pass without comment. I tried to return his attention to the identity of the torch. "What does your gut tell you about the perp?" I waved a hand at the scene. "You recognize a signature?"

He looked around. "I don't know a goddamned thing, except he was good."

"One of the best?"

"I'd say."

"All right, then. Suppose you had plenty of scratch and you wanted to hire somebody for a job like this. Among the local talent, who would you pick?"

He frowned at me, and I added, "I mean, of course, among the available candidates. Who's the best spark not pulling time at Huntsville?"

He cocked his head, laid a hand along one cheek and rubbed as if feeling for a jawbone under the layers of fat, sweat, and razor stubble. "Well, you put it like that, I reckon I'd go looking for Moline Bridgeman or maybe Darnell Toohey. I don't reckon I'd waste my money on anybody else."

I wrote these names down in my notebook, but it was rough going because my hands were so filthy my notes got smeared with ash. He was looking at me speculatively, so I played out the line. "One bomb would be expensive, but two?" I shook my head. "If we pooled our salaries, you and me, I doubt we could touch it. But a guy with that kind of dough who wants a job done, what's he going to do? Look up arsonists in the yellow pages? He's going to ask around, and he's going to be careful, because he's got the jack to afford the best. He won't take the first recommendation he gets. So it stands to reason that he'd hit on one of the first names on your list. That is, if he used a local. If he hired an out-of-towner, then all bets are off."

"You got a point, son." He put a hand on my shoulder. I tried not to think about the black pawprint he was leaving on my shirt. I'd hand it over to Mr. Lum tomorrow.

"Bridgeman and Toohey. They known to use timers?"

"Hell, the real pros all use 'em," he said. "But I'll tell you what, those two bastards hang around, make sure of their work after. That's how professional they are. We got them on security cameras after the blast—sometimes even before. Not right there, you understand, but close by. What we don't have is a nice Polaroid of them setting the timer."

"If I wanted to find these bums, where would I look?"

Stubbs narrowed his eyes at me. "I reckon you can look for them at the station later today," he said, "once we pick 'em up."

"Fair enough," I said, "but chances are good you won't be able to hold them. Tell you what—first stiff to lawyer up, I'll bet you he's your man. He should be flush after these two jobs."

He grinned at me. "I ain't going to take that bet. But I'll tell you what, son, I like the way you think."

"You don't have the manpower to sit on these birds. I do."

"All right," he said. "I'll tell you where to find 'em. But you better stay clear out of my way, and I expect full cooperation from you. Anything you find out comes to me, comprende?"

I nodded. "You've got to dance with them what brung you."

Chapter 21

The Rodriguez brothers took Darrell Toohey, who lived with his mother and aunt in West University. Sly Halsey and I took Moline Bridgeman, who lived in a rooming house on Chenevert Street downtown. Halsey would be less conspicuous on Chenevert than he would be in West University. Not that Mexican Americans were inconspicuous in West University, where they usually drove pick-ups, pushed lawn mowers, and carried hedge clippers.

"Hey," Danny had said, "how 'bout me and Turk wear our Hawaiian shirts, bring our ukuleles, and do our Hawaiian imitation? Gringos love Don Ho."

Now we were all parked outside the main police station on Riesner, Danny and Turk in their Pontiac and Sly and me in my Impala. The building looked like a tall cement waffle folded into a box.

By now it was early evening and the rain was pouring down. Our visibility was less than ideal.

We had a friendly bet going about which pigeon would be the first to fly the coop. Sly and I won it when Bridgeman came out, accompanied by a tall geezer wearing suspenders and carrying a jacket and umbrella. In a spirit of camaraderie, Stubbs had provided booking photos of both Bridgeman and Toohey which resembled them about the way her second-grade school picture resembles Marilyn Monroe. Bridgeman shook hands with the tall ghee, presumably his lawyer, and they went their separate ways. After giving the sky a hostile look, Bridgeman hunched his shoulders and stuck his hat on his head and his hands in his pockets. He was small and wiry, with a bad haircut and a worse shave. He wore khakis and a short-sleeved shirt, neither of them singed or smoke-stained, as far as I could see. Danny's voice came through on the walkie-talkie. "So you win. So what. Our old man can beat up your old man, cabrón."

We followed Bridgeman to a nearby bus stop, where he stood under the shelter and let two busses pass before taking the next one. We followed the bus down to La Branch, where Bridgeman got off. He stopped in a greasy spoon on the next block, and we sat, passing a flask back and forth and wishing we had hot dogs.

I drummed my fingers on the steering wheel. "One of us should get out and check to make sure he's alone in there."

Sly just looked at me.

"Okay," I said, "just so you know I support desegregation."

I sloshed up the sidewalk and looked through the window as I passed, but the window was steamed up and I couldn't make out the interior. So I went in. The bored-looking blonde with a haystack for a hairdo cracked her gum at me and directed me, upon my request, down the street to the nearest bus stop. At first I didn't see Bridgeman and I was afraid I was going to have to talk the blonde into letting me use the john when I spotted him in the back, using the telephone mounted on the wall. Just as I noticed him, he hung up and went back to his table, and I couldn't think of a good excuse to stick around, so I beat it. I told Sly what I'd seen.

"Either he's reporting in," he said, "or he's fixing up a date for later."

Danny reported that Toohey had left Police Headquarters about ten minutes after Bridgeman, and that an older woman had picked him up.

"Just sit on him," I said. "He might decide to take a walk after dinner."

"Okay, boss," he said. I heard crackling, but it didn't sound like static.

Sly looked at me. "Damn," he said. "They're eating."

"Are you eating?" I asked Danny.

"Ain't against the rules, is it?" Danny said.

"No," I said, "but Sly wants to know what it is so that he can enjoy it vicariously."

"Vi who?" Danny laughed. "Hombre, no need to intimidate us with big words. Sly, we got chorizo cut thick, smothered in salsa, and rolled in a tortilla. It's the mamacita special. But it ain't for gringos, man. It would burn a hole in your stomach. Lucky we got a cooler full of Lone Star in the back."

Sly was holding the now nearly empty flask and he gave it a mournful look, then looked at me.

"Don't look at me," I said. "I thought you were going to handle the catering."

"Sure," he said. "Blame the negro."

The rain beat down on the car and every now and then a truck would pass and a tsunami of dirty water would hit the windshield. Then the rain let up just in time to let two cops in a passing cruiser give us the fish eye.

We looked at each other.

"Black guy and a white guy sitting in a car in this neighborhood," Sly said, "they going to think it's a drug deal."

"Will they call in the plate?"

"Probably. You could be somebody."

"Not in this car."

He looked at his watch. "I give 'em five minutes, ten tops."

It took them five. They pulled up past our rear bumper to box us in. I watched in the rearview mirror as a stocky middle-aged brown-haired flatfoot climbed out of the cruiser as if he was dismounting a horse and put his hat on. He tapped on my window.

"You boys waiting for someone?" he said. He leaned down and squinted at Sly. He had the dead eyes and veined nose of a cop who spent his off duty hours trying to drown the memories of his workday.

"No, we're working," I said.

The other cop tapped on Sly's window, and when Sly rolled it down, he leaned down and joined the conversation. Although he was younger and had a bigger paunch, he looked a lot like the first cop, the way old married couples start to look alike. Frick and Frack.

"He says they're working," Frick said.

"That so?" Frack said. "Don't look much like work to me."

"Why don't we just show you our licenses and save you a lot of trouble?" I said.

"He wants to show us their licenses," Frick said.

"I'd admire to see 'em," said Frack.

I was feeling like the net at Wimbledon.

It took all I had to keep my temper in check, but I knew that if we got arrested they'd go harder on Sly than on me, so I kept a lid on it. We reached for our wallets, moving slowly and carefully. We handed them our PI licenses along with our driver's licenses.

"Well, whaddya know?" said Frick. "It says this one's a private dick."

"I be damned. Nigger's a dick, too," said Frack. "Ain't that something?"

"So what we got here is a couple of dicks sitting in a car," Frick said. "Y'all get paid for this? I should get me a PI license."

"A little over an hour ago, an arson investigator named Stubbs cut a guy loose after a conversation about the Union Station bombing," I said. "Stubbs doesn't have the manpower to sit on him, but he knew I'd do it for him."

"That so?" Frick said. "You hear that, Ernie? These dicks are performing a public service."

"Union Station, huh?" Frack said. "Where's your pigeon?"

"In the diner there, up the street," I nodded in that direction.

"Over yonder?" Frick said, following my head.

They both stood to look at the diner, then leaned over again to continue.

"Your man white or black?" Frick said.

"Let the nigger answer," Frack said, "if he can talk. Seem to me like he ain't pulling his weight here."

"He's white," Sly said.

"He's white," Frack echoed.

Frick said, "That don't sound right to me. They got them nigger students made for them two jobs—Union Station and the theatre."

I shook my head, as if we were having a free discussion. "Jobs were too professional. Ask Stubbs."

"I might just do that," Frick said. "Ernie, what you thinkin'? Maybe we best let these public-spirited dicks get on with their work. What you think?"

Frack gave Sly the fish eye again, but Sly didn't look at him. Then Frack shrugged. "It don't seem right to me to have two men on a job like this. I hope the city ain't footing the bill."

"Nah, it's private," I said. "City couldn't afford our rates."

"You got that right, brother," Frick said. He handed back my licenses. Then he slapped the edge of the window and straightened up, stiff like a robot. "Y'all stay out of trouble, hear?"

Frack handed Sly his licenses without comment. They got in the cruiser and drove off.

"I owe you one, Harry," Sly said as he watched them go.

I looked at him in surprise. "What for?"

"For not being your usual wise-cracking, cop-baiting, pain-in-the-ass son-of-a-bitch self."

"Give me some credit. I can show restraint."

"I guess you can at that," he said. Then he pointed up the street. "Big man in a trench coat went into the diner while you was waltzing with Matilda. Got kind of a funny walk—not a limp exactly, more like one leg's shorter than the other. Bad scar across his cheek—knife or bullet, could be either. Looked like muscle to me."

I squinted through the windshield. "You could see all that from here?"

"You can't?" he said. He shook his head. "Gettin' old, Harry."

"That's what my daughter tells me."

"Course, it helped he came up the sidewalk behind us and turned to watch the sideshow," said he added.

I grimaced. "I guess one of us has to go find out if he's dining with our boy."

"Don't look at me. I wouldn't make it past the front door before they'd be calling the fuzz back."

So I went. At this point the sun was trying to put in a late appearance before it flopped for the night. It was a July-in-Texas sun, and had its reputation to consider. Steam rose off the sidewalk and the air was thick and glimmering.

The blonde looked surprised to see me again—or as surprised as she was capable of looking about anything that didn't involve the celebrities she was reading about in the movie magazine she had open on the counter next to the cash register.

"I thought the number 10 bus came by here," I said, wagging a thumb over my shoulder. I looked accusingly at her as if she'd been the one to give me a bum steer. "I been waiting half an hour. I don't think it comes anywhere near here."

This outburst didn't rate an answer and she didn't give it one. She just shrugged. The shrug said that if I wanted a table and a fly-specked menu and an order of the pot roast special, she'd take an interest in me, but otherwise, nothing doing.

"Is there any place around here I can get a cab?" I went on.

She shrugged and her eyes drifted back to her magazine. "I don't take cabs," she said. It was a dismissal. She could have suggested I use the public telephone to call a cab, but she'd had enough of me and I didn't blame her. Houston wasn't a cab city anyway; people who didn't own a car either took the bus or walked. Cabs were few and far between and depended on airport runs for their income.

I returned to the car. "They're not sitting at the same table," I said, "or anywhere near each other."

"Don't mean nothing. Scarface looks like trouble, but whether it's the same kind of trouble as Bridgeman's trouble, we don't know yet. I don't guess a torch stay out of Huntsville unless he's cautious.

Here's our boy." He nodded up the street where Bridgeman had just come out of the diner and turned away from us. "Case you want to put on your glasses, grandpop," he added.

"You got a lot of nerve calling somebody 'scarface,'" I said, craning my neck to follow Bridgeman. I was sore because the crack about my eyesight hit home, but I couldn't afford to do anything about it until I got my kids through adolescence with straight teeth. I started the car, put it in gear, and eased out into traffic, which was light for the tail end of rush hour.

He ran a thumb over the scar on his lip. "Yeah, but mine just adds distinction. Anyway, who died and made you Emily Post?"

"My daughter would say that, too." Then I slapped the steering wheel as it hit me. "Damn! Dizzy's got a softball game and I'm supposed to be there." I glanced at my watch. The game had started fifteen minutes ago.

"Want me to tail him on foot?"

"Let's see if he goes home first."

"Kid's softball game's important."

"So's a bomb in Union Station." I handed Sly the Motrac mike. "Find out what Danny and Turk are up to, why don't you."

"We having a ball," Danny said. "We got a scenic view of the neighborhood. We taking bets on which house going to put out the garbage next. Plus we got two Lone Stars riding on whether any of these folks going to mow their lawns between now and sundown. I say no, it's too wet, but Turk, he's an optimist. Oh, wait, I better sign off now. We got us a dog walker at twelve o'clock, and I don't want to miss it."

"Any sign of Toohey?" Sly asked.

"Who?" Danny said. We heard Turk's voice, and then Danny said, "Oh, him. Nah, I figure he's full of his mama's fried chicken and potato salad and now he's sitting on the couch between the two ladies of the house, watching *Wagon Train*. Ask the boss if he wants me to sneak up there and find out if it's *Wagon Train* or *The Aquanauts*."

Up ahead, Bridgeman had turned in at a sagging gate and was

making his way up the walk to a large two-story frame house that hadn't seen paint since the Allen brothers landed at Buffalo Bayou and founded the Houston real estate market.

Sly saw the indecision on my face. "Look, why don't we pick up my car, and I'll come back here and sit on Bridgeman, at least till midnight. You tell Danny and Turk to do the same. If one of these geeks is the bomber, he ain't bombing nothing tonight because the kids didn't protest today. We can gamble that whoever's running the show won't want to meet at three in the morning because he needs his beauty sleep. You come back in the morning and watch Bridgeman."

"We're putting a lot of eggs in one basket," I said. "Well, two baskets."

Sly rubbed his chest. "I got a good feeling about this. I like Bridgeman and I like Scarface for his handler."

"Are your feelings usually right?"

"Yeah, man, 'bout half the time. Now all we need is for the kids to stage a protest somewhere."

"Well, you've got more pull with them than I do."

When I got to the ball park, Dizzy already looked like she'd lost the mud wrestling contest and she was sporting a smear of blood and a new bandage on one leg. The mothers all shot me dagger eyes that said I should have been there to rush the fence and weep over my fallen daughter—a spectacle which Dizzy herself would never have forgiven me for.

Chapter 22

"What happened to your leg?" I asked as I walked her to the car. I'd made it to the game by the top of the third, and she didn't seem all that sore.

She shrugged. "Big girl slid into me at home."

That was Dizzy. She was not one for drama. A certain amount of pain and injury came with the territory, that was how she saw it.

"They should have you wear knee pads." I laid a hand on her shoulder on one of the few patches that wasn't caked with mud. It felt hot through the fabric of her shirt.

"Don't start," she said, giving me the eye. "The stupid chest protector is bad enough. You know how much that thing weighs with ten pounds of mud on it? And then the mask on top of that? Someday I'm just going to keel over in the heat and it's going to take both coaches to pull me up."

"I'd like to see that," I said.

She rolled her eyes. "That'll be the day."

Not that I was the only villain in the piece. Even though her mother was always on time for the games, she had been known to miss crucial plays and even injuries because she was grading papers or correcting page proofs in the stands. She wouldn't know it was her own daughter who'd been hit until she pulled her glasses down and looked around. If there was no blood, she'd go back to her papers. If there was blood, she'd wait to see if an ambulance showed up. And if her daughter was carried off the field, she'd been known to check her watch and wonder whether she could collect Dizzy and go home.

Lucky for me, Hal had decided not to play baseball this summer because of his job at the Y. It was lucky on two counts, because while I would never have forbidden baseball outright, the thought of a hardball flying at his mouthful of expensive teeth gave me the willies.

In the car, I said, "I have to go by the apartment and pick up something." This living in two places at once was getting old.

She rolled her eyes but didn't comment. I knew she was perfectly content to visit Stanley, the downstairs cat, as long as I didn't take too long.

"Have you talked to Mrs. Heffelman yet?" I asked.

"No, tomorrow. B.D. had Bible camp today."

I liked talking to Dizzy in the car at night. Being in transit from one place to another with no eye contact seemed to encourage us to say things we wouldn't otherwise have said. The dark outside helped, and now a new contingent of storm clouds had bumped the sun and blanketed the sky with black.

"Do you ever wish you had Bible camp?" I asked, staring straight ahead. I felt her eyes on me, so I glanced over. Utter disbelief.

"What would I do at a Bible camp?"

"I don't know. I've never been to one. Maybe read the Bible?"

She made a noise.

"You ought to read it some time," I said. "Just because your mother and I don't go to church doesn't mean we're not Christian."

This was lame and we both knew it. We were Christian because we'd been taken to church a few times as children, and because what else would we be? Buddhist? Zoroastrian?

"I know," she said. "You have to read the Bible to read Shakespeare."

After a beat, I said, "Okay, no Bible camps for you. Is there anything else you're longing for? Piano lessons?"

"What are you going to hock to buy me a piano? Or lessons, either?"

"Why don't you let me worry about that? I just meant that if there's something your friends are doing that you wish you could do—."

"Like ballet."

I looked at her. In the light from a passing streetlamp her eyes were sparkling.

She looked at me. "What? You don't think I'd look good in a tutu?"

"You know what I mean. I want you to be happy."

"I'm the envy of the neighborhood," she said. "I'm a businessman."

I laughed. "So you girls are really raking it in?"

"We do okay," she said. "There is one thing I want, though."

"What's that?"

"I want you to take me to the shooting range again."

I smiled. "What will your mother say?"

"Who says my mother has to know anything about it? She's miles away. In fact, I'm feeling pretty abandoned."

"Really?"

"No, Harry. She's already called twice. Jeez, for a detective, you're pretty bad at telling when somebody's yanking your chain."

I nodded. "It's a real drawback in my profession."

We pulled up in front of my building, a small, three-story brick structure on a forgotten little street where all the houses and apartment buildings had the faded, old-fashioned air of great-aunts. We both got out.

"Want to come in and wash up a little?"

"Nah, I'll just wait till I get home."

At the sound of her voice, the black cat, Stanley, came bounding out of the bushes. I left them to it, went in and climbed to the second floor. I unlocked the door, pushed it open and stepped in.

I never saw it coming. By the time the stars burst on the inside of my eyelids, it was too late.

I woke up sitting in a straight chair that had been dragged out from my dinette. Apart from the throbbing at the back of my head, where Goliath was drumming his fingers against a particularly sensitive nerve, I could feel the icy bite of steel at my wrists. Eyes still closed, I watched tweeting cartoon birds circle my cranium and took inventory. My feet were free—that was good. They'd used cuffs instead of rope—that was bad. I didn't think I'd been out for long, but I wasn't sure. The thought of Dizzy downstairs playing with Stanley kicked my eyes open.

A gun—not my gun—was on the coffee table. It was a Browning Hi-Power 9 millimeter. There were two parties in the room with me and they both had mob written all over them—dark hair shiny with oil, pinky rings, tailored suits. More than that, they smelled like mob, like the expensive colognes a native Texan wouldn't be caught dead wearing for fear he'd be tagged as a pussy—a pardner light in his Tony Lamas. Anything on the floral side of leather and sweat would be regarded with suspicion by the local talent. These two could have been kissing cousins to my previous two nocturnal visitors.

One man was seated in an armchair—the one calling the shots, I figured—and the other was standing. The latter had shed his jacket to display a set of arm muscles so overdeveloped they looked like water wings.

"You should get a better air conditioner," said the guy in the chair. He had a hoarse voice, a Roman nose, a full head of hair, and a tic in his right eye.

"Here in Houston," I said, "we like to think it takes cojones to put up with bad air conditioning. If I caved in and bought a new one, it would be seen as a sign of weakness."

The two men looked at each other. Italiano, si, español, no. They probably had a word for cojones in Italian, but I didn't know it. We were at an impasse.

"We need to talk," said the boss.

"What about?" I wanted to hurry this along and get them out of here before Dizzy came looking for me.

"We heard you was asking about somebody," he said. "Somebody from the Texas Chief wreck."

I was surprised and I let my face show it. "I was asking about somebody who got killed. The family wanted to know more about his death, that's all—his last minutes on earth, that kind of thing."

"And who might that be?" he said.

I shook my head. "I'm sorry, mister. I can't tell you that. My clients are confidential."

The boss didn't even look at his sidekick. The sidekick stepped forward and delivered a backhand across my jaw that rocked the chair and made my ears ring. I tasted blood. It was time to make some noise.

"Say, what is this?" I shouted. "You can't come in here like this and demand information." I tried to rattle the bracelets, but they were tight.

The beefy one hit me on the other side. Now I had a concert in my ears, like Christmas. The cartoon birds returned and set up a squawk.

The boss's eye twitched. "Keep your voice down," he growled.

"Or what?" I shouted. "Who the hell are you to come barging in a man's apartment—."

The next one was a jab to the ribcage that knocked the chair backwards. It fell on the rug with less of a thud than I would have liked, in case Mrs. Furnivall downstairs was listening and didn't have her hearing aids out. I had a good view of expensive Italian leather before it connected with my stomach.

I yowled.

The muscle set the chair upright and picked up the Browning. "You make any more noise, pal, and I'll plug you," he said.

"Okay, okay." I let my voice rise. I knew they didn't really want to kill me—at least, not until they had what they came for. "I hear you, okay? Just don't hit me again, willya? Jesus, I'm bleeding!"

"Let's try again," the boss said. "Who were you asking about and why?"

"Give me a fag, would you?" I said. "Jesus, I'm all shook up."

The sidekick stepped in again. At least he'd put the gun down. "I'll shake you up, you yellow punk. Answer the boss's question!"

"Aw, give him a fag," the boss said. "Maybe it'll shut him up."

"Yeah, that's right," I said with enthusiasm. "It'll help me think. You're all right, mister. You and me, we could get along."

The sidekick stuck a fag in my mouth and lit it. I kept up the patter, which was no mean feat. I dropped the fag and the sidekick had to bend over to pick it up. I could've kicked his lights out, but then what?

Maybe I should've been going to church all along and sending Hal and Dizzy to Sunday school and Bible camp. Maybe I should've gotten in more practice at the altar and less at the range. Now, when I wanted to bargain with God, I found that he had all the aces and I had a hand full of nothing. But I asked anyway. Please keep her safe. Please keep her downstairs.

"That's better," I said, when the fag was in place again. Talking around it made my words mushy. "Now what was it you wanted to know?"

"About the guy on the Texas Chief—the one you were asking about," the boss said.

A new voice spoke up from the doorway. It was high-pitched and quavery, but it sounded loud in the sudden stillness of the room.

"Actually," it said, "Harry wasn't asking about anybody, I was."

Dizzy – July 5, 1961

Chapter 23

"What do you do at Bible camp?" Mel had asked B.D.

"Oh, you know—," she said. "We talk about the Bible and play games and sing songs and draw stuff. My favorite part is Bible charades. But most of it's pretty juvenile. I'm really too old."

"Then why don't you tell your mother?" Mel said.

"Oh, you know—," B.D. said. "It makes her happy to send me. It's just, maybe, four times a year, and it gives her a whatchacallit—a false sense of whatever."

"Security?" Mel said.

"Yeah," B.D. said. "It gives her a false sense of security. I figure if I go to Bible camp, she worries less about what I'm up to when I'm with y'all—you know, with heathens."

Mel took offense. "I'm not a heathen. I'm Jewish."

"Same difference, as far as my mother is concerned." B.D. gave Mel an apologetic look. "I'm sorry, but it's not her fault she's so ignorant. She doesn't know any Jewish people."

"Not any?" Mel said.

"I don't think so."

"Mrs. Baumgardner, your third grade teacher, was Jewish," I said.

"I don't think my mother knew that," B.D. said. "Anyway, I'm going, so don't y'all have too much fun without me, hear?"

Now, Mel and I were sitting in lawn chairs playing Go Fish and listening to the rain beat down on the roof. We had played Jacks, Hearts, and Clue. The transistor radio was on, and when "Travelin' Man" played, we agreed that Ricky Nelson was dreamy. That pretty much exhausted the subject.

“At least we’re not having too much fun without B.D.,” I said.

“These games all work better with three people,” Mel agreed. “If B.D. was here, she’d be crabbing about the rain.”

“Yeah.” We both sighed.

“What does Hal do at the Y when it rains?” Mel asked. “They can’t take the kids outside for archery or dodgeball or anything.”

“He says they just throw ‘em all in the pool, unless there’s lightning. They spend the day in the pool and come out all shriveled.”

“Sounds boring.”

I agreed. “Want to play Battleship?”

“I guess so.”

So that was how my day went. To top it all off, the rain stopped and the sun came out just in time for my softball game. By the time Harry showed up in the third inning I looked like Clayface and I was limping from blocking a steal at home. The chest guard felt like an anchor around my neck. My leg hurt like heck and every time I squatted down, the cut opened up again and bled a little. My coach had taped a bandage over it, but the tape wouldn’t hold.

Harry wanted to stop by his apartment after the game, which was okay by me since I could visit with my feline pal Stanley and catch up on the news. Stanley was a man about town who acted like he had to beat off the ladies with a stick, which might have been true, although he always seemed to be hanging out in the bushes near the front door of Harry’s apartment building. Harry said that cats didn’t do their prowling until late at night and early in the morning, and he figured that Stanley made his rounds in the wee hours. Stanley was a tuxedo cat, black with an immaculate white bib, so it stood to reason that he was a night owl. He was almost as handsome as he thought he was, too, unlike most of the males I know.

When Stanley heard my voice, he came running. But then he pulled up short, the way he always does, pretending like he could take me or leave me. He found a spot on his shoulder to lick as Harry went through the door, but then, he never gives Harry the time of day anyway.

"How's the boy?" I said to him. I sat down on the top step and let him make the first move.

The mud on my uniform had dried and now it was flaking off in little bursts of dirt that followed me around like Pig-Pen. Stanley approached me warily, stopped a foot away from me, and stretched his neck so that he could sniff at my tee shirt. He wore an expression that made him look like a snooty wine taster at a posh restaurant and I would have given a lot to know what he was thinking. Did he recognize dirt as dirt even if it didn't come from his neck of the woods? He took a step closer and inhaled more deeply, then opened his mouth as if he was going to sneeze.

"It's not *that* bad," I said. I ran a hand down his head between his ears and along his spine to his tail. He arched his back into my hand.

Then he went back to his survey. He stepped down to the next step and sniffed at my shin, where the bandage had slipped again. Since he was taking such an interest, I told him how it had happened. Then I gave him the highlights of the rest of the game, and some of the lowlights, too, like my pop fly in the fifth. I asked him about his day, and he leaned against me and purred.

I was about to tell him about our adventures at the train station when it occurred to me that Harry was taking a long time for somebody who was just picking something up, and I thought I'd better go up and hurry him along. I held the door for Stanley, but he hung back. He flattened his ears and looked up the stairs with an expression I couldn't read. He made a sound in his throat and looked at me, his eyes yellow slits in black wells.

"What's wrong?" I said. And then I heard it, too—a thump coming from overhead. When I looked back at Stanley, his eyes were wide and the fur at the back of his neck was standing at attention. He wasn't going in and clearly thought I shouldn't either.

"All right," I said softly. "Well." I could hear Harry's voice now, and it was louder than it should have been.

I went back to the car and got the Colt out of the glove

compartment. Under the dull glow of the porch light, I released the magazine, the way Harry had shown me, and made sure it had plenty of bullets in it. It did, as long as I didn't run into the Texas National Guard up there. I studied the safety. Was it supposed to be up or down? Pulling the trigger to test was not an option. Harry always preached the importance of keeping the safety on when you weren't actually using the gun, so I hoped he practiced what he preached. I would have gone back and searched the glove compartment for a user's manual, but I knew it was no dice. I was on my own, and I didn't have time to waste.

Stanley crouched on the top step, looking worried.

"That makes two of us," I said. "Wish me luck."

I climbed the stairs slowly, hugging the wall the way Harry had taught me, and reached the second-floor hallway. I crept to Harry's door and listened. I heard a loud thud and the floor vibrated under my feet. Then I heard a dull noise and somebody yelled. I thought it was Harry, but I couldn't be sure.

I put my hand on the doorknob and turned. I opened my mouth to breathe past the golf ball stuck in my throat. I could hear two voices besides Harry's. Then I could see them. There was a flat-faced man sitting in a chair across from Harry, who was seated with his hands behind his back, probably tied. The other man was muscular and had a long nose.

I was the only person holding a gun. Nobody had seen me yet. Harry was too cheap to buy brighter light bulbs and I guessed I should be grateful now but I wished I could see better.

Then the flat-faced man said something that surprised me. He wanted to know about the man from the Texas Chief that Harry had been asking about.

I stepped forward and raised the gun, holding it with both hands. "Actually," I said, "Harry wasn't asking about anybody, I was."

My voice sounded funny, and at first I thought maybe they couldn't hear me because I could barely hear myself over the rush of blood in my ears and the kettle drum in my chest.

But they all looked at me.

Then Bignose turned and bent to pick something up off the table and as he brought the gun up I shot it out of his hand. The kickback rocked me and I did a little dance to steady myself, but the big surprise was that I'd actually hit what I was aiming at—a lucky shot that would probably earn me more respect than I deserved.

I saw movement out of the corner of my eye and turned my head and fired again. In the split second before the glass exploded and the mirror fell in pieces to the floor, I caught a glimpse of a stranger with matted hair and mud-streaked cheeks, and I saw myself as they must see me, mud-crusted with torn shorts and blood-smeared legs and sagging socks and shaking hands, blown sidewise from the blast but already swinging the gun back in their direction.

My ears were ringing but I could see Flatface talking and heard his voice faintly, as though my ears were stuffed with cotton gauze. He said, "Who the hell are you?"

My own voice sounded hoarse. "I'm his daughter, and also the one with the gun."

The two men looked at each other. Flatface's look said, "Get rid of her." Bignose's look said, "*You* get rid of her." Bignose was holding one bloody hand in the other.

When Bignose had dropped the gun, Harry had kicked it in my direction. I advanced a few steps and heeled it backward in the direction of the door. I didn't want to pick it up. One gun was an advantage. Two were a distraction—a liability.

Even now, in the time it took me to kick the gun out of the way, Bignose stepped behind Harry and bent as if he had something in his shoe he wanted. I fired again, aiming high so I wouldn't hit Harry and hitting nothing useful. At the same moment, Harry bucked and slammed the chair back into Bignose's midsection. He grunted and the two of them went down, with Harry on top, on his back, still attached to the chair.

"Knife!" Harry shouted, and I ran over, spotted it, and kicked it toward the door, keeping the gun trained on Flatface. When

Flatface made a move for the door, I drew a bead on him and fired just left of his shoulder. The kickback made me stumble again and I felt something soft under my heel. Somebody groaned. Could have been Harry, but probably not.

"Goddammit, sit down!" I ordered him.

Flatface sat.

I was breathing hard but at least things had come to a standstill and I was still standing. Flatface hadn't reached for a gun so maybe he wasn't packing but I knew better than to make any assumptions.

"Enough, Dizzy." Harry's voice came from behind the bottom of the chair and that was all I could see of him except for his shins and feet. "No more shooting."

I felt anger rising like lava. "I don't think you're in any position to assess the situation, Harry," I said. "I've got my hands full here, and you're no help, but if you can think of a better way to get the police here, I'm all ears."

There was a pause, and then he said, "Fair enough. I withdraw the suggestion."

"Is your guy conscious?" I asked. "Do you think he knows that if he raises a finger I'll blow him away?"

"I don't think he's conscious," Harry replied, "but if he wakes up I'll give him the message."

"Now," I said, giving Flatface my full attention, "who the hell are you?"

"Lark, you teach her to use such language?" Flatface said.

"I taught her to shoot," Harry said. "The rest she picked up on her own."

"You should be more careful how you talk around your kids," Flatface said. "Kids pick up stuff."

"Don't tempt me," I said to Flatface, making a point of drawing a bead on his chest. I could hear sirens in the distance and I hoped they were coming here, but they didn't give me much time for explanations. "I asked you a question. Why do you want to know about the man on the Texas Chief?"

He spread his hands. "I was just asking your father why you were asking questions about somebody, that's all."

Harry said, "I told him the widow just wanted to know more about what happened the day her husband died—last words and such."

"That's right," I said. "And you still haven't answered my question. What's it to you?" The sirens were coming closer.

He shrugged. He could hear them, too, and figured he could wait me out. "Let's say I'm a security consultant for the railroad, and I take an interest in anybody who's nosing around."

"Let's not." I squeezed off another shot that whizzed past his ear and finally drained some of the color from his face. He didn't want to be dead when the cops arrived. His high-priced shyster wouldn't do him any good then.

"I'm going to count to five, and I want to hear your real reason," I said. "One."

"Okay, okay," he said. "Jesus!"

"Two," I said.

"Somebody on the train was carrying something valuable that belonged to me," he said in a rush. "It was never recovered. I'm just trying to recover my property is all."

The sirens, deafening now, suddenly died. We could hear the chatter from police radios coming through the open door downstairs.

"What property?" I sighted down the gun barrel.

"A briefcase," Harry said. "Full of what? Money?" It was hard to get used to hearing Harry's voice coming from an upended chair.

"Four." I tried to appear crazy enough to have forgotten what the original count was for. I heard voices downstairs, more sirens on the way.

"Yeah, that's right," Flatface said. "Dough."

"Five hundred grand?" Harry said.

"You know about it," Flatface said.

I stepped to the door and leaned out, keeping my eyes trained on the room. "Up here," I called. My voice sounded squeaky. "Apartment 2-B. I'm the only one with a gun now, and we could use some help."

"Only because you bozos keep sending thugs to look for it," Harry said. "I never heard of it before that, and I'm damned if I'm going to find it for you."

"Step out here where we can see you," somebody said from the hall.

"She's just a kid, officers," Harry called. "Don't shoot!"

I didn't know why they couldn't just push the door open wider to look, which would have suited me better, but I backed toward the door, reached behind me to pull it open, and backed out into the hall.

I glanced at the nearest officer, a paunchy brown-haired flatfoot with a gun in his hand. "There's another gun on the floor and a knife," I said. "Nobody's armed but me, as far as I know."

"We'll take it from here," he said. "Just set the gun down on the floor in front of you and step back."

I did it, and he nudged me toward his partner, who didn't look like he knew what to do with me. His sour puss said that he didn't want to frisk me, and it wasn't just because I was a girl. He looked me over with disgust and I realized he didn't want to get his hands dirty. I was still shaking and the movement created a little cloud of dirt like a dust devil.

"Well, I be damned," his partner said from inside. "Ernie, it's the public-spirited dick we got here."

His partner joined him and stared down at Harry, tilting his head to get a better look. "Well, ain't that a pisser. I'm glad the city's not paying his big salary, sure enough. Seem like he always sittin' down on the job."

Whatever that was supposed to mean, they both thought it was funny.

Chapter 24

The place was crawling with cops. The original comedy team stood over Harry and made smart remarks until Bignose woke up and started thrashing around. Then they set Harry upright again and I saw him grimace. Two cops held Bignose while they searched for the key to the bracelets that were holding Harry to the chair. I was sitting on the couch watching the commotion when I felt something soft against my leg. Stanley jumped up on the couch next to me, light as a bubble, and I gathered him up in my arms and pressed my face against his fur. He didn't object. He didn't even seem to mind the dirt. I closed my eyes and focused on the rumble of his purr and gentle vibration against my cheek. My hands finally stopped shaking and I found that I could swallow again.

I caught a faint whiff of Harry's aftershave. Then I felt his arm around my shoulder and I turned into his hug, with Stanley between us. When he finally pulled away, his eyes were sorry and sad and wet.

"I really loused up, Sis," he said. "I'm a world-class chump. I nearly got you killed."

"Well, don't do it again," I said. "Anyway, did you know those guys were after you?"

"I didn't know anybody was after me. Not this week."

I shifted Stanley a little to free one hand and fingered a bruise that was blooming red on his cheek. "You're bleeding."

He looked down at my bare leg half-folded under me. "That makes two of us."

I looked around. Flatface and Bignose were already gone, and I hoped they were on their way to the slammer.

"I'm sorry I shot up your place," I said.

He followed my gaze. "It could use some redecorating anyway."

"And brighter lights," I suggested.

He looked at me again, and I knew he was trying to figure out whether my aim had been affected by the dim light or whether I'd intended to miss the things I'd missed. He wasn't sure he wanted to know.

"Now will you take me to the shooting range?"

He rubbed my head and a cloud of dirt drifted down and settled on Stanley's fur.

"I'm not sure I can stand for you to get any better."

"If you don't take me, I'll tell Mama about tonight."

He grinned at me. "Deal."

"Cross your heart," I insisted, and he did.

We had to go down to the station next morning and make a statement, but Harry let me sleep in and Hal was already gone when I finally rolled out of bed. Rose must have known something, because she frisked me with her eyes when I sat down for breakfast. She and Harry are in cahoots and they mostly agree on what my mother should and shouldn't know.

She made me wear a dress and a slip. I'd kicked until she said that they wouldn't take me seriously in shorts, and I realized that she had a point and shut up. She dabbed my leg with Bactine and put a clean bandage on it. I took Judy Bolton with me at Harry's suggestion (I was saving Nancy Drew for a time when I could be sure to read uninterrupted) and it turned out to be a good thing because they parked me in a chair while Harry made his statement to a detective named Carillo. A young cop tried to make conversation with me under the mistaken assumption that I was a scared little six-year-old, but I kept going back to my book and he finally gave up. Then Harry came and got me and we went into a room about the size of a coat closet with gray cinderblock walls and a table with chipped veneer and a one-way mirror along one wall. I sat in a red plastic chair that had "Property of HPD" stenciled across the back. The station was pretty new, but it already smelled like stale coffee and cigarettes.

Detective Carillo was a tall, sad-looking man with deep lines in his face and a rumpled suit. A plain-faced woman whose suit could have come off the same rack sat silent in the corner with a steno pad even though there was a tape recorder on the table.

I glanced at Harry, who was settling into another red plastic chair. "Aren't you afraid he'll try to influence my story?" I said to Carillo.

Harry blew out a puff of air and muttered, "That'll be the day."

"He's just here to make sure I don't give you the third degree," Carillo said. "Which I wouldn't do anyway because I hear you're a pretty good shot."

There wasn't anything to say to that so I didn't say anything.

I told my story straight through. He only stopped me once and that was to ask who Stanley was. Then he asked me if I knew why the men were after Harry and I said that I didn't. Then he asked me why we were looking for Mr. Heffelman, and I told him the same story Harry had told the thugs, about the family wanting more information about his death. But when he asked me what I'd found out, I clammed up.

"That's privileged information," I said. "I don't see how it's relevant and my client has a right to expect confidentiality."

"That depends," Carillo said. "Has this client paid you?"

I thought about the Barbie doll stashed in our footlocker. "The client has given me a retainer."

"I see," he said. "And do you have a license to do business in the city of Houston?"

I swallowed. I figured he was just trying to mess with me, but I couldn't be sure. I could hear Harry shift in his chair behind me. "I have seen many garage sales in my neighborhood," I said. "I don't think any of those people have a license to do business in the city of Houston. I am also running a business out of my garage."

He opened his mouth as if he was going to argue, then shut it again.

"My advice, in case anybody's asking, is to leave it alone," Harry said. "You'll never win with her, brother."

Carillo's eyes shifted to Harry and then back to me. "I can see the resemblance," he said.

He complimented me on the clarity of my account and asked me to wait while the stenographer typed up the statement for me to sign. While we waited, I asked what was going to happen to Flatface and Bignose.

Carillo shrugged. "They've already been bonded out. My guess is that they're on their way home to Miami by now. The guy you shot, Antonio Bove, in case you're interested, spent a few hours at the ER getting his hand put back together. But he made it to court this morning."

"So they go scot-free after breaking into Harry's place and beating him up?" I wasn't surprised, but I let on that I was outraged. I felt bad about the hand, but not too bad.

Carillo looked Harry up and down, his arms folded across his chest. "He don't look too bad to me, your old man," he said. "A little banged up is all. And to be honest, I'd just as soon have those two gangsters out of the city. We got enough to do to keep up with the homegrown crazies."

"They were from Miami?"

"Miami mob, be my guess."

I thought that one over. The Texas Chief originated in Chicago. So why would a pair of Miami mobsters be in Houston squawking about losing something that belonged to them when the Chief wrecked? Harry seemed to think it was a briefcase of money—five hundred grand. I didn't know if Carillo knew about that, but I wasn't going to volunteer any information.

"You're not going after them?" I said. "What about extradition?"

His eyes shifted to Harry, who said, "She reads a lot."

"That's right," Carillo said, looking at me again. "Your

mother's a college professor, right? Well, Dizzy, I'm going to give it to you straight. Chances are good that the two meatballs who clobbered your old man have more resources than I do. So while I'm going to go through the motions of getting them back here to stand trial for assault, experience tells me that they're going to walk. And if nobody's told you yet that life ain't fair, I'm sorry to be the first."

He stood up and stretched. "I only took this case because it was your dad they had tied up. I'm a homicide dick. I don't usually get involved in assaults. But I got some history with your father, and this isn't the first time I've heard about this missing five hundred grand, if it's the same five hundred grand I heard about before—and I ask you, how many could there be? Anyway, I was hoping maybe your pop would give me a little additional information to work with, you know? So maybe I could find the dough before the next couple of mobsters blows into town and goes looking for him, maybe in your nice little suburban home." To Harry he said, "She got a nice little suburban home?" Harry must have nodded because he went on. "Only your old man is as close-mouthed as you are. What do you think of that?"

I didn't say anything.

He flapped a hand at us. "Aw, I had enough of both of you," he said, and left the room.

We signed our statements and skipped.

Harry was already late for a job so he dropped me off at home and split. Mel and B.D. had opened shop in the garage and were negotiating with Jimmy and Timmy Van Camp over a tennis shoe they'd found. They were both sitting in lawn chairs. Lucille was sitting upright on the footlocker watching the proceedings. Timmy was staring at an assortment of marbles in Mel's palm with a wistful look on his face. Jimmy was arguing with B.D. On the radio, Del Shannon was singing "Runaway."

"It's a size four and a half," Jimmy said. "It ain't no baby shoe." He was dancing from foot to foot in agitation.

"I see that," B.D. said. "Still, it would be better if we had the other shoe."

"This is a lost and found, ain't it?" Jimmy said, looking around. "The other shoe's not lost. We only found that one."

He had a point, but I knew that half the fun of this business for B.D. was the haggling, and I didn't want to spoil it for her.

"Two pairs would've been better still," I said.

Jimmy whipped around, his mouth open in disbelief. Timmy had taken a step closer to Mel and was petting the marbles in her hand as if they were baby gerbils.

"Aw, I say we give 'em all the marbles," Mel said. "What the heck." She had a soft heart.

B.D. cocked an eyebrow at me and I shrugged.

"You drive a hard bargain," B.D. said to Jimmy. Mel made Timmy cup his hands and poured the marbles into them. His eyes were big as basketballs.

"Need anything else while you're here?" Mel said. "We're running a special on golf balls—two for a dime."

Jimmy paused to consider. You could tell he was tempted by the low price—that was how it was supposed to work. But he thought about it long enough to wonder what he'd use two golf balls for. Mostly they were used by girls to replace those cheap rubber balls that came with a set of jacks.

B.D. turned up the heat. "You could give 'em to your girlfriend, make her think you were the last of the big-time spenders."

Jimmy blushed. "I don't got no girlfriend."

"Ooh, then you do need you a pair of balls," she said, "to help you get one."

I thought Mel was going to fall out of the chair, she was laughing so hard.

When the boys left, I told Mel and B.D. what had happened the night before. B.D. slapped her chest and gasped when I got to the part about the gun. Mel leaned forward and propped her chin on her fist. Even Lucille looked impressed.

“Are you telling me you actually shot a man?” B.D. said when I got to that part. “Actually shot him, with blood and everything?”

“Wow,” Mel said.

I told them the rest of it, and B.D. said, “Well, it’s a good thing I’m sittin’ down. Lucille, you hear what your mama just said? You better send this Stanley a case of Puss ‘n Boots or something.”

But Mel, who didn’t take as much pleasure in the drama of the thing as B.D. did, had already moved on to the implications. “So you’re saying these guys went after Harry because we were asking about Mr. Heffelman?”

“I don’t think they know about Mr. Heffelman specifically,” I said, thinking it over. “I don’t know whether they know his name. I never mentioned it, and I’ll bet Harry didn’t, either. They just knew that we were asking about somebody from the wreck.”

“But how did they know that?” B.D. said.

I shrugged. “Somebody squawked—maybe somebody we talked to, or maybe somebody who heard us talking to somebody. Maybe somebody thought they’d get paid for the information.”

“That is just low-down!” B.D. said indignantly. “That’s the person I’d like to shoot.”

“So these two guys, Flatface and Bignose,” Mel said, “they’re in jail now, right?”

I shook my head. I picked up a nearby paddle ball—one of the few we had that still had its ball attached—and began trying to whack the ball with the paddle. I wasn’t very good. Lucille’s ears twitched every time the ball made contact.

“They made bail this morning,” I said. “Detective Carillo thinks they’re Miami mobsters on their way back home by now.”

B.D. jumped up. “*Mobsters?*” she squeaked. “Are you telling me we got mobsters on our trail? Holy moly, Dizzy! I mean—holy moly!”

This counted as cussing for B.D., so I knew she was upset.

“But Harry just dropped you off here,” Mel said. “He left you on your own. That means he’s not worried.”

“I’m not too sure about that,” I said. “There’s a car parked in front of the Addisons', with a guy sitting in it reading a newspaper. Harry didn't mention him, but I think he might've sent somebody to keep an eye on us."

B.D. grabbed the paddle out of my hand. "Dizzy, would you please stop? You are gettin' on my last nerve. Now, listen. If Harry didn't mention this guy out front, how do we know he isn't a Miami mobster?"

"Because Harry didn't mention him," I said.

"But what if Harry didn't see him?" B.D. said. She was chewing on her lip.

"Harry sees everything. Well, unless it's hiding behind the door in the dark."

"But why didn't he mention the guy?"

"Because he doesn't want to scare us."

"Well, he did a piss-poor job of that," B.D. said, hands on her hips. "I don't know about y'all, but I'm scared, sure enough."

"Look, if it'll make you feel any better, we can go ask the guy." I turned toward the driveway.

B.D. grabbed my arm. "Dizzy, don't go out there. What if you're wrong and he is a Miami mobster? What then?"

"If he puts the snatch on me, call Harry," I said, moving away. "Or tell Rose and she'll call Harry."

The car was an old black De Soto with enough rust streaks to make it look like an overgrown tortoiseshell cat. The man behind the wheel watched me walking toward him. As I got closer, I recognized him.

"I'm sorry, I don't remember your name," I said through the open window.

"Turk," he said. "Turk Rodriguez."

I stuck my hand through the window. "I'm Dizzy. I guess Harry told you to keep an eye on us."

I turned around to see where B.D. and Mel were hiding behind a bush, their heads sticking up like perched birds, and gave them a big okay sign with my thumb and forefinger.

"He didn't want to make you nervous," Turk said as he shook my hand.

I nodded. "I got a friend that's real nervous. She'll be glad to know that you're on the job. Why don't you come on into the air conditioning and have a peanut butter and jelly sandwich with us?"

Turk looked around the car as if he expected to spot a lunchbox somewhere. "I don't think I should."

"Oh, come on," I said, leaning my arms on the window frame. "It must be hotter than Hades in this black car. Rose'll give you some lemonade. You can watch for button men out the kitchen window."

So he came, and B.D. calmed down considerably when she met him, though you could tell she wasn't sure how to take the gun nestled in his shoulder holster.

Rose already knew him, of course. Rose knows everybody.

Turk wasn't a talker, and B.D. said later it was like pulling teeth to get any information out of him. But Turk didn't think that Harry thought we were in any real danger. He didn't exactly say that it was against the rules to ice little girls, but he implied it.

"You could pick up a tail, though," he said at last.

"A tail," Mel said. "Cool."

B.D. looked at first like the idea of a tail could tip her into hysterics again, but Mel's reaction steadied her.

"But we're going to see the Heffelmans this afternoon," I said. "I don't want to lead any gangsters there."

"I haven't seen any sign of anybody," Turk said. "Where do these people live?"

"They live two streets over," I said. "We can cut through yards and give you the address so you can go there and watch the house."

He nodded.

"I still don't get what those guys are after," Mel said. "Harry thinks it's money?"

"Remember the man with the briefcase?" I circled my wrist with my other hand to remind them about the handcuff and chain. "Harry thinks he was carrying money—five hundred grand—and it's turned up missing. It must have been mob money because they keep sending thugs to ask Harry about it."

"But why would Harry know anything about that?" Mel said.

"And why would Mr. Heffelman?" B.D. said. "Unless—ooh, y'all, do you think they could have buried the money in the coffin with him?"

"Or without him?" Mel said.

Turk had stopped chewing and was staring at us. Rose was shaking her head. "Warped imaginations is what they got," she said to him. "Don't pay 'em no never mind."

Turk swallowed but his eyes followed the conversation.

"I read this one book where they buried some jewels in the coffin," B.D. said. Her eyes were shining. "Diamonds, I think it was. And everybody was looking all over for 'em, but couldn't nobody find 'em, of course. Until six months after the funeral when everybody had given up, the guy who put 'em there went out to the cemetery one dark night and dug up the coffin and got 'em back."

"Was it storming when he did it?" Mel said. "It usually is."

"Sure was," B.D. said. "Lightning and everything. That's how he could see the diamonds."

"Well," I said, "I think somebody would've noticed if they stuffed Mr. Heffelman's coffin with cabbage. Digger would've told us."

"I don't know," B.D. said. "He can be pretty close-mouthed about stuff he thinks is none of our business. I guess you get to be that way in the funeral business."

Turk wasn't smiling but the corners of his mouth were twitching.

Me, I was hoping the Miami mob hadn't decided to stick around and plug Harry before they blew town.

Harry – July 6, 1961

Chapter 25

"Wanna know what I regret?" Carillo said to me. He tipped his chair back on two legs. He made a gesture with his cigar. "I will always regret that I wasn't the first cop on the scene. They tell me that you were on your back in that chair, handcuffed like a nickel perp, and your daughter, Spring Branch Junior High's answer to Annie Oakley, was standing there, looking like she'd come straight from the Indian wars, covering two wise guys and her old man with a .38 Commander." He shook his head. "I woulda paid good money to see that."

"So would I. My view was pretty limited."

We were sitting in the sweat box the morning after Dizzy had gotten the drop on two mobsters—which is to say, the morning after the longest ten minutes of my life. The room was the size of a closet, with a battered table and wobbly red plastic chairs designed for the Seven Dwarfs. The steno had already returned to her cage to type up my statement and the recorder was off.

I picked up the Styrofoam cup and took a sip of coffee that tasted like Buffalo Bayou. I grimaced. "I thought you weren't allowed to torture prisoners anymore."

"You don't like it?" Carillo said. "I can ask our chef to make you something else." He set his chair down on all fours and sighed. "Anyway, you're not a prisoner, you're just a pain in the ass."

He stuck his cigar back in his face and bit down hard. "I'll tell you what I don't like. I don't like wise guys moving into the neighborhood. These guys were both from Miami—Cosimo Pittaluga and Antonio Bove. Bove's the one got plugged by your daughter."

I sympathized. The mobsters had all been run out of Houston in the past decade, and even Galveston was keeping its nose clean. The racketeers had moved on to Vegas. We still had plenty of vice and crime, of course, but it was the homegrown, loony Lone Star variety.

He leaned forward with his elbows on the table. "So what are they doing here? You say they're all looking for some five hundred grand they shipped down here on the Texas Chief. But what for?"

"Hell if I know. It's not enough to make an investment. You'd be lucky to get your own spittoon at the Chicken Ranch for that kind of dough. On the other hand, it's too much money for most other things I can think of."

"A high-priced hit?" Carillo suggested.

I shook my head. "If they're paying out that kind of scratch, we should both be considering a career change. Hell, there's local talent that would do the job for a pair of rodeo tickets and a six-pack of Pearl."

"Maybe they don't know that. Chicago prices."

"That was Graziano—he was from Chicago. But he was the pluggee, not the plugger, and I don't think he knew anything about the five hundred g's. These mugs were from Miami. You said the last birds were from Florida. Were they also from Miami?"

"Tampa and Miami. Same difference. They got higher prices in Florida, too. And that's another thing—it may not be enough jack to buy a baseball team, say, or a string of dance halls, but it's enough for Chicago and Miami to go to war over, Exhibit A being the deceased Mr. Smith, aka Graziano. I don't buy it that we got three sets of Sicilian tourists, and they're not all after the same score. You sure you don't want to tell me what Smith hired you for?"

I shook my head. "It was just a tail job—no connection that I can see."

He thought for a minute. "Okay, how about this? Political pay-off. They're both going after the same guy, Chicago and Miami."

"Could be," I said. "We've got some politicians who could be bought for that. Not Johnson or Thomas, maybe, but yeah, it could be that."

"You think of anything they'd want to buy a politician for?"

Smith's space center flickered in the back of my mind, but it made no sense, so I squashed it. "Maybe they want to open things up again," I said, "bring gambling back to Houston and Galveston. Maybe they're tired of the desert heat. Maybe they're missing the good old boys, the humidity and the hurricanes."

"They got that in Miami." The sides of his mouth turned down like a couple of clock pendulums. "I hope to hell you're wrong about that."

"Me, too."

He crossed his arms on his chest and cocked his head at me. "Tell me again why all these jailbirds think you've got their money. Do you?"

"No, but if I find it, Hal's orthodontist will be the first to know. I didn't know anything about it until they all came looking for it."

"But you were asking questions about a guy who got killed in the Texas Chief wreck?"

"Not me," I said. "Dizzy. I'm just her chauffeur."

"And she's asking questions because—?"

"There's a kid in the neighborhood—a little girl Dizzy knows. Her father died in the wreck." I felt my mouth go dry and it surprised me. Something about the dead fathers of little girls apparently froze up my vocal chords. I put it down to too much shooting and too little sleep the night before, and my own little girl sitting down the hall in the waiting room.

When I didn't go on, he looked at me. "What about him—the dead father?"

"The family just wants to know more about his death is all."

"Jesus, what's to tell?" Carillo said. "He was probably burned to a cinder or crushed by a half-ton of steel, unless he took a flying spike in his brain."

"I think they want to know more about his last day on earth, you know? Whether he was in a good mood, how he felt, who he talked to, that kind of thing."

It was lame, but Carillo's expression said he'd heard everything and there was no accounting for people's wishes.

"So what'd she find out?"

"What?"

"About the dead guy," Carillo said. "Was he in a good mood when he died?"

"She's not sure," I said. "She's going to tell the family he was."

"That's good," he said. "How's Dizzy taking all this? She must be pretty shook up."

"Hard to say. She cried a little last night, but then, so did I."

"She's not going to go all weepy on me now, is she? I mean, I'll go easy on her and everything, but I can't stand it when they cry. The kids, I mean—you can cry all you want."

I grinned at him. "You just better hope she's not packing."

"Let's invite her in."

I made a restraining motion. "Just a minute," I said. "Do you think she's in trouble?"

"With me? For illegal possession of a firearm?"

"With the mob," I said.

He stood up. "Nah. They don't go after kids. If somebody did go after her, and his pals found out he smoked a twelve-year-old for getting the drop on him, they'd laugh him all the way back to Sicily."

I nodded and stood.

He raised a finger. "Doesn't mean I wouldn't keep an eye on her, though. If they're interested in what she's up to, they'll watch her." His eyes crinkled into a smile that stopped me in my tracks. "Maybe I'll get a chance to see her in action."

Chapter 26

As I predicted, Dizzy gave as good as she got in the interrogation room, and I left wondering how soon she'd start lobbying for a partnership. I'd always hoped she'd take after her mother and choose a nice safe career like teaching English or nursing babies or demonstrating floor polishers. I imagined her husband with a sense of humor and the self-confidence to appreciate her brains, but also somebody I could go to ballgames and drink beer with. I always had trouble imagining the part that came before—when she walked down the aisle in white satin and lace. But I figured it was early days yet, and I'd heard that puberty turned girls into boy-crazy teenagers faster than you could tip a Stetson. The way things were going, though, Dizzy seemed more likely to find a life companion at the shooting range than the country club.

I dropped her off at the house and exchanged a few words with Turk Rodriguez, who was parked out front. I'd asked him to keep an eye on the girls today to make sure there were no repercussions from the night before. I'd told him he didn't have to show up until eleven, which seemed fair since he'd been keeping an eye on Darrell Toohey until midnight.

"We're dealing with wise guys," I reminded him. "Don't ask me why, but we are."

He nodded. "I see anybody sweating too hard, I'll sing a little opera, see how they react."

"You know any opera?"

"What's to know?" Then he opened his mouth and sang, in a squeaky mezzo soprano, "Figaro! Figaro! Figaro!" I thought I heard the faint pops of porcelain crowns shattering three streets away.

"I was about to say don't take any risks," I said, rubbing my ear, "but it's too late."

His face was as impassive as a highway exit ramp.

"You see anything," I said, "call Danny or me. Or both of us."

He nodded. "Kid packing heat today?"

"Who told you about that?"

He shrugged.

Probably every tough guy in the Houston Metropolitan Area, not to mention a few guys who weren't so tough, knew by now that my kid had saved my ass by getting the drop on a couple of mob enforcers last night. That was okay. It would give her an extensive fan club, which meant extra protection. There might be some locals who would be glad to shut her up, especially if they'd ever spent five minutes in a room with her, but Texans don't cotton to outsiders horning in on their show. If the mob tried to recommence operations on the Texas Gulf Coast, they wouldn't find anybody willing to hand them the keys to the city.

I was on my way to the office when I remembered Dizzy's fingerprints. And since I was beginning to have questions of my own about the wreck of the Texas Chief, I made a detour.

Irving Handy was Houston's answer to Sherlock Holmes. He worked out of an expanded garage behind his small house in The Heights. It had a lab upstairs and an area downstairs that was heavily populated by tall wooden tables, bright lights, and rows of boxes and file cabinets. Irv was known for his accuracy and his incorruptibility. Sometimes he testified for the prosecution, and sometimes for the defense, but his evidence never changed, no matter who was paying him. He had a tanned and weathered face in spite of his hours in the lab, but on the stand his wire-rimmed glasses gave him a scholarly air in spite of the white Stetson he set carefully on his knees. He was not a tall man, but he cast a long shadow.

He took the pictures to a workbench—the one of Barbie's behind and the one from a bottle of hair tonic—and fitted his eyeglass temples around his ears. "Polaroids," he said noncommittally as he studied them under the light. He made no comment on Barbie's anatomy, but I figured he was used to looking at stranger things.

"Not good enough?" I asked.

"Depends what you want 'em for." He reached for a magnifying glass.

"They don't have to stand up in court. At least, I hope they don't."

"Well, you got lucky. Feller who did the enlargements knew what he was doing. Ain't bad for Polaroids."

I didn't tell him that as far as I knew, the enlargements had been made by a female ninth grader.

"Could be better, though," he said, and tilted his head back to find the right focus.

"I just want your opinion," I said.

He looked at me over his glasses. "Would that be my professional opinion or an educated guess?" He turned back to the photographs. "'Cause if you want my professional opinion, that's going to take a few days and cost you more than a six-pack of Lone Star."

"How about you give me your educated guess and I'll decide if I want to raise the stakes?" I knew that there would be many more steps between a guess and verified evidence, and that these steps would involve further enlargements and meticulous measurements. But Handy's trained eye would be pretty accurate without all the rest of it.

"I'm assuming that the two sources bear some kind of relationship that make you think they were handled by the same person," he said.

I nodded.

He handed the photographs back. "Look the same to me."

I studied his face. "And if I paid you more for your professional opinion, would you expect that verdict to change?"

"Can't say that I would. But you never know."

I saluted him with the photos. "How about I leave you some beer money, return these to their owners, and await developments?"

"Suits me," he said. "I ain't settin' around twiddlin' my thumbs."

I flipped a coin and ended up taking a quick detour home to return the photos to Dizzy and tell her what Irv Handy had said, but I didn't hang around to shoot the breeze. I went to my office to check my answering machine. Sly Halsey was sitting on Moline Bridgeman at a pinball parlor on Preston Avenue. I drove down there and wandered in. As soon as my eyes adjusted to the light, I spotted Bridgeman playing a game against the right-hand wall. He was wearing a hat, maybe to cover the hack job his barber had done on him, but it looked like his jacket had been stowed on top of the game next to him. He wore brown trousers, a white shirt with rolled shirtsleeves, and brown suspenders. I spotted Sly playing a game farther up the aisle, facing away from Bridgeman. After a minute, Sly glanced in the direction of the door, then went back to his game.

I made a slow tour of the place as if I was picking my game. Bridgeman was playing a game called "Kewpie Doll." Sly was playing "Straight Shooter," a game featuring a blond babe in a cowgirl outfit astride a white horse, holding a smoking six-shooter.

"Glad you're here, man," Sly said in a low voice. "I'm fixing to die of boredom. He been in here more than an hour, and he still going strong." He shook his head. "Don't know how he do it." He flipped his flipper and missed the ball, which dribbled down the side and out of play. "And another thing." He fished into his pocket, which jingled. He brought out a quarter. "Somebody gonna owe me a shitload of expenses." He slid the quarter into the slot.

"I hope Leda Wardlow has deep pocketbooks," I said. "But I don't know what you're squawking about." I pointed to the backbox. "Looks like you've made thirty thousand."

"Naw, but I spent two million, though," he said.

My gaze shifted to Bridgeman, who seemed so absorbed in his game I didn't think he'd look up if the Kilgore Rangerettes came high-kicking through the front door. Sly's own play didn't make enough noise to drown out a caterpillar's whisper, but Bridgeman's machine pinged and dinged and whirred and popped, and two other customers more skillful than Sly were adding to the concert.

I nodded in Bridgeman's direction. "He have any visitors?"

"Uh-uh, just him and his kewpie doll."

"You want to take off?"

"Wouldn't mind. How you make out at the cop shop, you and the amazon?"

"Okay," I said. "Tell you about it later."

He glanced at my face. "Well, I sure hope the other guys look worse than you do. That ain't no mouse you got there, it's a full-grown rat."

I touched my cheek. "The other guy looks worse. Maybe lost some fingers."

He stopped playing. "She shot his fingers off?"

"She was aiming for the gun in his hand," I said. "Or maybe his forehead. I'm not sure."

After Sly left, Bridgeman and I spent another half hour playing pinball before he decided it was time for lunch. Once he was sitting in a diner, I went back to the car for a change of clothes. I pulled on a short-sleeved shirt and suspenders, set a white fedora on my head and a pair of sunglasses on my nose, and draped a seersucker jacket across my arm. I had a small camera in my pocket, one that I could palm if I needed to. I settled on a bench at a nearby bus stop to watch the diner and listened to my stomach growl while he fed his face. Afterward we caught a bus for the short ride to Busch Stadium, where the Buffs were playing an afternoon game against Denver. I sat three rows behind Bridgeman and had a swell afternoon, but if anybody passed him a coded message along with his Cracker Jacks and beer, I didn't see it.

I kept him in sight as we left the stadium but before we got to the bus stop, he bumped shoulders with a young colored kid who fell into step with him. The kid was a junior fashion plate, in pale yellow pants, a short-sleeved white shirt with a wide yellow tie, and an open vest in a black and yellow weave. He was light-skinned, with pale freckles and a ginger cast to his wavy hair. Bridgeman hardly seemed to be listening to him, but the kid radiated anxiety like a luminescent jellyfish. His arms and legs were in constant motion, and he kept looking around. I saw Bridgeman nod once, and then he passed the kid an envelope like an Olympic relay runner passing the baton—so smooth that I wouldn't have seen it if I hadn't been watching for it. The kid took off.

While Bridgeman ate dinner in a Mexican restaurant around the corner from the previous night's diner, I collected my car and called Danny on the Motrac.

"Hey, boss," he said, "I'm having a swell time. I'm looking forward to an exciting evening of watching the glow in Toohey's windows while he watches *Donna Reed*, *The Real McCoys*, and *My Three Sons*."

"You seen anything?" I said.

"Not a thing," he said. "Toohey could be an Eagle Scout an' I couldn't prove he wasn't."

"Okay," I said. "I've seen enough to think Bridgeman is our man. Why don't you go get some dinner and I'll talk to you after?"

"Diez-cuatro, hombre," he said. "Over and out."

Once I had my car in position again, I took a chance and crossed the street to a laundromat to use the phone. First I called Sly and told him what I'd seen. He whistled.

"This Progressive Youth Association that's behind the protests," I said. "Would you recognize a member if you saw him?"

"Naw, the only one I know for sure is Juney," he said. "And maybe the leader—cat name of Eldrewey Stearns. I've seen pictures of him. 'Course, he didn't look so good after the HPD got hold of him, but I think I'd recognize him. He's a little older than the others."

"This kid looks pretty young. Anyway, I don't think it's the leader we're after. I'm not that cynical."

He let that pass. "You want company?" he asked.

"I got no objection. But I don't guarantee any action tonight."

"We could still have fun."

Dizzy – July 6, 1961

Chapter 27

Harry showed up with our photographs right before lunch and gave me the news that his expert considered the prints a match. I knew he was secretly pleased that I was taking an interest in his profession, though he would never admit that.

After lunch, we went to see Sissy and Mrs. Heffelman. We asked to see Sissy first because we all agreed that we needed her permission to speak to her mother. Sissy was our client, after all, and we had to respect her wishes. We didn't want to talk to Sissy over the phone because we weren't sure she'd understand what we were asking and why.

Mrs. Heffelman came to the door wearing a light blue shirtwaist and a striped apron she was wiping her hands on. The apron had a heart stitched on it in wobbly red stitches and inside the heart a little handprint made with red paint and inside that the word "Mother" printed in crooked letters with Magic Marker. She was blond like Sissy, with flyaway curls and a dollbaby face and a little red Tiny Tears mouth. We asked for Sissy, and when she came to the door we asked her to come outside with us. There was a white wrought iron bench by the sidewalk and B.D. sat down on the bench with Sissy while Mel and I sat cross-legged in the grass. Turk was parked in front of the house and I gave him the high sign.

Sissy got right to business. "Did you find my daddy?"

"No, sugar," B.D. said. "We're still not for certain he's alive. But we need to talk to your mama now and maybe go through some of your daddy's things."

Sissy scanned our faces, frowning. "Didn't you look for him?"

"We did," I said. "We've talked to several people who knew him and saw him on the train. We haven't found anybody who saw him after the accident." I didn't add, "Except the guys in the funeral parlor who laid him out," partly because I didn't know if I believed that anymore.

"Would it be all right if we talked to your mama now?" B.D. asked.

Sissy's pouty lips said that she was considering firing us and looking for a more competent team of investigators.

"Everybody thinks he's dead except you," Mel said bluntly. "A good investigation takes time, especially when everybody already thinks they know what happened."

She chewed on the end of a pigtail and thought some more. "Okay," she said finally. "You can talk to her. But it won't do any good 'cause Mama thinks he's dead, too."

Meaning that maybe, just maybe, Mama's too satisfied with the life insurance money to want to dig up her dead husband?

Mrs. Heffelman could have modeled for a laundry detergent or floor wax ad, and as if to prove it, she was mopping the kitchen floor when Sissy took us into the house. She blinked her big eyes at us, looking a little skeptical. We didn't look much like Sissy's usual playmates.

There was no sign of Tommy, Sissy's brother, but since he was almost Hal's age, he probably had better things to do than hang around the house while his mother waxed the floor.

B.D. suggested we sit down at the dinette for a chat. The floor was pale yellow linoleum and the cabinets were all painted aqua and the wallpaper was yellow and aqua with bowls and spoons and beaters on it. The curtains were aqua with little yellow circles that could have been flowers. Some of Sissy's artwork was taped to the refrigerator. On the stove was a pan covered with aluminum foil that could have been a roast judging from the hump in the middle. There was a strong smell of Mr. Clean, as if she'd poured half the bottle into her bucket. I glanced at Mel and saw her nose twitching.

We each took a chair. I sat in the daddy chair, which meant I had armrests to grip if the going got rough and I had to restrain myself. Sissy perched on a stool.

B.D. explained about Sissy's visit to the Lost and Found, and the job she'd hired us to do. Mrs. Heffelman stared at her as if she was speaking Swahili. Then her eyes shifted to Sissy and she frowned, but she wasn't frowning at Sissy, she was just thinking. Her hands were folded on the table in front of her.

"My husband is dead," she said. "I know she doesn't accept that, even though I took her out to Woodlawn to see the grave. I don't think you girls should be encouraging her."

"We didn't intend to do that." B.D. raised a hand for emphasis. "We surely didn't. We thought we could help you convince Sissy is all. But we've found some things we can't explain." She let that hang in the air, where it fought with Mr. Clean to make an impression.

"What do you mean?" Mrs. Heffelman said. "What kinds of things?"

"Maybe you could tell us first how you recognized your husband when you identified him for the police," Mel said. "Did you see his face?"

Her eyes opened wide as she shifted her attention to Mel. "No," she said quickly, and swallowed. "No, I couldn't do that. I—." She glanced at her daughter. "He was very badly injured." Her voice quavered.

Mel persisted. "So how did you recognize him?"

She looked baffled. "I know my own husband."

"Did you look for moles or birthmarks or old scars you knew about?" I asked.

You could tell that she thought we were ganging up on her, and it flustered her. "No. No. Why would I do that? He was—." She pressed her lips together and crinkled her forehead. Then she repeated, "He was very badly injured, and I don't think we should be discussing this in front of—."

"The police told you that it was your husband," I said, "and you didn't have any reason to question that."

"Well, of course it was my husband. He was the right size, and—."

"Your husband was unusually tall, maybe," I said, "or fat or thin or—?"

"No, of course not. He was about average height and build."

"Uh-huh." I let it sink in.

She gripped the edge of the table and leaned forward. "It wasn't just that, though. He was wearing Leo's clothes—his jacket. And he was wearing Leo's wedding ring and watch and signet."

"Okay," I said, "so you recognized the jacket, shirt, pants and tie?"

"I said I recognized the jacket. And the tie was one Tommy gave him last Father's Day."

"And the shirt and pants?"

"I didn't notice. They were just ordinary—brown pants and a white shirt, that's all. Anyway, Leo generally bought his own clothes. He was particular, being a salesman and all, and sometimes he bought clothes while he was traveling."

"So you wouldn't necessarily recognize everything he had on," Mel said.

We were all thinking the same thing. If you wanted to dress somebody up to look like Leo Heffelman, and you didn't have a lot of time to do it in, you'd pick the things that were easiest to put on a dead person—jacket, tie, and jewelry. And then you might cross your fingers and hope that nobody wanted to take a good long squint at the bloody stiff.

"No, but this is just crazy," she said. "I don't know why you girls are asking all these questions, but it's not very nice. Anyway, it was my husband I saw. I don't understand about the things you say aren't right. What things?"

"Sissy brought us the doll she received in the mail," B.D. said.

Mrs. Heffelman sighed. "I know what she thinks, but it just isn't true. Her father did not send her that doll." She folded her hands on the table again.

"Do you know who did?" Mel asked.

"No," she said, looking down at her hands. "But it could have been anybody. Anybody could hear about a little girl who lost her father just a few weeks before her birthday and decide to do something nice for her."

"It was mailed from Topeka," I said. "Plus, we fingerprinted the doll. It has his fingerprint on it."

"You what?" She stared at me.

"Dizzy's father is a detective," B.D. said, "so we checked the doll for fingerprints."

"The only one besides Sissy's was your husband's," Mel said.

It took her a minute to process, then she turned to Sissy and said, "Darlin', I think you best go to your room and play while I talk to the girls."

But Sissy was not to be diverted from her mission. She leaped from her stool and stood defiant. "They're *my* girls," she said. "I hired 'em."

"She's right," I said. "She's our client. We're having this conversation on her terms."

Mrs. Heffelman put her hands to her cheeks and shook her head. "This is just crazy. I don't know what y'all are talking about. Sissy can't hire anybody, she's seven. You're too young to be hired. I don't know why you're talking about fingerprints. My husband is dead."

B.D., ever patient, tried a new tack. "You understand about fingerprints, don't you? Everybody's fingerprints are unique. You know that, right? That's one way police detectives solve crimes. They match up fingerprints."

"Yes, of course, but what does that have to do with my husband?" She seemed to have given up on sending Sissy to her room, who, pleased with this, settled back onto her stool with a smug look that boded ill for the future of discipline in the Heffelman household.

"We dusted the doll for fingerprints," B.D. said. "We asked Sissy to bring us some things that belonged to you and Mr. Heffelman so that we'd have your prints and your husband's for comparison."

"And mine," Sissy said, holding up her hands to demonstrate. "They made mine, Mama, with ink."

"That's right," B.D. continued. "And we found your husband's fingerprint on the doll."

"Barbie wasn't wearing the bathing suit she came in," Mel said. "She was wearing the Enchanted Evening ensemble—that's one of the most expensive outfits they sell. Somebody had to buy that outfit and change her clothes before they sent her to Sissy. It would make sense for the fingerprint to belong to the person who changed her clothes."

"Look," she said, smoothing her apron over her lap, "maybe y'all mean to be helpful, but you're not experts. And I have work to do."

"We know we're not experts," B. D. said soothingly. "That's why Dizzy's father took the prints to a fingerprint expert—someone who studies fingerprints and testifies about them in court."

She had started to rise but she sat back down and turned her eyes on me. "Your father? You told your father about this?"

I couldn't tell whether she knew who my father was or not, but I could tell that she was heating up.

"My father knows a fingerprint expert," I said, "and we needed an expert opinion. So I asked my dad to show the two fingerprints—the one from your husband's hair tonic and the one from the Barbie doll—to Mr. Handy. He thinks they're a match."

"And so people are talking about this?" she said indignantly. "About whether my husband is really dead or not?"

"No, ma'am," B. D. reassured her. "Mr. Lark hasn't talked to anybody except Mr. Handy, and Mr. Handy didn't know whose fingerprints he was looking at. We haven't talked to anybody."

She left Digger out of this account, but it was just as well.

"Well, I still say it's none of y'all's business," she said. "Or anybody else's."

"Yes, ma'am," B.D. said, "we can understand why you feel that way. When Sissy first came to see us, we thought we could help you convince her that your husband was dead. But then we started asking questions—not just about the fingerprints, I mean, but other questions, too."

"What questions?" She was still steamed, and I couldn't blame her. In her place, I would've given us the bum's rush.

B.D. shrugged. "Just different kinds of questions about your husband on the train. We can't find anybody who saw him after the accident, or right before."

"Well, of course you won't find anybody who saw him after the accident," she said. Now she was blinking back tears. "He was—." She glanced at Sissy, then away. "He was lying on the ground."

"Mrs. Heffelman, exactly when did Mr. Heffelman take out the life insurance policy?" I said, and earned a dirty look from B.D. "We heard it was a big policy, worth a lot of money."

She turned on me. "Now, why would you want to know a thing like that?"

"We're interested in any changes in Mr. Heffelman's behavior in the period before the accident," I said. "Did you notice anything?"

The new question deflected her attention from the life insurance and gave her something else to think about. "I certainly didn't! Everything was the same as always. This trip—it was just like all the others. There wasn't anything to notice."

I nodded as if she'd just given us valuable information. I didn't expect her to tell us anything useful, like that he'd been getting phone calls in the middle of the night or withdrawn enough money from their savings to finance a trip to Tahiti. I just wanted to plant a seed of doubt in her own mind.

"Would you be willing to show us his things?" B.D. asked. She was using the kind of voice they must use with the bereaved in the funeral home, whispery like in church.

You could see Mrs. H. turning things over now. To look at her, I didn't guess that thinking came naturally to her and the pressure of all those ideas was a new sensation, and not an especially welcome one. If I'd previously entertained any theories about whether Mrs. Heffelman was a shill in some elaborate scheme of Mr. Heffelman's to defraud the insurance company, I'd given it up by now. She might be left holding the swag, but I doubted she had the moxie—and she definitely didn't have the brains—to be in on the con.

"His things?" she echoed, frowning.

"Do you have any of the clothes he was wearing when the accident happened?" Mel said.

She flinched. "Oh, no, I don't have anything like that. They—the funeral home—they—well, they disposed of the things he was wearing at the time. The only thing I have is his shoes."

"But you have other clothes," Mel said. "Other clothes he took with him? Did they give you back his suitcase?"

She shuddered. "I haven't touched it."

"Maybe you could let us see that," B.D. said gently. "We wouldn't bother anything. We'd be real respectful."

She seemed to be making up her mind. "If I do, will you leave afterward and stop talking about this to Sissy?"

"Yes, ma'am," B.D. promised. I tried to keep my face expressionless.

"Well, I don't think I should encourage you."

But to my surprise, she led us to their bedroom. It had pale green walls, a heavy blond bedroom suite and dark green carpet. It smelled of lemon Pledge. She slid open the closet door. She pointed to the back corner, where a battered brown houndstooth suitcase lay huddled against the wall. It had several big dents in it. One wooden corner and a wooden reinforcing strap were scorched, and all of the wooden reinforcing corners were split, but it was closed.

"Was it like that when you got it?" I asked. If so, I'd check the brand so that the next time Harry needed luggage that could survive a train wreck, he'd be prepared.

"Yes," she said. "It's still locked. The key was in his pocket."

She handed over the key and turned to leave the room. Her look said that she didn't want to watch while the buzzards picked the bones.

"Are those the shoes?" I asked.

She nodded and left. We managed to shut the door against Sissy by telling her that we didn't want her to contaminate a potential crime scene, and she didn't know enough to argue. But I was pretty sure her elephant ears were glued to the door.

We all put on our white gloves. I examined the shoes while Mel and B.D. opened the suitcase. Men's shoes mostly look alike to me, and these were no exception. They were brown lace-ups, nicely shined, with no bloodstains that I could see. They even smelled of shoe polish. I looked inside, but I didn't find any claim checks hidden in the bottoms that could lead us to a secret stash at the Chicago train station. I turned them over. Somebody had scrawled on the bottoms in pencil: U13.

"Hey," I said, and my own voice sounded hoarse to me. "Hey, you guys."

They turned to look at me and I held up the shoes, soles out.

"What's that say?" B.D. said, squinting.

"It says 'U13,'" Mel said. Then her mouth dropped open.

"U13," B.D. repeated, thinking. "U13. What does it mean?"

"It means," Mel said slowly, "that a porter—Mr. Petry or the guy he replaced—shined these shoes and made a note on the bottom so he knew which passenger to return them to." She leaned forward and sniffed. "You can still smell the shoe polish."

"It means," I said, "that these shoes didn't belong to Mr. Heffelman at all. They belonged to the man in Upper Thirteen."

"The guy with the briefcase," Mel said.

Chapter 28

"Gee, whiz!" B.D. said.

"Let's see what you found in the suitcase," I said.

As if she was pulling a rabbit out of a hat, Mel reached in and pulled out a wad of cash.

We stared at it.

"Did you count it?" I asked.

"Not yet," she said. "I found it just before you showed us the shoes."

She began counting it out and laying down stacks on the green carpet. The bills were all sawbucks.

"Five hundred," she said when she finished.

"That's a lot of dough to be carrying around in a suitcase," I said.

"It was folded inside his socks," Mel said.

"Shoot! I never find the good stuff," B.D. said. "Let's see if there's anything else hidden in there." She slid her hands into one of the suitcase side pockets.

Mel and I watched her search. If there was anything left to find, she deserved to find it—and she did. The first thing she found was a claim check from a neighborhood laundry.

"Better give that to Mrs. Heffelman," I said, "in case there's still something to pick up."

But the next item was more interesting. I gave her credit for taking another look at the socks where the money had been hidden. I wouldn't have thought of it.

"There's something else here in the bottom." She produced another small rectangle of cardboard. She studied it. "It's another claim check. It's from the Union Pacific Station in Topeka, Kansas."

We looked at each other.

"Do we give this one to Mrs. Heffelman?" Mel asked.

"It's probably just a suitcase full of cleaning products," I said.

"Or Barbie clothes?" B.D. said.

"Or cash," Mel said.

"Tell you what," B.D. said. "We can't any of us head out to Topeka any time soon." She slipped the ticket back into the sock. "And Mrs. Heffelman isn't about to throw this suitcase away any time soon. So we put it back where we found it."

"I'd give anything to know what he checked," Mel said wistfully.

"Well, *we're* not going to Topeka any time soon," I said, "but we know some people who are."

"The porters?" B.D. said. She was still holding the sock. "Do you think one of them will pick it up for us, whatever it is?"

"Probably not," I admitted. "Technically, it would be theft, and they're all pretty sensitive about that. We don't want to get them in trouble. Maybe Harry has a contact there. I'll ask."

B.D. put the sock back in the suitcase.

"So what do we think about the cash?" Mel riffled the stack.

"We have to give that to Mrs. Heffelman, too," B.D. said.

"I know that," Mel said. "I mean, why did he have it? Is it normal to travel with that much cash?"

We looked at each other. None of us had ever traveled anywhere on our own. If we went out of the neighborhood without our parents, we were supposed to stash a dime in our shoes, but half a grand seemed like a lot of dimes, even if you were going all the way to Chicago and back.

"Maybe he made some sales along the way," B.D. said.

"All in tens?" Mel said skeptically.

"Maybe he sold something that cost ten dollars," B.D. suggested.

After we all thought for a while, Mel said, "Y'all realize this blows a hole in our theory that he might have done a bunk. He wouldn't have walked away and left this kind of money behind."

"Unless," I said.

"Unless what?" B.D. said.

"Unless he happened across something so valuable that he could afford to leave it behind."

"You mean like a briefcase full of jewels? Or cash?" B.D. said.

"Something like that, yeah."

"So what are you thinking, Diz?" Mel said. "That after the train wreck he woke up on top of the man with the briefcase? And he just took it? How did he know there was anything in it?"

"I don't know," I said. "He might've figured that anything that was chained to a guy's wrist must be valuable, but I doubt it. That doesn't feel right. If he did what we're thinking, he had to dress the briefcase stiff in his own jacket, tie his own tie around the dead guy's neck, and put his rings and watch on the guy. I don't think he'd do that on a gamble that the briefcase was worth more than five C's."

"Back up." B.D. held up one hand. "If the briefcase was chained to the guy's wrist, how did he get it off? Or are you thinking maybe the dead guy lost his arm or his hand in the wreck?"

"In which case Mr. Heffelman walked away with an arm under his arm?" Mel said. "Doesn't seem likely. Creepy, too."

I shrugged. "Maybe the chain broke. Or maybe the briefcase popped open. I'll bet most of the luggage on that train looked a lot worse than Mr. H's bag after the wreck."

"But if the stiff still had a chain around his wrist," B.D. said, "they would've known it wasn't Mr. Heffelman."

"Nobody's given us specifics about the condition of the body they buried," Mel said speculatively. "You think we should ask Mrs. Heffelman if it was missing an arm?"

"Don't you dare!" B.D. said, horrified.

"We'll ask Digger," I said. "He should know."

B.D. sighed. "It surely would be helpful if Mr. Petry could remember the name of the passenger in Upper Thirteen. Then we could check the newspaper again to see if he was listed as dead."

"What now?" Mel said.

"Let's show the cash and the shoes to Mrs. Heffelman," I said, "and see how she reacts."

Sissy was sitting on the floor in the hall when we came out and we told her we had to talk to her mother again, so she tailed us.

Mrs. H. was in the kitchen, gloved up and armed with a can of oven cleaner that made us keep our distance. There were newspapers spread out on the floor under the oven.

I asked about her husband's shoe size.

"Nine and a half," she said without hesitation. "Why?"

I held up the shoes. "These are size eights."

She blinked. "They can't be."

I held a shoe for her to see the size stamped inside. She set down the oven cleaner. To her credit, she didn't try to explain it away, didn't try to tell us that a man with big feet taking a train ride that would cause those feet to swell might choose to wear shoes a size and a half too small for him. She was baffled, and she didn't try to hide it. "What are you saying?"

"It's possible somebody returned the wrong pair of shoes to you," I said reasonably. "There was probably a lot of confusion at the scene. It's probably just a mistake. If not—." I let it hang.

"We found some other things we thought you might want," Mel said. The first hand she brought out from behind her back held the laundry ticket. She handed it over without comment. Mrs. Heffelman barely glanced at it before tucking it into her apron pocket. When Mel brought out the wad of dough, her eyes widened. She looked as though we'd slapped her in the face with a mackerel.

"There's five hundred dollars here." Mel held it out to her.

She cradled it in her Playtex gloves as if it was a newborn baby. She looked up at us. "I don't understand."

"I found it tucked inside one of his socks," Mel said.

"Five hundred dollars?" she repeated.

"Yes, ma'am," Mel said.

"Did your husband usually travel with that much cash, Mrs.

Heffelman?" I asked, though the answer was written all over her face.

"No, I—I don't think so," she said. "We didn't—that's a lot of money."

"Maybe you'd like to sit down," B.D. said gently.

We resumed our seats at the table. My plan was to skip before she got the Easy-Off uncapped.

"It surprises you that your husband traveled with this much cash," B.D. summarized.

"Yes," she whispered. "We don't have that kind of money. And anyway," she said, looking up, "traveler's checks are safer." When we didn't say anything, she added, "Leo—my husband—was a cautious man."

"I have a question," I said, which earned me a warning look from B.D. "When you identified your husband's body, did you notice any marks on his wrists?"

"On his wrists?" she said. "I didn't look at his wrists. Why would I?"

"I just wondered," I said. Another question for Digger: if the body they'd buried had two intact arms, were there any marks on one wrist where a cuff had rubbed the skin raw? It was possible the cuff had been padded—I would've made sure of that if it had been me—but if not, it might have left a mark.

Mrs. Heffelman's eyes teared up. She leaned forward and put her face between her hands. "I don't understand any of this," she whispered.

Sissy jumped down off her stool, went to her mother, and patted her back. "It's okay, Mama."

I was pretty sure now that it wouldn't be okay, and I wondered if Sissy was beginning to regret she'd ever hired us.

"Mrs. Heffelman," I said, "we need to ask you again whether you noticed any recent changes in your husband."

B.D. spotted a box of Kleenex on the kitchen counter and set it in front of her. Mrs. Heffelman took a few and dabbed at her eyes.

"He was worried about money," she said. "We—we were always

short on money. But I suppose we'd been having more—disagreements—than usual. He'd fly off the handle over the least little thing, like if I had my hair done or took the kids to the picture show or made steak for dinner. He'd say, 'You're not Mrs. Midas!' But it wasn't like that, honestly." She looked at us and I could see she was winding up to argue her case again. "I was always careful about money. But you've got to live a little, everybody's got to live a little."

"Sure," I said by way of encouragement. "Everybody."

"It's like he was afraid of something all the time," she said. "I'd say, 'What are you afraid of? You've got a good job. We don't live high off the hog.'"

"Did he ever get any unusual phone calls?" I asked. "Or visitors you didn't know?"

She frowned. "There were phone calls about work. He was always on the phone. It seems like maybe there were one or two calls that upset him. I don't know why, he didn't talk much about his business. I—I even wondered whether there was something wrong at work. But he was a very good salesman."

"Did you keep track of the family finances?" I asked. "Would you have noticed a five hundred dollar withdrawal?"

This turned on the waterworks again. "I've never paid attention," she said. "I've never had to. Leo took care of all that. Now my brother says he'll help, but he says I'll have to learn how to do it all myself—balance our checkbook, pay the bills. I don't know anything about that."

Mel said, "Maybe I can help you out sometimes." She was the only math whiz among us. If I offered to help, Mrs. Heffelman would cry harder if she knew what was good for her.

She was blowing her nose, but when Mel said this, she dropped her hands in her lap and gave Mel a melty look. "Oh," she said, "that's so sweet! Thank you."

We beat it because there was nothing left to say except what we couldn't bring ourselves to say: maybe it was time for somebody to dig up her husband's grave and find out who was buried in there.

Chapter 29

Turk was still sitting in the car out front, but he wasn't alone. As soon as I saw that, I put out an arm to restrain the others.

"Don't look now," I said, "but Turk's got company. Could be it's unwelcome company. So just in case, I'm going to say goodbye and head back the way we came. Y'all need to find out what's going on, and who's holding the heat, if there is any. If you see anything wrong, give me a sign."

I put some distance between us without ever glancing in Turk's direction. I rounded the corner of a neighbor's house across the street, then crouched down and looked back. The girls were approaching the car, one on either side. That was smart, dividing up the potential targets, and I thought they'd probably picked it up from watching Westerns. They talked for a minute, and then B.D. turned in my direction and waved me in.

I approached Turk's window. He said, "Dizzy, you know this bird?"

Turk had the drop on his pal, I was glad to see, so I leaned in, propped my elbows on the window frame, and copped a look.

"Hey, there, Mr. Bove," I said. "How's your hand?"

"It hurts like hell, you want to know," Bignose said. He held it up so I could see that it was the size of a kickball, with all the bandages wrapped around it.

"Maybe you should consider another line of work," I said.

He scowled at me. "You shouldn't ought to go around shooting people. It ain't nice."

"You want I should hold him?" Turk asked. "Maybe give your old man another go at him?"

I thought about it. On the one hand, I was pretty sure Harry would like a piece of him. On the other, Harry was pretty sure that he and his partner were wise guys, so it was better not to stir them up unless we wanted to take the heat. More important, I didn't want them to think we were up to anything suspicious. I sure didn't want to sic them on Sissy and Mrs. Heffelman, especially now that the briefcase man had popped up in the middle of our case. Bignose and Flatface were looking for a briefcase, and according to Harry, they were the second wave of thugs to come looking for it. Now they knew we had protection—that was the important thing.

I'd probably already blown my cover with this stiff, but maybe I could still con him into thinking we led such boring little-girl lives that he would give up and go tail someone else.

I shrugged. "It's no skin off my heinie if he wants to follow us around all day," I said. I was glad now that we'd left the shoes in the closet. "Maybe he wants to help us look for lost merchandise. Or maybe he's in the market for something—baseball cards or matchbox cars or jacks for his little girl." I couldn't resist. "We don't have any spare fingers in stock, though."

"Cut him loose?" Turk said.

"Sure," I said. "Without his gun though, if he had one."

Turk's look said, what do you take me for? Then he nodded at Bignose and B.D. opened the door for him. He got out and strolled off down the street—Attila the Hun, stretching his legs on a walk through suburban Houston. I saw him fish a handkerchief out of his pocket and wipe the back of his neck with it, angling his head up at the sun.

"Is he a real, honest-to-God Mafia hit man?" B.D. said with awe in her voice. She was hugging herself. Even Mel looked a little pale.

"He's not a hit man," Turk said. "They don't waste that kind of talent tailing kids."

"You mean when they take out the contract on us and arrange the hit, they send for the professionals," she said.

Turk grinned at her. He didn't smile very often, so when he did, it was like a full moon you weren't expecting.

"No chance of that, kiddo," he said.

"How do you know?"

"I know," he said. Turk didn't waste words like he didn't waste smiles, and when he said something, you believed it.

We didn't actually go hunting, like I told Bignose, because Mel thought we needed to go back and tend the store. They opened shop while I put in a call to Mr. Boudet to ask about the shoes.

"We're only supposed to take one pair at a time when we shine shoes," he said. "That's what the rules say. But everybody breaks that one. You don't want to be running back and forth all the time, so you pick up all the shoes that need to be shined and take your pencil and write down the berth number on the bottom. The passengers don't care."

"So if we find a pair of shoes with 'U13' written on the bottom," I said, "we can assume they belonged to the passenger in Upper 13?"

"That's right," he said.

I thanked him and hung up. I'd have to track down Arthur Petry's phone number through Rose, or maybe put Harry on it, since Mr. Boudet didn't know him.

I finally tracked down Digger at his friend Brian's house. I had to pry the information out of him.

"I don't think I should be telling you this stuff, Diz," he said. "It ain't right."

"Just tell me if Mr. Heffelman was wearing shoes when he came in, and if he had two complete arms with hands attached," I said. "Come on, Digger. I'll save the best baseball cards for you."

There was a sigh on the other end. "Okay, he was wearing shoes—the same ones we gave to Mrs. Heffelman. And the answer to the other question is no," he said. "That's all I'm going to tell you."

"Was there anything attached to an arm?" I said. "I mean—."

"That's all I'm going to tell you, Diz," he said, and hung up.

Out in the garage Loretta Newman was trying to trade her

sister's lipstick and eyeliner for a pair of sunglasses she'd dropped on the sidewalk in front of the Dad's Club Y.

"Come on, B.D.," she said. "Y'all ain't even supposed to pick things up at the Dad's Club. Anything we lose there is supposed to go in the Dad's Club lost and found." She was wearing a tee shirt over her bathing suit and thong sandals. She was carrying a towel. She'd probably just come from the lost and found in question.

She had a point, so we gave her the sunglasses.

"And if Lorraine comes looking for her makeup," she said as she slipped the sunglasses on, "you didn't get it from me."

"Silence unto death," B.D. said, and we all held up our hands like we were taking the Girl Scout pledge. But Lorraine was sixteen and I was pretty sure we weren't on her radar.

I filled them in on what Mr. Boudet had said.

"It could have been a mistake," Mel said, "just like B.D. said. Somebody found the shoes and put them on the wrong body. Maybe they didn't notice that the shoes didn't fit, or maybe they just didn't care. Lots of stuff probably got mixed up after the wreck."

"Sure," I said. "It could happen. And p.s., Digger says that Mr. Heffelman didn't have two complete arms."

"What's that supposed to mean?" Mel said.

"Don't know," I said. "He wouldn't say anything more."

I brought out the Barbie doll in her shoe box coffin and looked at her. We'd made her a sarong out of Kleenex to preserve the fingerprint and then wrapped her neck to toe in Saran Wrap like a mummy.

"Too bad she can't talk," B.D. said.

I nodded. "Too bad we can't give her the third degree."

I held her in both my hands and shook her. In my tough-guy voice, I said, "Give it up, toots. We know you're in on the con. You went to bat for him, okay, but the whole thing's gone too far. Time to squeal."

To my surprise, she rattled. I stopped shaking and stared at her. B.D. looked horrified, Mel, interested. I shook her again. We heard the faint but distinctive tap of something small and solid against plastic.

Lucille stood up on her hind legs, placed one paw delicately against my wrist, and sniffed Barbie's head. Then she sat back down wearing that superior expression cats always wear when they know something you don't. She wrapped her tail around her paws and half-closed her eyes.

"You broke Barbie," B.D. said.

"You ain't seen nothing yet," I said. I grasped her head in one hand, and looked at B.D. "If we had to find a replacement—one that looked just like this one—you could do it, right?"

She swallowed. "Well, yes. But it wouldn't be the same, Diz, you know it wouldn't."

"Then we'll take her to the doll hospital," I said, and yanked.

Barbie's head popped off in my hand and something small and shiny hit the footlocker and rolled till it bumped against Lucille's paw. Startled, Lucille raised her paw. I took advantage of her surprise to snatch the thing before she could take a whack at it and send it sailing across the garage.

"What is it?" Mel said. They both leaned in.

I opened my palm to show a brilliant light, like Tinkerbell. It was a small cut stone that sparkled even in the dull interior light of the garage.

B.D. gasped. "Is that what I think it is?"

"Wow!" Mel said. "Can I touch it?"

I held it out to her. "Be my guest. There might be more."

She took it between her thumb and forefinger and held it up for her and B.D. and Lucille to examine. I looked inside the doll's head. "We need tweezers," I said.

I went and got some from the medicine cabinet and then used them to pull a tail of tissue from inside the head while Mel held Lucille. As the tissue unwound, more stones tumbled out. Most were clear like the first one, but there were also a few green ones and red ones.

"How many?" Mel said, ever practical.

We all counted. "I got twelve," B.D. said.

"Same here," Mel said, and I nodded.

"Do you think they're real?" Mel asked. "I mean, they could be leftovers from some Barbie jewelry."

"I've seen a lot of Barbie jewelry," B.D. said, "and I've never seen anything like these before. Look at the way they sparkle! They must be diamonds."

"Son of a gun!" Mel said. "Upper 13 must have been a jeweler after all."

"They could be fake," I cautioned. I bent and sniffed one. "It smells plastic."

"But just look at them, y'all," B.D. said. "If those are fake, I'll eat 'em."

I picked one up, took it to the workbench, and picked up a glass jar filled with screws. I tried the diamond on the glass. "It cuts glass," I said. "But maybe even phonies would do that. Maybe we have to find something harder. Anybody ever seen emeralds or rubies before?"

Mel shook her head. B.D. said, "Not close up. Just in a jewelry store window." She shivered. "I sure am glad Mr. Rodriguez is on guard duty."

"Yeah," I said, "but I almost wish Bignose was here."

"Why on earth would you wish that?" B.D. said, raising her eyebrows at me.

"According to Harry, all the goons are looking for a briefcase full of cash. If they think we know where it is, they're barking up the wrong tree." I waved a hand at the glittering pile of jewels. "It's the wrong briefcase. We haven't found five hundred g-notes, but we have found ice. Mel's right. Upper Thirteen was a jeweler, not a mobster."

Harry – July 6, 1961

Chapter 30

All around me, washers churned, dryers made faint clicking sounds as their loads revolved, and women gossiped. I checked my watch. I figured Bridgeman was probably still eating, so I called home to check in and spoke to Dizzy.

"Juney's been trying to get hold of you," she said. "You got her number?"

I said I did.

"Also a Lieutenant Stubbs called. He's looking for you, too."

I grimaced. I didn't like cops calling a house that wasn't even my house anymore and talking to my kids.

When I tuned in again, she was saying, "We need to talk. I got something to show you. Are you coming home for dinner?"

"Not tonight," I said. "What've you got?"

"Not on the telephone," she said.

This made me smile. I could hear the excitement in her voice. Maybe Sissy Heffelman had received another doll in the mail, and this one had a fingerprint on her tit.

"It's about the briefcase," she said. "I think there were two."

"What do you mean?" I said.

"We'll talk about it when you get home," she said. I heard a voice in the background and then she said, "Rose wants to know if Turk is staying for dinner, and p.s., did it ever occur to you that having a strange car parked out front would freak us out more than being told that Turk was on guard duty?"

"Not really," I admitted. "Put him on, will you?"

She dropped the receiver on a hard surface and my hearing was just about restored to normal when Turk came on the line.

I asked him if he'd seen any trouble.

"Nothing I couldn't handle." He added that a bird with a bandaged hand had tailed the girls to the Heffelmans' house.

"Sounds like the Mafia muscle from last night," I said. "He do anything?"

"Could have been the muscle 'cause he sure wasn't the brains of nothing," Turk said, "unless the mob's getting pretty hard up. He mostly just tippy-toed around and hid in the bushes."

"He packing?"

"Not any more he ain't."

I felt the sweat pop out along my hairline and start making its way down to my jawline.

"Dizzy said to cut him loose, though, and I did what she said," he said. "Haven't seen him since."

I leaned my forehead against the cool plaster of the nearest wall. "Probably the right call."

"They just curious what she's up to, you think," he said.

"Probably so," I said.

"Might send a smarter guy next time."

"Might," I agreed. "Let me talk to her again."

I told Dizzy to tell Hal to stay close tonight. I heard her relay the message and heard him grumble something in protest on the other end.

"He wants to work on his soapbox racer over at Greg's house," she reported.

"Not tonight," I said.

I checked my watch again and decided to risk another phone call. I dropped a dime in the slot and called police headquarters. Stubbs was in his office and he picked up.

"Lark," he said. "Where the hell are you?"

"I'm sitting on Bridgeman, like I told you I would."

"Where?"

"Mexican restaurant on Capitol. It's a couple blocks from his house."

"Got anything for me?" he said.

"Nothing definite, but I'm pretty sure I saw him pay off a tipster earlier outside Busch Stadium."

"Yeah? Who was the tipster?"

"I can't go into it now," I said. "Like I said, I'm sitting on him, and I'm solo. He's liable to come out any minute and I don't want to lose him. I'll call you when I know more."

I hung up on his squawking. It was the usual problem—I had clients to protect and I didn't trust the HPD to do their own thinking. Maybe Stubbs had brains and maybe he didn't, but there was a good chance that if I mentioned a young negro he'd draw the wrong conclusion. On the other hand, I didn't want any more bombs going off on my watch, and there was also a good chance that if Stubbs got his mitts on the young negro in question he'd sweat the whole set-up out of him. Anyway the kid, whoever he was, was not my client.

I sat in the car, slick with sweat, eating a candy bar out of the laundromat machine and contemplating my life. Leaving the bombs aside, I still had problems. The Miami mob had a torpedo tailing my daughter and the ghee's low IQ was no consolation. I had to figure out how to get the wise guys off her back.

A tap on the passenger's side window startled me. Then Sly opened the door and slid in. He handed me a Whataburger bag stained with grease. When he closed the door, the scent of fried burger filled the car. If we'd been Italian, I could've kissed him without violating multiple sections of Texas statutory law.

I'd just finished inhaling the burger and fries when Bridgeman emerged, picking his teeth. We tailed him to his house and watched him go in.

It was about ten o'clock when Bridgeman came out again and headed for his car. He was wearing a trench coat and a fedora and carrying two shopping bags. He glanced around, but we were too far away to draw his attention, and we'd slouched down as soon as we'd spotted him. He wasn't really looking for us, anyway. He moved with the nonchalance of someone thoroughly acquainted with the HPD's manpower shortages.

"Don't like the look of the shopping bags," Sly said.

"Could be he's returning a couple shirts," I said.

Bridgeman got into a brown-and-white De Soto with a rear fender so crumpled it looked like it had been playing bumper cars with King Kong. I put the car in gear and we followed. He drove down Alabama. We were now in the Third Ward, headed toward South Central. He turned off onto a side street where most of the houses were tidy brick crackerboxes with an occasional eyesore mixed in.

"Texas Southern's around here, isn't it?" I asked Sly.

"Not too far," he said. "There's some student housing mixed in hereabouts."

Bridgeman cruised slowly, though he didn't appear to be rubbernecking. As we passed a house with a dim porch light on, I recognized two figures on a small front porch and cursed under my breath. Juney was sitting in a lawn chair talking with the yellow-vested kid, who was perched on the porch railing.

"That was Juney," Sly said, like I didn't know.

"And our tipster."

Bridgeman circled the block, and Sly and I hung back. He eased the De Soto over to the curb across the street and down from the house. The house had white siding that was jagged along the bottom edge, as if it was being devoured by drunken termites from the ground up. A downstairs window was boarded up, and a gutter sagged above the mossy roof covering the small porch. It had all the markings of student housing. We parked around the corner on a side street, from where we could see Bridgeman's car and the house, though trees obscured our view of the porch.

"We've got company," Sly said. "Tan sedan. They on the same merry-go-round we're on."

I looked up at the rearview mirror. I caught a glimpse of a tan car parallel parking, but I couldn't see the driver from this distance. That was all I needed—a pair of goombahs in the mix.

"Can't worry about them now," I said. "You've got to get Juney out of there."

He didn't argue. We both knew that he'd attract less attention in this neighborhood than I would. "How do I do that?" he said.

"I don't know," I said. I reached across him to open the glove compartment. "Tell him her Uncle Harry is visiting up the street and wants to talk to her." I removed the Colt. "She wants to talk to me apparently, so I don't expect you to have any trouble."

He got out of the car but he didn't close the door all the way. He crossed the street at the corner behind Bridgeman and sauntered up the sidewalk. Lightning showed dark clouds against a black sky and the cracks of thunder said that the storm was close. It didn't take long for Sly to return with Juney.

"Get in the front with Harry," he was telling her, "and don't close the door all the way."

She looked puzzled but she didn't object. She had other things on her mind. She was wearing white pedal pushers and a navy-and-white striped shirt, as if she'd mugged a sailor. She smelled good, too, causing me to wonder about her relationship with the kid in the yellow vest.

"I've been trying to call you all day," she said, as if it was my fault I hadn't been sitting by the phone. "I thought about what you said—about the kind of person who might be tipping off the bomber. I think that's him." She nodded in the direction of the house with the porch light on. "His name is Oscar DeWitt. He's kind of new to the group, kind of quiet, but there's something funny about him."

"I think you're right," I said. "I saw him take a payoff today."

In the dim light from a streetlight I saw her face fall. She'd wanted to be the one to tell me.

"So what are you doing hanging out with him?" I said. "It's dangerous."

"I can handle myself," she said. "Anyway, Oscar's a wimp. He couldn't hurt a fly."

"Maybe not," I said, "but he's got acquaintances that pull wings off flies just for entertainment."

"Anyway," she said with a toss of her head, "if you know so much, you probably already know where we demonstrated today. That was the other thing I wanted to tell you."

"I don't know," I said. "Where?"

"At the Metropolitan and Loew's," she said.

I turned to look at Sly, who was leaning forward with one hand on the back of my seat. Our eyes met. The Metropolitan Theatre was in the Lamar Hotel building. If the Brown brothers spit out of the window in 8-F, they'd probably hit the marquee. A bomb blast there would take several dozen people and a considerable chunk of Houston history down with the building. Loew's State Theatre was right next door.

Sly's eyes shifted up the street.

"We got another problem," he said. "While y'all were squabbling, Bridgeman got out of the car with one of his shopping bags and went up the street. Here he comes back again, and no shopping bag."

"Christ!" I said. I was already fumbling for the car door handle. "You drive," I told Sly. "Don't lose him."

"What about me?" I heard Juney say, but I was already sprinting up the sidewalk toward the house.

The kid had gone back inside, so I hammered on the door until he opened it. I reached in and yanked him out. I bent one arm behind his back before he had a chance to protest and threw him down the steps. He was still saying "What the hell?" when he hit the pavement.

I didn't make it that far. I heard a whoosh, like a Zeppelin with a bad leak, and the world exploded behind me. Something hard slammed into my back and then I was airborne. I landed on the kid and was grateful for the cushion.

The first thing I saw when I raised my head was the spectacle of Jumbo Stubbs charging us like a water buffalo. He had a walkie-talkie pressed to his face.

I was slow getting up and the kid was slower. He was still lying on the ground moaning when I hauled him to his feet and began propelling him toward Stubbs. My back was doing its best to get my attention but I didn't have time for it. Despite the cushion I'd come down hard on my right knee and it was throbbing like a drumbeat.

In the flickering light I could see Stubbs's angry face. I didn't doubt that anger was directed at me. Still, I let go of the kid with one hand and snagged Stubbs's elbow with it. I was now towing two people.

"Come on!" I shouted at Stubbs. "It's a diversion. He's got another target."

"Damn it, Lark!" he said, pulling back. "I've got to clear those houses on either side."

I didn't have an argument for that, so I just said, "Well, hurry it up! I'll take this one."

I hadn't had time to ask the kid if anybody else had been inside the white house. At this point, the question was moot.

At the house next door, I met a middle-aged couple coming out. They were holding on to each other, the woman had blood running down her face from a contusion on her temple and the man was limping. But she'd had enough presence of mind to grab her pocketbook, I noticed, so I wasn't too worried about her injuries.

I got them to the curb and told them to stay put. I hadn't loosened my grip on the kid, but he looked too dazed to resist now.

The first ladder truck was arriving. Up and down the streets, neighbors had emerged from their houses. Stubbs was striding toward the truck but I cut him off.

"We've got to go," I said. "Let 'em do their jobs." I seized him by the elbow, but he shook me off. He led us to the tan Mercury sedan and I got in back with the kid.

"Where we going?" Stubbs said.

"Lamar Hotel," I said. "The Metropolitan and Loew's theatres. You want to catch your man, make it quiet."

He turned around in the seat and looked at me.

"But fast," I added.

He slapped a light on the top of the car and roared away, throwing me and the kid into a cozy pile in the back.

As we approached the theatres, he pulled over and retrieved the light. We circled the block.

It was after ten on a sultry summer night, with the wind picking up now and causing the electrical wires overhead to dance. Rain clouds were gathering, made visible by flickers of lightning behind them.

"See anything?" Stubbs asked, craning what he had for a neck.

"Not yet," I said.

He pulled over, put the car in park, and turned around to look at me. "Then what in hell makes you think he's going to be here?"

"Why don't we ask the kid," I said. "He's the one who tipped him off."

Juney was right about the kid being a wimp. With both of us staring him down, the kid crumbled. That could also explain the mop-up operation. Bridgeman didn't trust him to keep his trap shut under pressure, so he decided that as long as he needed a diversion anyway, why not whack him?

"He'll be here," the kid said sullenly.

Stubbs corkscrewed around in his seat, heaving his belly with him. "You named the target?" Stubbs prodded.

The kid shrugged, but he looked scared. "I want a lawyer," he croaked.

Stubbs got on the radio then and called for backup in two unmarked cars. They were to approach slowly, park on different sides of the building, keep a low profile and wait for further instructions from him. He described the suspect. I realized now that Bridgeman had worn the trench coat and hat not only to disguise his identity in downtown Houston, but to hide his race in the Third Ward.

Stubbs looked up the street at the two marquees.

"You reckon he's inside?" he said.

"You know him better than I do," I said. "But if he was inside, I figure Sly would be out front, looking for me. I haven't spotted my car. You said he likes to hang around after. He could still be in the Third Ward."

"He don't usually hit places that are open for business and full of customers," Stubbs said. "He's more of an after-midnight creeper—that's his style."

"He doesn't kill people," the kid objected in a shaky voice.

"Recent evidence to the contrary," I said.

The kid swallowed. "He promised—."

"Not to kill you, I bet," I said.

I suspected I might have just delivered a sucker punch to the gut. The kid stared at me as the realization dawned. No, I thought, Bridgeman never regarded you as anything more than an expendable liability. Not just weak, but stupid to boot.

To Stubbs I said, "Got any cuffs?"

He rooted around in the glove compartment. Finally he handed me a pair.

I looked around. "Nothing to cuff him to," I said. "We'll have to stash him in the trunk."

Stubbs nodded, considering, while the kid cowered against the door. If he'd had the courage of a mosquito, he would have just opened the door and bolted, but he was probably afraid that Stubbs would shoot him in the back right there in the middle of Main Street.

"Aw, hell," Stubbs said at last. "Throw him in the front seat and I'll cuff him to the steering wheel."

As soon as I got out of the car, the bottom dropped out of the rain clouds, so I was dripping by the time I returned to the back seat. The kid was trying to put as much distance between himself and Stubbs as he could, but it was hard with his left wrist cuffed to the steering wheel. Stubbs glowered at the kid, and I didn't blame him. What he wanted was a commie he could sink his teeth into, and what he had was a greedy gerbil.

"What's your name, son?" he growled.

"Oscar DeWitt," the kid said.

"Jesus," Stubbs said, "Oscar DeWitt." He swiped a hand over his face. "Oscar fucking DeWitt. You a member of that nigger protest group?"

The kid flinched but nodded his head.

Stubbs nodded up the street. "This their idea?"

The kid shook his head.

"You thought it up all on your own?" Stubbs said.

"Mr. Black came to see me," the kid said.

"Mr. who?" Stubbs said.

"Black."

"Small fella with a bad haircut?"

The kid shook his head. "That's my contact, Mr. White. Mr. Black was somebody else."

"Hoarse voice, bushy hair, nervous tic in his right eye?" I guessed.

"I guess so," the kid said. "I only met him once. After that I just talked to Mr. White."

"And White paid you," I said.

By way of answer, he said, "I have to pay my own way through college. It's not easy."

"Uh-huh," I said. "So you got a part time job as a mob spotter. That was very industrious."

To my surprise, he showed some spunk. "Listen, Mister, you ever try to work your way through college flipping burgers?"

Stubbs and I exchanged glances. "Touché," I said. I wasn't sure that either one of them knew what that meant, but neither one was going to ask.

Stubbs ran a hand across a face dripping with sweat. "Jesus," he said. "Mr. Black and Mr. White. Jesus."

We sat listening to the rain pounding the car roof and the police dispatcher droning in code. Stubbs wanted some coffee, and since I was already wet—and in Dutch for withholding evidence besides—I went after it. When I climbed out of the car, my knee almost buckled under me and my back chimed in, singing harmony. The coffee shop found me a battered tin of aspirin that must have been handcrafted during the Iron Age. The pills inside were probably Bayer prototypes, but I downed a few and hoped for the best.

The storm blew itself out around one, and in the sudden stillness I heard a church bell chime the hour. Before the echo had died, I saw a familiar car pass us and turn the corner.

"There's our pigeon," I said. I got out and jogged to the corner, but I hung back and kept out of sight. That's where Sly caught up with me.

"He's using the service alley," I whispered, and Sly nodded.

"We got backup?" he asked, and I nodded.

Stubbs came puffing up, walkie-talkie in hand, so that we looked like a trio of first graders playing hide-and-seek. He pulled me back, but not before I'd caught sight of Bridgeman coming up the sidewalk with his shopping bag. The next time I looked, there was no Bridgeman but two shadowy figures crossing the street at a run. Metal glinted in their hands before they disappeared into the service alley, shouting.

As we rounded the corner to join them, a single gunshot rang out. But by the time we reached the entrance to the alley, the two plainclothes already had Bridgeman down on the ground. He didn't appear to be resisting the cuffs, but it was dark so I couldn't tell if he'd been shot.

"Did he set it?" Stubbs asked.

"Not unless he set it in the car," the standing cop said.

"Well, hell," Stubbs said. "Give me some damn light." Sly produced a flashlight and turned it on.

Stubbs was kneeling next to Bridgeman. He had a gun, and he now cocked it and pressed it to Bridgeman's forehead. The click bounced off the alley walls, magnified. "The bomb," he said. "Is it set?"

Bridgeman must have shaken his head because I heard Stubbs

pull the trigger on an empty chamber and then saw him struggle to his feet.

"Who fired?" Stubbs asked, whirling around to survey the crowd of police officers.

"I did," said the cop with the handcuffs.

"Jesus, don't you know any better than to fire up a blind alley at a man holding a bomb?" Stubbs said in a voice that made the man take his time with the handcuffs so he wouldn't have to stand up and meet Stubbs's eyes.

A back door opened and Marty Brenner stepped into the alley from the hotel building. He had a bigger flashlight and a smaller gun. "Who's that—Harry?" he said as he played the light over our faces. "What's going on?"

"It's okay, Marty," I said. "Most of us are cops."

By now we looked like a small convention. I introduced Marty to Stubbs, who gave him a brief account of what had happened.

"A bomb?" Marty said, bewildered. "Somebody was going to firebomb the hotel?"

"The target was the theatres," Stubbs said, "but it would probably have blown a hole in your lobby. We'll know better when the experts take a look at the bomb there."

He nodded at the shopping bag that now stood abandoned on the pavement, up against the building wall. It looked wet and miserable and harmless.

I pulled Sly aside. "Juney still with you?" I said.

He nodded. "I told her to stay in the car."

We both turned toward the entrance to the alley, where a feminine figure was silhouetted against the light from the street outside.

"You ever notice how women don't listen to a thing you say?" Sly asked.

"Tell me about it," I said.

Chapter 31

When I finally got home around two-thirty, Danny and Turk were still sitting in Turk's car out front, quizzing each other on baseball records.

"Hey, I bet even the gringo knows this one," Danny said. "Who holds the record for the most shutouts?"

"Season high or career high?" I said.

"Career."

I took a swipe at my face to clear the fog induced by too many hours of sitting in a car. "I don't know...The Big Train?"

"Hey, that's right! Walter Johnson." He turned to Turk and crooked a thumb in my direction. "He's not as dumb as he looks."

I thanked them and sent them home and stumbled into the house and went to bed. When I woke up the sun was glinting through the blinds. I was bone tired, like I'd been stomped by a rodeo bull and kicked by the clown for good measure. A shower gave me enough energy to pull my pants on, but when Rose set a cup of coffee in front of me I stared at it, not sure I had the strength to pick it up.

"You just going to look at it?"

"I was thinking maybe you could just inject it."

"The girls have something they want to show you when you're done with your breakfast," she said. She set a plate of eggs in front of me with a side of bacon and two pancakes. She always feeds me well when I've had a late night.

"Rosey," I said, "I'd marry you if I weren't divorced already."

I picked up a fork that weighed as much as a steel girder, but after I'd shoveled in a few bites, it went better. My back still felt like it had been run over by a bulldozer and my knee was threatening to go on strike, but I was feeling almost human when I limped out to the garage to see what the girls had.

Dizzy frowned at me, crossed her arms, and shook her head, but she wouldn't chew me out in front of her friends. B.D. told me to sit in one of the lawn chairs while Mel reached for something. It turned out to be a Popeye Pez dispenser. She bent over the footlocker and tipped back Popeye's sailor hat with her thumb. Something small rolled out, came to a stop and sat glittering in the dim light. She did it again. And again.

I looked up at them. "How many are there?"

"Twelve," Mel said.

"Not all of them diamonds," B.D. said.

"If they are diamonds," Dizzy said.

"Some look like emeralds and rubies," Mel said.

I picked up one of the stones between my thumb and forefinger and examined it. I took it outside into the daylight and scrutinized it some more.

"Is it real?" B.D. asked.

"If it's not, it's missing a good opportunity," I said. "Where'd you get these?"

"They were inside Barbie's head," Dizzy said.

"You pulled off Barbie's head?" I asked. Further proof that my daughter was not a typical girl. Maybe I was being overprotective. Maybe I should just turn her loose on the Florida mobsters and see who came out on top.

Dizzy ignored the question. "So what we figure is, the briefcase guy in Upper Thirteen—he was a jeweler, like Mr. Petry guessed he was. We think somehow Mr. Heffelman got hold of the briefcase after the wreck, found the jewels, and lammed."

I frowned. "That's kind of a leap, isn't it? How do you know the jewels were in the briefcase?"

"Because of the shoes," B.D. said.

They explained to me then that the shoes the body had been

wearing when it was delivered to the funeral home—the shoes that had been returned to Heffelman's widow—were marked in pencil with a "U13" on the bottom.

"Mr. Boudet says that the porters mark the shoes like that when they take them to be shined, so that they can return them to the right person," Dizzy said.

"In this case," B.D. said, "the right person was the briefcase man in Upper 13. It wasn't Mr. Heffelman because he wasn't in a Pullman that night. He got on in Topeka and sat in a chair car for the rest of the night."

"They weren't even the right size for Mr. Heffelman," Mel said. "Two sizes too small."

"This five hundred grand that the goons are looking for," Dizzy said. "They never said it was inside a briefcase chained to somebody's wrist. It could have been in another briefcase, or not in a briefcase at all. We just assumed it was being carried by the briefcase man because it was so much money and because the briefcase was chained to the bird's wrist."

"Well, I'll be damned," I said. I sat down again in the lawn chair and ran a hand through my hair. Here I was, wearing my shoe leather down to a communion wafer in my efforts to drum up business, and this trio of aspiring Nancy Drews had sat around the garage until a case fell in their laps, then practically solved it in the time it takes a check to clear.

"So what do you think?" Dizzy said.

"I think you're a handful of smart cookies," I said. "But your theory doesn't explain everything. It doesn't explain why the Florida mob keeps sending goons to keep an eye on you."

Dizzy shrugged. "They're just wrong, is all. They're not very bright."

"Could be," I said. "But they think they lost something valuable on that train, and they must have a reason for thinking so."

B.D. sat up straighter and closed one eye. "Maybe somebody else on that train was carrying valuables—that five hundred thousand dollars y'all keep talking about. When the train wrecked, he got the same idea as Mr. Heffelman. He could disappear with the loot and wouldn't nobody ever know what happened to him. Maybe he even left his wallet in the pocket of a dead person, like Mr. Heffelman did. How about that?"

"Two birds in the same wreck boosted a fortune and did a bunk?" I said. "That's a little hard to swallow."

"But not impossible, though," B.D. said.

"No," I admitted. "Not impossible."

B.D. clapped a hand to her forehead. "Or, wait, y'all. I just thought of another one. Maybe the briefcase guy was a jeweler who made stuff for the Miami mob. You know—like he was an exclusive jeweler for mobsters who wanted to buy jewelry for their wives. Maybe these goons just got the story wrong. Maybe the jewels were *worth* five hundred thousand, but they thought they were supposed to be looking for cash."

"Or maybe Upper 13 was carrying cash as well as jewels in his briefcase," Mel said. "No reason he couldn't be."

"There's only one way to find out," Dizzy said. "We've got to find Mr. Heffelman and ask him."

I couldn't argue with that. I took it a step further and promised I'd help. They gave me the Pez container full of rocks to lock up in my office safe. I hoped the next pair of goons who showed up didn't hit me harder than I could stand to be hit.

Chapter 32

I sat with the girls until Danny Rodriguez came jogging up the walk. "Hoo, boy, I love this summer camp," he said. "Are we going to have fun today? I been practicing my hopscotch, and can't nobody touch me at jump rope."

I found the office just as deserted as I'd left it except for a fly that seemed to have made his way through the mail slot and was now exploring the outer office. Seemed he didn't like what he saw because he never stayed anyplace long, and I didn't blame him. There were dust bunnies that could flatten him if he landed in the wrong place at the wrong time. He buzzed his displeasure with the whole set-up.

"I hear you, brother," I told him, "but if you don't like the low-rent district, you should pick a classier mail slot next time."

Against the wishes of my back, I stooped over to pick up the mail from the floor and dumped it into the trash can next to the secretary's desk. Then I thought better of it and stood over the can to paw through it, but my first instinct had been correct. There were no notifications that I'd won the lottery, no checks, no letters from long-lost well-heeled uncles, no telegraphs from Washington offering to put me on the federal payroll. On the bright side, there were no window envelopes from one Morton P. Gooch, DDS.

My answering machine testified to Juney's many attempts to reach me the day before, along with Stubbs's growing annoyance that he couldn't locate me. There was one job prospect from an impatient bird who had probably called the next gumshoe in the yellow pages by now, and one from a woman who sounded drunk and who didn't answer the phone when I returned her call. I put in a call to Leda Wardlow, who I figured deserved a report from me on last night's developments, but she was in court for the day.

I went to the police station to talk to Stubbs and Carillo about the previous night's festivities. They told me that Stubbs was down on Truxillo Street at the bomb blast site, but Carillo was in.

I told him that the Florida mob was tailing Dizzy.

"Well, what do you want me to do about it?" Carillo said. He was smoking a small cigar with a big odor somewhere between Roquefort and bug spray. "It's a free country, unless you want to get a restraining order. Me, I wouldn't bother. I'd just strap a pair of six-shooters to her skinny hips and let 'em take their chances. She plugs one of 'em I ain't gonna arrest her, I'm gonna give her a medal."

I found Stubbs under a tent on Truxillo Street. The scowl on his face reminded me that I didn't even know if anybody had died in the blast there, and it made me wonder about casualties.

He shook his head. "Lucky bastards. The housemates were either working or at the movies or out chasing co-eds. That dumb fuck DeWitt 'bout peed his pants when he realized how many people could've been killed."

"He cooperating?" I said.

"What do you think?" Stubbs's white short-sleeved shirt soaked up the sweat that was pouring down his face and dripping off his chin. He stopped to mop his face with a handkerchief, replaced it in his pocket, and hitched up his pants. He was wearing a string tie that hung limp as a noodle from his unbuttoned collar. "We come damn close to having to scrape him off his neighbors' brick walls and garage doors. I don't believe he's realized yet that we can't get the death penalty for Bridgeman without any bodies. He'd like to be the one to throw the switch on Old Sparky."

"Who hired Bridgeman?" I said. "Does the kid know?"

"Aw, hell, you heard him last night," Stubbs said in disgust. "He don't know shit. And Bridgeman won't talk—not yet, at least."

"You boys must be losing your touch," I said. "No percentage in terrorizing the mice."

"We just getting warmed up, son," he said. "Don't you worry about that. We just getting warmed up."

"Does Bridgeman have a lawyer?"

"Hell, yes," Stubbs said. "Barnett Hathaway. Ever hear of him?"

"Maybe," I said. "Wears hundred-dollar suits and parts his hair with a razor?"

"That's him," Stubbs said. "Sumbitch is slicker than a mud wrestler. And I'ma find out who's paying his bills."

"Let me ask you something else. What's Bridgeman's background? He got any connections in Chicago or Miami?"

"Wait a minute, lemme think." He propped two meaty fists on his hips and stared off into space. "They got a La Grange in Illinois, just like we got in Texas, but I don't know if it's near Chicago or not. That's where he comes from. Got a juvey record in Illinois. I reckon juvey was a real educational experience for him, 'cause his adult jacket's pretty thin, all of it in Texas. Couldn't tell you why the sumbitch moved south, though. We just got lucky, I reckon."

I thanked him and headed back to the car. I felt Stubbs's eyes on my back as I limped away.

"You might could get something for that limp in civil court, son," he called after me. "No reason Bridgeman's shyster should get all his money."

I went back to my office and tried to pretend that I had a business to run. I filed a few of the things that were piled on the secretary's desk, but in no time I was sitting in the sweatered chair with my feet up, reading a catalogue from a surveillance equipment outfit while the dust settled around me. I answered the phone three times. The first was a wife who cursed me out like a drunken stevedore. I promised to give me the message. The second was from the wife's husband. They seemed not to be speaking to each other but they wanted to continue the argument they'd be having if they were speaking to each other. They apparently wanted me to referee. They were shouting so loud I don't know why they bothered with the phone; if I'd turned off the air conditioner and opened a window, I would have heard them just fine. I hung up on them. The third call was from a client who expected to see me in court the following Wednesday. I told him I'd be there in spats and Stetson.

I regarded a small pile of bills that needed to be paid, but when I smelled them, they weren't ripe enough, so I left them alone.

The fly and I were both bored but too lazy to get up and do the things we should be doing. The fly marched up and down the desk blotter for a while and flicked his wings at me.

The phone rang again and this time it was Leda Wardlow. I told her what had happened the night before and referred her to Juney for additional information on the kid.

"But who was behind it all?" she asked, her voice like thick honey. "Did you find out?"

"Not yet," I said, as if I had a plan for tracking down the information.

"It's horrible," she said. "The poor neighbors. The blast must have done some damage to their homes."

"Probably," I agreed.

"But who will they sue?"

Everybody loves a lawsuit. "They can try suing Bridgeman," I said, "but he may not be convicted in criminal court for the Truxillo Street fire."

"Does he have money?"

"He's not setting fires to earn his Boy Scout badge," I said. "Arson jobs are expensive."

She sighed. "At least nobody was killed," she said. Then, as an afterthought, she said, "You risked your life to save that young man, DeWitt, didn't you?"

"I didn't think of it that way," I said.

"Well, you ought to start thinking about it," she said, and her voice was sharper than I expected. "You have two children, don't you?"

"Yes."

"Then you have no right to risk your life to save a criminal," she said, "especially when that criminal has risked other lives."

"He's just a dumb kid," I said.

"That doesn't let him off the hook."

"Say, you wouldn't be standing for judge any time soon, would you?" I said. "I just want a little advance warning is all."

I heard the smile in her voice when she said, "I'm too soft-hearted to be a judge."

"Now there's a scary thought," I said.

"But, seriously," she said. "If we don't know who hired Bridgeman, we don't know why he was hired. And if we don't know why he was hired, we don't know if he'll be replaced. What's your opinion on that? Will they try a new tactic?"

"I don't know," I said. "You ask me, last night was supposed to be Bridgeman's last job. He probably didn't want the cops breathing down his neck any more than they already were. To make sure they wouldn't be waiting for him at the movie theatre, he needed a distraction, and he figured he'd take out DeWitt in the bargain. Maybe he figured the cops would finger DeWitt and his friends for the other fires if DeWitt's house went up in smoke. Say his pals had already removed one bomb from the premises, and DeWitt was just cleaning up when kablam!"

"But the police would be able to ascertain the point of origin, wouldn't they?" she said. This is the kind of gold-plated legal talk that ordinarily drives me nuts, but when she said it, it made my scalp tingle. If she ever did become a judge, I might have to get arrested just for the pleasure of listening to her voice.

"Sure," I said. "They might even figure it out right away, and they might even be suspicious if it turns out to be a trash can behind the house. But the press might fumble the information, and the citizens of Houston might be encouraged to draw the wrong conclusion."

She sighed again and said in a tired voice, "Well, please see what you can find out about who's behind this campaign. Keep me posted. And—don't take any more foolish risks."

I stopped by a bar on McGowen for a beer and sat down on a stool next to one of the regulars, a dour old bird named Pappy who had a face like a fallen cake. Pappy was reading the *Post* and shaking his head. I figured he was reading about the firebombing, but that wasn't it.

"You see this story about the trouble down at the docks, Harry?" he said. He talked through his cigarette, showing teeth like relics. His battered Stetson sat on the bar next to his beer.

"Which one?" I said. I now realized that since he was reading the morning paper, the *Post*, and not the evening paper, the *Chronicle*, he might not know about the bombing. Well, I wasn't going to be the one to tell him.

"Aw, they had a riot down there on the picket lines," he said. "Winders got broke and hot tar slung around. Police had to bust it up. They pinched some of the boys. Cracked some heads, too."

"Yeah?"

"I don't like it," he said.

Since Pappy never liked anything he read in the paper, this wasn't news and I refrained from comment.

He took a swig of his beer and set it back down. He laid the paper down with an air of dismissal. "No, I don't like it one bit," he said. "Town's going to hell, Harry."

"Uh-huh."

"Firebombings downtown, bloody riots on the docks—why, if I didn't live here, I sure as hell wouldn't move here, and that's God's truth. And as for the mayor and the city council—." He waved a hand. "They are the sorriest bunch of nincompoops ever been elected to public office. It ain't enough we got us a biblical flood nigh on every week. It ain't enough we can't drink genuine alcohol—I'm talkin' about a shot of whiskey, now—in a neighborhood bar of an evening." He curled his hand around his glass and frowned at it as if someone had slipped him a pint of turpentine when his back was turned and expected him to drink it.

As I listened to him, I felt the rusty wheels grinding into motion in my brain.

"I'm fixin' to run for city council on the storm-drains-and-Jack-Daniels ticket," he said. "And you just turn me loose on them strikers and them protestors and all them other commie agitators—why, they ain't seen no agitation like my agitation. I'll agitate ever' last one of 'em down to the Harris County booby hatch, you see if I don't."

"What makes you think it's communist agitators behind all the trouble?" I said. I knew the answer, but I asked it anyway, just to wind him up another notch. Communist agitators were behind every breach of the public peace that came down the pike and you didn't have to look further than the local newspapers to find that out. Still, the locals had taken pains to distinguish between other places, which were hotbeds of communist activity, and Houston, an all-American law-and-order town where we'd just as soon string up a communist as spit at him.

"I'll tell you why," Pappy said. He hitched himself up on his stool and leaned toward me. He removed the cigarette from between his teeth and balanced it on the edge of a glass ashtray that resembled an overcrowded burial ground. "We ain't never had these kind of problems before, not never. But you don't think Castro is a-settin' down there in Cuba just waiting for the next invasion, do you? Hell, no! It's a known fact that him and his Russky pals are busy with their own invasion. Why, they got infiltrators all over this country, just looking for an opportunity to turn the tables on the U. S. of A. It's like a disease—a—a—plague! All these secret commie agents just looking for people to infect. We didn't never have no trouble with the nigras before. It's like LBJ said last year, our nigras didn't have no complaints—not until the commies stirred 'em up."

I raised my eyebrows as if in surprise. "You don't think negroes have any cause for complaint? You're complaining because you can't get hard liquor in here, but a negro can't even walk in here and get served a glass of water."

"Hell, they don't need to come in here," Pappy said. "They got their own colored bars in their own neighborhoods. You better believe they can get anything they want in those places." But he'd jumped the track as if racial unrest no longer interested him. "But not me! I want a whiskey, I got to go join me a club and pay a membership fee. Why should I have to do that? It's a free country, or it ought to be! You don't want to drink whiskey, why, that's fine and dandy with me. But you shouldn't ought to go passing laws about what other folks can drink and when."

By now some of the regulars were egging him on.

"You tell 'em, Pappy!" one called.

"Pappy for Governor!" another shouted.

A man in a string tie and a cowboy hat that looked custom-made for Bigfoot was slapping him on the back. Pappy took another swig of beer to lubricate his vocal chords.

But as the thoughts whirred inside my cranium I was beginning to feel like a major league chump, like the MVP on the all-star clown squad, and I wanted to go off by myself and contemplate my own stupidity. I sat in the hot car for a while and smoked a couple of cigarettes and watched women in their pastel summer dresses come sashaying down the sidewalk, their purses swinging from their elbows like Christmas tree ornaments. I found that I could add up one and one and one for a change and get three. In fact, the big picture, now that I could see it, was so pretty, I'd be bitter as a dose of cyanide if it turned out to be wrong.

I put the car in gear and headed home. I was on dad duty, and I had a tent to put up in the back yard.

I knew a guy who knew a guy who knew a guy who worked for the local Maritime Union, so on Sunday I drove out to Jacinto City to meet him. I had a disgruntled Dizzy riding shotgun because I was afraid to let her out of my sight, but all of the togetherness was wearing on both of us. Every time I pressed the clutch my knee complained about middle-aged men behaving like John Wayne's stunt double, especially when the other knee had already been taken out of commission. The place we were looking for was a diner tucked between a pawnshop and a washateria on Market Street. I limped through the door, trailed by my daughter, who was worrying that she might finish the book she was clutching and have nothing to read.

Gavin McHugh looked like he was auditioning for the part of Ahab in a *Moby Dick* remake, but the mutton chop whiskers, moustache, pipe, and seaman's cap didn't go with the yellow polyester shirt he was wearing or with his high-pitched Texas drawl. His ruddy complexion looked like evidence of a pending heart attack rather than a recent sea journey. His whiskers were wet with perspiration. I introduced Dizzy and then she went and found a back booth where she could read undisturbed.

Once we'd ordered coffee and sandwiches, I began.

"It's about the recent trouble on the docks." I kept my voice low. I was the one who had suggested we meet somewhere away from his office. "I'm curious to know whether the outbreaks of violence were spontaneous or whether they might have been provoked."

"Provoked?" He frowned and puffed on his pipe.

"By an outsider, say. By someone who had an interest in seeing things take a wrong turn."

His eyes flared. "You mean communists."

"No," I said. "I don't mean communists at all. I'm working on a theory that whoever is behind the recent firebombings in the city could also be stirring up trouble at the ship channel."

He looked surprised. "I seen in the paper they caught that fellow. But they didn't seem to know why he done it. I don't see what it's got to do with us. We haven't had anything of that kind. We've got good relations with the colored. We've got colored members."

"The people behind the firebombings recruited a young man to join the civil rights group and provide them with information so that they could bomb only those places where the group had held protests," I said. "I'm wondering if they recruited someone to join your group, or recruited someone who was already a member, so that they could promote violence."

"What for?" he said.

Our food arrived and he put down his pipe.

"It just don't make no kind of sense to me," he said when the waitress had gone. "We don't want violence, the ship owners don't want violence, and the port police sure as hell don't want violence. Two men like to got killed the other night, and for what?"

He dumped half the contents of the salt shaker on his French fries before I wrestled it away from him and emptied it on mine.

"We got a legal right to strike, and we're exercising it is all," McHugh said.

"I'm not saying it makes sense," I said, "at least, not to you and me. But suppose someone wants to make Houston look bad?"

"Who would want to do a thing like that?" he said. He was trying to stuff half the sandwich in his face. I watched with interest, rooting for him. But I found myself wondering if he swallowed enough of his moustache on a daily basis to give him hairballs, like Dizzy's cat.

"Someone who does business in a city competing with Houston for a big contract," I said.

"Are you telling me that there's some kind of business deal in the works that would be big enough to make someone do a thing like that?" he said through a mouthful of sandwich.

"I think so."

He stopped chewing and looked at me. He laid the other half of his sandwich carefully on his plate as if to reduce distraction. I didn't blame him. I was having a hard time believing it myself, and now that I'd explained my theory out loud, it sounded about as likely as a blue norther in July.

He swallowed, then boosted my confidence by asking, "You sure about this?"

"No," I said, "that's why I'm running it by you. I was hoping you'd tell me if it's possible that someone, or a small group of someones, could be behind the violence at the ship channel—maybe someone who doesn't have the best interests of the sailors at heart."

He seemed to be gazing at the woman seated behind the cash register at the front of the diner.

"It's funny you should say that," he said slowly. "They's one fella I been wondering about. He works for one of the tug outfits—an ornery, unfriendly cuss who don't usually have time for nobody. He ain't never been interested in joining the union, ain't never had a good word to say about the strike. But don't you know about two weeks ago, why, here he comes along and pays his dues. Said he had a change of heart. 'Wally,' my boss says—it's what they call me, on account of the walrus whiskers—'Wally,' he says, you keep a weather-eye on that one. He's trouble.'"

"And is he?"

"He's always where the trouble is happening."

"But you never worried that he was a communist agitator?"

"Abe Sullivan? Don't make me laugh." He shifted on the seat. "Abe likes money too much, and he ain't about to share it with nobody, neither, not even the seamen's emergency fund or the widows and orphans fund."

"Sounds like a good prospect if I wanted to buy myself an inside agitator," I said.

I looked up when the waitress set a glass of milk down in front of me. "What's this?"

She nodded toward the back. "From the lady in the back booth. She says you ought to try eating something healthy for a change."

I turned to look at the back booth, but the lady in question had her nose in a book.

Book Three

Chapter 33

I went down to the office on Monday morning to work on the problem of how to contact some people. But I started by working my way through the *Chronicle* from the night before and I was still reading the morning *Post* when one of them walked in the door. I felt the stir of air around my ankles that told me the outer door had opened, and before I could get the paper folded, George R. Brown was standing in the doorway. He was in his sixties with a face like a topographical map of all the building sites he'd supervised over the years for Brown & Root, with a fan of laugh lines at his eyes to indicate that he'd enjoyed doing it. He wore a coat, tie, and hat, and carried nothing in his hands, one of which gestured at the newspapers spread out on the desk as he said, "Well, I'm glad to see you don't discriminate."

George and his brother Herman were particular pals of John Jones, the editor and official owner of the *Houston Chronicle* and head of the Houston Endowment—his uncle Jesse Jones's legacy to the city. John also owned the Lamar Hotel and was himself a member of the 8-F group.

"No," I said, "I read both papers. I like to stay informed." I stood and extended a hand to him. "How are you, Mr. Brown?"

He removed his hat, uncovering neatly trimmed white hair. He extended his hand, and said, "I'm doing fine, Mr. Lark, thanks to you," he said. "The boys over at police headquarters, they told Mr. Jones we all owe you a debt of gratitude, and I came around to thank you on our behalf." His speech impediment was slight, a barely detectable curl at the ends of some words.

Brown shook my hand warmly and I offered him the client chair. He sat down, holding his hat in his lap.

"I appreciate the visit, Mr. Brown, but I wasn't working for you or Mr. Jones at the time," I said.

"No, I believe you were working for that nigra group, if I understand correctly," he said.

I smiled at him and didn't say anything.

"That Mrs. Wardlow," he went on, shaking his head, "she's a force to be reckoned with."

Again I smiled. "It would have been a shame to see the Lamar Hotel go up in smoke." There probably wasn't much about this business that Jones and the Browns wanted to know and didn't—down to my underwear size—but if there was, they wouldn't get it from me. Not that Jones was likely to publish anything until he'd decided what was in the public's interest to know. That's why he'd sent Brown and not a reporter.

"Oh, I know it," he said. "There's a lot of Houston history in those walls." He chuckled. "Of course, Herman and I are mighty glad the walls can't talk."

"How is your brother?"

"Oh, fine, fine. He's up in Austin, you know. But he was mighty glad to hear they caught the bomber before he could do any more damage. Sends his regards."

I nodded.

"I don't mind telling you we're all pretty puzzled by this whole business," he added. "We surely would like to know what this bomber was trying to accomplish and who was paying the fella."

"I might be willing to speculate," I said, "but before I do, I need to ask you a question."

"All right," he said.

I leaned back in my chair. "This big space center that NASA wants to build," I said. "What other cities besides Houston are in the running to build it?"

You don't found a company like Brown & Root and then keep

it going for more than forty years if you go around advertising your private business on your face, so I wasn't expecting much of a reaction and I didn't get much of one. The muscles around his eyes tensed and his head made a slight movement, as if he'd been slapped by a fairy.

He cleared his throat. "What space center would that be, Mr. Lark?"

"Nuts to that," I said. "I can't speculate on what you want to know if you're going to clam up on me."

He seemed to give this some consideration. Then he said, "You read about it in the newspaper?"

"Your pal Congressman Thomas was shooting his mouth off about it a couple of weeks ago. He seemed to think that Houston was a shoe-in." This was true. Both papers had made that point in their front-page articles around the middle of June.

He grimaced. "I told Albert that it was ill-advised to mention the possibility so early in the game. But you know what politicians are like."

I shrugged. "Doesn't seem early to me, not with NASA representatives down here already looking over the property," I said. "But if you want to call it the first quarter and not the fourth and goal, that's jake with me, only I still need an answer to my question."

His eye muscles flickered again. "Well, I—I don't really have an answer, Mr. Lark, not an easy one." He shifted in his chair. "From what I hear, ever since this thing was announced, every congressman from every damn district in the country has been hearing from constituents hot to see the thing built in their neighborhood."

"Not every congressman chairs the committee that oversees NASA's budget."

He smiled then. "Well, maybe that's so."

"And not every district has a major industrial builder sitting on the Space Committee."

He looked uncomfortable at that. "Now, Mr. Lark, the federal government has rules about bidding out contracts."

"So if the space center comes to Houston," I said, "Brown & Root will submit their bid just like every other outfit in Texas. Okay, that's jake with me, too. And if that builder happens to be chairman of the board at Rice University, I got no beef with any of it. I just need to know who the competition is, if you can call it that."

He hesitated again, frowning. He wasn't used to having someone tell him his business, especially someone who hadn't even been on his radar three days ago. "Well, now if you're asking me what city besides Houston has the best chance, in my estimation—," he said.

"That's what I'm asking."

"It has to be a large metropolitan area," he said. "It has to be able to transport large, heavy equipment to the launch site at Cape Canaveral. That could mean rail transport, but more likely water, so a port city. NASA favors sites with an existing military base that could accommodate military aircraft—not a fully active base, you understand, but facilities already in place. A major university would be an advantage."

"Uh-huh."

"I would say, then, that given those requirements, our biggest competitors are likely to be cities in California, Florida, and Louisiana," he said, "not counting other cities in Texas like Corpus."

"Miami?" I said.

He shook his head. "I haven't heard it mentioned."

"Where in Florida, then?"

"Jacksonville and Tampa would be the likeliest."

I looked up at the ceiling for inspiration, but I saw nothing but old water stains and peeling paint—not even the fly who had been so vocal a few days ago. He'd probably already checked out, and I'd find him later, wings down and toes up, turning to dust on the windowsill.

"Okay," I said. "Here's my best guess. You've got some mobsters in Florida who want the new space center built there. They've already got the launch site, but if they can score the space center too, so much the better. A space center means jobs, which means more customers for mob activities. The mob can add up the likely profits—they've got Jewish accountants to do it for them—and they can see that Houston has an edge. But they don't want to share with Houston, and short of rubbing out a high-profile congressman like Thomas, they're not sure how to tip the decision their way."

"I don't think of Jacksonville or Tampa as hotbeds of Mafia activity," he objected. "Now if it were New Orleans, that would be a different matter. Why are you assuming it's Florida?"

"I've got my reasons," I said. "Look, the Mafia probably owns the statehouse in Florida. They've got branches all over the state. If Jacksonville or Tampa need a fix, they call up Miami because Miami has more manpower." I left Chicago out of it for now. Chicago would just confuse him. Hell, it confused me.

"All right, but how does all this lead to firebombing the Lamar Hotel?"

"It's all about image," I said. "Houston is a law-and-order town. We don't have violent confrontations between civil rights protestors and police. We don't have violent confrontations between striking union members and police. At least, we didn't, until somebody decided to manufacture it."

He got it. "They're trying to make the city seem like a dangerous place for a major federal facility like a manned spacecraft center." He stood and wandered over to the window.

I took the opportunity to do some thinking of my own. I'd been calling this new joint a space center. This was the first time I'd heard it referred to as a "manned spacecraft center," and the implications were multiplying like West Texas jackrabbits. I'd known it had something to do with Kennedy's promise to put a man on the moon, and the Rice connection had made me envision laboratories, but now it sounded like more than that.

"Tell me more about this manned spacecraft center," I said. "What goes on there?"

He turned from the window. "Astronaut training. Mission planning. Mission control. Lots of other things that you and I probably wouldn't understand, but those are the essentials."

"So the first man to walk on the moon, if we make good on the president's promise, and if the center gets built here, will be a Houstonian?" It gave me chills.

"That's right," Brown said. "Not native, of course, but then, you and I aren't native, either, are we? Albert believes that the manned spacecraft center would be the making of Houston. We'd become a world-class city. It will all be on television someday, like Alan Shepard—not just the launch, but everything. There will be cameras inside the mission control center. Rice University will have the top aerospace engineering program in the country."

I smiled at the chairman of the board who couldn't resist thinking about his alma mater. Everything was beginning to make sense. "Even more reason for Florida mobsters to take an interest. Eventually, this space center will be a tourist destination, just like Cape Canaveral is, and the mob likes tourists because they support mob enterprises like gambling and prostitution. We've managed to run the Mafia out of Houston, so they don't have to start a mob war to improve their chances. They just have to make sure that every decision maker in Washington views Houston not only as a cowboy backwater but as a Wild West shooting gallery where racial tensions and labor battles turn ugly."

He tapped his hat against his palm absentmindedly. "What can we do about it? We've arrested the firebomber, but won't they just hire another one? And you mentioned the maritime strike. You think they've got a paid agent inside the union who's inciting the violence? What do we do about that?"

"I might have a line on him," I said. "But I don't have a client for that part of the investigation."

He looked surprised. "The union hasn't hired you?"

"Not yet."

"We'll hire you," he said. "I can write you a check for the retainer right now." He returned to his chair and pulled it closer to the desk so that he could write.

"The firebomber is part of another investigation," I said. "I haven't established that he's working for the mob, and I may not be able to do that. I believe that the Metropolitan and Loew's would have been his last job anyway—that and the house on Truxillo. The pattern he'd established was making it too risky for him to keep going. The question is whether they'll try to hire someone else at this point, or figure out a new strategy. I'm guessing they'll come up with a new idea, but we might not know what it is until the NASA decision is about to be made. What's the timeline on that?"

Brown was writing a check. "Well, things are moving pretty quickly for Washington. But they haven't named a site selection committee yet. I believe it will take another month or two for them to get around to making a decision."

"In the meantime, somebody on the inside is feeding information to the mob," I said, "but we'll probably never know who. Whatever information they get will probably determine their next strategy."

He frowned. "On the inside of what? The Space Group?"

I shrugged. "Anybody who works in a NASA facility that might have to relocate to the new site. There will be some of that, right?" I didn't mention Virginia and his connection to Goddard. I didn't want to cause any more trouble for the poor schmuck.

"Sure," he said. "That's one of the goals of the manned spacecraft center—to consolidate some existing facilities."

"So you've probably got more than a few people who don't want to be relocated. Or people who are particular about where they get relocated to."

"Yes, I see," he said. He tore off the check and held it out to me.

I didn't take it. "Are you sure your brother will approve of paying me to clear the union's name?" George's own sentiments probably weren't far from his brother's when it came to unions, but he was generally less vocal about it. As LBJ's principal financial backer, George bore some responsibility for Johnson's mixed record on labor.

He smiled. "I think I can talk him into it."

I took the check. It was for five hundred.

"I might owe you change," I said.

He started to wave a hand, then seemed to remember something and reached inside his coat.

"I forgot why I came," he said. "John and I wanted to give you a token of appreciation for saving the Lamar."

He handed me an envelope. Inside was a check for one grand.

I put it back in the envelope and held it out to him. "Like I said, I wasn't working for you at the time."

"I know you weren't. And I suppose Mrs. Wardlow can raise enough money from her supporters to pay your usual fee? Let's just say it's a reward for going above and beyond the call of duty." He stood up. "I believe you have a couple of kids to support, not to mention your beautiful ex-wife."

I left the check on the desk and stood, too. "My beautiful ex-wife could support me," I said dryly.

He chuckled. "Mr. Lark, I'm chairman of the board. I know what she makes. And I'm sure those Shakespeare books bring in something. But it's not enough to send two kids to college on, even if one of them decides to go to Rice."

Chapter 34

I deposited the check and wrote checks of my own to Danny and Turk Rodriguez, delivered them, then drove back to the house. Danny was seated cross-legged on the garage floor, playing jacks with B.D. Dizzy and Mel were haggling with a tall tow-headed kid over a baseball glove.

"It was me, I'd make him take it out in the back yard and prove he could catch something with it," Danny said, and missed his own catch. At least he swore in Spanish.

The kid gave the girls a nickel and two unopened baseball cards. I gave Danny the two checks.

He grinned up at me. "Hey, I like this job," he said. "You got any more like this one, boss, you be sure let me know."

At noon I met Leda Wardlow and Sly at a small soul food joint in the Third Ward called This Is It. I was gratified to see that Wardlow wasn't shy about eating in front of men. A whole team of oxen had sacrificed their tails for her lunch and she honored their sacrifice. Today she was wearing a cream-colored suit and a pale peach blouse, pearls and pearl earrings. I don't know what Sly was wearing. I didn't notice him much.

I outlined my theory about the mob's involvement in the firebombings. Wardlow reacted with consternation, but she didn't let it spoil her appetite.

"White was Bridgeman, of course," I said. "The kid told him what targets to hit—where the group had protested that day. Black was Florida mob—wise guy name of Pittaluga."

I didn't mention the Chicago mob because again, I didn't want to overcomplicate things, and to add Chicago to a cast list that had already grown longer than a list of Alley Theatre patrons would only confuse them. It might also convince them that I was paranoid and delusional. I was beginning to have thoughts of my own about the Chicago connection, but I'd keep them to myself until I had more information.

"But what interest could the Florida mob possibly have in the Houston civil rights movement?" Wardlow said.

I told her. It wasn't just that my original client, Mr. Smith, was dead. Congressman Albert Thomas had made the NASA project public information by talking to the newspapers about it, so I didn't see how talking about it now would violate any confidences. Smith sure wasn't going to object.

"So you saying that these bombings were supposed to make Houston look bad?" Sly sounded skeptical. He was wrestling with a pork chop, and the pork chop was winning. "Like we another Selma or Montgomery, only more dangerous for white folk?"

"I think so," I said. "I don't think it's the only way they're trying to make us look bad, though."

He thought about that, then raised his knife. "Trouble at the docks?"

I nodded.

"Oh, just use your fingers," Wardlow said, nodding at the pork chop. "This is a soul food restaurant, not Maxim's." She had polished off her oxtails and lit a cigarette.

Sly smiled at her and picked up his pork chop. I took her observation to be general and hoisted a piece of fried chicken in both hands, savoring the sensation of grease on my fingers.

"So now Houston's got race trouble and labor trouble," Sly said. "The maritime strike is national but we got us a nasty homegrown variety down here. No telling what would happen if they wanted to ship a moon rocket out of the Port of Houston."

"Uh-huh," I said. "No telling."

"So what will happen next?" Wardlow said. She flicked her ash into a cheap tin ashtray. "I mean in terms of the PYA, our local civil rights group. I'm sympathetic to the maritime union, but they're not my problem. What I want to know is whether these instigators will try to stir up more trouble."

"Worst case, they switch to the other side," Sly said. "Hire some local crackers with shotguns to shoot some kids on the national news. What you think, Harry?"

I explained my theory about timing. "They might cool it for now, start up again next month. Washington bureaucrats have short memories when they want to. If this were my show, I'd wait a month and then remind them. Will they use the civil rights movement again? I don't know."

Wardlow made an angry gesture with her cigarette. "Hell, why don't they just buy themselves some politicians and bureaucrats like everybody else does?"

I shrugged. "Maybe they thought they could get off cheap, local rates being what they are. Maybe they'll rethink that now that they have legal fees to pay and court appearances to make."

She looked at me thoughtfully. "If you could prove the connection between Bridgeman and the mob, I could sue them on behalf of the PYA for character defamation. I've already offered to sue Bridgeman on behalf of the Truxillo Street property owner. I can add other defendants if you can prove the connection."

Sly set down his bone and waved greasy fingers. "Wait a minute!" he said. "Hold on! Time out, y'all!" He turned to Wardlow. "Are you out of your mind? You want to sue the Miami mob? Girl, you want to take a swim in Buffalo Bayou wearing that nice Chanel suit and a pair of cement shoes?"

She squinted at him through the cigarette smoke. "I'm not afraid of the mob."

"Then you crazy!" Sly said.

"He's right," I said. I held up my hands. "I admit, it's tempting. But I've now got a twenty-four-hour watch on my daughter because she shot off a goon's finger. Stirring them up was a boneheaded move and I wish we'd had more options at the time. Besides, a lawsuit would be a minor inconvenience to them—at worst—and it would ruin your life."

"If it don't end it," Sly muttered.

"So what are we supposed to do?" she said. "Let them get away with it?"

"They the mob," Sly said. "It's what they do—get away with stuff."

"You can call the DOJ hotline and leave an anonymous tip for Bobby Kennedy," I said, "but I doubt it will go anywhere. Look, we've disrupted their plans for now. I'm working on doing some further disrupting down at the ship channel. Let's take what we can get."

"Okay," she said, and shook her head to acknowledge the defeat. "But none of us would ever risk our lives on a picket line the way those young people are doing now. They're the ones who are going to change the world."

"If they survive," Sly said.

"You get no argument from me," I said.

The waitress appeared then, her pad at the ready. "How about some dessert?"

Wardlow turned to her with a smile. "I thought you'd never ask."

In the afternoon I called an army buddy of mine who worked as a PI in Kansas City, and he put me in touch with a PI in Topeka. Then I went down to the *Post* to talk to Sam Jeeter.

"There he is, the man of the hour," he said. "I heard you single-handedly saved the Lamar Hotel. Get my messages?"

I'd had a bunch of messages on the answering machine in the office that morning, and a few taped to my office door, but when I'd realized they were all from reporters, I'd stopped listening.

"Where'd you hear that?" I said. Cops don't like to share credit so I doubted that the press had heard anything from Stubbs. But every reporter keeps a string of tipsters on the payroll.

"Word gets around," he said. "Here for your interview?"

He got up and filched a chair from behind somebody else's desk and wheeled it over. The newsroom was as crowded as a cage of lab rats. There was paper everywhere and the smell of printer's ink and tobacco smoke. Phones rang and typewriters tapped and canisters thumped inside pneumatic tubes that resembled post-industrial sculpture. This was the new *Post* building, just about five years old, and everything was made out of metal, which contributed a whole new level of clanks and creaks and bangs to the general commotion and made me miss the old wooden desks and chairs. Jeeter's own desk looked worse than my secretary's desk, except I had a feeling he knew what was on his.

He poised his fingers over his typewriter and blinked at me through squarish dark-framed glasses. "Now, tell papa. How did you finger Bridgeman?"

I laughed. "You know I can't say much before the case gets to court. Stubbs will have my license. Anyway, I don't want my name in it."

"Okay," he said affably, "we'll call you 'a source close to the investigation.' How did you know that Bridgeman would try for the movie theatres?"

"That's easy," I said. "That's where the kids were protesting on Thursday. He always hit targets of civil rights protests."

"Except for the house on Truxillo. Or was that a mistake?"

"No comment," I said.

"He's a professional torch," Jeeter said. "That lets the kids off the hook. They don't have that kind of dough. So if he wasn't working for them, he must've been working against them, right?" His fingers jumped on the keys. I shifted uneasily, not sure what I'd given him to type.

"No comment," I said.

"But who for?"

I shrugged. "Don't know. Maybe we'll find out in court."

"I've checked him out," he said, and paused in his typing. "He's not political, he's strictly mercenary. So that suggests somebody hired him who wants to give the local movement a black eye."

"Who's got that kind of dough?" I said.

"Are you kidding?" he said as he resumed his typing. "John Birch

Society, the Klan, the Young Americans for Freedom, a good third of the oil-rich bubbas driving around with shotguns in the back of their pick-ups…"

"Bubbas with shotguns like to do the damage themselves," I pointed out.

"True enough," he said and cocked an eyebrow at me. "So what aren't you telling me?"

"No comment. But if you do me a favor, I might have a bigger story for you within the week." I was talking through my hat since there wasn't much I could tell him in the end, even if I could prove any of my theories. But I might be able to offer him the maritime angle if I could confirm a mob shill inside the union.

"Might?" he said. "Might? You don't win Pulitzers on stories that might get written."

"Here's what I can tell you. The kid who was arrested with Bridgeman—."

"He lived in the house Bridgeman torched on Truxillo Street," Jeeter said.

"Right," I said. "He was Bridgeman's source inside the PYA. He joined so that he could provide Bridgeman with the targets."

His fingers did their dance on the keyboard. "Is that the straight goods?" he said.

"From the horse's mouth," I said. "But remember—."

"I know," he said, "I didn't hear it from you." His fingers paused while he stared into space. "So the blast on Truxillo—that wasn't a mistake, that was a clean-up operation."

"No comment," I said.

I gave him the photograph of Heffelman, asked him to wire it to a reporter at the *Topeka Capital*, who would pass it on to Art Demarest, the Topeka PI, and fended off his questions about it.

"It's private," I said. "Wouldn't interest you."

He sent the wire and returned the picture. He nodded goodbye with the phone receiver already wedged between his jaw and his shoulder, fingers on the keys.

Chapter 35

At four o'clock, after a visit to Mr. Grossman's pawnshop, I met Gavin McHugh and Sly Halsey at McHugh's office at the Port of Houston. Sly had volunteered to help me with the maritime angle, and since I needed the Rodriguez brothers to watch Dizzy, I was glad to have him along. The Port was one of those rare Houston locations where nobody would be surprised to see a white man and a black man palling around together. Apart from the colored sailors, a large contingent of colored stevedores worked there, and some of these had refused to cross National Maritime Union picket lines to load and unload the ships in port.

McHugh raised his eyebrows when we walked in, but there were several people working at desks in the outer office, so he just shook Sly's hand, took us into a back office and shut the door.

"I didn't recognize you," he said to me.

"Good," I said. I was wearing a shaggy white wig that gave me an Einstein air, and a pair of overgrown white eyebrows to match. I'd traded my belt for navy suspenders, and my necktie for a navy bow tie. I wore a blue seersucker suit and wire rims with a bifocal line for added authenticity. I didn't necessarily expect to run into anybody I knew, but I didn't expect not to, either. Either way, it was best to be prepared.

If the state of the union office was anything to go by, the seamen could use a raise just so the union could hike its dues. The inner office was a dull beige that might have been chosen by Jean Lafitte, it was so fly-speckled and discolored. Against the back wall a rusty pipe ran from floor to ceiling and a lopsided pedestal sink had been squeezed into one corner. The mismatched file cabinets looked like they had been salvaged from Davy Jones's locker. There was something on the floor that resembled green carpet, but in places it had given up trying to cover the floorboards altogether. The venetian blinds had slats missing and slats hanging at odd angles like drunken sailors.

"This is the boss's office," McHugh said. "He's out this afternoon."

We sat in folding chairs around a wobbly wooden table and shared a chipped glass ashtray.

"You're sure Sullivan isn't working today?" I said.

McHugh shook his head. "He worked right up to the day he joined the union. If that don't make you suspicious, I don't know what would. He didn't have no trouble crossing our picket lines before, and then all of a sudden, you'da thought somebody went and lit a fire under him, the way he talked. The shipping companies this and the owners that, and what we ought to do about it. He gits all riled up and then he riles the boys up. And I'll tell you something else: he ain't applied for no strike benefits, and he's got a wife and a handful of kids."

"Okay," I said. "That's what we need to do—light a fire under him. We don't have time to wait around for him to contact his handler, we've got to give him a reason to do it."

"So you want me to tell him the police have been asking about him?" he said.

"Let's make it the feds," I said. "Sounds scarier."

"Also more likely," Sly said, "if he's suspected of subversion. And they got more resources."

"You mean the FBI?" McHugh said.

"That's right," I said. "A couple of birds in suits and short haircuts. Tell him you came to see him in case his phone was tapped. That'll guarantee that he asks for a meeting in person instead of telling his sob story on the phone to whoever's paying him off."

McHugh nodded. "I can do that."

I thought he probably could, too—not that we had any good

options. You never know in a set-up like this whether an amateur is going to overplay his hand or fall apart. I liked the way McHugh sat smoking his pipe, impassive. He'd been irritated with me before, in the diner, but he'd never lost his cool and I didn't think he'd lose it now.

"Get him outside if you can," Sly said. "That way we can keep an eye on him."

McHugh nodded. It didn't seem to have occurred to him that this might be a dangerous assignment.

I brought out the paper bag Mr. Grossman had given me, and told McHugh to stand up.

"I'm wearing a wire?" He looked pleased, like he'd been recruited by James Bond.

"I doubt that you'll get anything useful," I said, "but we might as well try." The words of a man whose bank account had seen a recent infusion of funds. Otherwise, Sly and I would be wearing tree branches and standing around in the front yard.

I fixed him up and showed him what button to push when he got out of the car and we tested it. McHugh put on a lightweight jacket and a dusty sailor cap and we were ready to go.

Sly and I were driving separate cars, both equipped with walkie-talkies. McHugh led us to a street in Magnolia Park, not far from the port. It was a white ranch on cinderblocks with an attached carport and a chain link fence around the yard. There was a glider on the front porch and a picnic table in the yard. A rusty blue tricycle lay on its side at the front gate and a row of kids' sneakers decorated the top of the picnic table. When I turned the corner and passed the house, I saw a string of kids' tee shirts and pants on a clothesline in the back. I also spotted a weathered doghouse but no sign of its occupant, not even piles of dog turds in the yard. I hoped to Jesus we wouldn't end up with a wire full of interesting conversation we couldn't hear over a dog barking.

I parked around the corner and across the street. I couldn't see the porch from my vantage point, so I had to rely on Sly for the play-by-play. I figured he was watching through the rearview mirror.

Sly had his own narrative style. "They on the porch," he said. "Our man McHugh got his hand on Sullivan's shoulder. Now Sullivan's mouth is open so wide you could park a Buick on top of his tonsils. McHugh still talking. Uh, oh, now Sullivan is mad, throwing his arms around. McHugh saying, 'Don't be like that with me. I'm the one saved your sorry ass. I told them federals you was a fine, upstanding, dues-paying member of the union.' Oh, Sullivan sorry now, but not too sorry, though. He saying, 'But why them fibbies come after *me*? Who fingered me?' McHugh shrugging. He don't know. 'But maybe the Bureau got somebody on the inside,' he say, 'like a paid informant tell them who threw the first punch or yelled the loudest about burning down the port or broke the first window.' Okay, now that give him something to think about. He not quite so uppity now. That real pale green color white folks get, that means y'all upset, right? Look like McHugh giving him little goodbye pats on the back. Yeah, there he goes. So long, snake! Hope you get what's coming to you."

The two men had talked for less than ten minutes.

"Get a picture?" I asked.

"Of what?" he said. "Couple of stiffs talking on a front porch? Yeah, I got it."

After a few minutes, I said, "Is McHugh gone?"

"Yeah," Sly said. "He didn't even wave or nothing."

I sat smoking in the hot car for maybe twenty minutes before the Motrac crackled and Sly said, "Here we go." Then he added, "Give it a minute. He's got to open the gate to get the car out."

I gave it a minute and then some. As long as Sly had Sullivan in his sights, I wouldn't lose him. When Sly told me to, I put the car in gear, turned the corner and followed them up the street, Sly in the lead and Sullivan between us, easy to spot in a shiny red Chevy pickup. If I'd wondered about Sullivan before, the new pickup convinced me that we were following the right bum. I pictured his wife driving the family car, maybe an old station wagon full of kids and dog, while Sullivan drove the dream car he hadn't been able to resist when he'd suddenly found himself in the money. Well, I knew all about that. And maybe all his kids already had straight teeth.

He led us downtown and pulled into a parking space on Main Street. Sly went on around the block and I parked a few spaces up from the red pickup. I watched Sullivan go into a coffee shop sandwiched between a Western Auto and a Thom McAn. I slipped on the seersucker jacket and grinned at myself in the rearview. I didn't even recognize myself. The miniature camera went into my jacket pocket. I got out, stretched, and tucked a newspaper under my arm. The wig made my scalp itch; it felt like a ski cap in the blazing Texas sun. I stooped a little and ambled into the coffee shop. I saw Sly pass me and park up the street in the next block. He had a camera with a telephoto lens that he could use instead of binoculars if he needed to.

When the hostess batted her mascaraed lashes at me over her armful of menus, I scanned the joint, blinked at her, and asked for a table in the back out of the sunlight that was streaming through the plate glass windows. When she tried to deposit me in a booth, I asked for a table instead, and indicated the one next to the booth where Sullivan was sitting. She conceded the match with a tight-lipped smile that said I'd just made a hash of her seating rotation and she'd hear about it from the next waitress in line for a table. If the place had been empty, as it might have been at that time of day, I wouldn't have chanced it, but enough people were taking advantage of the early bird special that the room was moderately crowded.

The second man in the booth had been showing me his back, but now he turned to flag down the waitress and I got a good look at him. It was Pittaluga, the one Dizzy called Flatface.

When you have that kind of luck, you hold your breath and wait for the other shoe to drop. I half expected the sidekick, Bove the Bignose, to materialize behind me with a gun to my ear. That was assuming he could find my ear under the sheepdog I was wearing on my head. But the two men in the booth, Sullivan and Pittaluga, barely glanced at me. I ordered a coffee and a piece of pie and unfolded my paper. I palmed the camera as I extracted a handkerchief from my pocket and checked it under cover of the newspaper. Parting my fingers to expose the lens, I shot a couple of pictures.

The two men were talking in low voices and the background noise, especially the clatter and clamor coming from the kitchen, made it impossible to hear. Pittaluga's face remained impassive. Sullivan's emotions were written all over his face. He was a big man, tall and powerfully built, and he'd draped that giant frame in a faded green polo and khakis. He had a head of thick black hair above a brow as wide and flat as a coastal plain broken by a set of heavy eyebrows like two lines of Texas sweetgrass. He was on the young side of forty.

Sullivan raised his hands in a gesture that seemed to say, "What am I supposed to do?" Pittaluga said something, and Sullivan shook his head, but Pittaluga kept on talking. My order arrived and I tasted the pie—apple—so I wouldn't arouse suspicion, but I couldn't say whether it was any good or not because all my senses were focused on the booth to my right. Sullivan raised a hand, palm down, in a gesture of impatience or disavowal. But the other man kept talking and Sullivan listened. Finally, the other man laid an envelope on the table. Sullivan picked it up, opened it, and tipped out a nice stack of green corners to riffle. I wanted to kiss the big dope, but Pittaluga practically lunged across the table and tried to snatch the envelope out of his hands. Sullivan turned his body away from me to guard the envelope, and Pittaluga's eyes scanned the room. All he got for his trouble was an old coot with a forkful of pie in his face. The camera lay under the hand resting on top of a newspaper—a hand that wasn't as old as the hair and eyebrows, but he wasn't a careful observer.

The envelope seemed to mollify Sullivan, though, because after that he did more nodding than shaking. When I thought things were wrapping up, I left cash on the table and went out the door, giving Sly a thumbs-up on the way. I got into the car, yanked off the eyebrows, and traded the wig for a hat and the wire-rims for dark glasses. I slipped off the suspenders. It was a relief to ditch the wig; even under the hat, I could feel some air circulation by comparison.

Sullivan was the first to leave and I let him go. He was Sly's game. I ducked down when Pittaluga came out and when I surfaced he was half a block up the sidewalk. He got into a blue Oldsmobile with a Hertz sticker in the back window and I backed out of my space and tailed him about half a mile to the Shamrock Hilton. He drove under the portico and let the valet park it. I skipped the valet and found a space at the curb not far from the main entrance. I needed to know if he was registered, and it didn't tell me anything that he'd used the valet instead of the parking garage.

I put the suspenders back on, traded my bow tie for a string tie and my fedora for a porkpie, and got a loud plaid sports coat out of the trunk. The dark glasses weren't really in character, but they would have to stay in case Pittaluga spotted me. I pinned an oversized name tag to my breast pocket; it said "Gulf Coast Realty," and under that, "Al Traub." I passed all the white coats congregated at the entrance who were hoping to be of assistance to higher rollers than I was and went in. I waded through a half mile of dense carpet to the registration desk, where an efficient-looking woman in a navy suit waited to be of assistance.

"Yes," I said, "I need to call up to Mr. Pittaluga's room."

"One moment," she said. She retrieved the glasses that were hanging by a chain around her neck and managed to set them on her nose without chipping her nail polish. She picked through the registration file, and said, "Room 507. The house phones are just there by the elevators." She pointed a talon in that direction and I thanked her. I went over to the house phones, pretended to dial one, and had a conversation with myself. Then I hung up and angled off in the direction of Trader Vic's, but halfway across the lobby I checked my watch, shook my head, veered toward the entrance and went out. I had just wanted to know if Pittaluga was registered, and if so, if he'd used his own name. I wasn't ready to resume our conversation.

I headed back toward the Ship Channel until I was within range of Sly's walkie-talkie. Sly was sitting on Sullivan in Magnolia Park.

"He came home to eat hot dogs with the wife and kiddies," he said, "which is what I should be doing."

I told him what I'd seen and we agreed to call it a night. I sent him home, dropped off the film at a processing lab that gives me speedy service, and went home to my own progeny.

Chapter 36

McHugh held the photograph in his hand and narrowed his eyes at it. Then he looked at us. "I'd like my boss to see this," he said.

I shrugged. "Your call."

Technically, the person who should have seen the photograph first was the man who had paid me to take it, George Brown. But before I went to see Brown, I wanted to know what all our options were. So Sly and I had met McHugh in the parking lot of his office building. After a brief confab, we followed him inside and into the office we'd visited the day before, except that now it was occupied by a brawny balding man with quick green eyes to match his quick movements. The energy field around him was so palpable that I thought his handshake might hand me a shock.

"This is my boss," McHugh said, "Ross Donnelly."

McHugh told the story as far as he knew it, and Sly and I told the rest. We were sitting at the same rickety table as the day before, so when Donnelly brought his fist down on the table, I flinched. The table's days were numbered.

"By God I'll tear the bastard limb from limb with my own hands!" he said. "That snake! I've never trusted him! Never!" There was a trace of brogue behind his Texas twang.

My best snapshot, the one that showed Sullivan trying to count the money in the envelope, jumped every time Donnelly's fist hit the table.

"Here's the thing," I said. "I still have to report back to the man that hired me to investigate Sullivan. He's not personally involved, he's just a businessman with an interest in the city's business climate. The evidence I've shown you would probably go nowhere in a criminal court. Whether or not you could collect damages from a sympathetic jury in a civil suit, I couldn't say. I'm not an attorney. But I think that you and my client share an interest in ending Sullivan's influence on the strikers. My client would like to see the situation become less volatile, and I'm guessing that you would, too."

"Sure, I would," he said. "But I'm not willing to see my men lie down and let the goddamn scabs walk all over us. If it comes to a fight, we're ready to fight. But we sure as hell don't need some paid agitator pouring fuel on the flames."

"So if we left the thing in your hands—?"

"We'd take care of it," he said. "I don't see how it's anybody's business but ours."

"By 'take care of it,' you mean—?"

"Like I said, nobody's business but ours," he said. "But since y'all brought us the information—you and Mr. Halsey—I can tell you that he'll be kicked out of the union, and when we're done with the kicking, he won't be trusted by anybody anymore."

"If there's violence," I said, "it'll look bad for the union."

"Damn it," he said, "I didn't say we'd kick him, I said we'd kick him out. But listen here, I can't answer for individual members, who have a right to express their opinion. He'll know that. If he doesn't feel safe down at the docks after that, that's on him. The union won't have anything to do with it."

"Yeah," I said. I looked at Sly, who sat with his arms folded across his chest. He raised his eyes to mine, and there was a shrug in them.

So we shook hands all around and Sly and I went off to pay our second visit of the morning. Sly wasn't sure he should come along, but I told him I wanted somebody to back up my story, which was true, and convinced him to come. I also wanted him to meet George Brown and vice versa, in case the Browns had business he could handle for them, always assuming it was business he'd consent to handle. If what they wanted was a snitch inside one of the colored unions, he'd tell them to go soak their heads, but I wasn't going to deprive him of the opportunity to do it.

The office we were finally ushered into after a twenty-minute wait resembled the previous office the way a rowboat resembles the Queen Mary. It was more lavishly if tastefully furnished than suite 8-F at the Lamar, probably because it wasn't a poker venue. It was a penthouse corner office with a view of the downtown so that George Brown could keep an eye on his buildings. The muted beiges and grays in the color scheme seemed intended not to compete with the view. The surfaces of Brown's desk, credenzas, and conference table were littered with paper, including plans and architect's drawings which testified to his close supervision of Brown & Root projects. The piles were tidier than the piles on my desk, though, and I was sure he employed a secretary just to straighten them.

He came forward and shook Sly's hand so cordially a person might think that a negro visitor was an everyday occurrence in the corporate offices of Brown & Root. We sat down at a table built solid as the Gulf Freeway and a secretary—maybe the paper straightener and maybe not—brought us coffee.

We told the same story we'd told at the maritime union. Brown gave us his full attention. I handed him the photographs and he put on a pair of reading glasses to study them. I finished by disclosing that we'd already left a set of prints with the head of the union.

He looked at me over his glasses. "And why did you do that?"

"Because I thought you just might ask me what I thought you should do about all this," I said. I gestured at the photographs. "If you don't want my opinion, you don't. But if you did, I wanted to be able to tell you what the union was likely to do."

"All right," he said with a smile. "What is the union likely to do?"

"They'll put Sullivan out of business."

"But will that solve the problem? Won't this Pittaluga go out and recruit someone else?"

"He might," I said, "just as he might hire another firebomber."

"But you haven't tied Pittaluga to Bridgeman, have you?" he said quickly. "Not definitively."

"No, and we might not be able to," I admitted. "What we've done, Mr. Halsey and I, is to demonstrate to Mr. Pittaluga and his gang that doing business in Houston might be more trouble than it's worth, or at least more trouble than they anticipated." I should have included Dizzy's role in the demonstrating, but that would have required more explanation. "I have reason to believe that they intended to invest five hundred grand in this campaign of theirs. By my calculations, they should be about out of money." I could have made him feel better by telling him about the extra five hundred grand that the mob lost on the Texas Chief. But I skipped it. There was a good chance I'd have to return that money to get them off Dizzy's back.

"You don't think they'll be willing to spend any more than that?" he said.

"I'm hoping they won't have the stomach for it," I said. "At least, not right away, like I said before. They might try something closer to the time when the decision gets made."

"And I take it that you don't think arresting Sullivan and Pittaluga would do any good," he said. He was a man accustomed to compromises, enough of a politician to keep his eye on the outcome he wanted most.

I shrugged. "On what evidence? A good lawyer would make hash of my photographs." I picked up my favorite by one corner. "It's just Uncle Cosimo handing over a loan or maybe some birthday money. Good enough for you, maybe, and for the union. But it wouldn't stand up in court."

He nodded. "It would cost them more money, though, to go to court."

"If you could get an indictment, sure," I said. "So if you want to throw money at it, be my guest. He's already due in court on an unlawful restraint and assault beef that he'll plea bargain down to a donation to the judicial rest and recovery fund."

He leaned back in his chair and looked out the window at the city skyline. "I'll tell you something, gentlemen. It would be worth a lot to me to see the manned spacecraft center built here. I believe Albert's right—a world class facility like that would make Houston hard to beat as the gateway city to the future." He laid his palms on the table. "On the other hand, I'm not interested in wasting money." His gaze shifted to Sly. "What about you, Mr. Halsey? What do you think?"

Sly met his gaze. "I don't believe in messing with the mob unless you've got a good reason to do it," he said. "It's like stirring up a nest of fire ants. You're bound to get stung, and it doesn't matter how many ants you step on, there'll be more ants. In this case, Bridgeman's arrest and trial will let everybody know that our racial violence was a put-up job. The union will get rid of Sullivan before he can do any more damage. Why not just leave it at that?"

"Well, I know you're right," Brown said thoughtfully. "I just hate to see the sumbitches get away with it."

Dizzy – July 14, 1961

Chapter 37

The train pulled out at seven-twenty in the morning, and we were all on it. B.D. and Mel were plastered against the window waving at their parents, and Harry and I were across the aisle. As I settled back in my seat and heaved a sigh of relief, I glanced at Harry and he winked at me.

We'd all thought that it would be B.D.'s mother who would be the biggest pain in the neck about the trip, especially with Bible camp in full swing, but she surprised us and said that it sounded like a great adventure. B.D. says her mother has a romantic soul. Mrs. Cooter's only objection was that she didn't have enough time to take B.D. shopping for new clothes, but we told her that my mother was coming home early next week and we needed to be back by then. So she was jake with everything.

It was Mel's parents that balked. It was such a long way, they said, and Mr. Lark might not be able to handle three girls on his own. Anything could happen, they said. I was well aware that most grown-ups we knew did not consider Harry a responsible adult. In the popular version of our family drama, he'd abandoned us. That wasn't the way I remembered it, exactly, but Harry always says people will think what they want to think, so let 'em. Anyway, Harry had a long talk with Mrs. Landau, like Rose suggested, and afterward Mrs. Landau convinced Mr. Landau to let Mel come along.

Of course, we left out the part about the Mafiosi who were tailing us.

We were a little disappointed to be in a chair car instead of a Pullman, but Harry said you only ride first class if your client can pay. I pointed out that Sissy Heffelman owned a Barbie with a biscuit full of diamonds, and he pointed out that we'd be in Topeka by midnight.

B.D. was the only one who had never crossed the state line before. Mel had been to New Orleans on a family vacation once, and I had been to Florida for the same reason, and once to the Midwest to see my grandparents. B.D. was excited to be crossing the Red River, but I think she was disappointed that the landscape looked pretty much the same on the other side. At lunch she read aloud from the train brochure, all about Ridemaster chairs and Fred Harvey meals. She asked our waiter who Fred Harvey was, but he didn't know. He made up for it by bringing us free ice cream.

Mel's parents had bought her a diary so she could record all the details of our trip, so whenever we came to a new city, we helped her with the description. We spent the afternoon playing cards in the lounge car while Harry smoked and drank Scotch, which is to say that he ordered two drinks and made them last all afternoon. He had the bartender make us drinks as well—not Shirley Temples, like the waiter wanted to bring us, but real drinks minus the alcohol. Mel had a whiskey sour minus the whiskey and B.D. and I drank Mai Tais without the rum and orange liqueur. Harry let us get off the train to stretch our legs at Oklahoma City and Wichita. According to the official schedule, the Chief was supposed to depart the station the same minute it arrived, but of course, that didn't happen. After dinner, we all slept through Emporia, with our dogs up and our heads back against the pillows that the attendant brought.

Harry woke us up outside Topeka and we scrambled for the Ladies' Dressing Room. When we saw ourselves in the mirror, B.D. said, "Shoot, y'all, we don't look like detectives, we look like roadkill." She remade her ponytail, Mel tried to tame her electric curls with water from the sink, and I rubbed at the pillow creases across my cheeks and slapped some color into them. My hair was bristling with static electricity from the pillow so I looked like a porcupine in distress. There was no help for our crumpled dresses, but we pulled up our socks and refolded them.

We were met at the station by Mr. Demarest, a man about Harry's height with slicked-back blond hair and a dent in his chin. He seemed reassuringly alert for the time of night, and was polite to us without being effusive, as if he had dozens of customers our age that he met at the train station at midnight. He shook hands with all of us, helped us collect our luggage, and took us to the hotel. He was not a chatty bird, Mr. Demarest, and wouldn't make much of a tour guide. We'd probably learned as much about Kansas from *The Wizard of Oz*. We couldn't see much in the dark, except that the Hotel Kansas had two tall wings on either side of a shorter part. But inside the lobby I wondered if Harry was expecting Sissy to pay first class after all. The lobby was crammed with armchairs and couches and marble tables and fringed lamps and fancy plant arrangements that Lucille could have hidden in. There was a balcony running all around the lobby on the second floor and a big marble fireplace on one end. The bellman in his red jacket and cap and the desk clerk in his dark suit and bow tie looked wide awake, so we tried to look the same. We had a suite on the sixth floor, with a bedroom for B.D. and Mel and one for Harry and me, and a sitting room that looked like a miniature version of the lobby.

When I hit the hay, Harry came and bussed me on the forehead and then stood grinning at me.

I sighed. "Okay," I said, "it's amazing. But I'd still like to sleep in a Pullman someday."

"Plenty of time, kiddo," he said. "Plenty of time."

Mr. Demarest came to the hotel for breakfast so that we could all hear his report. We ate in the Orchid Room, where the mounted fans barely stirred the sultry air and the tails of the linen tablecloths. I'd wanted to eat in the roof garden, but it was closed for breakfast.

Mr. Demarest, freshly scrubbed and smelling of aftershave, handed me a photograph to pass around.

"That your pigeon?" he asked us.

I took a long look at the photograph, then passed it to Mel, who passed it to B.D. It showed a man bending to talk to someone through a car window, but he'd looked up just as the picture was snapped. He was a balding, middle-aged man with a paunch and he wore a light-colored sports coat. A strand of hair had fallen over his forehead and gave him kind of a goofy look, and I noticed with some surprise that he was wearing a signet ring and wedding ring on the hand that rested on the car roof.

"That's him, all right," B.D. said, staring at the image.

"Are you sure?" Harry said. "Have you ever seen him before?"

Mel shook her head. "I haven't."

"I don't remember if I've seen him or not," I said.

"I've seen him," B.D. said. "Unless he's got a twin, it's him."

Harry nodded at Demarest. If B.D. was sure, it was good enough for him.

"Here in Topeka, he goes by Lou Haines," Mr. Demarest said. "He lives in Oakland—that's a neighborhood in northeast Topeka, near the airport. He rents, but he's been there for two years. Wife's name is Adele. They have a four-month-old baby named Billy."

We stared at him. "Four-month-old?" I said. "Are you sure?" As if this was the least likely part of the story.

He shrugged. "So she says. She was out wheeling the kid around in a buggy, and I chucked it under the chin and asked her." He passed me a photograph of a pretty young light-haired woman, probably a blonde, squatting next to a baby carriage. She was smiling, presumably at Demarest, and pointing up to draw the baby's attention. The baby was squinting up at the camera. His stubby arms were sticking out and suspended like the arms of a marionette.

I looked at Harry. "Did you know?"

"No," he said. "I asked Mr. Demarest to wait and give his full report when we got here. I figured you girls had the right to hear it first."

"Jeez!" I said.

Two years," Mel said. "He must have just been waiting for the right opportunity to walk out."

"On Sissy?" B.D. said. "I'm just finding this so hard to believe, y'all."

There wasn't anything to say to that, so after a minute of silence, Mr. Demarest went on.

"I checked the courthouse records, in case you were interested," he said. He was looking down at a small notebook. "Lou Haines married Adele Collins on May 10 of last year."

B.D. was counting on her fingers. "Sissy was five," she said sadly. "And all that time he was planning to leave."

"Why didn't he just get a divorce?" Mel asked. B.D.'s eyes flitted between Harry and her plate and she shifted uncomfortably in her chair. But Mel didn't have B.D.'s finely tuned sense of propriety, just boatloads of curiosity.

"It's not that easy to get a divorce in Texas, Mel," Harry said easily. "In the absence of cruelty, abandonment, or insanity, the only grounds are proven infidelity. That's why so many people go to Reno."

Now B.D. looked downright miserable.

Mel said, "But he did abandon her, and he was unfaithful."

"Abandonment takes three years to prove," Harry said. "Maybe he couldn't wait that long."

B.D. turned scarlet like a neon sign flashing on at dusk.

"As for infidelity," Harry continued in his reasonable voice, "he might not want to damage his reputation that way. He's a salesman, after all, and reputation means a lot to salesmen."

I couldn't help myself. "But not to private investigators." My mother's grounds had been infidelity, but both she and Harry maintained that they'd rigged the evidence between them just to move things along. I was never quite sure if I believed them.

He smiled and winked at me. "Not that kind of reputation." He turned back to Mel. "Besides, there'd be alimony to consider. Maybe he couldn't afford the alimony. It's expensive to support two families at once, which probably explains why he couldn't resist the temptation when he saw a chance to walk away with a lot of dough and start a new life."

"He'd already started it," I pointed out, "with another wife and a baby."

"True enough," Harry agreed. To Demarest, he said, "What else have you got?"

"He works as a salesman at a Chevrolet dealership on Topeka Boulevard," he said, and passed us another picture. In this one Heffelman was inside a showroom, with one hand on the shoulder of another man in a suit and the other on the hood of a car. He had a big smile on his face. "He's only worked there for about a month."

"Sure," Mel said. "Before that, he was selling cleaning products on the road."

"One neighbor told me he traveled a lot until recently," Demarest confirmed.

"He sure was lucky to find another job so quick." The flames had died down in B.D.'s cheeks.

"Maybe not so lucky," Demarest said. "The dealership is Collins Chevrolet Buick. I'm guessing Collins is a relative of the missus, maybe even her father." To Harry he said, "I can find out if you really want to know."

Harry made a dismissive gesture. "It's up to the girls," he said, "but I doubt it's important. I'd bet dollars to doughnuts the second wife doesn't know about the first one."

"Be my guess," Demarest said.

"What do you want to do, girls?" Harry said.

"Go car shopping," I said.

So we shoveled in our breakfast and Harry paid the bill and we followed Demarest to his car. Before we got there, B.D. turned around and said, "Holy smokes, would you look at that! There's a Greek temple on top of our hotel."

She was right. Perched on top of the building that connected the two wings, maybe seven stories above the lobby, was a Greek temple.

"I'ma sketch that in Mel's diary when we get back, y'all," she said, "but nobody's going to believe it."

At first we parked across the boulevard from the dealership and passed around the binoculars so we could look for Heffelman before we went in.

"He must be inside," B.D. said.

"Maybe he doesn't work on Saturdays," Mel offered.

"He's the newest salesman on the floor," Mr. Demarest said. "Sure he works Saturdays, even if he is related to the boss."

At last we saw him come out of the building with a man in shirtsleeves and a woman in a pale green suit and matching Jackie Kennedy hat. He walked them over to a bright yellow car.

Then he appeared to be handing over a set of keys to the man in shirtsleeves, so Mr. Demarest put the car in gear and we drove across to the lot. Heffelman was waving at the couple as we got out of the car.

Harry probably saw the ruddy-faced salesman in a tan jacket who was racing toward us, but he turned his shoulder and closed the distance between himself and Heffelman without appearing to notice the second salesman or even Heffelman himself. He was doing a good imitation of a man suffering from love at first sight as he zeroed in on a wide-bodied bright red LeSabre sedan with a white hardtop. It had two sharp projectiles like the snout of a shark on either side of the grille, and a pair of chrome torpedoes under them.

"Well, well," Heffelman said, standing back to give Harry more room to admire the car, "I can see that you're a man who knows what he likes. But how did you manage to persuade this bevy of beautiful ladies to come with you?"

"Just lucky, I guess," Harry said.

Heffelman introduced himself as Lou Haines, and shook hands all around as Harry made introductions. Demarest had disappeared, so it was just the four of us. But I discovered that I couldn't unglue my tongue to speak to him. Then I felt Harry's warning hand squeezing my shoulder, and I managed to croak, "Pleased to meet you."

B.D., who had all the thespian training that was normal for Southern girls, beamed at Heffelman and spoke her line with more enthusiasm.

Heffelman opened a rear door and gestured. "I know the ladies will want to inspect the beautifully appointed, luxurious interior while we men take a look under the hood."

This ticked me off, but it was Mel, whose father is a car fanatic, who said, "Actually, I'm more interested in speed. What's the top speed on this car?"

This question momentarily dammed the flow of Heffelman's patter, but then he chuckled. "Oh, I imagine it'll satisfy you, little lady," he said. He patted the car fondly. "This baby will go up to one hundred and ten miles an hour."

If he expected to impress her, he was disappointed. "That's kind of on the low end, isn't it?" she said, and frowned. "Seems to me the average is around a hundred and fifty."

"Well, I don't know about that," Heffelman said.

"But you should know, shouldn't you?" Mel said.

At this point, B.D. slid into the back seat and said in a loud, breathy voice, "Oh, it's just beautiful!"

But Mel persisted, an evil glint in her eye. "I think even the Impala will make around one-fifty. Of course, we should probably talk about acceleration and not just speed."

Heffelman shuffled his feet as he tried to regain his balance. "I'm happy to show you an Impala, but it has a very different look to it. I believe Mr. Lark is drawn to the sportier look of the LeSabre." He ran a hand through his sparse hair and turned his frozen smile on Harry.

Harry nodded affably at him.

"These seats are real comfortable, y'all," B.D. was saying from the back seat. "And there's plenty of leg room."

"Let's look at the engine," Harry said to Heffelman. "I'm also interested in acceleration."

They went to the front of the car and Mel went with them. B.D. raised her eyebrows at me, but I just raised an eyebrow at her. Heffelman deserved as hard a time as Mel could give him, and more.

Eventually, we got around to the test drive and B.D. maneuvered Heffelman into the back seat between her and Mel. We drove down the boulevard with Heffelman leaning forward, one hand on the back of my seat, to continue his pitch. Then Harry turned into a shopping center, parked the car in an isolated space, glanced at the mirror, and then looked at me.

I turned around to face Heffelman, who was still smiling.

"Actually," I said, "we're not interested in buying a car."

He looked puzzled but not alarmed. "You're not?" he said.

"No," Mel said. "We came to talk to you."

"Sissy sent us," B.D. said.

He deflated so fast you could almost hear the whoosh of air escaping. He slumped back against the seat and ran a shaky hand over his head.

"It was that darned doll, wasn't it?" he said in a strangled voice. "But they printed my obituary in the paper—I saw it! There was going to be a funeral, they said."

"There was. But Sissy never believed you were dead," B.D. said. "The doll just confirmed it."

"My wife?"

"Which one?" I said dryly.

He looked at me and blinked.

"Your wife was convinced you were dead," Mel said. "She identified your body. But now she has her suspicions."

"And not just because of the doll," I said.

He looked at Harry then, as tears began to leak from the corners of his eyes. I realized that he was appealing to Harry as the only peer on this jury—as if any man would understand the logic of polygamy.

"It was a terrible thing I did," he said. "I know that. Christ, don't you think I know that? But they're better off without me. She got the life insurance, right? And maybe something from the railroad?"

Harry spoke for the first time, casually. "How deep were you in, brother?"

I bristled at the "brother" even while I admired Harry's strategy. We didn't want him to clam up if we were going to get the whole story out of him.

Heffelman fished a handkerchief out of his back pocket and buried his face in it. His voice was muffled. "It was bad," he said. "Real bad. I owed almost three grand by the end, with the vig. They would have come after me. You know what they would have done to me." He glanced up at Harry over the handkerchief. "Well, maybe you don't. But it would have been bad. They could have done anything—maybe burned down the house to collect the insurance money. I—I was so scared that I took out a life insurance policy."

"Only one?" I asked.

He hung his head. "I could only afford one."

"Maybe you shouldn't have acquired another wife if you couldn't afford the one you already had," Mel pointed out.

Heffelman just groaned.

"They wouldn't do anything to ruin your earning power," Harry said. "Wouldn't be good business."

"I don't know anything about that," Heffelman said. "Christ, I don't know anything! I was crazy, I tell you, crazy with fear."

Mel and B.D. rolled their eyes in unison.

"Didn't it occur to you that the thugs you were dealing with might go after your wife after you died?" Harry said.

Heffelman gave Harry a baleful stare. "They wouldn't do that, would they?"

"Sure they would," Harry said. "If you signed something, I'm sure she's seen it by now."

I looked at Mel and Mel passed the look to B.D. This was something we hadn't considered because we hadn't considered that Heffelman could be in debt to the kind of guys who keep knee-cracking gorillas on the payroll. But Harry, who had plenty of experience dealing with deadbeats, not to mention financing a household, had heard about the insurance policy and the phone calls in the middle of the night and the dead guy who maybe wasn't dead and drawn the most logical conclusion for a cynic to draw. We hadn't asked Mrs. Heffelman if any muscle had visited her to put the squeeze on, and she hadn't volunteered any information about that. But she had no reason to confide in us, either.

Heffelman swallowed. "You don't think—."

Harry shrugged. "House could still burn down."

I was pretty sure he was giving Heffelman a hard time, but that didn't make it untrue, what he was saying about the house burning down.

Heffelman suffered a relapse into self-pity. "Look, I was crazy—just crazy. I didn't know what to do. They were hounding me and I didn't have the money, I didn't know where I was going to get it. I felt like I was being watched all the time—followed. You don't know what it's like. Everywhere you look you see tough guys, and you spend your life wondering when your legs are going to get broken. After a while, you just wish they'd get it over with." He was rubbing his head now so that he looked like a mangy hedgehog with a bad hairstyle. "And then, the train wrecked. And—and—and there it was! Practically sitting in my lap."

"A briefcase full of money," Harry prompted.

My eyes shifted in his direction. That wasn't how I saw it, but he must have known something I didn't.

Heffelman spread his arms and closed his eyes as if he was reliving the moment. "The solution to all my problems. Right there! The guy was dead—he wasn't going to be needing it. The chain was broken—well, practically broken. His arm was a mess. The lock had snapped and the lid had fallen back. It was like it was meant for me—almost as if, I swear to God, somebody was whispering in my ear, 'Take it, Leo. It's all yours. Take it and your troubles will all be over.' It was so easy."

He opened his eyes and heaved a sigh.

Harry said, "But it wasn't that easy, was it, Leo?"

"Christ," Heffelman said, "I haven't had a minute's peace. I'm living on borrowed time. Don't you think I know that?"

"What happened?" B.D. asked.

He looked down at his hands, where they'd collapsed into his spacious lap. "I've been waiting for you," he said. "Maybe not you, but somebody like you. Well, not like you at all, I suppose." His gaze took in the rumpled dresses, the sandals, B.D.'s little white basket of a purse and the bow in Mel's hair. "Jesus, I'm lucky it's you and not a pair of goons with clubs. At least if they show up again, I can afford to pay them off now. And that's what I'd do. There'll be more vig to pay, I know that, and they'll be sore that I ran out on them, but as long as they get their money, that should satisfy them, right?" He reached out in Harry's direction, as if Harry could tell him what to do and it was a relief to have a consultant to tell him.

"How much money, Leo?" Harry said.

"What?" Heffelman said. "I told you, almost three grand—more now, I figure."

"In the briefcase," Harry said. "How much?"

Heffelman retracted his arm and shifted on the seat. "Well, I—." He licked his lips.

"How much?" I said.

"More than three thousand," he said.

"How much?" Harry said.

"Maybe ten," Heffelman said, "or a little more."

Harry swiveled around and started the engine. "Can't help you, Leo," he said. "You're right about being lucky it's us this time. We're not crazy about you, but the next delegation will be much less friendly than we are."

"You'll be lucky if it's the goons with clubs," I said. "The muscle we've met, they all pack heat."

"Heat?" He stared at me.

"You own a gun, Leo?" Mel asked.

"Might be a good time to get you one," B.D. added.

His voice hit the car roof in a panic. "Wait! Don't take me back there! Please. I need—we've got to figure this out. You've got to help me."

Harry had turned his head to watch the traffic so that he could pull out of the lot. "Can't help you if you don't level with us, Leo."

I looked out the window, too. B.D. put in, "Lies always catch up with you in the end."

"Why would I lie to you?" he squeaked. "I'm not lying. That's just how it happened."

Harry turned onto the boulevard. But he was driving slowly. Well, slowly for Harry.

"Okay, maybe it was more than twelve grand," Heffelman said. "I'll pay you. Name your price. Just get them off my back, won't you?"

"How much more?" I said.

"Almost twenty," he said.

I looked at Harry, who kept his foot on the gas. We let the silence stretch. I didn't look at Heffelman but I dropped the visor and used the mirror to survey the back seat. Both Mel and B.D. were turned away from him.

"All right, all right," Heffelman said, "it was a hundred grand."

Harry snorted.

"We told you Sissy sent us," I said, "and she did. But we had to give her the children's discount."

"To be honest," B.D. said, "it wouldn't have been worth our while to come all the way up here for what Sissy paid us."

"And we wouldn't have come if we didn't know what we were dealing with," Mel said.

Harry flipped the blinker on to turn left into the dealership.

"Who owns this joint, Leo?" he said. "Your father-in-law?"

"Please," Heffelman said. "Don't take me back yet. And Christ, don't tell my father-in-law. I'll level with you. I'll pay you whatever you ask. It was five hundred grand." He mopped his forehead as Harry turned the blinker off and kept going.

I shook my head at Heffelman like a disappointed teacher. "See? That wasn't so hard."

Harry pulled into another parking lot and parked.

"How did you know?" Heffelman said.

Harry turned slowly toward him, shaking his head. "Leo, I sure hope you're a better salesman than you are a man of intrigue."

"What—what do you mean?" Heffelman said.

"What made you think that nobody would come looking for that briefcase?" Harry said. "Let me tell you the facts of life, Leo. When you see a man with a briefcase chained to his wrist—a big, heavy one—nine times out of ten, that man is a courier. He's not carrying his own loot, he's carrying somebody else's. If he kicks the bucket, the owner is going to send somebody to find his property."

"The owner?" Heffelman said.

Harry shook his head again. "I have to hand it to you, Leo, when you take to crime, you do it in a big way. Not many men would have the guts to steal from the mob."

Heffelman's eyebrows shot up and his eyes popped as if they were attached by cartoon springs. "The mob?" he squeaked. "You mean the Mafia?"

"That's the one," I said.

"But—but—but—but we don't have Mafia in Houston," he objected.

"They don't live there," B.D. said, "they just like to visit."

"They got big hearts," I said. "They like to send money to needy Texans when they want something done."

"Hire the local talent," Mel said.

"You're telling me I stole five hundred thousand dollars that the Chicago Mafia was sending down to Houston to pay somebody off?" Heffelman said, a thread of doubt creeping in.

"Hard to believe, we know." B.D. patted his hand.

He roused himself and shook her off. "Wait," he said. "I don't know who you are, mister"—this directed at Harry—"but if you want me to believe that you brought three little girls up here from

Houston to warn me that the mob is on my trail, well, I don't, that's all."

"I didn't bring them," Harry said. "They brought me. It's their case."

"Anyway," B.D. said, "we don't give a rat's ass what you believe, the fact remains that we tracked you down. And if 'three little girls' can do it, other people can."

"Especially if we help them," Mel said.

He threw up his hands. "Okay, okay, look," he said. "What do you want from me? Name your price."

"We don't have a price," B.D. said.

"We don't need money," I said. "We've already got about thirty-five grand in gemstones. Isn't that what you said, Harry? About thirty-five?"

"Uh-huh," Harry said.

"You found the diamonds." Heffelman's voice was hoarse now. All the color drained out of his face as he adjusted to his new position—not a wealthy man bargaining from a position of strength but a man whose fortune had evaporated before he'd had the chance to enjoy it. "Those were for Sissy—for Sissy and her brother. For my kids. In case something happened to me."

B.D.'s temper flared. "What makes you think that Sissy wants your gol-derned diamonds more than she wants her daddy, you low-down, no-count, sorry-assed son of a snake?"

She ignored his wet eyes and hangdog look. "You asked what we want. I'll tell you. We want to know how you had the unholy nerve to get you another wife and family in Topeka when you already had one in Houston. And then we want to know how you propose to straighten out this mess. That's what we want."

"I don't know how it happened," he blubbered. "Honest, I don't! It just did."

Mel raised a hand. "I move we take him up on the tallest bridge in Topeka and dangle him over the side until he takes some responsibility."

"Not a bad idea," Harry said thoughtfully, and eyed Heffelman as if assessing how much he weighed.

Heffelman gasped. "I just—I just—I just met this girl I liked, and, you know, fell in love. I thought it was the greatest thing that ever happened to me. And then the next thing I knew, we were engaged. That's all. I was a long way from home and Millie and I weren't getting along so well, and there were money problems even then, so I was worried and—and—and Adele made it all go away. When I was with her—."

"Yeah, yeah," I said, "bells rang and flowers burst into bloom and the damned bluebird of happiness floated down and perched on your shoulder."

"I hope it pooped there," B.D. said so savagely that the rest of us couldn't contain ourselves and soon we were laughing so hard the tears were streaming down our cheeks. Even Harry was laughing.

Heffelman just looked confused. As professional investigators, we had a lot to learn.

"So what's it going to be, Leo?" Harry said at last, wiping his eyes. "What are you going to do?"

Heffelman seemed to gather his feeble resources and said earnestly, "What do you think I should do? Can you get the mob off my back?"

"Get in line," I muttered.

"First things first," B.D. said severely. "You've got to tell your first wife you're alive, and you've got to tell your second wife about your first wife."

His expression said he'd rather go up against the mob than his two wives.

"You'll have to let Millie divorce you," Harry said, the only one in the car with any experience in the matter. "You've given her grounds—adultery and abandonment."

"Adele will be furious," Heffelman said. "What if *she* divorces me?"

"I don't know the Kansas statutory law," Harry said, "but

technically, you're not married to her. You can't be married to two women at the same time, no matter what your marriage certificate says."

"But—but—that would make our baby—," Heffelman sputtered.

"Illegitimate," Harry said. "Which is what he is."

I caught a glint in B.D.'s eye that made me realize she was now living inside one of her sister's drugstore romances. When she wasn't overcome by fury, she was thrilled.

Heffelman choked up. "You have to understand, I love my kids. All my kids. I'd do anything for them."

This last part was blatantly untrue but nobody bothered to point it out. Instead, Harry said, "It's possible that nobody in Topeka will ever hear about the Texas divorce. If your new wife keeps mum, she can marry you again in a private ceremony—maybe in Kansas City, maybe across the state line in Missouri—and nobody will ever have to know. It's up to her whether she wants to tell her family, including your boss. You know her better than I do."

Heffelman shuddered. "I need this job," he said.

"You'll need it more when the alimony comes due," Harry said, again the voice of experience.

"But what about the money?" Heffelman said. "Can I give it back?"

"That what you want to do?" I said.

He closed his eyes. "I just don't want to live in fear all the time any more. I'd rather give it back than wait for them to show up on my doorstep—or at the dealership—waving guns and demanding their money." He opened his eyes. "But I've already spent some of it. And of course, there's you—you have to be paid."

"You can pay my expenses," Harry said. "The rest is up to the girls."

"We've already collected," I said. "We work for Sissy."

"Do you think the—well, the Mafia—will take my note for the rest of it?" Heffelman said anxiously.

"How much can you pay?" Harry asked.

"If I sell the jewels—," he began, and looked to Harry for

confirmation that this would be possible. Harry looked at me and I nodded. "If I sell the jewels for what I paid for them, and empty the bank account I set up for the kids, I can pay at least four hundred and fifty, maybe a little more."

"You still owe three grand to the Houston sharks," Harry said. "You'll have to pay that as well, plus the vig." He cocked an eyebrow at Heffelman, and Heffelman nodded, defeated.

"I'll make an offer of four hundred and fifty to the Chicago boys, with your apologies," I said. "Let's see what they say. Maybe you could throw in a car—say, a Buick Electra. You can donate it to one of their charities."

"They have charities?" Heffelman said.

"Sure," Harry said. "Raffles to support the opera or the Italian-American league or the church, in case they want to gild a baby Jesus."

"Okay," Heffelman said. "Whatever you think best."

"You might ought to have asked somebody's advice about that before you got yourself into this mess," B.D. said.

"I know," he said meekly.

We took him back to the dealership, where Mr. Demarest was waiting inside an Electric blue LeSabre convertible, listening to a sales pitch. We made Mr. Heffelman pose for a picture, which Mr. Demarest took. Then Harry went inside and sat down with him as if they were making a deal, but instead Harry was dictating the terms of a contract we wanted him to sign for us to take back to Mrs. Heffelman. He wrote out a check for Harry's expenses. This included Mr. Demarest's fee, which Harry inflated the way he often does when his client is wealthy.

When Mr. Heffelman came out to see us off and shook our hands, he still looked shaken. But he looked relieved, too.

"What a jerk," B.D. said as we drove away. "It's a wonder Sissy wants him back."

"He's her father," I said.

There was no response from the front seat.

We spent the afternoon seeing the sights and then ate dinner in the roof garden. In the middle of dinner, Mr. Heffelman showed up with the things we had required him to produce. He handed two envelopes to Harry, and Harry handed them to me. I put down my fork and opened the first. Inside was a certified check, made out to Harry, in the amount of four hundred and fifty-four grand to pay back the money Mr. H. had borrowed and stolen. Since he didn't have the jewels yet, I presumed he'd taken out a loan of some kind, but that wasn't my problem. If Harry couldn't make a deal with the wise guys, the money would come back to him like a bad debt that had accumulated interest. I opened the second envelope and found three handwritten letters, one to each of Mr. H's Houston family members. This was good. We'd only required him to write to his wife, but he'd also written to each of his children. I nodded, put everything back in the two envelopes, and passed them to B.D., who inspected them and passed them to Mel. "We're satisfied," I told Harry.

Mr. H. was inclined to stick around and chat, but Harry gave him the bum's rush so we could eat our dessert in peace. B.D. stuck her finger down her throat as soon as his back was turned.

Later, we slept in the train station until the Texas Chief rolled in at two-thirty and we crawled into our Pullman berths, too excited from the luxury of it to sleep—or so we thought. But the porter sat guard on his stool while the sway of the car rocked us and the wheels hummed a lullaby and at last we fell asleep.

Harry – July 16, 1961

Chapter 38

We got into Houston at eight o'clock Sunday night. The girls made a rush for the waiting parents while I brought up the rear. I was distracted by the familiar miasma of the Bayou City and the rank odor of Pasadena refineries. But I knew I had less than forty-eight hours until the real trouble started. At high noon on Tuesday, D.F. Lark would step down off the plane and onto the tarmac, and I would have a lot to answer for.

I went home and called Carillo, who was, as usual, at the office.

"That guy Graziano, my late client," I said. "You got a contact?"

"Yeah, sure. Me and the Chicago wise guys, we're tight. Every few days they call me up to find out how my case against Neroni and Landi is going. What do you think?"

"If Neroni and Landi are still alive," I said, "it means that maybe Graziano wasn't much use in Chicago."

"Yeah," he said, "or maybe he wasn't important enough to start a mob war over. You making any progress on this thing? I still want to know why Chicago and Florida picked Houston as their O.K. Corral."

"Probably misjudged the intelligence of the local cops. Who claimed Graziano's body?"

"Widow and her brother," he replied.

"Got a number for the brother?" I said.

"And I'd be telling you this why?"

"Because you admire my work and hope that someday I can explain everything to you."

"That's right, I forgot," he said. "Hold the line."

I heard rustling noises and in the background the kind of noises you hear in a cop shop, even late on a Sunday night—shouting, moaning, drunken singing, the works.

Then he was back. "Brother-in-law's name is Luciano Marchetti."

"She married family, I bet," I said. "Cozy."

"Also safer, probably," he said.

He gave me a number in Chicago, and I hung up and checked the time. Chicago and Houston were in the same time zone, so it was getting late, but not, according to the rules of the aforementioned D.F. Lark, too late. I dialed.

When I got Graziano's brother-in-law on the line, I explained that I had been working for Mr. Graziano when he bought the farm and that since his death I had come across some information relevant to some missing property that Mr. Graziano had taken an interest in. I couldn't afford to be too explicit on the phone, especially now that Bobby Kennedy and his Justice Department had declared war on the mob.

I had no idea if what I told the brother-in-law was true, of course. The Florida mugs who had clipped Graziano had taken an interest in missing property, but whether Graziano himself had been looking for secret files, five hundred grand, the crown jewels or my personal dental records when he'd searched my office and gotten caught by Neroni and Landi, I had no idea. But I told the brother-in-law that I'd felt obligated to call and let him know about it out of respect for my late client Graziano. Marchetti might have known that Graziano and I hadn't parted in a state of mutual respect or he might not, but if he did he didn't say so. He thanked me and told me he'd call me back. Forty minutes later, he did. He informed me that a Mr. Zangari would call on me at my office the next afternoon.

I can never decide what it is that distinguishes one rank of wise guy from another. At the lower end, it's easy to tell the muscle from the brains, the bulging plaid suits from the whispered pin stripes and discreet diamond stickpins. But how did I know that Zangari was higher up the organizational chart than Graziano had been? Maybe it was the Rushmore jawline, the steel that hardened the brown eyes. It wasn't so much that his dark suit was lint-free as it was that it had the air of a suit that lint wouldn't dare to land on. He had graying sideburns and a threadlike scar under his right ear. The only thing I had on him was my amicable relationship with the Houston weather, but he managed to look cool even while blotting his forehead with a linen handkerchief. He had shaken my hand, parked his plaid sidekick in the outer office, and assumed as comfortable position as he could in my client's chair.

"We think it gets hot in Chicago," he said, "but my God."

I nodded. "Mayor Hofheinz wants to build a domed stadium, but we might just skip it and build a dome over the whole city so we can air condition it."

He put his handkerchief away and got down to business. "You told Mr. Marchetti that you had information about some missing property that Mr. Graziano was interested in."

"That's what I told him," I agreed, "though to be honest, I don't know if Mr. Graziano was interested in it or not. I know that the men who killed him were interested because they came to me next. They seemed to think I knew where it was."

"But fortunately for you, you were able to discourage them," he said.

"That's right," I said.

"And did you, in fact, know where this missing property was?"

"Not then. I didn't know anything about it. I do now."

"I see," he said. He uncrossed his legs and recrossed them the other way. "And how did you come to acquire this information?"

I shook my head. "I can't tell you that without compromising another client. I told you I didn't know anything about it when the goons came after me, and I didn't. But once they'd spilled the beans, I became curious. After that, I was on the lookout, you might say."

"I see," he said.

"I'm now in a position to arrange a return of the property—well, most of it," I said. "But naturally, I'm not keen to return it to the same thugs who killed my client and came after me."

"Naturally."

"I also have reason to believe that they sent a pair of their pals to try and persuade me to tell them what I didn't know," I said.

"And your daughter interceded, I heard." He was gazing at the ceiling as if the spiders had been chronicling my adventures up there.

"Uh-huh," I said.

"I would like to have seen that, Mr. Lark," he said, lowering his eyes to meet mine.

"Me, too," I said. "I didn't have much of a view."

"I admit that I'm still curious how you came into possession of this missing property."

"I didn't say that I possessed it," I corrected him. "I said that I could arrange its return."

"'Most of it,' I believe you said."

"Look," I said, "it's like this. Suppose you were a poor working stiff with a wife and kids and a mortgage and some installment payments coming due on your refrigerator. And one day the train you're riding in runs into a tank car and jumps the rails and you wake up with a briefcase stuffed with cash in your lap. You can see that the bird who was carrying the briefcase won't be able to use if anymore, and anyway the briefcase is no longer attached to him and no longer closed and locked. What do you do?"

He ignored the question. "What did he do?"

"He helped himself," I said. "I might do the same. You might do the same."

"And now?"

"He's got a guilty conscience," I said. "And he's entitled to it. He'd sleep better at night if he gave it back."

"Most of it," he reminded me again.

I shrugged. "There were those mortgage and refrigerator payments. He can't give it all back because he doesn't have it all."

"How much?"

"Four hundred fifty thousand," I said.

He relaxed a little, and tried to cover his relief by recrossing his legs. He'd probably been expecting half. What's fifty grand between businessmen?

"May I ask why you think that Mr. Graziano's family would be interested in this money?" he said.

"You're here," I pointed out. "And for another reason, I think that Mr. Graziano's employer may have had some business dealings with the Florida outfit. I think they may have killed him because they thought he knew where the money had gone. Maybe they thought he'd taken it. But if the money belonged to Mr. Graziano, it seems only fair that Mr. Graziano's family should get first crack at it, now that it's found. He was my client, after all."

"And what fee would you expect to facilitate this return?"

"No fee," I said. "A favor."

His eyebrows lifted, but you had to be watching closely to see it.

"The Florida torpedos are still after my daughter," I said. "Maybe they think she knows where the money is, or maybe they're just sore. I want them off her back."

"I believe that can be arranged," he said. He hesitated, then asked, "How old did you say your daughter was?"

"I didn't say," I said, "but she's twelve. Going on thirty."

He nodded once. "I'll take care of it."

"Can I ask another question to satisfy my curiosity?"

When he didn't say no, I went on, "You and Mr. Graziano are from Chicago. These other birds are from Florida. What are they, competition?"

He stood to go. "Let's just say that we have a business connection. We were doing them a favor, and it didn't work out."

"No good deed, huh?"

"You could say that."

When we went out into the waiting room, the goon was chuckling over a *Reader's Digest*.

The next day I told Carillo, "I hated to do it. I hated like hell to do it—give back the money they'd invested in giving Houston a black eye. But what choice did I have?"

"No choice," he agreed. We were sitting in a bar downtown at the time because he thought it would put him in a better mood to hear the story. "But at least you didn't give it to the Florida mob."

I contributed a butt to the logjam in the ashtray and lit another. "I still don't know how Chicago came into it in the first place—not for certain," I said. "Zangari said they were doing somebody a favor. I think Chicago must've offered to set everything up in Houston. They probably knew Bridgeman, after all. Then the Chicago courier lost their dough and relations went south. The money must have been Florida money or the Florida goons wouldn't have come after it. Maybe the Miami boys thought the whole thing was a set-up. Anyway, it's a cert they thought Graziano knew where their money had gone. When they said as much in my office that night, where Graziano was looking for more dope on the NASA business, things got hot."

"Yeah," Carillo said. "Heat's one thing we got plenty of here in the Bayou City."

"I'm sure when Graziano got himself croaked, that didn't do anything to promote amity between Miami and Chicago. Meanwhile, the Miami brass decided to run their own operation."

Carillo raised his head. "Promote what?"

"Amity."

"That's right," he said. "You were married to a college professor. What about the stiff who's buried in Heffelman's grave?"

"He's getting dug up and shipped home," I said. "He was the logical first suspect, of course, since his name never made it onto any casualty list after the Texas Chief wreck. I bet my license that maybe Chicago and definitely Florida thought he was the one who'd done a bunk with the boodle."

"And now they feel guilty about it, so they'll give him a hero's sendoff," Carillo said. "And maybe they'll return the dough to Miami or maybe they'll divide it between the widows."

We signaled the bartender for another round and cursed Texas liquor laws. It didn't do any good, of course. It was just what you did when you were drinking beer in a Texas bar.

"Say, who'd you collect from on this case?" Carillo asked.

I parked the cigarette between my middle and ring fingers and held up a hand for counting off. "The Chicago mob paid me to tell them what they already knew—that Houston had an inside track on the new NASA space center. Wardlow and her outfit paid me for ending the firebombings and clearing the PYA's name. George Brown paid me for putting Abe Sullivan out of commission and calming things down on the docks. Also for saving his clubhouse from being burned to the ground. Heffelman paid my expenses to come after him and force him to own up to his children and pay back the wise guys. The wise guys paid me out of respect for my work."

Carillo was studying my fingers as if he was having trouble keeping them in focus. "Christ!" he said. "That all?"

"Well," I said, reaching for my beer and cigarette, "the insurance company tried to pay me for proving that Leo Heffelman wasn't dead, but I made them write the check to Dizzy, and she split it with her pals. The only fee they'd earned prior to that was a Barbie doll, and Dizzy had ripped the head off that one. In the end they felt bad, so they bought their client a new Barbie."

He nodded. "Did the professor make it home okay?"

"Yup," I said.

"How much did you tell her?"

"Not a thing," I said. "She wouldn't want to know."

"Not a thing?" he repeated.

I shook my head. "Anyway, I crossed my heart."

Dizzy – July 17, 1961

Chapter 39

"So now that you're in the money," I said, "you should hire a secretary."

At breakfast I'd asked Harry about the permission slip I needed to travel with my team to a city tournament across town. He said that he'd left it at the office, which meant he'd never find it in this lifetime and I'd be sitting on my catcher's mitt and waving goodbye to my teammates.

"I don't need a secretary," he said. He was fiddling with the toaster.

"Excuse me?" I cupped a palm around my ear. "I can't have heard that right. How many times have your lights been cut off because you lost your electric bill? How many checks have you lost in your inbox? How many times have I helped you go through the wastebasket looking for the evidence you needed for court the next day?"

The toast popped up and he flinched.

"Your office is a pigsty," I said. "I mean, fundamentally. We could file every paper in it and underneath it all would be a pigsty. For starters, you have enough bug specimens to enter the junior high science fair."

"I like my bugs." He was frowning down at the toast he was buttering. "We're on a first-name basis."

"What kind of an excuse is that?" I said. "You're on a first-name basis with every crook in Houston."

When he didn't say anything, I repeated myself. "You should hire a secretary."

"Where would I find a secretary?" he said. He was raising the toast to his mouth when Rose spoke.

"I've been to secretarial school," she said. She didn't look up from the stove she was scrubbing.

He paused, mouth open, toast hovering. He blinked. "You have?"

"Yes," she said simply. "I have." She still didn't look at us. She frowned at a spot on the stovetop and rubbed.

Harry put the toast down and cleared his throat. "I didn't know that."

"Well, now you know." She started in on the sink.

Harry's eyes shifted to mine, then back to Rose.

He cleared his throat again, but he was just buying time. Finally, he said, "Who would look after the house if I hired you as a secretary?"

She had started running the water but now she turned it off. "Daisy's out of work right now," she said.

Rose had lots of sisters, and Daisy was one of them. I liked her. She was mischievous and fun-loving and talkative.

"Do you think Daisy would want a job like this?" Harry said. "And would you give her a reference?"

"Of course, she'd want it," Rose said. "It's a good job." She looked at him now. "As far as a reference, you don't have to be a genius to do this job. Daisy is a good cook. But you don't need a college degree to clean a house or do the laundry or iron a mess of clothes."

Harry cocked an eye at me. "What do you think, Sis?"

I knew that he genuinely wanted my opinion. But he also wanted backup when my mother came home and found out he'd hired her housekeeper right out from under her.

But this was Rose. And I knew where my loyalties lay. Besides, as soon as she got over her anger, my mother would agree that this was a good opportunity for Rose.

So I swallowed and said, "I think it's a good idea. Why not?"

There was an answer to that, but nobody was going to say it. If Harry hired Rose, she'd probably be the only negro woman she knew working as a secretary for a white employer.

"Why not?" Harry repeated. "Okay, Rose, you're hired."

"On what terms?" she said, and my cereal went down the wrong way.

After breakfast we went to see Mrs. Heffelman and Sissy. B.D. had called to warn Sissy we were coming, with progress to report, so that she'd have some time to prepare herself for news. We'd considered talking to Mrs. Heffelman first, and letting her break the news to Sissy, but Sissy was our client and we wanted to honor that.

"Anyway, Sissy is tough as nails, y'all," B.D. said, and Mel and I were inclined to agree.

Today the house smelled like wax and furniture polish. Mrs. Heffelman's blond hair had the tight, misshapen look of a beauty shop style that has been slept on a couple nights but otherwise left alone. She wore fresh pink lipstick and a pink floral print house dress with a checked apron like she was competing for Mrs. America. Sissy wore a tee shirt with a blue cottontail bunny on it that exposed her belly button and made her look two years younger.

We sat on the gray plaid couch in the den this time, facing Sissy, who was in a giant armchair that made her look like Fay Wray in King Kong's fist. Mrs. Heffelman sat in a rocking chair, but held it motionless by perching on the edge of the seat. Once again, there was no sign of Sissy's brother Tommy.

I looked at Sissy. "We've concluded our investigations, and we have a report to give. We think it's a good idea for your mother to be here to hear what we have to say. Is that okay with you?"

Sissy's gaze swept our faces, and then she nodded.

"Your father is still alive," I began. "He's living in Topeka, Kansas. We've talked to him."

Mel got up and handed Sissy a photograph of her father on the car lot. Sissy stared at it so long that her mother became impatient and got up to look over her shoulder. I noticed that Mrs. H. didn't look shocked or astonished, so I presumed she'd been thinking things over since we'd talked to her and gotten used to the possibility.

"When the accident happened," I went on, "he was knocked

unconscious, and when he came to, he found a briefcase full of money practically on top of him. The owner of the briefcase was dead. Your father needed the money because he was in debt to some —some bad guys, so he dressed the man in some of his clothes, put his wallet in the dead man's pocket, and walked away with the briefcase."

Sissy and her mother were staring at me, stone quiet.

"But then I guess he thought that he might keep all of the money instead of paying back the bad guys." I hoped that Sissy was getting the general idea rather than scrutinizing the logic of the whole story. I was cutting Leo some slack for Sissy's benefit—I didn't want her to think that he walked out on her without a thought.

"He decided that he wanted to just disappear," I said. "He knew that you would get the insurance money, Mrs. Heffelman. He says—well, he says he thought you would be better off without him. And he would make sure that Sissy and Tommy were well taken care of financially."

She flinched, and at first I thought that her reaction was sadness, but then her eyes narrowed and I saw them heating up like a stove burner. Sissy's eyes had melted and were threatening to overflow.

"Tell me the rest of it," Mrs. Heffelman said. She stood and crossed her arms over her chest.

"He owed money," I said, "and he was afraid of the people he owed it to."

When she didn't say anything, I continued.

I glanced at Sissy, but when I looked back at Mrs. Heffelman, her expression was hard and unrelenting. "He had another wife," I said. There was no way to soften the blow, and when I looked into her smoldering blue eyes, I knew she was expecting it, or something like it. "Another wife in Topeka, and a new baby."

"Son of a—!" she said, and I put a restraining hand on B.D.'s arm to keep her from running to Sissy to cover her ears, but Mrs. H. pulled up short anyway. "I need a cigarette."

"But Mama," Sissy said, turning in surprise, "you don't smoke." In a small voice, she added, "Only Daddy smokes."

"I do now." Mrs. Heffelman marched out of the room.

We listened to her slamming cabinet doors and drawers in the kitchen—surely more than she needed to slam for a pack of cigarettes and an ashtray—while tears slid down Sissy's cheeks. Sissy whispered, "Mama's mad." We heard the flick and scratch of a lighter.

"She's entitled," Mel said gently.

Mrs. Heffelman returned with a lit cigarette between her teeth and an ashtray and box of Kleenex in the other. She set the ashtray down, pulled a wad of tissues from the box, stooped, and began dabbing at Sissy's eyes. Sissy put her arms around her mother's neck, and for a few minutes, her mother held her close and let her sob.

When the sobs subsided at last and Sissy had blown her nose, Mrs. Heffelman straightened and asked, "You got a picture?"

Mel knew what she meant and handed her the photo Mr. Demarest had given us—the one of the second Mrs. H. out walking the baby in a baby carriage. I wondered if the first Mrs. H. noticed how much the second Mrs. H. resembled her.

Apparently she did because she nodded and said, "He always liked them pretty and blond—and young."

Sissy said. "Daddy has another wife? And a baby?"

"Let me explain it to you, sweetheart," her mother said, not without tenderness. "Your daddy is a louse."

Sissy's chin quivered like a performing flea. "But when is he coming home?" She turned wet eyes on her mother again. "I wanted to say thank you for my Barbie doll. I wanted to show him her new outfits, when the girls give her back."

I felt a pang of guilt and looked away.

"He wrote you a letter, sugar," B.D. said. "You and your mother and your brother. Maybe he explained it to you in the letter." B.D. handed the envelope to Mrs. H., who looked like she could burn it to cinders with rays from her eyes. B.D. knelt in front of Sissy. "The good news is that he's still alive and you can see him again some time."

We knew that this was a risky thing to say, since it would depend entirely on Mrs. Heffelman whether or not Sissy would ever lay eyes on her father again. But we'd decided to go on the record in support of a father-daughter reunion.

"But he's not coming home?" Sissy said.

"No, sugar, he's not coming home," B.D. said and put her arms around Sissy.

"I suppose I'll have to pay back the insurance money," Mrs. Heffelman said in a voice like a karate chop.

"I suppose so," I said.

"And then what will we live on?" she said. "I'll have to fight him in court for every penny, won't I? And I'll have to get a job. I'll have to go back to secretarial work."

I said a silent prayer of thanks to the gods of business arrangements that Harry had already hired a secretary. He didn't need Mrs. Heffelman's temper. What he needed was a firm hand to make him toe the line, and Rose would do it.

Mrs. Heffelman was so entangled in her own misery that she didn't think to ask about the dead man until we were saying goodbye at the door.

"So who's buried in Leo's grave?" she said. "I suppose they'll have to dig him up again. And then everyone will know—everyone who came to the funeral will know!" She gazed across the street to where a lawn sprinkler was circling, its staccato buzz the loudest sound in our quiet neighborhood. "But what am I talking about? I'm fixing to divorce the jerk, and everyone will know anyhow. I'm going to get the best darned divorce lawyer in the city." She raised her chin. "You tell your daddy I might want to talk to him, Dizzy."

Mel removed a box from the shopping bag she'd carried in and handed it to B.D. B.D. handed it to Sissy.

"Here's your present, sweetheart," she said.

Sissy stared at Barbie, resplendent in her Enchanted Evening get-up. We held our breath to see if she'd rumble the substitution or reject it out of anger at her father, but she just said, "Isn't she beautiful? And Daddy picked her out special for me—for my birthday." She whispered the last part of this sentence, as if reassuring herself.

And then we were back out on the hot pavement. A tickle of mist from the sprinkler reached our faces.

"Well," B.D. said as we walked away, "I hope she takes him to the cleaners."

And we didn't have to ask who she meant.

That was the last night Harry would be on duty. My mother was returning the next day.

When the news went off, I cuddled up against his shoulder to assure him that he hadn't messed up too bad.

He smiled at me and rubbed a hand across my head. "You'll be pretty glad to see your mother, won't you, Sis?"

"Sure. It will be great having her back. Only—."

"Only what?" He held up his palm and I matched mine to it, finger for finger.

"It's been kind of nice having you around," I said.

"It's been kind of nice being around," he agreed.

"Really? I thought we cramped your style."

"Sister," he said in a tough-guy voice, tightening his arm around me, "you *are* my style."

Book Club Questions

1. Harry and Dizzy Lark are versions of the hard-boiled detective and the girl detective, respectively; they're direct descendants of Philip Marlow and Nancy Drew. How do they compare to the predecessors with whom you're familiar? How does the father-daughter relationship affect both detective types? (For more about girl detectives and their detective fathers, see the Inquiring Minds section at dbborton.com.)

2. In her suburban Southern neighborhood in 1961, Dizzy is an anomaly because her parents are divorced. How do you think her unusual status shapes her as a character?

3. Like you, Dizzy and her friends are, above all, passionate readers. How does their reading influence how they think and feel?

4. In the book, Harry stops working for the mob because he foresees how important the new space center will be to his children. He appreciates that his children need heroes to look up to and emulate. Of course, Dizzy rightly elevates Juney Armbruster to hero status for participating in civil rights demonstrations. Who are today's kids' heroes? Do they measure up, in your opinion?

5. The book is set in the time before the Civil Rights Act of 1964 (in the days before "civil rights movement" was conventionally capitalized). What do you think has and hasn't changed in American race relationships since that time?

More Books by D.B. Borton

Hank Jones isn't kidnapped by aliens. He goes voluntarily. What does he have to lose? It's spring break. His freshman comp students have taken their bad grammar and bad attitudes to Florida. His dissertation is going nowhere. And his ex is sleeping with his dissertation director. So when two aliens walk into a bar in Bloomington, Indiana, looking for directions, he's their man.

And they need help, that's clear. It's 2007, and they haven't visited Earth since the 1950s, so their cultural information, like their clothing and their language, is sadly outdated. The android who's had an Elvis makeover doesn't even know that his idol is dead.

Hank finds himself riding shotgun to Washington and acting as consultant on a mission to save the Earth from annihilation. SECOND COMING is not so much about space aliens but about celebrity in 21st-century America, the seductiveness of consumer culture, the self-destructiveness of the human race, and the very human pleasures of friendship, dogs, and rock 'n roll.

Fun book. Very engaging characters. ... Well-paced story of anachronistic comedy of errors. Goodreads.com

Second Coming *is the perfect alien arrival science-fiction with loads of humor.* Goodreads.com

I loved this book. Goodreads.com

The message is foreboding, but the tone of this delightful and humorous book is anything but doom and gloom. Amazon.com

Very entertaining book; kept me laughing throughout. Amazon.com

D B Borton's book, Second Coming, *should seriously be required Freshman College reading. It's the most well crafted hilarious wake-up call I've read in a long, long time.* Amazon.com

Late one night during the fiery early days of the Iranian revolution, as rain washes smoke from the air, two dark figures raid the Tehran Museum of Contemporary Art and carry off twelve of the world's most valuable paintings. The theft is never made public. But even the Iranians don't know the surprising result: most of the paintings are forgeries.

Thirty-six years later, M.J. Smith still works for Quixote, Ltd., a secretive branch of Levesque Security that specializes in "extrications," when she is handed a list of paintings stolen from a deceased client. The paintings—a Picasso, a Monet, a Gaughin, a Degas, and others—are all familiar to her. She stole them herself three decades before.

Now she must find the paintings and steal them again, determine who wanted the paintings enough to murder their owner, and penetrate the fog that cloaks the past and guards its secrets, relying on a cast of characters who are never what they appear to be—just like M.J. herself.

Fantastic read. Goodreads.com

I love the sense of humor evident in Ms. Borton's writing. … The writing is wonderfully descriptive and often produces audible chuckles as the story weaves in an out of the many twists. Goodreads.com

A great escape! There are wonderful twists and turns in this mystery. Amazon.com

About the Author

A native Texan, Borton became an ardent admirer of Nancy Drew at a young age. By the time she was fourteen, she had acquired her own blue roadster, trained on the freeways of Houston, and begun her travels. She left Texas around the time that everyone else arrived.

In graduate school, Borton converted a lifetime of passionate reading and late-night movie-watching into a doctorate in English. She discovered that people would pay her to discuss literature and writing, although not much. Finding young people entertaining and challenging, she became a college teacher, and survived many generations of students. Later, during a career crisis, she learned that people would pay her to tell stories, although even less than they would pay her to discuss stories written by someone else.

Borton has lived in the Southwest, Midwest, and on the West Coast, where she planted roses and collected three degrees in English without relinquishing her affection for and reliance on nonstandard dialects. In her spare time, she gardens, practices aikido, studies languages other than English, and, of course, watches movies and reads.

www.dbborton.com